The

Long
Way
Back

Praise for

The Long Way Back

"For any parent, the most frightening nightmare is the disappearance of their child. In Nicole Baart's extraordinary novel *The Long Way Back*, not only is a mother tortured by this terrible circumstance, but she also becomes a primary suspect. Baart writes with a poet's eye for language and a storyteller's gift for suspense. Readers already won over by Nicole Baart's fine body of work will discover another sparkling gem, and new readers couldn't find a better place to begin."

—William Kent Krueger, *New York Times*
bestselling author of *This Tender Land*

"*The Long Way Back* is a beautifully written, atmospheric page-turner that brilliantly explores the complexities of the mother-daughter bond, finding it as fraught as it is profound."

—Kimberly McCreight, *New York Times* bestselling author of
A Good Marriage and *Friends Like These*

"In Nicole Baart's gripping new thriller *The Long Way Back*, a mother creates a perfect Instagram life for herself and her teenage daughter, traveling the country while chronicling their adventures for legions of fans. But despite doing everything right, never posting her daughter's face and never identifying their location until they've moved on, things go horribly wrong. Timely and provocative, Baart's marvelously relatable characters and gifted storytelling take the reader on a wild and unexpected ride. I loved this book!"

—Karen Dionne, #1 internationally bestselling author of
The Marsh King's Daughter and *The Wicked Sister*

"Riveting and timely, *The Long Way Back* is not just an unforgettable mother-daughter thriller, it's a deeply felt love story about the natural world. In beautiful prose, Nicole Baart has penned a novel that will stick with me for a very long time."

—Jo Piazza, bestselling coauthor of *We Are Not Like Them*

"Nicole Baart is the queen of the family thriller! This tender, propulsive story reveals a heart-twisting understanding of human nature and the risks we take to get what we want. Timely and thought-provoking, this "turn the pages as fast as you can" cautionary tale about the danger of the spotlight and the steep price of privacy will surprise you and haunt you, even after the gasp-worthy conclusion. Baart crafts her mother-daughter suspense not only with soul and passion and stomach-churning tension—but also a deep and important wisdom. Book clubs rejoice: this is the novel for you!"

—Hank Phillippi Ryan, *USA Today* bestselling author

"In *The Long Way Back*, Baart achieves the nearly impossible feat—writing that is tense and propulsive as well as poetically rendered. A beautiful story about the fraught relationships between parents and their children, the tension between growing up and learning the difficult truths about the dangers of independence, *The Long Way Back* will have you turning pages late into the night and holding your breath until the final, emotional scenes. I absolutely loved it."

—Danielle Girard, *USA Today* bestselling author

ALSO BY NICOLE BAART

The
Long
Way
Back

A Novel

NICOLE BAART

ATRIA PAPERBACK

New York · London · Toronto · Sydney · New Delhi

ATRIA
PAPERBACK

An Imprint of Simon & Schuster, Inc.
1230 Avenue of the Americas
New York, NY 10020

First Atria Paperback edition June 2023

ATRIA PAPERBACK and colophon are trademarks of Simon & Schuster, Inc.

For information about special discounts for bulk purchases, please contact Simon & Schuster Special Sales at 1-866-506-1949 or business@simonandschuster.com.

The Simon & Schuster Speakers Bureau can bring authors to your live event. For more information or to book an event, contact the Simon & Schuster Speakers Bureau at 1-866-248-3049 or visit our website at www.simonspeakers.com.

Interior design by Yvonne Taylor

Manufactured in the United States of America

1 3 5 7 9 10 8 6 4 2

Library of Congress Cataloging-in-Publication Data is available.

ISBN 978-1-9821-1510-4
ISBN 978-1-9821-1511-1 (ebook)

For all the free spirits, wild hearts, and brave explorers.

PART I

Charlie

INSTAGRAM POST #1

I must be a mermaid,
I have no fear
of depths and
a great fear
of shallow living.

Anaïs Nin

[IMAGE CONTENTS: A raven-haired girl
beneath a waterfall.]

It was a hollow caption, as empty and desolate as the husk of a seed. The photo had to be *experienced*, and Charlie felt sorry for anyone who couldn't see Eva with the water cascading down her face and across her narrow shoulders. She was thirteen, sleek and plump, with a pointed nose, pointed chin, and two perfectly pointed ears that hinted at what she would one day be. Not pretty, per se—at least, not yet—but arresting, and made all the more extraordinary by the cold disdain in her sapphire eyes.

Incongruous. That's what it was. The petal-soft blush of her full cheeks paired with the penetrating wisdom of her gaze. A child caught at the exact intersection between girl and woman.

"Mom," Eva said, in the moment before Charlie snapped the picture, "*don't.*"

But Charlie did. It was a moment of madness, of ferocious love, that disintegrated after the shutter snapped and Eva tumbled off the slippery rock, falling headlong beneath the foamy spray of the waterfall. There was laughter then, and Charlie carefully packed away her camera and dove in to join her daughter. But the moment was resurrected later, when the image lit up Charlie's computer screen.

Without a doubt, the picture of Eva in the waterfall was the most powerful portrait that Charlie had ever taken. Eva was just turning, framed between a wall of greenish water on one side and slick, brown stone on the other. One slender hand was on the rock, and one hand was tangled in her long hair as she pushed damp curls out of her eyes. Before that, she had been posing. All artificial smiles and a self-conscious thrust to her jaw. But the last click of Charlie's camera had captured a singular moment, an unexpected window into Eva's soul. Something wild lived there, raw and untamed, a whole world contained in her eyes.

Charlie couldn't print it, not something so intimate and vulnerable, but it also seemed cruel not to share. So she cropped it close—one shockingly blue eye, a wet ribbon of hair against the blade of her cheekbone, the sparkle of sunlit water—and showed it to Eva.

"That's me?" She couldn't suppress her grin, but tried by pinning her bottom lip between her teeth. "Wow, Mom. I mean, wow. Can we post it?"

Their Sutton Girls Instagram page had been the only thing Eva truly wanted for her thirteenth birthday. Allegedly, all the kids in her class were already on social media (age limits be damned), and Eva felt the pinch of isolation when they chatted over chicken nuggets in the school cafeteria about accounts they followed, funny memes they saw, and photo ops they were staging. It was obvious Eva thought that maybe *this* was her in. Still, Charlie couldn't stomach the thought of her daughter online at such a young age, so they had compromised: The Sutton Girls. A joint account to chronicle their life as a little party of two. At first Eva had argued, but it was half-hearted, and in the end the very first photo they posted was the close-cropped waterfall shot. Eva found and carefully typed out the mermaid quote all by herself.

They only had a handful of followers (mostly family and friends), but the photo took on a life of its own. Strangers liked it and commented, put it in their stories and archived it for later. Charlie's phone *ping*ed incessantly with notifications until Eva showed her how to turn them off.

Somehow the picture garnered a hundred likes within the first day. It quickly blossomed to two hundred. Then, suddenly, a thousand. Friends of friends and members of their Duluth, Minnesota, community and total strangers who double-clicked and then expressed their deep appreciation by sharing to Stories and hitting Follow—hoping for more. By the time ten thousand people had liked their post, and there were more comments than Charlie or Eva could ever hope to keep up with, everything had changed. Even if they didn't know it yet.

"I think we just went kind of viral," Charlie said. "They're calling you the Little Mermaid."

One side of Eva's mouth quirked in an abashed smile. "I know." Then she giggled. "Does that make you Ursula?"

And Charlie started to sing: "You poor, unfortunate soul!"

Four Years Later . . .

CHAPTER 1

Charlie is dreaming of mermaids.

Monsters of the deep. No wide-eyed, nubile princesses here. These mermaids are murderous and cold, grim with the flash of iron scales, sharp nails, a slash of razor teeth. Charlie can feel the bite of a powerful hand circling her wrist, a plume of liquid hair as it tangles around her neck. Then a sudden tug and she is drawn deeper still, drowning beneath the weight of leagues pressing down above her.

She can't wait a second longer. Her lungs are pulsing with the need to breathe, and the gasp propels her right off the chilly vinyl bench.

It happens all at once: the understanding that she isn't living a nightmare, that she is breathing and safe and dry, and that she is on Frank's offshore fishing boat. Belowdecks, to be specific, in the little cabin with the long, matching seats and the tiny marine toilet behind a half-sized door. She can smell the lemony-chemical tang of the tank treatment layered beneath gasoline.

Still, the tendrils of the black dream cling—she feels wrong. Her elbow stings and she knows without looking that the traction tape she spread across the narrow floor so many years ago has scraped her skin. It's a tangible hurt, easier to address than the malice of a nightmare, so she pulls her knees to her chest and leans against the bench to survey the damage. A patch of sanded skin, pink and already bubbling where the textured grips dug deep, but nothing a bandage won't fix.

"Eva?" Charlie's voice hitches. She swallows, stunned that her mouth can be so dry only moments after a potential drowning. But she wasn't drowning, was she? And then she tastes it. "Dammit," she groans, and covers her face with her hands.

How much did she have? A glass? Two? Surely not the whole bottle, because she can remember forcing the swollen cork back into the neck with at least half the wine still sloshing about inside.

"Eva?" Charlie tries again, regret curdling in her stomach. But of course Eva can't hear her down here. The hatch door is shut. Maybe that's for the best.

There's no mirror in the pocket-sized bathroom, just a bucket with a toilet seat, but Charlie doesn't need one anyway. She finger-combs her short waves into place and sweeps a bit of salve on her chapped lips. She hopes that Eva can't see straight through her—that her eyes aren't bloodshot, her skin isn't sickly sweet with the scent of wine. How long has she been down here?

A wave of nausea rolls over her, but it has nothing to do with her being tipsy belowdecks on a fishing boat, and everything to do with shame.

Charlie sucks in a deep breath and takes the few stairs bent at the waist. The door isn't latched, just resting against the T-Molding in a testament to the quiet day. She's remembering now. The uncharacteristic sunshine as the temperatures in Landing soared to eighty in May. The siren call of still water in the man-made bay, pooling out into Lake Superior like spilled honey.

"Let's go!" Eva had said, a spark in her eyes that Charlie hadn't seen in forever. "Come on—take the boat out with me. Just the two of us."

She hadn't even paused to think. It was Eva's idea, how could Charlie say no? The last few weeks had been exhausting, filled with drama and disagreements, and Charlie leapt at the opportunity for some (hopefully) fight-free time with her daughter. They slapped together ham sandwiches and snagged a half-eaten bag of baby carrots from the fridge. A couple of Frank's famous peanut butter cookies rounded out their impromptu picnic. They forgot sunscreen, towels, and live bait. But Eva had remembered the old bottle of yellowing chardonnay that had been collecting dust on top of the refrigerator. They were supposed to be celebrating.

"Hey," Charlie says now, pushing out into an unexpected dusk. A mere slice of sun is balanced at the edge of the horizon and a bank of purple clouds unfurl like a cape to the southwest. Storms rise from that corner of Minnesota, often fast and unpredictable, and Charlie makes some quick calculations to figure out how long it will take to get back to the harbor. A cold wind raises the hairs on her arms, and she opens her mouth to ask Eva to toss her a coat.

But the boat is empty.

Frank's offshore fishing boat, the reliable, if run-down *Summer Moon*, is as bare and vacant as the miles and miles of lake surrounding her.

Charlie whips around to search the small crow's nest above the cabin, but she already knows that Eva isn't there. Her daughter hates the height, the tremulous climb up a flimsy ladder. Forget it if there's even the hint of a breeze, and this wind is enough to clip the top off the small waves and send sprays of water against the side of the *Summer Moon*.

The boat trims aft and for a second Charlie loses her footing. Whether it's the wine or the crush of her growing panic, she slams into the transom. Pain zings through her hip, but it only fuels her. There's storage in the stern, insulated compartments for fish beneath the bench seats, and Charlie lunges for the hand loops, yanking off the lids with a stifled scream. It's ludicrous to imagine that Eva might be hiding there—small as she is, a seventeen-year-old would never fit—but it's all Charlie can think to do. Then she scours the inboard engine mount, crawls on her hands and knees to the helm, and touches every switch and dial as if there are clues hidden on the impassive faces of the *Summer Moon*'s tachometer and water temperature gauges. Nothing.

"Eva!" Charlie screams her name, the syllables fracturing apart as she scrambles port side and looks over. Gray water in a slow churn, white bubbles simmering across the surface. Starboard is the same. No life jacket, no flash of color, no telltale ripple.

"Eva! Eva! *Evangeline!*" She realizes she's been shouting the entire time, her daughter's name a howl ripped from her throat. It feels bloody and raw, but Charlie keeps yelling. "*Eva!*"

The wind swallows each word until it's as if she never called at all. It's hopeless, Charlie can feel that in every single bone, and it aches so much that she crumples to the deck. But just as quickly as she gives up, she galvanizes. She can just make out Split Rock Lighthouse along the southernmost edge of the western shore. They're only a few miles out, but the sky is turning dark and threatening.

Charlie's cell phone is in a waterproof compartment near the boat wheel, and she dives for it, scrabbling at the marine radio with her other hand. She's two-fisting it, managing 911 on her cell with her left hand—only two wavering bars of service—while tapping channel 16 with her right. "Mayday, Mayday, Mayday!" she shouts into both, her voice breaking. There's a protocol she's supposed to follow, a series of words and information to provide. But she can't remember any of that right now.

"Help us!" Charlie cries. "We're on the *Summer Moon*, and Eva . . . she's *gone!*"

. . . .

The boats come en masse, seemingly from every direction, their lights flickering over the growing swells. But by the time the first response boat is close enough to hail the *Summer Moon* over the intercom, Charlie is past the point of answering. She's crouched on the floor of the fishing boat, still clutching her cell phone in one hand and the radio in the other. The dispatcher is shouting that help has arrived, but Charlie can't acknowledge her. Or move.

Later, she won't remember the firefighter carry or the treacherous few steps from the *Summer Moon* to the recovery platform of the coast guard responder. She won't recall the cramped survivors' compartment where she was wrapped in a Mylar blanket and handed a cup of coffee sweetened with three sugar packets. "It'll help," an EMT told her, but she choked on her first sip and couldn't face another. Charlie won't remember that Ted and Paula Shepherd were the first people on the scene, or that they hedged the *Summer Moon* like a warden keeping safe a wounded charge.

But when they pull into Stone Harbor and Charlie can see the familiar aquamarine boathouse beyond the three short rows of docks, she comes to as if she had fainted dead away and is suddenly, stunningly conscious. Against the EMT's wishes, she goes to stand on the deck, arms curled tight against her body beneath the Mylar. Even in the growing dusk she can see they're all there: Sue and Edith, the Russells, Weston all by himself because Thea gets her hair done on Saturdays. And Frank, standing at the end of the *Summer Moon*'s empty boat slip, a wooden chest with flaking green paint behind his bowed knees. When he sees her, he wavers, swaying as if the waves have somehow crested the breakwater and are slamming against the mooring poles.

Charlie can feel everything inside of her turn liquid at the sight of her foster father. They never made it official, Frank and Hattie were just granted temporary custody when her mother died, but "temporary" turned into the three years between Rosie's death and Charlie's eighteenth birthday. Frank Morrow is the closest thing to a father Charlie's ever known. She can't decide if she wants to throw herself into his arms or throw herself over the side of the boat and sink to the bottom of the bay. She ran away nearly twenty years ago and broke Frank's heart. If he loses Eva—his unofficial granddaughter—now, it will be his absolute undoing.

Frank looks fragile from a distance—shoulders slumped, hair a scant tuft of white, hips so narrow his belt can nearly wrap twice around his waist—but Charlie's heart doesn't have room to contain his fear and grief, too. She turns away, but not before she sees him collapse. Thank God for the chest where they store extra life jackets, buoys, marine odds and ends. He lands on it, hard, and buries his face in his hands. He can't be sure of anything, not yet. None of them can. And yet, Charlie knows that even the sight of her without her shadow, without Eva at her elbow, toothy smile flashing and arm held high in greeting, is unnerving enough to fill them all with dread.

The world is nothing at all without Eva in it.

INSTAGRAM POST #2

Just a couple of girls completely floored
(get it?) that y'all liked our waterfall post.

We're new to Instagram.
Are we doing it right?

[IMAGE CONTENTS: Two pairs of feet
standing toe to toe on cracked concrete.
One pair of feet are in wide-strapped
sandals with the toenails painted red,
orange, yellow, green, and blue in color
wheel order. The other pair of feet are
in purple converse sneakers with bright
white laces. Together, they make a
double rainbow.]

"We're not from the South," Charlie told Eva as she stared at the phone screen, proofing the short text. She had an old smartphone with few bells and whistles, and it was already becoming a bit of a feat to upload pictures from her Canon to the computer and then send them to her phone. Still, it felt momentous to post again. Like there were now thousands of people breathlessly waiting to read what they would write next.

It wasn't an entirely welcome thought. "I'm not sure you spelled *y'all* right."

She gently lifted the phone from Eva's hand and thumbed open the internet search engine. As she typed, she said, "You know it was a fluke, right? What happened with the waterfall post, I mean. There was something about Gooseberry Falls that day, the way the light was filtering through the trees and—"

"Yeah, Mom. I know."

"I just don't want you to think we're going to be famous or something. Hollywood's not going to call because of a cool picture."

Eva bumped Charlie's elbow with her own. "An *awesome* picture," she countered, grinning.

Charlie couldn't help but smile back. "Well, yes. But it was a one-time thing."

"I know." Eva said it quickly, lightly, and that was how Charlie knew her daughter was far more invested than she let on.

Something inside of Charlie squeezed tight. It had been a hard year—the worst—with letters home from the guidance counselor and emails to fellow parents that she typed in a blind rage and then viciously edited before sending. Their replies were terse, formal, defensive. And nothing changed.

The kids were subtle in their cruelty, but certainly not original. A handful of mini candy bars left on Eva's desk when she got up to sharpen her pencil, a stifled cough that sounded a lot like "Tubby." In the lunchroom, girls shuffled and slid, making sure that there was never room at their table for Eva. As if the invisible disease that made Evangeline Sutton untouchable at Lincoln Park Middle School was somehow catching.

To Charlie, Eva was ample in the most perfect way, soft-

cheeked and rounded in the belly like a well-fed kitten. It reminded Charlie of when Eva was a toddler. Of how she used
to cup her little girl's sweet tummy in the palm of her hand
to feel it rise and fall as she fell asleep. It would all disappear,
Charlie knew, melt off when Eva hit a growth spurt just like
Charlie's own baby fat had done twenty-some years ago. They
were late bloomers, that's all. But that was cold comfort now,
especially when boys started to call her Evangeline the Blubber
Queen when no teachers were near enough to hear. Eva heard.
Every time.

Charlie put the phone back in Eva's hand and kissed her
temple. "You're perfect. And you spelled *y'all* exactly right."

Eva grunted in response and let her finger hover over the
Share button. "Ready?" she asked.

"As I'll ever be."

And then it was live. Their feet—matching size 9s—for all
the world to see. It felt a bit like the first drop of a roller coaster
to Charlie, a mix of adrenaline, delight, and fear. Almost immediately, notifications began to *ping*.

"Here we go!" Eva said, and the hope in her tone tipped
Charlie off another ledge.

"Let's go." Charlie reached for the phone, suddenly desperate to turn it off. "I want to walk the Aerial Bridge. When's
the last time we had ice cream from the Boxcar? I'm craving a
strawberry shake."

But Eva wasn't listening. Angling away from Charlie, she
pulled the phone just out of reach. "What's this?" she asked,
pointing to the upper righthand corner of their social media
mailbox. "It says we have twenty-seven requests."

Before Charlie could utter a single word, Eva had clicked it
and opened the first message. Tilting their heads together, they
read.

Hi! We love your look and are seeking new influencers
to help us reach our 450K followers. We'd love to
have you on board!

Charlie took the phone from Eva and scrolled. They were all
the same. *Wear our swimming suit, sandals, scarf. Try our shampoo, body lotion, eco-friendly soap.* And they all echoed the very
words that Charlie had said only mere minutes before.

The perfect look.

The perfect fit.

You're perfect.

Perfect.

"Mom?" Eva asked, looking over Charlie's shoulder. "What
does it mean?"

But Charlie didn't know how to answer.

CHAPTER 2

SATURDAY

The wind howls down the dock and whips Charlie's short hair against her cheeks as she's ushered toward land. She's never seen the small Landing Marina like this before: crowded with people, emergency vehicles, and lights. Her friends are huddled together on their boats, clearly trying to give the emergency workers space. Weston has gone to comfort Frank and is sitting with one arm draped around the old man, holding him close. Weston comforting Frank? When pigs fly. Eva would giggle, roll her eyes at Charlie and the ancient, bewildering grudge between the two eightysomethings. *She would love to see this.* The thought rips a sob from Charlie's lips.

Then suddenly they're off the dock, Charlie and her entourage, and the steady ground beneath her feet is enough to make her stumble.

"We just want to make sure you're okay, Ms. Sutton." The young man who is holding her elbow sounds grim. "The ambulance is going to transport you to Landing Memorial—"

"No," Charlie croaks, her throat sore from screaming. She plants her feet. "I'm not hurt."

She drops the Mylar blanket from her shoulders so that the small crowd gathered around her can see that she's not bleeding, nothing is broken. But that's not true. Charlie feels splintered, like a piece of glass that has spiderwebbed into a thousand tiny shards but is somehow, impossibly still whole. One shiver and she'll shatter. Almost the moment the blanket has puddled at her feet, it begins: huge, convulsive spasms that judder through her body.

An EMT catches her. His shout is carried on the growing wind. "Let's get her inside. Who has a key?"

It's a mad scramble as several people hurry toward the loose shingle, the not-so-secret hiding spot for the key to the ramshackle boathouse. In seconds the door is open, the lights flung on, and a musty, rolling chair is procured by Ted, who must have beat the coast guard responder to his slip. He catches Charlie's hand and squeezes it hard before ducking back outside.

Charlie is pushed into the chair with a blood pressure cuff wrapped around her upper arm. She is aware of the growing pinch, the way her fingertips feel disconnected from her body, but not much else as her vision shrinks to a pinprick. The boathouse is crammed and humid, and a snippet of conversation reaches her ears.

"The helicopters are out, but no one could survive in that water."

"You'd have to be a hell of a swimmer."

"The water's barely forty degrees. Doesn't matter how well you swim."

Charlie's pierced with a sudden, ice-cold clarity. "What time is it?" She doesn't mean to yell, but it gets everyone's attention.

The EMT at her side keeps pumping the blood pressure cuff.

"Eight fifty-eight," a man in a black sweater answers, consulting the oversized chronograph watch on his wrist. His eyes narrow as he takes a step closer and squats down to come face-to-face with Charlie. She doesn't recognize him; he's not Landing Police Department.

But he's nothing more than a momentary distraction. She

closes her eyes—8:58? She and Eva got to the marina around two. They were planning on a lazy afternoon on the water, the wind in their hair and the sun—after a long, cold winter, and unusually rainy spring—warm on their skin. At just after three they eased the *Summer Moon* out of the bay and puttered a couple nautical miles from shore before tossing in the first few lines. When did the sandwiches come out? The wine? When did Charlie go below and leave her daughter alone on the deck of the boat?

A tap on her knee makes Charlie's eyes fly open.

"You feeling better, Ms. Sutton?" The man in the sweater is still crouching before her. "Are you ready to answer some questions?"

"Please," the EMT cuts in. "I can't get an accurate reading."

"I'm fine." Charlie rips the cuff off her arm, and the sound of Velcro crackles through the small room.

"But—"

"She said she's fine."

With a huff of frustration, the EMT tosses the blood pressure cuff into his medic bag and zips it shut. The three paramedics that escorted Charlie into the boathouse withdraw, letting the wind slam the door behind them. Through a grimy window she can see them stop just outside the low building, the flash of their ambulance lights still dancing on the dark water of the bay and illuminating their profiles. The marina teems with unfamiliar vehicles and people.

"How many people are here?" Charlie isn't even aware she's voiced the question until the man across from her clears his throat.

"We brought out the full cavalry," he says, shifting his linebacker frame into a folding chair that a short woman with a drooping ponytail has carried over for him. He holds up his hand and begins ticking off his fingers. "Coast guard responded from the port in Duluth. Landing PD, fire, and ambulance are all here, as well as several civilian volunteers. We've got crews in cold water suits searching an area around your last known coordinates, and the coast guard helicopters have been called out. They should be on-site by now. We take an SOS call very seriously. Especially when the victim is a minor." His hand is in a fist now, and Charlie can't help but stare at it.

Victim. It's such a grisly word. She thinks of police tape, forensics teams, body bags. "Who are you?" she asks through the sting of bile at the back of her throat.

"Detective Mitchum James, Duluth PD. Missing Persons division. I was nearby when your call came in. Just lending my services." He considers his fist, the white-knuckled severity of it, and shakes out his hand, giving Charlie a tight-lipped smile. "We all just want to find your daughter."

She watches him for a moment, the buzzed hair, square jaw, heavy brow. It's not surprising that the tiny Landing PD was more than happy to let someone with more experience take the reins—a missing person case is a far cry from their usual duties of handing out speeding tickets and the occasional DUI—and Detective James exudes confidence and competence. He's a middle-aged All-American boy with a permanent dimple in his left cheek and shoulders that wrestle the fabric of his sweater. It's clear he knows exactly what he's doing. But something feels off. He's studying her too intently, and his gaze fastens on her crossed arms. Brushing the underside of her elbow with her fingers, she feels the torn skin and dried blood from her tumble off the bench in the belly of the *Summer Moon*. Suddenly, Charlie knows exactly what he's thinking.

"I fell," she says lamely.

"Looks recent."

"On the boat. Just a bit ago." Guilt blooms in her chest, a suffocating swell that makes tears spring to her eyes. Detective James doesn't trust her. He's already imaging the worst—that her scrape is a defensive wound, or something even darker. Charlie didn't do anything, but whatever happened, wherever Eva is, Charlie *does* know it's her fault. Because she drank and slept and got careless. For once she didn't micromanage every little thing, and look what happened.

A tear slips down her cheek. She knuckles it away and says, "I'll tell you anything you want to know."

The woman with the ponytail hands Detective James a tablet in a protective case that makes it look like a piece of tactical gear. He balances it on his knees and swipes the screen a few times before taking a stylus and beginning to write. Charlie hasn't answered a single question and already she feels like a suspect.

"Full name and age," he says, not looking up from the tablet.

"Charlotte Greer Sutton. Thirty-nine."

One eyebrow quirks, but he goes on. "And your daughter's?"

"Evangeline Rose Sutton. Seventeen."

"Occupation."

Charlie clears her throat. It's hard to talk. Hard to focus on the questions when Eva is . . . But that line of thinking is a black hole of pure terror. She digs her fingernails into her palm and makes her mouth form words. "I'm a photographer. And freelance writer. I write articles for magazines sometimes. *Outside*, *Wanderlust*, *Midwest Living*."

At this, Detective James looks up. "That's interesting," he says, then squints back at the tablet. "Because it says here you're a social media influencer."

Charlie has no idea what he's looking at or where he got that information, but she doesn't have time to dwell because she can feel the heat creeping up her neck. The boathouse is chilly and damp, and she knows her blush is telling. She almost says: "It's complicated." But that sounds like an excuse better suited for Match.com. She decides to keep her answer simple. Neat. "We were. Not anymore."

Detective James is already flipping through screens. "Looks like your account is still live. Eva Explores. You have quite a few followers." He whistles low. "Over a quarter million on Instagram. That's really something."

It's not. Not really. There are thousands—maybe tens of thousands—of accounts with more followers, more influence than Eva Explores. But it paid the bills. It allowed them to live the sort of life that dreams were made of. The Sutton girls' dreams, anyway.

"I don't see how this is relevant," Charlie says. Hearing Eva's name on his tongue makes panic sizzle across her skin. "My daughter is missing."

"Just gathering information," Detective James says, writing away. "Everything is relevant at this stage. Can you tell me what you and Eva were doing on the boat today?"

"It was beautiful out. Eva wanted to be on the water."

"It was her idea?"

"Yes." Charlie nods, suddenly unsure whose idea it was to take out the *Summer Moon*. Did it matter? But yes, she can picture Eva thundering down the stairs and pointing at the glittering lake framed in the window above the kitchen sink. "It was her idea."

"Go on."

"There's not much else to say. It felt like summer, and we wanted to enjoy it. We were celebrating."

"Celebrating what?"

"Graduation. It's a week away," Charlie says. But of course, that was only part of it. She doesn't explain that they had been fighting for weeks. That after a months-long stalemate, Eva had finally agreed to one last summer of Eva Explores. Charlie was ecstatic. But she can't tell Detective James any of that. She says, unnecessarily, "Eva's a senior."

"A seventeen-year-old senior? She's pretty young to be graduating."

"Eva was homeschooled for most of high school. She finished all her coursework early. Could have graduated last semester." A note of pride creeps into her voice, but Charlie doesn't have the capacity to feel sheepish about bragging about her girl.

"Why didn't she? Graduate early."

It's a simple question with a complex answer. Charlie settles on: "She wanted the experience. You know, homecoming, prom, graduation."

The detective stares at her for a moment, but apparently decides not to press this line of questioning because he changes tack. "Do you and Eva get along?"

"Yes," Charlie blurts. "She's my best friend. I mean, she's my daughter, but we're very close."

"Ever fight?"

A blush rises as Charlie thinks about the night before. The angry words. The yelling. "Everyone fights."

"How about recently?" Detective James asks, his look boring right through her.

He knows, Charlie thinks. But she never gets the chance to answer. From across the room someone calls: "Detective James?" His tone is sharp enough to silence all the chatter in the boathouse. "I think you should take this."

Charlie holds her breath as the stranger hands over a cell phone. Detective James thrusts the tablet at the ponytailed plainclothes officer—her name is Mia and she's Landing PD;

Charlie recognizes her now—and takes the phone into the far corner. It's a small building, one low-ceilinged, open room separated by a few desks, a bookshelf or two, and a pair of glass cases that hold artifacts of a time long gone. Stone Harbor was dug out by hand in the fifties, courtesy of a group of young men who wanted to put Landing on the map. Some of the things they found in the process now collect dust in the display case where Detective James drums his fingers. Charlie focuses on what she knows is there instead of the military-straight line of the detective's back. A brass gimbal compass, a copper cup, a thick, ugly ring. There's a sextant of questionable origin and a small wooden mermaid carved by hand.

Charlie is picturing the curve of the mermaid's hair, the way the wood ripples as if it was once water, when the detective turns and strides back to where she's sitting.

"Is there a life raft on the *Summer Moon?*"

She blinks, trying to clear her head. "Yes. Of course."

Detective James gestures for her to continue.

"It's a, a . . ." Charlie stutters, trying to remember. "It's a compact life raft. Inflatable. Yellow. For up to four people."

"Where is it stored?"

"In a seat locker."

"Are you sure?"

"I put it there myself." Charlie's heart begins to thunder. "Just a couple weeks ago when we dewinterized the boat."

But he's shaking his head. "It's gone."

INSTAGRAM POST #57

Living our best life on the slopes of Lut
sen! It's a winter wonderland here and
we may never go home. We've already
told you all about where to get the best
pizza (yes, the kitchen is in the back
of a gas station, but TRUST US), who
makes the best white chocolate mocha
(we love you, Will!), and that you should
definitely buy a bag of copper shavings
for some truly spectacular nighttime fire
magic. But, if you want to know which
runs to hit and miss, stay tuned. There
are four mountains and ninety-five
runs, and the Sutton Girls have three
days left to hit them all. We live to give.
#charlieandevaexplore #nofilter #lutsen
resort

Always take the long way back,
Charlie & Eva

[IMAGE CONTENTS: Two sets of snow
skis sticking up in the air. They're
angled together to create a triangle

that frames a gorgeous snowscape
with Lake Superior in the background.
The water is a deep, Prussian blue
against a silvery, winter sky.]

Their first paid gig was a stay at Lutsen Resort. Well, technically, it wasn't a *paid gig*. They didn't earn a dime. But they were
comped four nights in the resort lodge with a complimentary
breakfast buffet every morning in the Strand—a waterfront restaurant with a glass wine cellar, leather chairs, and linen table-
cloths that they immediately decided were far too fancy for their
dumpy two-bedroom apartment and shabby backpack tastes.
Still, there were Swedish pancakes with lingonberry compote
and maple breakfast sausages that were positively swoon-worthy,
and they decided they could be fake-fancy long enough to stuff
themselves full of eggs scrambled with aged cheddar before hitting the slopes.

The Sutton Girls Instagram page had continued to grow in
the six months since Eva's mermaid portrait made a lucky splash.
Charlie had no idea what they were doing, but Eva turned out
to be unexpectedly savvy, picking up on trendy hashtags and
following up-and-coming accounts that helped her and Charlie
create an aesthetic that resonated with more people than they
could have ever imagined. In many ways, Charlie felt like they
had caught the tail of a comet and were just along for the ride.
It was fun and exciting, a temporary side hustle that resulted in
some fun freebies.

Line-minimizing facial masks. Body lotion. There were
leggings and graphic T-shirts and candles. "Gifts" for "micro-
influencers" Eva told her (they were micro-influencers?), and

there was more where that came from. But while Charlie wasn't ready to pump the brakes on the modest success they'd experienced, she was also unintentionally creating a code that governed what and how they posted.

No full faces. If Eva or Charlie appeared in one of the Sutton Girls photos, it was almost always cropped, off-center, blurred, or from behind. Charlie didn't like the idea of strangers poring over her daughter's lovely face—and she had no desire to showcase her own—so they were usually just beyond sight. The accidental result was that the Sutton Girls were shrouded in a veil of mystery.

Nothing artificial or retouched. In a medium where virtually nothing was authentic, the Sutton Girls were real. Charlie's secondhand Canon EOS Rebel T7 was nothing special, but it got the job done, and she played with aperture and shutter speed the way an artist blended paint. A swirl here, a dab there, the result something new and unpredictable. Her unfiltered photographs were raw and arresting in a way that made people stop their scroll.

Emphasize the outdoors. Photographing their adventures had been a part of their lives since Eva was born. It was them against the world, a mother-daughter duo that stood with their backs together and their arms open wide. When Eva was still a baby, Charlie saved up for a Kelty child carrier so she could strap her daughter to her back and take her anywhere. They hiked, cross-country skied, swam in Lake Superior when it was still cold enough to take their breath away, and camped curled up together in a single sleeping bag while coyotes howled outside. Little changed as Eva got older, other than that they bought a second flannel-lined sleeping bag.

Showcasing where they went and what they loved in such a unique way earned them a private message from the Lutsen Resort's director of marketing. They were local, causing a bit of a stir, and in exchange for six positive posts (tagging the resort, of course), Charlie and Eva could enjoy everything Lutsen's had to offer. It was an easy yes.

"I don't want to leave," Eva said as they packed up on the last day. Her cheeks were pink with sun and windburn from long days on the slopes, and her eyes tired but happy. They had gone all out, posting eight times in the four days that they spent playing in the snow. But they had also sat in the hot tub late at night (with no camera in sight), watched Marvel movies in bed after luxuriously long showers, and slept in. It was the first non-camping vacation they had ever taken.

"I hear you, sister." Charlie reached out to tug the end of one of Eva's long braids. "But reality calls."

Eva turned to yank the zipper closed on her duffel. Carefully, with her back turned to Charlie, she said: "What if this was our reality?"

"Living at a resort?"

"Traveling."

Charlie's exhale was more of a sigh. Although they could probably hand-draw a map to every worthwhile hike, swimming hole, and spot of interest in Northern Minnesota, the gorgeous *National Geographic* magazine spreads that they cut out of old magazines and taped on the walls of their dingy apartment in Duluth had created a shared longing for *more*. More to see, more to explore, more variety than their little—albeit beautiful—corner of the world had to offer.

Of course, Eva's question was about so much more than travel. As their online popularity grew, Eva had only become more of an outcast at her Duluth middle school. She'd dared to aim higher than the bottom rung she'd been assigned, and nobody liked it.

But Charlie was a single mom working full-time in a warehouse and shooting a handful of senior photos and the occasional family portrait on the side. They couldn't afford to travel. Eva had never even been on a plane.

"If wishes had wings . . ." Charlie smiled softly.

Eva sank to the unmade bed and flicked both of her dark braids over her shoulders. "It was dreamy, though, wasn't it?"

"The dreamiest."

And then Charlie took her camera out of its battered case and set it up on a chair. She grabbed Eva's hand and dragged her to the balcony where a copse of tall evergreens wreathed in white created a backdrop worthy of a greeting card. They crouched in the snow, grinning at each other instead of the camera, and just before the timer hit zero and the shutter clicked, Charlie kissed her daughter's forehead.

They posted one last time from the resort. The snow was stacked five inches high on the railing behind them, and the sun shining off all that white gave their matching dark heads halos. They were in profile, unobscured for the very first time, and they only wrote two words: *Where next?*

CHAPTER 3

The two-story farmhouse that Charlie and Eva have called home for the last five months is dark when the police cruiser turns down the long, gravel drive. The lane is sloped, treacherous in winter, but currently rimmed with lupines in extravagant purple bloom. As the headlights sweep the tree-lined property, they glint off the silver side of a vintage Airstream trailer parked beside a small, detached garage.

Mia, the Landing police officer who has been tasked with driving Charlie home, speaks for the first time in miles. "Is that—" she stops abruptly and clears her throat as if somehow she can erase the question she was about to ask.

Those two short words tell Charlie that Mia knows exactly who she is—who Eva is—and that she recognizes the iconic Airstream. Maybe it was Mia who told Detective James about Eva Explores.

"That's Sebastian," Charlie says. Because of course it is. The motion-sensor activated floodlights have kicked on now and are illuminating the small yard. The garage is on the south side of the narrow property and painted red to match the 1940s farmhouse that can't seem to decide if it's Victorian or Colonial. It boasts the clean lines of a Colonial, but the wraparound porch and bay windows of a Victorian. Framed between the two buildings is a generous wedge of Lake Superior. Beyond the trees the

32

night is black, but the movement of the water is unmistakable. A squat stone wall separates the green lawn from rough-hewn boulders and a slip of rocky beach. But newcomers—at least, those in the know—bypass the view to hone in on the Airstream.

The trailer—lovingly nicknamed Sebastian—is fully illuminated, practically sparkling in the fluorescent floodlights. The white-and-black checked buffalo curtains and Norway pine silhouettes subtly etched on the front are clearly visible. When they were refinishing Sebastian, Charlie had intentionally included several nods to their Minnesotan heritage so that they could take a piece of the North Shore with them wherever they roamed. But she didn't realize that the scarlet-colored Lake Superior agate that she had carefully drilled a hole in and hung from the wide rear window would become a calling card of sorts. They had made themselves recognizable before they ever realized that notoriety might be a problem.

Mia puts the cruiser in park between the house and the garage and openly gawks at the Airstream. "Why Sebastian?" she asks.

So she isn't a groupie who's been with them since their Sutton Girls days. "Because in the beginning, people called Eva the Little Mermaid," Charlie says. Her answer is rote, her soul numb. "And Sebastian was the friend who helped her get the life she always wanted."

Mia makes a sound that could be interpreted as sympathy or schadenfreude, but Charlie is past the point of caring. She's staring at Sebastian too. She'd give anything to be somewhere—*anywhere*—in that Airstream with Eva right now.

On the back of the trailer, beneath the window with the agate, are neat rows of decals that they lovingly, meticulously placed throughout their two and a half years on the road. All the likely suspects are there: Glacier, Yellowstone, Zion, Sequoia, the Great Smokey Mountains, the Everglades. But they didn't just stick to the well-beaten paths, and Charlie can't help but smile thinking of the road to Denali National Park and the weeks they spent on the Alaska Highway. Or the days they lounged in Dry Tortugas. They had to leave Sebastian behind to take a boat across the turquoise water. They pitched a tent the old-fashioned way and explored the island from the home base of the first-come, first-served campground. It was the first time they swam with sea turtles.

The silence in the car is suddenly deafening, and Charlie realizes that Mia is studying her. The smile freezes on her lips, then melts away as quickly as it came. Her daughter is missing and she's *smiling*? Even in her grief-stricken, muddled state, Charlie understands how that must look.

"What now?" she asks quietly. She hadn't wanted to leave the marina, but after Detective James took the call about the life raft, things seemed to intensify. Deep down, Charlie knew this shift was because the likelihood that Eva was alive had increased by a few percentage points. She couldn't even go there—life, death, probabilities. Not yet. In the ruin that was her broken heart, the world could simply not exist without Eva in it. So when the detective kicked it into overdrive—he had no more time for an impromptu interview—Charlie was thrilled. They tried again to get her to take the ambulance to the hospital, and when she refused, she was sent home.

"Try to get some sleep," Mia advises her now. "Someone will be here when you wake up."

Detective James had already explained that someone would be around all night "just to keep an eye on things." He didn't elaborate and he didn't need to: if Charlie had done something to Eva—or knew what happened—they didn't want to risk her slipping away. But the presence of Landing PD in her driveway doesn't comfort Charlie, and she knows there's no way in hell she can sleep. Whether she likes it or not, she's playing a momentous game of chess. Eva is missing, and the last person to see her was her mother. This will explode online, and in no time at all the whole world will know. Charlie just wants Eva home, safe, whatever the cost. The thought of the yellow life raft bobbing on the waves is a thread of hope that she clings to like a lifeline. She can't even consider the *why* of it now.

Of course, Charlie realizes that to anyone from the North Shore, a missing life raft does not necessarily equate hope. Decades ago, a man had been convicted of murder when his wife's body washed ashore after some alleged boat trouble. Later, when the raft was discovered with five distinct puncture marks, the defendant's story began to deflate. The narrative is ubiquitous along the banks of Lake Superior: a horror story, cautionary tale, or tongue-in-cheek joke, depending on the company. Still, a frisson of dread sparks through Charlie at the thought that even now, people might be drawing comparisons between Eva's disappearance and that infamous case.

When another vehicle turns down the driveway, Charlie lets herself out of the police cruiser wordlessly. It's a second Landing officer, driving her truck with Frank buckled in the passenger seat. She hadn't talked to her foster father at the marina—they escorted her into the waiting cruiser before she had a chance—but she gave instructions for him to be brought here instead of to his apartment in the independent living section of the Landing Retirement Home. She couldn't stand the thought of him alone in that tiny one-bedroom apartment surrounded by the smell of cooked cabbage and the ghost of his recently deceased wife. Hattie had passed just before Christmas, and her sudden, precipitous decline was the reason Charlie and Eva came home to Minnesota in the first place. Charlie had never intended to stay, but the snow had been falling like a Hallmark movie when Eva stepped foot in Landing for the first time in years, and as she lifted her face to the sky and breathed deep, Charlie knew that an anchor had been dropped. Now Eva considered the lake house—not Sebastian—home.

The officer parks Charlie's truck beside the patrol car and kills the ignition. Charlie can see that he is talking to Frank, but she opens the passenger door, unconcerned about their conversation.

"Oh, Charlotte," Frank sighs, his eyes welling at the sight of her. "What are we going to do?"

He slides from the cab of the truck and she steadies him, wrapping him in her arms. When she was fourteen, and for all intents and purposes orphaned, Frank and Hattie Morrow had been her safe harbor. Charlie hadn't always been appreciative, but they never wavered in their commitment to her. In response, she loved them bluntly, solid and straightforward. There was little need for tenderness between them—Charlie had never been the touchy-feely type—but she holds him now, inhaling the scent of pipe tobacco and peppermint from the roll of sweets he keeps in his breast pocket.

Frank patting her back is almost her undoing, but Charlie pulls away before she can wither to the ground.

"I thought we should be together tonight."

"Of course," he says, taking her arm and falling in step beside her. Frank is eighty-four, but fit and bright—he had only agreed to the retirement home a year ago because he could no longer handle Hattie's care. By the time she stopped eating, and Charlie and Eva came home, he insisted he was happy where he was. And the Morrows' waterfront property on the outskirts of Landing became the Sutton girls' temporary haven.

The wind is fierce and the sky heavy with rain, but it refuses to fall. Charlie glances at the lake as she mounts the steps to the porch and tries to picture Eva in the raft, riding the white-capped swells. She prays for a hand to hold the inflatable platform—to draw back the rain and illuminate a path for the helicopters and bring her daughter *home*—but her heart is submerged before she can believe for even a second that everything will be okay.

A high-pitched whine from behind the front door reminds Charlie that Eva isn't the only life she's responsible for. "Scout!" she cries, lunging for the handle. Their golden mutt loves the trailer and life on the open road, but hates boats. He won't step a single paw on the *Summer Moon*, preferring to sleep in a patch of sun on the hardwood floor in the kitchen while waiting for his people to return. But's he's been locked in the house for hours longer than intended.

"Sorry, old boy," Charlie lets him out with an apology and a scratch behind the ears. Then he races into the yard, running a few circles around the two Landing police officers who are deep in conversation beside Mia's cruiser, before disappearing into the trees. Charlie wants nothing more than to bury her face in her dog's caramel fur, but it'll have to wait.

"You can sleep in the main floor bedroom," Charlie says, flicking on the lights as she steps inside.

"I can't sleep." Frank follows her through the living room to the eat-in kitchen at the back of the house. The bay window framing the small, round table looks out over the water, but there's nothing but darkness beyond the panes. "I haven't slept in years. You know me. Coffee?"

"Yes. Please." Charlie sinks into a chair at the table. The sounds of Frank moving about his own kitchen—opening and closing cupboards, running water into the glass carafe, and setting a pair of mugs on the counter—rewind the years. How many mornings did they spend together sipping strong coffee as the sun came up over the lake? For a moment Charlie wishes she could be sixteen again.

"Have you called her?"

"Goes straight to voice mail," Charlie tells him, but she slips her phone from her pocket and tries Eva's number anyway. Like the last dozen times she called, Eva's cheerful "Hey, leave a message!" plays almost immediately.

"I bet they'll do that triangulation thing. You know, where they use cell towers to figure out where a phone is?"

The hint of a smile tugs at Charlie's mouth. Frank loves his cop shows. "Yeah," she says, but his casual observation makes her mind spin off in other directions.

On the way back from the marina, Charlie had tried Find My Phone to see if she could locate Eva's cell. Unfortunately, the app simply said: No location found. Either the phone had been switched off or Eva had disabled location services, a thought that makes her physically sick. But the location of Eva's phone isn't the only thing that's turning her stomach. As Charlie sits at the table, she scrolls through the last few texts from her daughter.

It's stunning to her how a screen can give people permission to write things they would never dare to say. The epic fight she and Eva had just last night is a secret Charlie would like to keep, but Eva's texts to her tell a pretty damning story. An ugly story. Can Charlie just delete them?

Of course, the world had been a very different place when Eva came downstairs in the morning. She was happy, radiant even, in a pair of cut-off jean shorts and a loose tank top that revealed the lacy line of her bralette. She had hugged Charlie from behind and kissed her on the cheek. Begged her to take the *Summer Moon* out because the day was shaping up to be perfect in every way. Most important—in a shocking, completely un-anticipated turnaround—Eva had confessed she'd had a change of heart. "Let's do it," she whispered, her mouth close to Char-lie's ear. "One more summer on the road with Sebastian. Where should we go?"

It was all Charlie wanted. One more summer, a few more months with her daughter. She read once that you only get eighteen summers with your kids. And then they're off, grown into their own miraculous personhood, self-sufficient and inde-pendent and *gone*. Charlie wanted to cling to every moment like the final few grains of golden sand in her palm. It was selfish, maybe, but the truest thing about her in the months that she and Eva spent settled in Landing. She wanted *more*.

And Eva wanted less. At least, less of Charlie. Less time to-gether, less intrusion, less involvement in her day-to-day, her decisions, her world. It was the way of things, Charlie knew that, but it hurt all the same. She hadn't meant to push Eva so hard.

Now, she hates herself for not questioning her daughter's about-face. For believing Eva wholeheartedly because she *wanted* to, not because she was convinced everything had magi-cally resolved itself in a few short hours. But rather than press-ing it, Charlie had blissfully agreed, and they'd had a chatty, happy morning.

None of that is documented in Eva's angry texts. None of their jaunty banter is recorded, the familiar back-and-forth as Charlie made sandwiches and Eva entertained her with an end-less supply of giggle-inducing memes. And the feeling in the kitchen couldn't be captured and bottled up, offered as evi-dence of the very real joy and relief that had permeated the lake house in the warm glow of their sudden reconciliation. Instead, the last things Eva wrote to Charlie were a handful of seeth-ing words that kept them both up well into the night nursing regrets and cursing their own stubbornness. Charlie traces them with her thumb, wishing down to her marrow that she could erase them all. But she knows it can't be undone.

I can't believe you won't let this go

I said no

I'm not changing my mind

The most damning one was the last message Eva had sent. It was from a mere twenty-four hours ago, after Eva slammed the door to her bedroom so hard the light fixtures in the ceiling of the main floor rained dust.

I will never forgive you for this

INSTAGRAM POST #188

We can't believe the day has come, but
Sebastian is finally ready to hit the road!
We know you're dying for a tour, but
we'll reveal some (not all!) of our secrets
as we go. For now, peep our favorite
spot in the whole trailer. Dreamy, right?
We're locked and loaded, ready to roll,
and every other cliché and catchphrase
you could imagine. Drop your favorite
"we're ready" expression in the
comments below and we'll pick a lucky
winner to receive one of Charlie's prints
(your choice). Can't wait to see you
on the road, everyone! Oh! And don't
forget to say "hi" to the newest member
of the family, our rescue dog, Scout.
#ontheroad #newadventure #rescuedog

Always take the long way back,
Charlie & Eva

[IMAGE CONTENTS: A clean, white
couch beneath a wide, curved window
in a renovated Airstream trailer. The

couch is plush with pillows in soft
textures and muted colors. The window
frames a summery forest view and is
flanked by white-and-black buffalo plaid
curtains. A macramé planter hangs from
the ceiling with a large pothos plant
inside. On the butcher block table in
front of the couch, a handful of items
are carefully arranged: a tattered map
of the United States, a pair of black
binoculars, an antique brass compass,
and two stoneware mugs with steam
rising from the rims. On the floor is a
scruffy-looking dog with floppy ears and
a friendly face.]

Renovating the Airstream was a six-month endeavor, and one
that swallowed up Charlie's entire life savings. She didn't have
much—barely five figures collecting pennies on the dollar in an
account at the bank in Duluth. By the end, her hands were calloused and her joints sore, but she didn't mind. Restoring the trailer
wasn't just a cosmetic remodel, it was an absolute resurrection.

The Airstream was the only thing that Charlie's mother had
left her when she died. Officially, Rosie Sutton's cause of death
was listed as a heart attack brought on by acute cardiomyopa-
thy, but everyone in Landing knew that she had pickled her
liver—and every other organ in her body—over the course of
twenty-some years. Charlie had lived most of her childhood
understanding that her mother was not long for the world. How
many times had she called 911 only to be told to let Rosie sleep

it off? The EMTs underestimated how difficult it was to watch her mother "sleep it off" when the space they often shared was a twenty-seven-foot 1977 Airstream Overlander.

For years, the trailer had been parked in the trees on a piece of property belonging to Frank and Hattie Morrow near the outskirts of Landing. Exactly how the Airstream came to rest in the shade of the Morton building where Morrow Construction stored their trucks and equipment had been long forgotten. Rosie called the trailer their "summer home," but there were years when they were still there when the snow began to fly. Winter was when they couch hopped. One of Rosie's friends would put them up for a month. A new boyfriend for two, or if they were really lucky three. A homeless shelter in Duluth was good for a while when they were in between, and then the revolving doors of tolerant acquaintances would swing open and closed all over again.

Gutting the Airstream was an exhumation, and Charlie savagely exorcised all the ghosts of her past as she took a crowbar to the interior. She sobbed when she demolished the platform where her mother had slept, and the cupboards in the galley kitchen came down with a scream. It felt like holy work, a purging, and both her sweat and her tears baptized the hollow core of the trailer. When it was empty, and she began to carefully mend everything that had been broken, there was not a single floorboard that went down without intent. Charlie bound up her pain and her love, her loss and her hope, and poured it back out as an offering. The Airstream wasn't just their future home or Eva's dream brought to life, it was a promise that her daughter would never live like Charlie had: alone and afraid.

Uprooting the trailer from its decades-old spot on the property of Morrow Construction was one of the most exciting things Charlie had ever done.

"It needs a name," Eva said, when the Airstream was parked by the curb in front of their apartment building in Duluth. It sparkled in the hot July sun, looking for all the world like it was as ready for an adventure as they were.

"Really?" Charlie quirked an eyebrow.

"For sure. We need to be able to call it something in our posts." Eva lifted her fingers in air quotes. "'Bob needs gas.' It'll keep us on the road."

Charlie laughed. "Bob? We can do better than that." But she couldn't argue that Eva had a point. Involving their ever-growing audience in their escapades wasn't just a fun way to stay connected, it was turning out to be lucrative. The Sutton Girls had secured their first partnership with a Minnesota-based company that sold hiking gear and had signed a short contract that gave them access to merchandise and a hundred dollars per post, featuring the products. Eva's fingers gripping the straps of a charcoal-colored daypack as it dangled over a worn forest path had garnered thousands of likes—and exactly the kind of out-of-state exposure the company was hoping for. Still, a couple hundred dollars from photographing the daypack, poncho, and canteen they'd been gifted wouldn't get them very far. They needed more partnerships. More people invested enough to Venmo them a buck or two after they found one of the Sutton Girls' hidden gems or hiked an undiscovered trail that they'd shared.

"How about Sebastian?" Charlie suggested.

"Sebastian?" It was Eva's turn to wrinkle her nose.

"Like the crab in *The Little Mermaid*. It's perfect. They both have hard shells, are a little cranky, and ultimately obsessed with your happiness and well-being."

Eva tucked herself under Charlie's arm. "I thought that was you."

"Guilty as charged."

"I like Sebastian," Eva admitted. "It's kinda perfect. We could call him Seb for short."

Charlie planted a kiss on the top of her daughter's head as they studied the Airstream. It really was a sight to behold. Frank had helped her along the way, and Hattie had sewn the curtains, pillows, and bedding. Other friends and acquaintances had stepped in when different aspects of the remodel exceeded her limited knowledge. All their efforts had rendered the trailer unrecognizable from what it once had been. And it was all for Eva. To whisk her away, to allow her to see the world—or at least the continent—to give her all the things that Charlie had never even dared to dream about when she was Eva's age.

"I think we need to change the name of our account, too," Charlie said.

"Why?"

"Because this is *your* adventure. Your coming of age on the road. I think we should call it Eva Explores."

CHAPTER 4

SUNDAY

A blade of sunlight cuts through the slotted blinds and carves a path across Charlie's cheek. She startles awake, gasping in pain. She's fallen asleep sitting on the living room floor with her upper body draped across the coffee table. For a disoriented moment she can't imagine why she's here, why her body feels like it's on fire, and when she remembers, she's gutted all over again. Eva's gone.

Scout shifts from his resting place beside her and licks Charlie's hand. There's comfort in the way he curls his warm body against her—he knows something's wrong. The house feels strange without Eva in it. Never mind the old man snoring softly in the recliner.

Charlie cups Scout's head and presses her cheek to the velvety curl of one ear. He's really Eva's dog—after they rescued him, he attached himself to Eva like a trusty sidekick—but he'll take affection from anyone, and he whines softly at Charlie's touch. But she can't fix what's troubling him, so she gives him a scratch and then carefully lifts herself from the hard floor. Frank doesn't stir, and Charlie tiptoes to drape a blanket across his lap. She hopes for his sake that he can catch a few more hours of rest.

A quick glance at the clock on the mantel tells her it's just after six. The last time she checked in with Mia (who insisted

46

on spending the night in her cruiser even though Charlie invited her inside) was four a.m. Two unwelcome hours of sleep brought on by grief and pure exhaustion. It's nowhere near enough and far more than she wants or deserves. Charlie hates herself for sleeping while Eva is missing. What kind of a mother is she?

"You're just like *her*," a voice inside her head sneers.

Charlie stumbles to the bathroom and splashes her face with cold water. In the mirror above the sink her brown eyes stare back, bloodshot and swollen from crying. Her skin has a sickly gray cast, and the dark smudges in the hollow above her cheekbones make her look like she's been in a fight. The ghost of her dead mother stares back at her. She looks just like Rosie the morning after.

But whether she can ever forgive herself for letting this happen is irrelevant. The sun has risen on a new day, and she has one job and one job only: to find Eva.

Charlie brushes her teeth, changes into a clean sweater, and sneaks outside with Scout on her heels. Mia is leaning against the patrol car, yawning into the back of her hand. In the other, she holds what looks like a fresh cup of gas station coffee. It's steaming in the chilly morning air, and Charlie's mouth waters in spite of herself.

"If I'd known you were up, I would've told Ellis to bring you one too," Mia says as Charlie stares at the coffee.

"Any news?"

Mia shakes her head, but there's a hitch in the movement that makes Charlie think she's holding something back. She's about to press her when the sound of distant voices drags her attention toward the road.

The lane that leads from the dead-end street to the Morrows' farmhouse is long and cavernous, framed by an arch of trees tangled overhead. But at the crest of the low hill that draws away from the water, Charlie can just make out a handful of vehicles parked in the shallow ditch. "What's going on?" she asks, motioning toward the ruckus. Someone is shouting now.

Mia looks sheepish. "It's the media. The news about . . . well, about what happened got out."

"Already?" Charlie sways a bit, vertigo from shock and lack of sleep kicking in. "It's been less than twelve hours."

"There were a lot of people at the marina. One text can snowball like *that*." She snaps her fingers and Charlie starts.

Charlie knows this. She understands the interconnectedness of the digital age better than most. The way a story can start the size of a pinprick and balloon to Hindenburg proportions. How a handful of people can make so much noise it's deafening. What happens when the truth becomes something unrecognizable. She's battled more than her fair share of trolls and rumors gone wild, she just never imagined she'd lose control of her own narrative. Charlie has no idea what they're saying, how they're spinning this particular story, but separated by the trees and an invisible property line, she feels completely helpless.

"I want to talk to them," she says.

Mia laughs. "No. Bad idea."

Charlie bristles. "I don't think you can tell me what to do, Mia."

The officer narrows her eyes. "You can call me Officer Grady. And you're right, I can't tell you what to do. That was a bit of free advice from me to you. But I suggest that at the very least you consider how this must look from an outside perspective. And then ask yourself how they'll spin it."

Charlie feels her heart thump high and hot in her chest. She's doing it wrong. She's doing everything wrong. Mia's right. Everyone will be calculating whether or not Charlie had anything to do with her daughter's disappearance and come up with little evidence to the contrary. She stepped off the *Summer Moon*—alone—bloodied and still raw from a knock-down, drag-out fight with her daughter less than twenty-four hours before. But Charlie can't have people looking at her when they're supposed to be looking for her girl. Eva is out there, she can feel it in her bones. If her daughter was gone—*dead*, she makes herself think the word quickly, like ripping off a Band-Aid—wouldn't she sense it? Wouldn't she *know*? She can feel Eva in the world like a whisper in her soul.

"You're right," she says, letting her shoulders slump. She nods toward the small crowd at the end of the drive. "Who's there?"

"Some local reporters, the *Tribune*, and Fox 21 came up from Duluth with a couple of cameras. They're hoping for a clip to spice up the local news at seven." Officer Grady takes a sip of her coffee and studies Charlie over the rim. She seems to soften a little. "It's small now, Charlotte, but this is going to be big. You might want to go back in the house before someone spots you."

She knows. Eva Explores' modest fame is confined to a very particular community, but they have followers from all over the world, in all age groups. A majority are outdoor enthusiasts, hikers and bikers and people who like to consider themselves free spirits. And while neither Eva nor Charlie has to wear floppy hats and sunglasses in public, they have been recognized from time to time. Hiking the Narrows in Zion National Park. At a diner in a small town on the Georgia coast. It happened again in California and Jackson Hole and near the Adirondacks. In Landing, they are the local girls made good. People have long memories in small towns, and they take one look at Charlie's face and see Rosie. Who could have imagined the town drunk's daughter would one day be semi-famous? Charlie starts to tremble.

"Come on, let's get you inside," Officer Grady says, setting her cup of coffee on the hood of her car.

Charlie doesn't have the strength to protest, nor does she try to stop the policewoman from taking her by the elbow and leading her toward the house. But she pauses at the steps and sinks to the porch floor. "Frank is sleeping," she explains. "I don't want to wake him."

Officer Grady shrugs and leaves her to it, walking back to the patrol car with her arms stretched overhead. When the radio at her shoulder crackles and she answers it, Charlie wishes she was close enough to overhear.

Scout lopes out of the trees and bounds up the steps to flop down next to her. She wraps her arms around him for a moment, and then takes her phone out of her pocket. Out of habit, she tries Eva's number (straight to voice mail again), and when that fails, she opens up a search engine and types in her daughter's name. *Eva Sutton.* She pauses, afraid to hit enter and see what's being written. But this is her life now. What choice does she have?

Thousands of hits appear, so Charlie narrows it down by navigating to Tools and selecting *Past 24 hours* as a timeframe. Thankfully, there isn't much. Just a scattering of links, and only two of them seem relevant. The first is a tag on the Eva Explores Instagram account.

After they parked Sebastian six months ago, they only posted occasionally, and only because Charlie insisted their break was a sabbatical, not retirement. But if she was honest with herself, sharing about their life in Landing felt strange and hyperintimate because what they were suddenly doing was living a normal, rather uninteresting life. They enrolled Eva in high school, went grocery shopping, and spent time with Hattie in her final days. All boring, deeply vulnerable stuff that didn't photograph well and that Charlie refused to display on their feed. Yes, they had lived the last two and a half years very much in the public eye, but they gave the world a carefully curated glimpse of a fantasy life. Sure they took all the hikes and swam in the cold rivers and saw buffalo up close on the plains, but those pictures captured a split second in time. What happened before and after the shutter snap was off the record. Returning to Charlie's childhood home and documenting their often-rocky reentry into society felt like posing nude.

So they stopped. Or at least cut back dramatically. Charlie shot and uploaded the occasional porch view—making sure that there were no identifying landmarks in the photo—or the row of their new succulents on the kitchen window ledge. But it wasn't the same, and Eva wasn't exploring anymore. Not in the way their audience wanted. Her discoveries (the numbing routine of tardy bells and homework with a strict deadline) were not the stuff of social media esteem. They lost a lot of followers in those first few, rooted weeks, and many who stuck around had no qualms about sharing their disappointment.

The first search engine hit is a disgruntled former fan. Someone has tagged the @EvaExplores account in a list of influencers who "lost the magic touch." *Whyyyyyyy?* the user whines. *I don't know where to go (vicariously) or what to do (vicariously) without them. Thanks a lot, Charlie and Eva. You ruined my life.*

Charlie rolls her eyes. Clearly not much has changed in the land of social media.

The next hit takes her to a Reddit thread helpfully titled Charlie/Eva Sutton, The OG Lewis & Clark. Charlie knows that there are several Reddit threads dedicated to Eva Explores, but she learned long ago to give them a wide berth. There seems to be little oversight (or basic human kindness) on the platform, and after reading a particularly nasty conversation that made her want to lay waste to someone who referred to herself as *Instasnark*, Charlie swore it off. But this entry is recent, less than an hour old, and as Charlie clicks through, her palms go damp.

bebemama18

The dynamic duo we know and love (or love to hate) has been AWOL for months now, leaving us biting our finger-nails as we wonder: Where next? (We all know they haven't hit Kentucky yet. Got something against the deep south, girls?) Will Eva ever grow up? (Seriously, how do you survive in a 27-FOOT TRAILER with your mother, chica?) And, most importantly, will the Sutton girls ever learn to take a selfie??? (Welcome to the new world, bitches.) BUT, HYH all, did you hear? Is Eva missing? If you know, spill all, but please read the rules before posting, and try to have at least a little chill.

There are already fifty comments and counting. As Charlie watches, the number ticks up to 51, 52, 53. She scans the first comment (it's something about how *pushingupdaisies* would in-tentionally go missing if she had to share a 27-FOOT TRAILER with her mother) and quickly scrolls through a few more, look-ing for something of substance.

She hits it about halfway down.

blairstichproject

Are we surprised? Tell me no one is surprised by this. You spend 2+ years tripping all over the country in a trailer and DOCUMENT it and you think you can go back to life as normal??? Somebody finally caught up with that pretty girl and did bad, bad things to her. Or she ran away (you go, girl). All I know is that her mama should lose custody because

WHO DOES THAT? When I have kids, I will NEVER post their pictures online. She was asking for it.

 bebemama18
Define IT. I agree, they dug their own graves, but do you really think something bad happened to her?

 blairstichproject
IT is whatever bad thing happened. Mark my words. Credit where credit is due, and when the truth comes out you all have to admit that I called it. She ran, she was taken, or her mama did something to her. Didn't you always think that there was something not right about them? This won't end well, and Evangeline Sutton will be just another cautionary tale. Write it down kids: Mamas (GOOD mamas) don't let their babies grow up to be Instagram stars.

The severity of their collective judgment is staggering. But it shouldn't be. This is the way of things: a dizzying fall from grace can turn even the most beloved public figure into a scorned pariah.

Charlie's shaking so hard she can't hold the phone anymore. It slips from her fingers and topples down the stairs, coming to rest in the rocks of the gravel path. But she doesn't really care about the condemnation of a bunch of strangers. She's trembling because she hasn't even considered that anything truly unthinkable has happened to Eva. Drifting alone in a life raft on Lake Superior in May is bad enough. Never mind—God forbid—drowning. But *what happened?* The appalling possibilities replicate like sores and fester in Charlie's mind, each one more horrific than the next.

It's true, they have their fair share of obsessive followers and fanatics. A few creepy spin-off sites that fans set up to try and track them. Of course, Charlie and Eva were always just out of reach—they never posted about where they were until they had moved on, and there was no discernible path or pattern to their wanderings. If anyone showed too much interest, or posted something inappropriate, they blocked them immediately.

Still. They're sedentary now. Rooted in the same place and veritable sitting ducks. It wouldn't be nearly impossible to find them anymore. Has someone slipped through the cracks? Could Eva be in danger from more than just the elements?

Panic claws at Charlie, but before the tears that are threatening can fall, a commotion from the road interrupts her near hysteria. She stands on shaky legs to get a better view. A police cruiser with lights flashing but siren off is driving slowly down the lane. Officer Grady's replacement. But at the apex of the hill, reporters crowd the property line, pushing each other in their excitement to get the money shot. There are zoom lenses and people shouting questions over the distance between them—Charlie's been spotted. And because there is no gate, they spill down the road, following the cruiser. Lights flash, a boom mic surges forward, and Charlie freezes.

"Get in the house!" Officer Grady shouts.

But it's too late. The first few frames are already captured. Charlotte Sutton is bent and disheveled, her short hair impossibly mussed and her eyes red-rimmed and seeping. She looks wild. Angry. Maybe just a bit mad.

They'll call her: *Crazy Charlie.* The story is already being written.

INSTAGRAM POST #325

Everything they said is true. Yellow
stone is superlative. And if you consider
yourself a lover of the great outdoors,
we think you should definitely put this
national park on your bucket list. There
are so many things to see and do—and
we'll break them all down for you over
the next few days—but for now, we'll
share a view from Mount Washburn,
one of Yellowstone's most iconic peaks.
From the Dunraven Pass parking lot,
it's a 4–6 hour, moderate difficulty, out
and back hike (took us 5 hours, so
we're decidedly average), and from the
summit you can see the Tetons and all
the way to the Grand Canyon of Yellow
stone. Worth. Every. Step. Stay tuned for
so much more! And don't forget to drop
your guesses in the comments . . .
Where next? #yellowstone
#washburnsummit #evaexplores

Always take the long way back,
Charlie & Eva

[IMAGE CONTENTS: A young woman is pictured from behind at the top of Mount Washburn in Yellowstone National Park. She is sitting on the ground with her arm around a taffy-colored dog. She's wearing a yellow tank top and a red hiking backpack, and her long, dark hair is in two loose braids. Snowcapped mountains and lush, green hills roll away in the distance, and there are bright white clouds scattered across an extraordinarily blue sky.]

Charlie and Eva posted about Yellowstone from a campground near the Montana/Idaho border. It was a hidden oasis, set far back from the nearest paved road and alongside a wide, shallow river. A pair of fellow adventurers at a diner in Wyoming had hand drawn them a map.

"You won't find it online," the woman told them, scribbling on a napkin. Her skin was baked and leathery from hours spent in the sun and wind, but her smile was soft. Genuine. Her partner called her Honey. "It's the greatest little spot. Mostly a hub for fly fishers, but September is pretty slow. You'll have no problem finding a site. Right, Crew?"

"Yeah, but the map's not quite right." Crew reached for the napkin and made a few topographical corrections. "Here," he said, tracing the path with his finger when he was done, "you'll want to take I-90 through Butte, then take the exit just past Rock Creek . . ."

THE LONG WAY BACK

Their conversation had been light and easy, but when Eva excused herself to use the restroom, Honey had pursed her lips. "You're alone?" she asked.

"Hardly alone if we're together." Charlie smiled.

Crew gave her a quizzical look. "That's not what Honey means. Two pretty, young women traveling by themselves . . . Do you own a gun?"

A gun? It had never crossed Charlie's mind to arm herself. Even if she had a firearm, she highly doubted she'd be courageous (foolish?) enough to point and shoot when it mattered. "No." She laughed. "No gun. Pepper spray and a trigger-happy nine-one-one finger."

Honey and Crew exchanged a look. "Don't get me wrong," Honey said, "ninety-nine percent of the campgrounds you'll encounter are perfectly safe. Great lighting, decent security, lots of regulars, and managers that live on-site and truly care about their travelers."

"But it doesn't hurt to travel smart," Crew cut in. "Avoid South Dakota during Sturgis, Lake Mead in the height of summer, and anywhere that just doesn't feel right."

"Trust your gut." Honey nodded. "You'll know."

"Have you had problems?" Charlie asked, a slight quiver in her voice.

"No!" Honey quickly replied. "No. We've been camping for forty years. We've never had anything stolen or been confronted by vandals or . . . worse."

"But it's not unthinkable. And you're . . ." Crew trailed off.

Two women alone. Young. Easy targets. Charlie could fill in a dozen vulnerabilities that she and Eva possessed. Not that she hadn't thought of these things before they hit the road. It was just sobering to hear someone else say them out loud.

"We'll be careful," Charlie said. And then, Eva was sliding back into the booth and the conversation was over.

When they parted ways in the parking lot—Charlie and Eva into the steel-colored 4-wheel-drive truck that had already conveyed them nearly two thousand miles, and Crew and Honey into a Mercedes Sprinter—Crew beckoned Charlie to follow him. He dug around in a compartment in the back of the camper van and came up with a Louisville Slugger.

"Here," he said, handing it to Charlie. "Just in case."

Thanks to Crew and Honey's map, the hidden campground had been easy to find. And their newfound friends were right: it was an oasis. After three weeks in Yellowstone—hitting all the touristy spots and hunting for hidden gems—they were ready to slow down a bit, and the sleepy, half-empty Crooked Creek Campground tucked between a circle of tall mountain peaks fit the bill perfectly. The peculiar mix of their "on the road" yet "in the public eye" new life was fun and exhilarating, but also exhausting.

They picked a site beside the river and angled Sebastian so that when they sat around the fire ring at night, it felt as though they were the only people in the world. High above, the stars pooled like cream between the mountains that hemmed them in.

They felt fierce and free.

"I liked them," Eva said as they were lying in the Airstream late one night.

Charlie had retro-fitted Sebastian with both heat and air-conditioning, and it was the first night that they turned on the heater. They were snuggled under plush quilts in their respective beds: Charlie's a queen beneath the big window on the hitch-side of the trailer, and Eva's a twin perpendicular to her mother's and across a narrow hallway from the bathroom.

"Liked who?" Charlie asked, rolling over so she could better hear Eva. She had been half-asleep when her daughter started talking.

"The couple in Wyoming. The ones who told us to come here."

"Me too," Charlie agreed. "We've met some pretty great people so far." But a prickle of unease made her pull the blankets tighter.

"Do you think everyone will be so nice?" Eva whispered into the darkness.

So Eva had overheard. At least, a little.

"Maybe not," Charlie admitted. "But we can handle whatever—and whoever—the road throws at us."

It wasn't false bravado. Charlie was no Pollyanna—her life with Rosie had made sure of that—and she felt prepared to face pretty much anything. She had planned ahead. In addition to a new, heavy-duty Keeler lock, she had outfitted Sebastian with a bolt barrel slide lock that they secured every night. Charlie had signed up for Platinum AAA, and their phones had unlimited coverage all over the United States. They carried an emergency survival kit on long hikes, equipped with everything from a small hatchet to a fire starter and a thermal blanket. There was pepper spray within easy reach in the truck, trailer, and affixed to Charlie's key chain. And they hiked with bear whistles and mini GPS radios in case they were separated from each other—which hadn't happened yet. All in all, Charlie felt they were doing everything they could to stay safe as they adventured.

Still.

"Why did Crew give you a baseball bat?" Eva pressed.

Charlie took a deep breath. "An overabundance of caution. And pure and simple kindness."

"But, you don't think we'll need it, do you?"

Charlie sat up and crawled to the end of the bed to smooth the errant curls that always tickled Eva's cheeks. "No," she said, pressing a kiss to her daughter's warm temple. "Definitely not. But if we did, you need to know that I once hit a home run in PE."

Eva giggled. "You did? How old were you?"

"Doesn't matter."

"How old?"

Charlie sighed. "Fine. I was ten and it was only a home run because Mickey Erikson fumbled the ball when it bounced and hit him in the chin. He started to cry instead of chasing the ball."

"That's tragic," Eva moaned. "Poor Mickey."

"Not: poor Mickey! Try: yay, Mom! You're supposed to be impressed by my skills. Awed by my strength and prowess."

"Because you hit a home run in fourth grade? Whatever. Go to sleep, Mom."

"Yeah, yeah. Goodnight, Evangeline Rose."

"'Night, Mom."

Charlie shuffled back under the covers, grateful that Eva's breathing was already starting to slow. She was grateful for the heavy locks on the door and the hum of the heater as it beat back the chill in the autumn air. But most of all, she was grateful that Eva was asleep when the wolves started to howl, an eerie cry that echoed through the canyon and made the hair on Charlie's arms stand up. She listened for a while, torn between loving the sound and fearing it: she felt so unrestrained out here, wild and resonant, elemental and alive. Whole and fully present on a swiftly tilting planet beneath an infinite sky. In stripping away the trappings of a life that hadn't been very joyful anyway—Charlie was a single mom working a miserable job and living in a crappy apartment with a daughter who was bullied—she was starting to become her essential self. So was Eva. They were connected to the world and to each other. Unconcerned about the expectations of a culture and community that had more or less forgotten them. Charlie wasn't sure she had ever felt happier.

But as she rolled over to smooth her cheek into the pillow, she reached with one hand to feel for the baseball bat that she had secreted away at the head of her bed. She rubbed the smooth wood with her thumb until she fell asleep.

CHAPTER 5

Charlie understands that she is under a sort of house arrest. No charges have been filed, and no one has told her as much, but the officers stationed outside of the lakeside home and the fact that Detective James won't answer her calls is evidence enough. Presumably, Officers Grady and Martinez are here because they know what's coming—a tidal wave of attention that will swell and grow as the news of Eva's disappearance spreads—but they also suspect that Charlie should not be *going*. Anywhere. The marina is off-limits, as is the police station. Not that heading there would change much of anything—nearly half of Landing's small force is mere yards away from where she stands peering out from behind closed curtains.

The invisible shackles are unsettling.

She paces the main floor, rounding the chair where Frank is alternating between watching her and watching TV. Before they were forced back off the property, Fox 21 got what they wanted: Charlie looking like a deer in the headlights and guilty of *something* as she turns tail and runs into the house. The clip is played over and over again, and made all the more incriminating because, in her haste, Charlie slams the door on Scout and leaves her faithful companion standing alone on the porch. He turns to the eager reporters and growls. The sound underscores the scant brief: Local "Celebrity" Miss-

62

ing. The quotes around *celebrity* feel at once patronizing and accurate.

"I'm going outside," she announces when the news goes to commercial.

"I don't think that's a good idea," Frank says, holding up the remote control as evidence. His meaning is clear: *Don't give the armchair detectives any more fodder. Don't give them another clip to play.*

"I just need a little fresh air."

Frank looks skeptical, but he pushes himself out of the recliner and clicks off the TV. "I'll make us something to eat."

It's midmorning, less than fifteen hours after Eva went missing, and neither of them has thought to eat or drink anything besides coffee—and that's pure necessity. They feel trapped and helpless, indifferent to food. Still, it will be good for Frank to have something to do, even if she can't stomach a bite.

The back door is through the laundry room. It opens on two wide steps and a patch of hard-packed dirt that is perpetually damp and mossy because it's on the north side of the house. A thicket of trees separates the Morrows' property from their neighbors, the Greenes, but a narrow path through the underbrush has made borrowing eggs or a cup of sugar a simple endeavor for more than fifty years. It's quiet here, brisk in the shade and completely separate from the bedlam that is the driveway. Charlie could almost lean against the clapboard siding and forget that her world is unraveling. That on the other side of the house, cops and reporters and concerned citizens wait anxiously for the smallest scrap of news or a fleeting glimpse of Eva's mom. Eva's bad mom. Her terrible, irresponsible, negligent mom. Charlie knows that whatever happened, the world will believe that it's all her fault. She doesn't think they're wrong.

The morning is crisp but warming at the edges, the sun sparkling furiously off the water as Charlie climbs over the low stone wall and drops to the rocky beach below. It's not really a beach, more like a thin strip of rugged coastline, covered in smooth pebbles and bits of driftwood. When she was Eva's age, it was her favorite place on the Morrows' property. Forget the widow's walk on the roof (accessible only through a pull-down ladder on the second story) or the porch swing with a view of the lake and the sailboats that scudded across the waves on hot summer days. Charlie loved the slice of land between the fresh-cut grass and the ferocious rush of water. She could think most clearly in the space between tame and wild, home and away.

Lake Superior is calm this morning, the waves lapping at the stones gentle as a kitten with milk. Usually, Charlie loves this particular mood of the water: peaceful and somehow sated. There was no storm last night, not a single drop of rain fell, and still Eva was lost on a raft (Charlie's favorite theory) in the vast expanse of water and sky. Maybe if it had been still, if these idyllic conditions had existed last night, they would have found her easily. Charlie can almost picture it: her dark-haired daughter waving in the yellow raft. Laughing at her own joke even though nothing about it is funny. Later, telling Charlie that she *had* to run, that it was the only way to get her mother's attention. Why? But the why of it all is still as incomprehensible as a black hole, and Charlie knows she has to take this one step at a time. Step one: find Eva.

The waterfront that stretches the length of the Morrows' modest estate is its own little cove, a shallow curve that is bordered on the south end by trees spilling over and into the water and a rocky outcropping to the north. Loosely speaking, the jagged peninsula correlates to the Greene's property, but technically no one owns the beach. Charlie's relieved that the reporters haven't figured that out yet. Although, if they did try to hike down from the tiny, lakeside park a half mile south, the terrain wouldn't make it effortless. The rocks are slippery, the boulders sharp. Ice-cold water on one side and a tangled forest on the other make the hike an adventure. It would be hard to navigate with cameras and equipment.

"You've got a great view."

Charlie's heart skips as she spins to see who's found her. How long has she been out here? Ten minutes? Twenty? How did they know she was here?

But it's not a determined reporter who's joined her on the beach. It's Detective James. "Didn't mean to startle you," he says, burying his hands in the pockets of his jacket and squinting out across the water. It's clear to Charlie that he meant to do exactly that. "Chilly morning."

Charlie doesn't really feel it until he says it, but all at once the breeze off the water lifts the fine hairs on her arms and sends a tremor down her spine.

"Have you found her?" Charlie hardly dares to ask, and yet the words tumble from her tongue in a rush.

"No."

He doesn't offer so much as a scrap of news to soften the blow, but it's better that way. Charlie takes the report like a clean right hook, absorbs the pain, and moves right past it.

"What next? Let me help. Let me take a boat out. I know Eva better than anyone and—"

"That's exactly why I'm here," Detective James cuts in, giving her a sideways glance. "We didn't get a chance to finish our conversation last night. I have a few more questions."

"I don't see what good talking will do. Shouldn't we be out looking for her?" Charlie can feel frustration coming to a head, foaming up and out of her chest in a fizz of frantic energy. But the detective cuts it with a single sentence.

"Perhaps you'd be more comfortable at the station?"

The implication is clear: cooperate here and now, or we'll make you. Nothing she can do to help behind bars in the local jail.

"Frank is making breakfast," she says, turning toward the house. It's hard to leave the water, the place where Eva is. She snags one last look over her shoulder, taking in the spill of blue and the dark smudge of tiny islands crouched in the distance, and leads the way back to the kitchen. Detective James follows.

They find Frank and Sophie sitting at the table overlooking the lake, and for a few seconds Charlie can't square the scene before her.

Sophie Greene is the Morrows' longtime next-door neighbor and friend. She's in her mid-sixties, short and sturdy with a neat, silver bob and blue eyes that usually glint with a mischievous twinkle. There's no joy in her expression today, though, and she pushes back from the table to wrap Charlie in a hug that's almost suffocating in its intensity.

"I brought food. I can't fix a damn thing, but I can make sure you're cared for and fed," Sophie says, giving Charlie one last, hard squeeze. "We're going to get through this, okay?"

Someone—Frank or Sophie?—has opened the blinds at the back of the house, away from the drive and the reporters, and lifted the sash windows. The breeze is light and fragrant, laced with lake water and springtime. On the table there is a generous griddle of fried eggs, hot blueberry drop biscuits with a drizzle of white glaze, and a plate of sausages. A full pot of steaming, black coffee stands in the middle of the table. Charlie's stomach betrays her by grumbling.

It's as if Sophie can read her mind. "You need to eat. And rest and keep taking care of yourself. You'll be no good to anyone—least of all Eva—if you don't cover the basics." She fills a plate for Charlie and slides it across the table in front of an empty chair.

"Sit down, Charlotte." Frank's eyes are pleading, and he looks as if he's aged ten years in a night. It scares her.

Because Charlie feels thick-headed, her thoughts muddled

and unsure, she does as she's told. It's only when Sophie starts filling a second plate that she remembers Detective James. "Oh," she says belatedly, motioning toward where he hovers in the door between the laundry room and the kitchen, "this is Detective James."

"We've met," Frank tells her. "We sent him to call you for breakfast. And the other gentleman is already eating."

As if summoned, a tall, Black man in jeans and a dark gray blazer ducks into the room. He's startlingly handsome, with a wide, white smile and bottomless eyes. His natural hair is cropped in a tight fade with neat, razor edging at the temples and along his high forehead. He's holding a nearly empty plate. "Didn't mean to disappear on you," he says. "This is absolutely delicious, Mrs. Greene. Thank you."

The older woman blushes, and Charlie finds herself looking between Sophie and the stranger who seems so at home in her kitchen. To add insult to injury, Scout pads out of the living room and flops down by the newcomer's feet as if they are the best of friends.

"Excuse me," the man says, setting his fork on the plate so he can offer Charlie his hand. "I'm Agent Jude Turner. FBI."

FBI? And as she slips her hand in his—unexpectedly calloused, firm grip—any appetite she had is suddenly gone. But she doesn't want to make a fuss in front of Frank and Sophie, so she pulls off a corner of her still-warm biscuit and puts it in her mouth. It tastes like dust on her tongue.

Ignoring the detective and FBI agent, she says to Sophie: "I want you to take Frank home when we're done eating."

"That's the plan," the older woman agrees. "We can walk back to my house and we'll go from there, okay, Frank?" He looks for a moment as if he's about to protest, but Sophie is already going on. "That way we won't have to run the gauntlet. I'll just take the long way back."

Charlie's heart hitches at Sophie's casual words. She studies her friend for just a moment, weighing if she said it on purpose or not. It wasn't intentional, she decides, but she has to put her fork down and take a sip of the scalding coffee to ease the knot in her throat anyway.

The Sutton girls carefully curated well over a thousand social media posts, and all but the very first few are signed: *Always take the long way back*. It's their family motto, something that Charlie said to Eva when she was just a babe in arms. "Let's take the long way back, shall we?" If she's honest with herself, it's a tiny stab at Rosie and the way that Charlie was never allowed as a child to linger. Their followers love it. They put it on T-shirts and use it as a sort of code to separate the true devotees from casual fans. One woman even had it tattooed on her arm in her grandmother's graceful cursive. She tagged the Eva Explores account in all the stories she posted about the process.

Charlie tosses a napkin over her plate and takes it to the sink before anyone can inspect how much she's eaten. Three bites, to be exact. And they're churning in her stomach.

"If you're done," Agent Turner says, joining her at the counter, "perhaps you could show us Eva's room." He tucks his practically licked-clean plate beneath her full one and carefully places his fork in the sink.

Who is this man? And who says *perhaps*? Charlie finds herself staring at him, but when he looks back, she can't hold his gaze. "Why are you here? Why is the FBI involved?"

They're wasting time here, eating Sophie's homemade biscuits when they should be out looking for Eva. Lake Superior is roughly the size of Maine—the Coast Guard has thousands of square miles to cover, and though she's sure they can calculate wind speed and waves to coordinate approximate distances covered, it feels as if every moment allows Eva to slip farther and farther away. Don't they understand the urgency? Don't they feel the ticking bomb that is time spent unprotected against the elements? If they don't find Eva soon, there will be nothing left to find. The thought rips through her like a flame.

If Agent Turner can sense the sudden acrid heat of her fear, he doesn't let on. But he does say calmly, "The FBI field office in Duluth is often utilized in missing person cases, especially when the victim is a minor. We lend tech assistance and resources and offer an objective perspective when needed."

"They handle high-profile cases," Detective James adds, and there is an edge in his voice.

Charlie clocks the fissure between the two, but she doesn't much care if they hate each other like she suspects. "You want to see Eva's room? Why?"

"It'll help us understand her better," Agent Turner says. "What motivates her, who her friends are, how she sees the world."

"We're going to need her computer and her phone." Detective James takes a far more direct route. "We need to know if she was suicidal."

Fury turns Charlie's blood to ice. "Eva was not suicidal," she says coldly. "Her room is this way."

The stairs to the second floor are through the living room. They're narrow and creaky, something Charlie hated when she was a teenager, but loves now that her own daughter is of sneaking-out age. At the landing, there's a ninety-degree turn and a lead glass window that is always the first to frost over in winter. Charlie glances through the diamond panes to see if more crews have joined the melee at the end of the drive, but the glass is warped and smoky at the edges. All she can see is a watercolor of green and blue.

There are two bedrooms and a small bathroom on the second floor, and Eva's room is at the very end of the hall. After living in close quarters for so many years, the expanse of the house feels immense to Charlie, and she still finds it hard to fall asleep without the sound of Eva's breathing in her ears. Eva talks in her sleep—nonsense words and phrases that sound like a one-sided conversation. Or, she used to. Charlie hasn't fallen asleep close to her daughter in nearly six months.

"Here it is," she says, swinging open the door and stepping inside. She resists the urge to follow it with: *You won't find anything*.

The room is cramped but tidy, with sash windows and a slanted roof over the twin bed. Eva painted everything in shades of yellow when she moved in—buttery walls and honeyed doors and trim in a shimmery, frothy cream—and the bedspread is tufted and white. The overall effect is of unbridled optimism, happiness, and hope. *See?* Charlie wants to say. *The girl who lives in this room can't possibly be suicidal.* Her gaze catches on a dark swath hanging over the frame of the closet door. Eva's graduation gown. Navy with gold cords draped around the neck. She came home with it yesterday. The day before? Time seems irrelevant, and Charlie sinks to the edge of the bed.

"You okay?" Agent Turner asks. "You don't need to stick around."

Charlie assumes it's a polite way of asking her to leave, but she's not going anywhere. She shakes her head and stays put.

So the two men begin to sweep the room, casually at first. Detective James opens the closet and peers inside, careful not to disturb the graduation gown. He flips through Eva's hangers with a knuckle, but it seems half-hearted. When Charlie turns her attention to Agent Turner, she realizes that he has slid a pair of leather gloves over his long, slender hands. They're black and expensive, but she knows he's not wearing them to be fashionable.

"No one has been in here," Charlie offers. "I mean, besides me and Eva."

"She didn't have friends over?"

"No. I mean, yes. Sometimes." Rarely. "But they mostly hung out downstairs. There's not much room in here." The truth is, Eva has only ever had one girl over: Piper Berkley. She came exactly twice, and Charlie despaired of her daughter ever making a good, true friend. But after those first awkward homework sessions, Eva found her groove in Piper's world. Piper's fancy house and friends and preferred weekend activities. Charlie couldn't complain. She'd had Eva all to herself for two and a half years on the road—she could hardly grumble now about her daughter's regular absences, especially if they were friend-related.

Agent Turner uncurls his body from a crouch and clips his head on the slanted ceiling. "I'm going to need the names and numbers of Eva's closet friends," he says, rubbing the spot.

"Okay." But she isn't sure she has that information. Eva's friends are all new, a gaggle of long-limbed girls with dewy skin and hair so shiny it looks like they've stepped from the pages of a magazine. *Teen? Seventeen?* Charlie doesn't even know if those magazines exist anymore, and she isn't sure she could name Eva's friends. She hasn't even met them all, just seen cropped photos on Eva's phone when she prodded her daughter for details. How many texts did Eva send over the last six months telling Charlie she was *going out with the girls* or *@Piper's house?* Why didn't Charlie pay closer attention to who and where and when?

"Boyfriend?"

"No," Charlie says a little too quickly. One of Agent Turner's eyebrows quirks, but he doesn't press it.

"Job?"

"She works at Mugs. It's a little cafe on Badger Street."

"I'm assuming she goes to Landing High."

"Yes. Since January."

"Homeschool before that," Detective James interjects as if trying to prove himself a valuable asset.

They're quiet for a few minutes, both men concentrating on a more thorough investigation of Eva's room. Detective James has pulled a pair of latex gloves from his pocket and is feeling along the bookshelf that's crammed with everything from Jane Austen to Rick Riordan. Agent Turner has drawn the short stick and is rifling through Eva's drawers, starting with her underwear drawer at the top of the small bureau. There's a certain chivalry in the way he carefully lifts and shifts her things, putting it all back exactly where he found it. But the invasion of her daughter's privacy unearths something in Charlie all the same, like black rot beneath the blade of a shovel, and she pushes herself off the bed before she loses control and screams at him to stop.

"Where's her computer?" Detective James asks.

Charlie is clenching her fists so tight her fingers are going numb. "What?" she manages, barely comprehending.

"Eva's computer. Landing High is entirely digital. They issue a laptop to students at registration. She's gotta have one. Where is it?"

Yes, Eva has a school computer. It usually sits on her desk, and the power cord snaking across the surface only accentuates its absence. "In her backpack?" Charlie tries. But it's clear to them all that there's no backpack in the room. Still, they look under the bed and in the closets, behind the door and in every corner. Eva's backpack is missing.

"Did she take it on the boat?" Agent Turner asks.

Charlie can't remember. "I don't think so. Why would she take her school computer on the boat? It must be downstairs somewhere." But she already knows that it's not. After years of living in Sebastian, of having a dedicated place for absolutely everything, Eva is not the kind of girl to toss her backpack on a chair or leave her coat draped over the back of the couch. Her backpack belongs beneath her desk, the top zipper open and ready for the computer that spends every night connected to the charger so it's ready to go the next day. Eva is meticulous.

"We need to find that computer," Agent Turner says, and for the first time there is something flinty in his voice. He's kind, but Charlie gets the sense that he is also very good at his job. A phrase from her sporadic Sunday school days slips unbidden into her mind: *gentle as a dove, wise as a serpent*. It fits the FBI agent like a tailored suit.

"I'm sure it's around here somewhere," Charlie repeats, though the air in the room is brittle with doubt.

"Does Eva keep a journal? A diary? Anything of the sort?" Detective James is now rummaging through the three tiny drawers of her desk, rattling #2 pencils, plastic boxes of paper-clips, and tacks that Eva kept neatly sorted and stacked.

Looking through his eyes, Charlie can see that her daughter's room is almost preternaturally clean and organized. What seventeen-year-old alphabetizes her books and sorts her T-shirts by color? One who spent the last two and a half years in a twenty-seven-foot trailer with her mom, Charlie wants to explain. They had to compartmentalize their inner lives, find ways to express their individuality and process their emotions and *exist* in careful, unobtrusive ways. Of course, they lived loud and open with each other, sharing things that other mothers and daughters would probably consider a sort of willful violation of acceptable boundaries. And it worked for them. It was special and beautiful. It was good. But Charlie doesn't know how to say any of those things.

"Eva Explores was our diary," she says instead.

Detective James looks unimpressed. "No phone, no computer. No diary or journal or even a note from a friend. There isn't even dust on her windowsill. Eva's life looks pretty sterile."

Charlie's tears are swift and mortifying. She blinks them away, but not before one slips down her cheek. Eva's life is the farthest thing from sterile. "I don't think you'd understand," she whispers.

"Maybe I'll understand this." Detective James takes a step toward her. "Did Eva use drugs? Did she party? What about alcohol? Did she drink a lot?"

For a moment Charlie is too stunned to even reply. "No. Absolutely not."

"So the alcohol on the boat was yours?" This question comes from Agent Turner, and when she turns to look at him, his gaze is steady. There is no pity in his eyes, but also no rancor.

"Yes," she admits to him, not Detective James. She thinks, *My mother was an alcoholic. I battle my own addictions. Mostly, I win.* But of course, she doesn't say that. Charlie knows how it will look, and that they will shift their full attention to her. She can't have that—they need to keep focusing on the water. The raft. The hope that somewhere out there Eva is okay and waiting to be found.

Charlie needs them to believe that it's true. *She* needs to believe that it's true. So she changes the subject. "I'll make that list for you," she says, crossing the room to grab a pad of paper and a pencil from Eva's desk. "Of her friends. And her boss at Mugs. She rides to school sometimes with the kid who lives at the end of the road. I think his name is Andrew?"

They let her scribble, jotting down every name she can think of, and then referencing her phone to see if she has their contact info. But Agent Turner's question lingers in the room like an odor. It's just another piece of circumstantial evidence stacked against her.

INSTAGRAM POST #401

With love from Arizona!

The Sutton girls don't do snakes, but
we've been told that the rattlers down
here "brumate" (a fancy word for their
special form of hibernation) in winter. So
we left the West Coast for some
southern sunshine—and Tucson is making
our hearts go pitter-patter! Everything
here is a study in contrasts: hot days
and cold nights, harsh landscapes and
the most delicate of flowers, arduous
trails but moments of true serendipity.
Can you believe we just stumbled across
this purple prickly pear? A perfect heart
in the middle of the toughest path. If
that's not a metaphor for life, we don't
know what is. There are tons of great
hikes around here, but we especially
loved Bear Canyon to Seven Falls (this
photo was taken about halfway in). It's
an 8-mile out and back with an elevation
gain of just over a thousand feet. The
trail features several stream crossings
(you will get wet shoes!) and ends at

a gorgeous pool (definitely plan ahead
for a much-deserved swim). Bookmark
it for your next Arizona trip. And Happy
Valentine's Day from us. We hope you
enjoy this little love note in the wild!
#bearcanyon #sevenfalls #valentinesday
#evaexplores

Always take the long way back,
Charlie & Eva

[IMAGE CONTENTS: A pair of hands
curled in the shape of a heart
frame a prickly pear pad that is also
heart-shaped. The cactus is bright
purple and green, and there are tall
saguaros and jagged mountain peaks in
the distance. The hands are tanned and
lightly freckled, and around the right wrist
there are several handmade friendship
bracelets in a rainbow of colors.]

They spent just over a month in Arizona. It was supposed to be a pit stop on their way from southern California to Florida, but Charlie and Eva ended up loving the desert in a way they couldn't have predicted. It wasn't at all what they expected it to be. Though it was hot, the air felt clean and crisp in their lungs, and the endless sunshine in the dead of winter was welcome. They wanted to be outside all the time and created their own little haven in a campsite shadowed by the Rincon Mountains.

An outdoor rug ringed by plastic Adirondack chairs in an array of primary colors became their unofficial living room and a place of fellowship for their neighbors in the campground. Late afternoon was their impromptu gathering time, and Charlie found herself looking forward to this hour with strangers who became quick friends more than she cared to admit.

There were the requisite snowbirds, older couples from freezing northern states who wintered in Arizona and inevitably missed their children and grandchildren—they took great pleasure in spoiling Eva. And there were younger families who came on weekends to enjoy the two sparkling pools at opposite ends of the campground—Eva took great pleasure in spoiling their small children. Sometimes, as people began trickling over with icy drinks in hand, Eva would offer to take the kids to the pool by herself and let the adults have "grown-up" time. Because the campers felt a bit like family, and because Eva was so clearly kindhearted and dependable, the parents inevitably (gratefully) said yes, and sank to the bench of the picnic table in the shade of Sebastian's awning with exhausted smiles.

"She's incredible," Diane, a thirtysomething mom with five-year-old twins, told Charlie. "You're raising an amazing young woman there."

"Yeah, she's pretty great." Charlie grinned. "But she is fifteen—she can be a total pain in the butt, too."

"I just can't believe that your teenager agreed to hit the road with you. How long have you been gone, again?" Diane's husband, Tim—a man almost ten years her senior and with far less social grace than his lovely bride—stopped dealing the Rook cards long enough to arch one eyebrow at Charlie.

She didn't answer. He had asked this question before. Somehow, the lifestyle that Charlie and Eva had chosen for a season was suspect to Tim. He gave Charlie the impression that he thought they must be on the run from something, and he was forever trying to ferret out what he considered to be the "real" reason for their itinerancy. But Diane wasn't having it.

"Stop it," she said, smacking his arm with the back of her hand. "I just hope we have as good of a relationship with our boys someday as Charlie has with Eva."

"It's inspiring," Ingrid said, joining the circle. "Your relationship is beautiful." She was pushing her adult daughter, Lydia, in her wheelchair. There were already a half dozen lengths of colored floss taped to the arm of the chair. Eva and Lydia would braid friendship bracelets later, enjoying quiet camaraderie before tying their creations on each other's wrists. They were amassing quite the collection.

"It's not inspiring," Charlie demurred. "It's just us. This is something we've always wanted to do, and we're lucky to be able to do it."

"So how long do you think people will bankroll your adventures?"

"Tim, seriously!" Diane grabbed the deck of cards from his hand and shooed him off the picnic table. "I need a drink. Why don't you go grab us some margaritas? Charlie?"

Charlie shook her head, but Ingrid, and Leo and Kyle (who had just turned up), all indicated that they'd take one of the sugary canned concoctions that Diane favored. Tim left the circle in a bit of a huff.

"Ignore him," Diane told Charlie when Tim was out of earshot. "He's just jealous."

"Of some company goodies and Venmo contributions for gas?" Charlie chuckled, but it was hollow. The truth was, one of the reasons they had settled in Arizona for so long was because they were running low on cash. The mail forwarding service they had employed before they left Minnesota kept them flush in outdoor gear and trendy T-shirts, but the few checks they received were small. Once, Charlie had uploaded a gas station photo to their Instagram stories and joked: "Will trade travel tips for gas money!" Enough people ponied up a few bucks that she was able to fill the tank and grab some pre-made subs from the convenience store. They weren't destitute, but they certainly weren't rich.

"Nah, he's jealous because you like each other enough to want to be together, day in and day out, week after week, month after—hey!" Leo broke off when Kyle hit him.

Everyone laughed because Leo and Kyle had been together on location for nearly two months. They were filmmakers working on a documentary about ocelots in southern Arizona and northern Mexico, and their lives consisted of tracking the rare mammal and hurrying off to remote locales when sightings were reported. Unusual footage of one of the sleek cats peering at a trail cam had them tenting for a week, but they were back at home base—a worse-for-the-wear fifth wheel circa the late 1980s—while they pored through footage and decided where to go next. Like Charlie and Eva, they were their own solitary duo.

"I didn't choose this life," Kyle joked. "It chose me. And believe me, I'd take anything with a pulse over Leonard here."

"That's a low blow," Leo mused, reaching for the Rook cards he had been dealt. "Don't tell people my real name is Leonard unless you're ready for everyone to know that your Tinder profile claims you're five foot nine."

Ingrid got the giggles at this, and Kyle's protests only made her laugh harder. "Honey, we see eye to eye and I've been five five since the seventh grade. Whoever swipes right on you is in for a surprise!"

Charlie loved their banter, the comfortable back-and-forth of this potpourri of people. The campground was a level playing field where their backstories were often irrelevant; they lived in the present moment and rarely discussed much beyond their plans for the very next day. An outing to a fabled taco truck on the outskirts of a nearby small town, a midday movie at the cinema to get a break from the heat, a nighttime trip to the local observatory.

Stargazing was how Leo first managed to get Charlie alone. "Did you know the entire state of Arizona has light pollution laws?" He told her that one night as the sun went down and everyone filtered back to their trailers. "It's a worldwide hub for astronomy, so they cut down as much unnecessary light as possible. You've never seen the Milky Way until you've seen it beneath an Arizona sky."

He was cute, a little younger than Charlie, with a hipster beard that he kept carefully trimmed. Leo wore lightweight hiking pants with zippered pockets and T-shirts that hugged in just the right places. At first, Charlie thought that he and Kyle were a thing. But when she agreed to walk over the ridge with him so they could watch the first few stars prick the purpling night sky, and he laced his fingers through hers, any lingering doubts vanished.

They had sex a handful of times, usually on a coarse, wool blanket that Leo carried along during their star-gazing excursions. It was hurried but sweet, a guilty pleasure like stolen candy. Charlie and Leo were more friends than anything, but when he slid his body against hers, Charlie felt a spark of longing so white hot it made her claw her fingers into his skin as she bit back tears. She was lonely, she realized, and maybe he was, too. For a few weeks outside of Tucson they had each other, but around the circle with their friends in the afternoons, they treated each other with the same neutral warmth they employed with the rest of their patchwork group.

Charlie thought she had everyone fooled.

It wasn't until Leo and Kyle were packing up to head for the Mexican border that she realized her whirlwind romance with Leo wasn't exactly a secret.

"So I guess we're going to Mexico?" Eva asked, watching as Leo and Kyle struck camp only a few sites away.

"I thought we decided on Florida." Charlie was barely paying attention as she worked on a crossword puzzle in the local paper. She and Eva were side by side at the picnic table. "What's a four-letter word for a lover's clash? Starts with a *T*."

"Tiff," Eva said automatically.

"I think that works, I need a—"

"Is that what happened with you and Leo? Did you have a *tiff*?"

Charlie looked up. "What do you mean? Leo and I are friends."

Eva snorted a laugh, but it was a bitter sound. "Is that what they call it nowadays?"

"*Evangeline.*"

Charlie watched as her daughter deflated, curling over the innards of the portable gas stove that she had spread across the picnic table. It had stopped working suddenly, and Eva had insisted she could fix it. A few FaceTime chats with Frank later, and she was soaking the sealed burner base in vinegar while she cleaned the burner holes with a straight pin. It never ceased to amaze Charlie how this child could be so like her and yet so wholly *other*. Sure, Charlie had renovated the Airstream, but every single upgrade had been a mortal battle. She hated it. Eva, on the other hand, was curious and nimble, quick to see the problem and then puzzle out how to mend it. Eva was a fixer, but she wasn't much of a fighter, never had been. "Sorry," she muttered, responding to Charlie's mild reprimand.

"You don't miss much, do you?" Charlie wrapped an arm

around Eva and pulled her close. She wondered why her daughter was upset. Was she jealous? Angry that Charlie had kept a secret from her? Afraid that her fling with Leo would change everything? "I guess Leo and I didn't do a very good job of hiding our"—she fumbled for the right word—"relationship."

"Everyone knows. Do you like him? I mean *like him* like him?"

"He's not going to be your new daddy, if that's what you mean." Charlie tried to put a smile in her tone. "Leo's a great guy and I really enjoyed hanging out with him—and everyone—these past few weeks."

"Me too."

There it was. A wistful note in Eva's voice that matched the melancholy in her own spirit. Eva was lonely too. Apparently, it was catching.

"Do you want to stay?" Charlie asked. "Ingrid and Lydia will be back next weekend, and the twins are already making plans for an epic bean bag tournament."

"No," Eva said.

Charlie paused for a moment, gathering her courage for the next question. "Do you want to go home?"

Eva didn't answer right away. Instead, she put her head on Charlie's shoulder and watched an oriole land on a branch of the lime-colored paloverde at the edge of their site. Ingrid had sliced an orange and put some grape jam in the cap of an old sour cream container to lure the bright birds to the tree. It worked like a charm. "No," Eva said after a while. "Do *you* want to go home?"

"Home is wherever you are," Charlie said. She pressed her cheek against her daughter's warm head. "Home is the wide-open sky."

"The stars at night," Eva chimed in after a minute.

"The beginning of a new trail."

"The *end* of a new trail."

"Sebastian." Charlie felt herself choking up, but the spell was broken when Scout poked his head between the two of them. "Feeling left out?" She laughed, rubbing his broad head.

"Home is wherever Scout is," Eva finished, wrapping her arms around the dog's neck. "We'd never forget about you, good boy."

Charlie's heart ballooned in her chest and strained against her ribs in a bittersweet ache. She didn't know if she was making the right choices for herself and for her daughter, but it was the best that she could do. It was a free-range, joyful and joy-filled life, and if they had to document and share scraps of it here and there, so be it. She'd take a picture of the oriole and the grape jam, talk of strangers who became friends, and follow the road wherever it led them next. So what if they were lonely? There were much worse things to be.

They had each other.

When Leo turned and caught her staring, she lifted her fingers in goodbye.

CHAPTER 6

Charlie pulls a baseball cap over her long, layered pixie and slips on a pair of sunglasses. It's not a disguise—not really—and yet, she doesn't want to draw any unnecessary attention to herself. With her hair pushed behind her ears and the glasses taking up half of her face, she's sexless and forgettable, an average-sized person in nondescript jeans and a gray sweater.

After Detective James and Agent Turner left—the list of names and numbers in hand—Charlie hurried downstairs to catch Frank and Sophie. They were already gone, but Sophie had left behind a loaf of her homemade sourdough bread and a jar of apple butter with a Post-it Note stuck to the lid: *Call me if you need anything. Anything* was underlined twice, and Sophie had helpfully written her cellphone number at the bottom. It would've been thoughtful if she and Charlie didn't text back and forth on an almost daily basis.

Stress makes people do strange things, Charlie thinks as she crumples up the note and shoots Sophie a text.

Can I borrow Mack's truck?

Mack, Sophie's late, beloved husband, has been gone for nearly five years, but Sophie can't bring herself to get rid of his truck. As far as Charlie can tell, she keeps it around for hauling branches to the dump, and for her once-a-month solo trip to get a slice of rhubarb pie at the greasy spoon Mack frequented on the outskirts of town. Charlie has always respected her neighbor enough not to inquire about the significance of the truck, but apparently when her daughter is missing all bets are off. She has no compunction about asking to borrow what had once been Mack's pride and joy.

Sophie doesn't hesitate. *Sure thing,* she texts back almost immediately. *Keys are on the hook just inside the mudroom door.*

Nobody knows when Charlie slips out the side door and follows the path through the trees to Sophie's house. If her handlers—the cops still stationed on the Morrows' property—decide to check in on her, they'll find her gone, but Charlie doesn't care. Let them put out an all-points bulletin and scour Landing for her. Let them think whatever they want. She has things to do.

Because Charlie needs to see how bad it's gotten, when she pulls Mack's truck out of the Greenes' driveway, she turns south toward the crowd of media vans and journalists camped at the end of the lane. With her baseball cap and sunglasses, she's hard to recognize, but it doesn't really matter because no one gives her even a passing glance as she drives by. They're clumped in small groups, chatting away with their eyes trained on the house overlooking the water. Charlie guesses there are a dozen journalists and cameramen, and the hoods of their vehicles are littered with paper coffee cups and bags of takeout. An unmistakable air of anticipation wafts through the open truck window. It's as if they can tell she's close. Too bad Charlie is driving away from them instead of preparing to make a statement or—even better—offering up another juicy impromptu clip.

Lakeside Road is exactly what it sounds like, a path that dips down from Highway 61 and Landing proper to give locals access to Black Bear Park and the long row of lakefront homes. A few are fancy, new builds that were constructed after old cottages were torn down, but the farther out the houses are, the less they've changed. The Morrows and the Greenes are at the very end, and heading northwest there's not much beyond the trees of Finland State Forest on one side and the lake on the other. But driving southeast, Charlie hits a brand-new chalet-style apartment building with a view of the water, and then a succession of colorful homes on both sides of the street.

The parking lot of Stuart's Smokehouse on the corner of Lakeside Road and Highway 61—Landing's only real landmark—is packed as usual. Stuart really does sell the best smoked salmon and sugar-cured lake trout that Charlie has ever tasted, but just the thought of all that fish makes her stomach flip today. She drives past quickly, hoping that nobody notices when she runs the stop sign as she makes the turn into town.

Landing isn't much, and maybe that's why Charlie hated it when she was younger. The gas station sells five-pound bags of wild rice and maple syrup in leaf-shaped glass jars, and everything feels rugged and outdoorsy in a straightforward, unassuming way. From the chainsaw carving of a beaver on the corner by the pharmacy to the rough-hewn logs that hold up the sign for Mugs, Landing confirms every stereotype of rural Minnesota.

Mugs looks busy on a Sunday afternoon, and Charlie makes a mental note to stop later so she can talk with Eva's boss. Of course, what she really wants to do is head to the marina and take the *Summer Moon* out. She knows the water like the back of her hand, and many of the little islands and outcroppings that dot the shore of Lake Superior. Surely she could *feel* Eva out there. Surely she could sense her daughter's presence and follow it like some genetically connected homing beacon. Charlie knows her daughter. But the marina is no doubt still crawling with rescue workers, the *Summer Moon* wreathed in electric-yellow police tape.

If she can't actively search for Eva, Charlie wants to do the next best thing: try to understand what happened and why.

Charlie might not know much about Piper Berkley—other than she's wholesome and happy, with flaxen hair and eyes the color of the lake in winter—but she knows where Eva's best friend lives. Months ago, when the girls were working on a school project together, Charlie had to bring Piper home.

"Thanks, Ms. Sutton," Piper had cooed as Charlie drove the steep hill toward the swankier part of Landing. Well, considering anything in Landing *swanky* was a stretch, but there was one newish subdivision with a handful of expensive homes. Piper's was the imposing brick monstrosity at the end of a cul-de-sac.

"You can call me Charlie." She had given the girl an expansive smile. Charlie didn't mean to be so overeager, but the fact that Eva had invited a friend over was cause to celebrate. True, they were working on a project, but a friend was a friend.

Now, pulling into Piper's stamped driveway on a sunny Sunday afternoon, Charlie is nearly effervescent with hope. Why didn't she think of this earlier? She has no doubt that Piper will know what's going on. This—whatever *this* is—is just a part of growing up. And when the entire melodramatic story is known, Charlie will be quietly mollified that they survived Eva's teenage rebellion. At least, she hopes.

She parks behind one of the three garage doors and hurries up the walk toward a vaulted entryway, eager to see Piper and begin the process of putting this whole godawful ordeal behind them.

The doorbell chimes prettily through the massive house, and though the front door is frosted glass, Charlie can see a shape moving behind it. A dog? A child? She will have to be gentle but firm, and she expects there will be tears. Perhaps she and Piper's mom will eventually have coffee to discuss their daughters' antics, and Charlie is so deep in the throes of this particular fantasy that when someone wrenches the front door open, she startles.

It's a towheaded boy of maybe eleven or twelve. He's wearing a Golden Gophers sweatshirt and eating what looks like a bologna sandwich. "Yeah?" he says around a mouthful.

"Hi." Charlie sticks out her hand and then quickly retracts it, eyeing the mayonnaise that oozes from between the slices of bread. "I'm Charlie Sutton. Eva's mom?" It comes out as a question.

The boy takes another bite of his sandwich and stares at her.

"Evangeline?" Charlie tries. "Long dark hair, blue eyes. Piper's friend. Is Piper here?"

At this he shrugs, then hollers over his shoulder: "Piper! Someone's here to see you!"

Job done, he walks away without a backwards glance, leaving Charlie to stand on the threshold with the front door propped open. She's not sure what to do, so she steps inside the palatial foyer and quietly closes the door behind her. The rug beneath her feet is expensive-looking, and the Hunter boots she tugged on are crusted with sand and dirt. She holds herself very carefully, willing her boots not to mar the beautiful rug.

Piper comes tripping down the stairs a moment later, dressed head to toe in Lululemon, with her hair pulled back in a high ponytail and looking just as fit and virtuous as she did so long ago. She pauses at the base of the steps as she considers Charlie, a kaleidoscope of emotions fluttering behind her eyes. Surprise wins. "Ms. Sutton. What are you doing here?"

"I'm so glad you're home." Charlie can barely get the words out. She feels herself slipping, all the assurance of only minutes ago seeping away as she considers the girl before her. "It's Eva. I need to talk to you about Eva."

"I heard," Piper says, crossing her arms over her chest as if to ward off the terrible news. "Everyone's saying . . . I mean, anyway, it's really sad."

She's talking as if she already knows the outcome. "What's everyone saying? Do you know where she is?" Charlie croaks.

Piper looks stricken. "I thought . . . The news said she's missing."

"I know. But do *you* know where she is?"

"No, I—"

"Did she tell you anything about what was going on? About why she would—"

"What's going on here?" A woman in an olive-green nap dress interrupts Charlie by hurrying into the foyer. Her dyed blond hair is pressed flat on one side, and she looks as if she was indeed taking a nap.

From the way the woman rushes to Piper's side, it's clear that Charlie was making a scene. She doesn't remember shouting, but she had to work so hard to get her questions out. They were thick as tar on her tongue. Maybe she was being a little loud—Charlie can hardly hear a thing over the sound of her own blood pumping in her ears.

"I'm sorry," Charlie manages. "I'm Charlotte Sutton, Eva's mom."

"Jane Berkley. Piper's mom." She doesn't offer her hand, and somehow the introduction feels like a challenge.

"Look, I just want to talk to Piper about Eva."

Jane just gapes at her, and after a few beats Piper tells her mom in a stage whisper: "The girl who's missing. The one on TV."

"I'm here to find out if Piper knows anything about where Eva might be," Charlie tries to explain. "I would have called, but I didn't have your number."

Piper tucks her arm through her mother's and ducks her head to whisper something in the older woman's ear. Charlie wants to shake her, but she stands her ground, belatedly registering the fact that she has stepped off the rug and is tracking grit across the hand-scraped hardwood floor.

"Ms. Sutton," Jane finally says, "Piper has absolutely no idea what happened to your daughter. And frankly, *I* have no idea what made you think she would."

This isn't going at all how Charlie planned. Even more concerning is the fact that Piper seems almost defensive. Charlie decides to address the teen directly. "I just need to know if Eva was acting strange. Did she seem different to you? Did anything happen at school that was out of the ordinary?"

The serious look in Jane's eyes tells Charlie that she's getting loud again. She balls her hands into fists and digs her fingernails into her palms in an effort to wrangle back some control. "I'm sorry," she says again. "I'm not trying to scare you. I'm just trying to find my daughter."

At this, Jane softens a bit, but she doesn't move from the foot of the stairs where's she's wrapped around her own daughter. It's not lost on Charlie that Piper is safe and sound—in her mother's arms—while Eva is missing. Charlie's hands itch with the longing to pull Eva into a hug and never let go.

"I'm so sorry about . . . what's happening," Jane says. "But I don't think Piper can tell you anything about Eva's whereabouts."

Standing beside her mother, Piper seems braver. "Eva's nice and all, but why would I know where she is? We're not even friends," she says quietly.

The edge of Charlie's vision sparks black. "What? I don't understand. You're Eva's *best friend*. You guys hang out all the time. You pick her up from Mugs and go driving until all hours of the night. You were together Friday! She texted me from . . ." Charlie trails off, fumbling for her phone and the text that will prove to Piper that she was just with Eva—that they were together, having fun—only a couple nights ago. Eva told her as much. But as her fingers claw at the screen, Piper is assuring her mother that it's simply not true.

"I haven't spoken to Eva since we had to do that world cultures project together," the girl says, her voice high and frantic. "That was *months* ago. Mr. Peterson assigned partners and she was mine. I swear we haven't seen each other since. I don't know anything about her disappearance. We only have the one class together and we sit on opposite sides of the room."

Jane Berkley's eyes are huge and glassy with unshed tears; she's clearly torn between compassion for another mother and the desire to protect her own child. She studies Piper for a long moment and then looks up, her decision made. "I think you need to go," she tells Charlie. "Truly, I'm so sorry that your daughter is missing, but you heard Piper: she hasn't talked to Eva in months."

"But—"

"You need to leave now." Jane seems deeply unsettled by the whole situation, and conflicted about what exactly to do, but she steps around Charlie to open the door anyway.

Charlie can feel the fear radiate off them both, these women who were supposed to be her allies and friends. They're afraid of *her*, of her desperation and their sudden, shocking proximity to her tragedy. But Piper is also afraid of what Charlie is claiming, and as Charlie searches the teenager's face for any sign of deception, she understands that what Piper is saying is true: she and Eva were not friends.

"I'm sorry I bothered you," Charlie whispers around the lump in her throat. "I guess I was . . . I didn't know . . ."

"We'll be praying for you and Eva," Jane says as she holds the door. There is real sympathy in her eyes.

Charlie can't say *I'm sorry* or *thank you* or even squeak out another word. She leaves quietly, flinching a little as the door thumps shut behind her. The unmistakable click of a dead bolt sliding home punctuates her departure.

In Mack's truck, Charlie manages to back out of the driveway and crawl to the end of the road before she has to pull over. The Berkleys might be watching her from behind their locked door, but she can't be bothered to care. She can't drive, not safely. If Piper isn't Eva's friend—the girl who she allegedly spent countless nights with: playing games in a booth at Mugs, getting ice cream from the Dairy Dandy, watching movies in the Berkleys' basement—what has she been doing for the past several months?

And what else has Eva lied about?

INSTAGRAM POST #456

"There is meaning in every journey that
is unknown to the traveler."

Dietrich Bonhoeffer

The world is our classroom.

Well, it's Eva's literal classroom, and
Charlie takes more of a metaphorical
approach. To say these past months
on the road haven't been chock-full
of learning experiences would be the
understatement of the century. Don't
misunderstand us: traditional education
is important, necessary, transformative,
and all the other adjectives we
forgot to employ. (Please don't @
us. We love school!) But our blend
of homeschool and distance learning
has opened up a world of possibilities
for us both. Eva can follow passion
projects and explore the topics that
pique her interest (provided she keeps
up with curriculum requirements as
outlined by the Minnesota school

board), and Charlie gets to play
the part of guide and co-learner
depending on Eva's trending
curiosities. Our current obsession?
The writings of Dietrich Bonhoeffer.
Who knew a German theologian and
anti-Nazi dissident would so capture
our imaginations? We recommend
Letters and Papers from Prison as well
as his biography written by Eberhard
Bethge, his best friend. Fair warning:
it's not for the faint of heart! We're
slowly, methodically working our way
through it. Of course, it helps when the
gulf waves are our soundtrack.

#dietrichbonhoeffer #everyjourney
#sanibelisland #evaexplores
#wherenext

Always take the long way back,
Charlie & Eva

[IMAGE CONTENTS: A dog-eared copy
of *Letters and Papers from Prison* lays
closed on the sand. Tiny calico scallop
shells dot the cover and a spectacular
black-and-white striped king's crown
rests on one corner. The sand is
pearl-colored and fine as flour, and in
the background, waves break against a
Sanibel Island beach.]

Florida was humid. So humid that when they woke up in the morning, everything was wet and sparkling. Water pooled on the hood of the truck, collected on the palm fronds that edged their campsite, and puddled on the picnic table. Eva took the side of her hand and swooped it off, spraying sheets of water that made tiny rainbows in the bright slant of early sun. Charlie and Eva were perpetually damp, tendrils of hair clinging to the sides of their necks, and it was in Fort Myers that Charlie decided to chop it all off.

"Are you sure?" the hairdresser asked, holding the warm heft of Charlie's long waves in her hands. "I can't glue it back on."

Charlie looked at her reflection in the mirror, at Eva standing just over one shoulder, and nodded. Eva had always been her little copy, and Charlie was grateful that her daughter didn't look much like the man who shared her bed for a couple of weeks in her early twenties and then disappeared to the East Coast. But she didn't want to be mistaken for Eva's sister anymore. The months on the road had been kind to Eva, and their outdoor lifestyle had contoured her body and turned her skin golden in all the ways Charlie knew it would. Her daughter was sturdy and strong, with more than a sprinkling of freckles across her nose, and a lopsided grin that was toothy and infectious—and somehow it didn't feel right for Charlie to match this new, growing up version of Eva.

So the hairdresser wrapped an elastic band around the hair at the base of Charlie's neck, and hacked off her thick, sable mane. She clipped close to the scalp beneath Charlie's ears, then added a few face-framing layers, and in less than an hour Charlie emerged from the salon a completely different version of herself.

"You look like a movie star!" Eva enthused, practically dancing around Charlie as they headed to the truck.

"I was going for rock star."

Eva walked backwards, framing Charlie in a rectangle with her fingers and squinting. "I'd buy it. All you need are a few tattoos."

"Nah."

"Temporary," Eva countered. She'd been begging for a tattoo for months, and practicing with a set of custom designs that they'd received from an upstart company. The motifs were all boho chic, mandalas and arrows and crescent moons. Eva was currently sporting a tiny feather on the inside of her left wrist. It was beginning to flake off. "Just try one. You're going to love it. We could get matching ones. You'd be the coolest mom ever."

"I'm already the coolest mom ever, and I'm not letting my fifteen-year-old get a tattoo," Charlie said.

"Buzzkill. Spoilsport. Party pooper."

"Check, check, check," Charlie punctuated each word with a flourish of her finger.

She had given Eva freedom, independence, and a life crammed to bursting with incredible experiences, but Charlie had to draw the line somewhere. Tattoos could wait until Eva's frontal lobe was fully developed. Still, Charlie felt a prick of remorse when Eva avoided her for the rest of the day, opting instead to join a pickup game of volleyball at the campground's sand court, and then walking away deliberately when Charlie came to watch.

It was then that the niggling doubts crept in. Would it really be so bad if Eva got a little tattoo? Something small and understated to remind her of their travels?

By suppertime, Charlie had *almost* convinced herself that the tattoo was a good idea. Eva had even suggested matching ones. What fifteen-year-old wanted to get a matching tattoo with her mother? Charlie smiled to herself as she threw hamburger patties on their charcoal grill and sliced a ripe tomato nice and thin, just the way Eva liked it. They were out of buns, but they had plenty of romaine, and with some sautéed mushrooms and onions she reasoned they wouldn't miss the carbs one bit. Thinking of her daughter and cataloging all the ways Eva was extraordinary had made Charlie soft and sentimental, anxious to love her girl in some tangible way, and her favorite burgers fit the bill.

But when the sun began to dip low in the sky and paint the downy clouds watercolor pink, Eva was nowhere to be found. The hamburgers were starting to blacken at the edges, the tomato limp and seeping on a well-worn plastic plate. Scout was moody and restless, complaining at passersby in a rumble that was just shy of a growl.

"Stop it," Charlie warned, tugging his collar to pull him away from the edge of their campsite. He was the friendliest dog she had ever met; she hardly knew what to do with his sudden belligerence. So she shut him in Sebastian, wrapped the well-done burgers in a square of tinfoil, and sent Eva a passive-aggressive text. *The burgers are burnt. Where are you?* It *ping*ed almost immediately, alerting Charlie to the fact that her daughter's phone was tucked next to an overturned washbasin on the picnic table, but Eva herself was nowhere to be seen. Charlie rolled her eyes and took off on foot to find her.

She wasn't worried. Not really. Eva hadn't given her reason to be, and although she still kept the baseball bat tucked between her mattress and the hard side of the camper, there had never been grounds to use it. But as the sun set over the Gulf, and an unexpected chill stole through the air, Charlie wished for a moment that she had taken it along.

"Have you seen Eva?" she asked her neighbors. They weren't nearly as tight as the circle they had formed in Arizona, but they knew each other's names. One by one they shrugged.

"Not since volleyball."

"On the beach this afternoon."

"Nope."

The farther Charlie got from their site, the quicker her pulse skipped. She didn't realize she was breathless and hurrying until she stumbled and almost fell headlong into the railing of the boardwalk that led to the beach. Her hands took the brunt of it, and she felt splinters from the old wood rough up her palms.

"Eva?" she called, against her better judgment. The wind was whining, the crash of waves a resonant boom that only intensified the closer she got to the water. She'd have to shout to be heard over any distance. Those prettily airbrushed clouds were changing and gathering on the horizon, turning from pink to purple to the menacing plum of a deep bruise.

A couple with two children hurried up the boardwalk away from the beach. The dad was holding a toddler wrapped in towels, and the mom had a small child in one hand and an insulated cooler on wheels in the other. When one of the wheels caught in a gap between boards and they jerked to a stop, the little boy began to wail.

"Have you seen a teenage girl on the beach?" Charlie asked the woman, bending to free the wheel for her. "Long, dark hair. She's wearing a Glacier T-shirt and a pair of khaki shorts."

"It's getting really windy down there," the stranger said over the cries of her son. "Everyone's gone. I think we were the last people left."

Charlie didn't wait for a thank-you or ask any more questions. She couldn't explain the beat of panic that throbbed hot and sudden in her chest, but something about Eva being gone felt wrong.

She had never disappeared like this before; not once in the eight months they had been on the road. Of course they wandered off on their own, but they always took their phones. They were Lorelai and Rory, Thelma and Louise. Not just loyal, but astonishingly close, and definitely not prone to vanishing in order to make a point. But this. This was something new and unnerving.

Over a tattoo?

Charlie toed off her sneakers when she hit the sand, preferring to run barefoot rather than contend with the fine dust that would undoubtedly sift into her shoes. She wished for a sweatshirt as the wind whipped her newly shorn hair around her cheeks. Past a cluster of sea grape trees, Charlie could see where the beach curved away in both directions. She was standing on the lazy bend of the south side of the island, and as far as she could tell, she was alone.

"Eva!" she yelled, but the wind seized the word and hurled it over the water.

Every nerve ending in Charlie's body sparked white hot, a fluorescent charge of pure terror and adrenaline that sent her sprinting over the sand. She *knew* she was overreacting. That even now, Eva was probably stepping into Sebastian and grumbling to Scout about what a nuisance her mother was. But Charlie's mind had short-circuited, and all she could imagine was every worst-case scenario: death by drowning, abduction by a stranger, an accident that left Eva wounded and alone, unable to call for help.

Waves crashed against the shore, spilling up the sand and staining the beach umber in the growing twilight. Charlie stuck to the damp shoreline, where the ground was hard packed and easier to navigate. There was no point in yelling, but she raced along the headland, searching for any sign that Eva had passed by. Flip-flops, her beloved Glacier cropped tee, *anything*.

It took Charlie a few minutes to realize that the smudge nestled in the low-hanging fronds of a joewood tree on the farthest edge of the beach wasn't a shadow, but a person. And not just one person, but two. As she squinted in the dusky light, a wave caught her unsuspecting and almost swept her feet out from under her. By the time Charlie righted herself and was back on solid ground, her shorts were soaking and she was shaking, but more important, the couple had peeled away from the tree. They were watching her.

Charlie knew it was Eva before she could make out any distinguishing features. It was in the way she stood, the way one shoulder hung lower than the other and one hip jutted. Heedless of the stranger, Charlie gulped the distance between them in several long strides.

"Where have you been?" She seized Eva by the shoulders and searched her face for any evidence of harm.

She was wide-eyed and a little rumpled, but seemed fine. She shook Charlie off. "I've been here," she said. "Studying."

Satisfied that Eva was okay, Charlie turned her attention to the person standing in the shadows. He was tall and lanky, with wrinkled clothes and a University of Michigan baseball cap. Charlie had seen him around the campground with a small group of coeds, but they had never met.

"She's fifteen," Charlie spat, suddenly sure of what she had stumbled upon. Eva's rosy, just-been-kissed lips; the boy's inability to meet her eyes.

"*Mom.*" Eva's hand shot out and grabbed Charlie's arm. "*Stop.*"

But Charlie's blood was still frothing in her veins, and finding Eva had flipped a switch inside her: in a couple of seconds she went from ice cold to boiling hot. "How old are you?" she demanded, taking a step closer to the boy.

To his credit, he didn't back up. "I'm nineteen, ma'am." He held something out to Charlie, and when she looked down she realized it was the Dietrich Bonhoeffer book that she and Eva had been reading. "Just finishing up my freshman year at the University of Michigan, majoring in history with a minor in moral and political philosophy."

When he shoved the book into her hands, Charlie was rendered speechless. She took it from him, turning to Eva as he brushed past.

"Bye, Eva. Good luck with your Holocaust unit." To Charlie he said, "She told me she was eighteen."

Mother and daughter stood there for a moment, watching him walk away as the roar of the waves muffled the dissonant drumbeat of their hearts. After a moment, Charlie put a hand on Eva's shoulder. "Hon—"

"*Don't.*" Eva jerked away and spun on Charlie. "Nothing happened. *Nothing.* We were talking about genocide and how those who don't learn history are doomed to repeat it. We lost track of time."

The heat—fury and fear and sickening relief—snuffed out in Charlie's chest. "I'm sorry," she tried, her voice breaking from the rush of adrenaline. "I was worried and—"

"Just don't." Eva glared at her, eyes brimming with furious tears, and took off after the boy. He had already disappeared down the boardwalk.

Charlie didn't even know his name.

CHAPTER 7

SUNDAY

Mugs is bustling when Charlie swings open the front door and steps inside. She's forgotten that it's Sunday, that the after-church throng likes their brunch, and the Sunday lunch shift is always the busiest of the week. There's a crowd gathered in the vestibule, waiting for tables to become available, and some guy helpfully turns to Charlie as she tries to edge her way to the front of the pack.

"Twenty-minute wait at least," he tells her, his smile fading quickly when he realizes who she is.

Charlie is used to being recognized in Landing and then tact-fully ignored. When she and Eva first moved in to the Morrows' house, the townspeople were curious. Some were thrilled that the semi-famous Eva Explores duo had settled down in pictur-esque Landing—Charlie's hometown! Their expectations were clear: "Put our quaint, little village on the map." Others regarded Charlie and Eva with thinly veiled hostility. It was obvious that their Sutton Girls brand of allegedly attention-seeking fame did not impress. Charlie quickly learned to keep her head down and disregard the extremes. Most people accepted that she was just a single mom living her own quiet life in the best way she knew how. But none of that stopped the inevitable whispers when Charlie and Eva were recognized.

By the way the atmosphere in Mugs crackles, Charlie knows that the gentleman at the door isn't the only one who has clocked her entrance.

"I'm not here to eat," she tells him belatedly, then elbows past the crowd queued up in the entry.

The restaurant is hot, stuffy with the scent of buttermilk pancakes and crisp bacon, and Charlie can feel the heat rise in her cheeks. She tells herself that it's because the tiny, packed room is stifling, not because everyone is looking at her. She's still shaken from her encounter with the Berkleys, and as her vision blurs for just a moment, she wonders if coming here was a terrible idea. But Charlie doesn't have the luxury of time, of going home to regroup and recover. Each second that peels off the clock is irretrievable—and she needs every single one she can get.

"I need to see Peter," Charlie says, catching a nearby waiter by the elbow. He's about Eva's age, dressed in black jeans, a white button-up, and a trademark royal-blue Mugs apron with the logo embroidered in the corner. Charlie has to stop herself from reaching out to straighten the crooked bow of his apron string. Eva was supposed to work today. She always works the Sunday lunch shift.

"You want Peter?" the boy echoes, stumbling over the name. It's clear that he, too, knows exactly who Charlie is, and he isn't sure that she should bother the boss. "I don't think—"

"You don't have to think anything," Charlie interrupts. "I just need to know where he is. The kitchen? Does he cook on Sundays?" Without waiting for an answer, she begins to weave around tables, heading in the direction of the kitchen door at the back of the buzzing dining room.

Peter Cole is the middle-aged owner of Mugs, a man who

was once the star of the Landing hockey team when he was a senior and Charlie was a timid freshman. She had nursed a painful crush on him for a few months, and his kindness toward her only made matters worse. Now, he's barrel-chested and balding, married with three teenagers of his own. But when the Sutton Girls moved in, he remembered Charlie and generously gave Eva a part-time job even though she had no work experience to speak of. He's a good man and a good boss, but Charlie doubts he'll welcome an impromptu, lunch-hour interview with the daughter of Landing's infamous Rosie Sutton. Thirty years ago, Charlie was just the wide-eyed little girl of the town drunk. And then a socially awkward orphan who left town as soon as she could, only to work menial jobs until she got knocked up by a stranger. Even Instagram fame can't erase a past like that. Charlie knows she walks a fine line between disdain and grudging respect.

The door to the kitchen snaps open as she approaches, and she holds it for a young waitress whose arms are laden with steaming plates.

If anything, the kitchen is even hotter and busier than the dining room. Two girls fill plates at an expo station, and another waiter snags orders from a long counter. At a large range, a pair of cooks stand side by side with their backs turned to the cramped room, flipping blueberry pancakes and scrambling eggs with stainless steel spatulas. One of them is Peter.

Now that she's made it this far, Charlie finds herself frozen. She pauses to get her bearings, but before she can even catch her breath, the two-way door swings into her shoulder with a resounding smack. The pain is quick and fortifying.

"Stand clear of the door!" Peter hollers over the noise of sizzling oil, range fans, and chatter. He scoops a trio of pancakes onto a waiting plate and turns to see who was caught unaware. His eyes go wide when he sees Charlie rubbing her arm.

For a moment, she's afraid that he's going to send her away. But then Peter gives his spatula to the man beside him and says a few words that she can't hear. Wiping his hands on a dish towel tucked into his apron, he walks past Charlie and motions for her to follow.

His office is down a narrow hallway at the back of the kitchen. It's cooler, as Peter has thrown open the window behind his cluttered desk. The view is nothing to speak of—the dingy back alley and a volunteer birch sapling that is fat with round, green buds—but Charlie takes a shuddering breath of the fresh air. She's surprised when Peter wraps her in a hug.

"I'm so sorry," he says.

Charlie's resolve frays, and all at once she feels completely undone. Peter helps her into the lone chair, then leans against the rounded edge of the desk and surveys her.

"I'd ask you how you're holding up," he says after a moment, "but I'd be an absolute basket case if I was in your shoes."

Charlie nods, burying her face in her hands. She can hardly remember why she came, but now that she's here, she's so grateful for Peter's compassion that she could cry.

"Any news?" he asks. "I would've stayed glued to the TV today if I could, but Sundays . . ."

Charlie waves away his would-be apology. "You don't have to explain anything. And no, no news."

"So they haven't found . . ." he trails off, unwilling or unable to finish the thought. They both know that if Eva drowned, they may never find her body. Lake Superior does not easily give up her secrets.

Charlie shakes her head. "I'm just trying to put the pieces together. Figure out what happened. The unknown is the worst, you know?"

"What do you think happened?"

"She didn't drown," Charlie says definitively, even though she can't possibly be sure. "She's smart, she's strong, and she knows that lake. She would never have gone for a swim and . . ." She trails off, unable to finish.

"Where could she be?" Peter asks gently.

"In a life raft on Lake Superior for reasons I can't begin to guess." She levels him with a serious look. "I keep asking myself: Was there something going on with Eva that I didn't know about?"

Peter puts his palms on the desktop as he seems to genuinely consider her question. "Not that I know of," he says after a while. "Eva was normal at work. Happy. Hardworking. She's one of our best servers, you know."

This tugs Charlie's mouth into the ghost of a smile. "I don't get it," she says, mortified by the wobble in her voice. "Eva graduates next week. And we're going to do one last summer on the road. We're so excited." She doesn't mean to admit that part. They haven't told anyone that they reached an agreement. Charlie wishes she could erase the confession.

But Peter is looking at her strangely. "You are? I thought Eva Explores was over."

"It is. I mean, it was. We changed our minds. But please don't tell anyone. We hadn't announced it yet."

Peter heaves a sigh and crosses his arms over his chest. "If you're looking for something out of the ordinary, that might be it. At work on Friday afternoon, Eva was telling us all that she plans to work full-time this summer so she can save up for college. I promised her forty hours a week plus overtime."

"Things change," Charlie says, irritated. What does he know about Eva and her plans? But this is exactly why she came—so she can learn if there is anything that doesn't add up in her daughter's life. Until yesterday, Charlie was convinced that Eva's world consisted of school, work, friends, and home. If Eva has been lying about her friendships, what else isn't as it seems?

It's obvious that she's hurt Peter's feelings, so Charlie gives him a rueful smile and stands. "I'm sorry, I didn't mean to be short. You're right, Eva was planning to stay here and work all summer. We actually fought about it. But we figured everything out. Just yesterday. We're really happy about where we landed."

"Then I'm glad to hear it. We'll miss her at Mugs, of course, but we wish you both the best of luck."

It's the kindest thing he could possibly say. So normal and filled with the casual certainty that *of course* they'll find Eva. Charlie's glad that she came, even if it stings to be talking so nonchalantly about the upcoming summer when Eva is gone. On the boat yesterday, Charlie and Eva had discussed doing a highlight reel of all their favorite destinations, with a college-bound angle that would spotlight traveling on a budget. It was sure to be a huge hit, and announcing their encore should have been a reason to celebrate. But nothing is certain anymore. Nothing is okay.

"Thank you for your time," Charlie says, wavering between sticking out her hand and just walking away. In the end, Peter leans in to give her one more brotherly hug.

"Of course. Please let me know if there's anything else I can do."

"I will."

"And I'll talk to all of my employees," Peter adds as Charlie walks away. "You know, just to see if they know anything. I'm sure you've already reached out to her school friends and her boyfriend, but sometimes things slip out at work. Let's stay in touch, okay?"

"Boyfriend?" Charlie nearly chokes on the word, spinning so fast that Peter looks taken aback.

"Yeah," he says slowly.

"What do you mean, boyfriend?"

"I figured you knew. She talks about him sometimes. Not much, but it was obvious she was seeing someone."

Charlie's mind is ricocheting. As far as she can tell, Eva has never had boyfriend. Not that Charlie would be upset about it. She's encouraged Eva to find good friends, say yes to date invitations, experience her first kiss. If she's being honest with herself, she eagerly awaited the day that Eva would come home and share her feelings for some cute guy in her homeroom. She imagined they'd make popcorn and curl up on the couch to gossip about it, and Charlie would offer whatever paltry wisdom she could about men and relationships and the ever-elusive thing called love.

"What's his name?" Charlie finally manages.

Peter still looks uneasy. "I don't know."

"How long have they been dating?"

"A couple months? Look, Charlie, I really don't know. I don't pay too much attention to the love lives of the kids who work for me. But I also can't help but overhear conversations in the kitchen. Eva was definitely seeing someone."

Charlie's heart is a fist in her chest, clenched and aching. "Do you know anything at all about him? What he looks like? Where he lives? Does he go to Landing High?"

Peter is already shaking his head. "I can't tell you anything. I never saw her with him and she never talked to me directly about him. You could try Lennon. I think she and Eva were pretty tight. They worked a lot of shifts together and liked to talk."

Lennon is a name that Charlie has never heard before, but

she leaves with a scrap of paper printed with the girl's cell phone number. In the alley, she leans against the cool bricks and swallows huge mouthfuls of air until her breaths turn into sobs. She's alone on the gravel drive with the dumpsters and the weeds, and she finally lets go, crying until there are no tears left.

Beyond a work buddy, Eva has no real friends. Of that, Charlie feels absolutely certain. If her daughter had to make up meetings with Piper and pretend that the popular blonde was her bestie, it has to be the closet, most meaningful connection Eva has—even if it's just an illusion.

But, Eva *does* have a boyfriend. A secret boyfriend that she talked to her coworkers about and never once mentioned to her mother. They'd been together for months. *Months?* Who was this boy? And why didn't Eva think she could tell Charlie about him?

The road hadn't ruined everything. Roots had. They should have never come to Landing.

Charlie wants to throw things, to punch the brick wall— even if it is the only thing holding her up—or yank the cheerful sapling growing beside her out of the ground. She wants to break something, just to feel it crumble in her hands, because the destruction inside of her feels so terrible and absolute. Charlie fears that even finding Eva healthy and whole won't mend what has been torn. Of course, she'd give everything she has and ravage the world itself to make sure her daughter is still safely in it somewhere. But she knows in her soul that nothing will ever be the same.

God, being a mother is agony, Charlie thinks. *Bittersweet and aching and inexpressibly beautiful.* And hard. Never mind the raw indignity of pregnancy and birth, from the moment Eva's tiny fingers curled around the very tip of her thumb—the nails translucent and tiny as a grain of rice—Charlie was no longer her own person but wholly her daughter's. It was as if she existed for the sole purpose of being Eva's sun, the center of her universe and the axis she would spend her life orbiting around. But that was never true. From almost that very first spark of contact, Eva has been slowly slipping away. In that brightly lit delivery room, her diminutive hand held her mother's for a second, two, and then she broke the connection, flung her skinny arms overhead, and screamed.

Motherhood is push and pull, back and forth, I love you even when you disobey, walk away, keep secrets. *Maybe especially then*, Charlie thinks, *because I know you. I know you like I know the rhythms of my own body.* A mother doesn't have to think about it, the innate knowledge of her child in the world is a part of who she is. Until it isn't. Until one day you wake up and there's an entire cosmos contained in your child's eyes, a galaxy you do not have a map to.

They should be together, the Sutton Girls, on the road. None of this would be happening if they were in the Adirondacks, watching the mist evaporate in the morning sun. Or the Poconos, Cumberland Island, Havasupai.

Charlie dries her tears with the sleeves of her sweater, readjusts her baseball cap, and steps out of the alley. Keeping her head down, she hurries past the large side windows of Mugs, digging for the keys to Mack's truck in her pocket as she goes. She doesn't want to see anyone else—to bump into one of Eva's coworkers or some random acquaintance who might tell her more things she doesn't want to hear.

Charlie is so intent on getting in the truck and going home, that she doesn't realize a crowd has formed on the sidewalk until she nearly bowls over a little boy clutching his mother's hand. At least thirty people have gathered, and no one notices her because their attention is all focused on a woman at the heart of the small mob. Charlie falters, trying to make sense of the spectacle before her. It's only when she sees that there's a CNN field van parked by the curb that everything clicks into place.

"I'm standing in front of Mugs Cafe, a busy diner and beloved community fixture in Landing, Minnesota," an attractive woman with a neat chignon and a dove-gray suit says into a microphone. "Mugs is also the place where high school senior Evangeline Sutton works part-time as a waitress. Many people—especially in the hiking and outdoors community—are familiar with Evangeline as the titular Eva of the popular Instagram account Eva Explores. Eva and her mother, Charlie, spent two and a half years crisscrossing the continent and sharing their adventures as well-known Instagram influencers. But now, it seems that Eva is missing."

Charlie's ears begin to ring, and she can't hear the rest of what the reporter with the perfect hair is saying. She has to get out of here, *now*, before someone realizes that Eva's mother is only feet away from where a live broadcast is being filmed. She can't explain why she's here, not in a way that would make sense. How could she let this happen? How could she let *any* of this happen?

Tripping over her own two feet, Charlie tries to back away without causing a scene. But it's too late. Someone has already turned and realized that she's lurking at the edge of the crowd, and a swell of whispers ripples toward her. When the reporter turns her head a fraction of an inch and they make eye contact, Charlie knows she's in trouble. She tries to flee, but not before the reporter points and a husky cameraman swings the slick camcorder her way.

"Charlotte Sutton!" the reporter calls. "Do you know where

Eva is? Is it true that she went missing on Lake Superior? Where are the police focusing their investigation? Have any persons of interest been named?"

By the time Charlie rounds the corner of the building, the whispers have grown to shouts. She's not sure if they're yelling at her or the reporter, but she doesn't intend to stay and find out. Sprinting down the block, she doesn't pause to look back or check if they're following. She's fast, and they can't move easily—not with the van and the equipment and the press of the crowd.

But when she turns down a side street, there's a car at her heels. For a moment she thinks about trying to outrun it, zigzagging through backyards and over fences, but that's insane. She's not a criminal. Just a mom who wants her daughter back.

Charlie slows and glances at the car. The tinted window is already rolling down.

"Get in, Charlie," Agent Turner says from the passenger seat.

Detective James is behind the wheel, and for a moment Charlie wavers. But then someone hits the locks and she can hear the invitation in the snick of metal. It's a tempting getaway. Somewhere behind her there is a reporter and a camera rolling, a group of people who may or may not think that she had something to do with her daughter's disappearance. She's not sure what to do with James and Turner, but they're better than what's waiting for her back at Mugs.

Swinging open the back door, Charlie slides in. Almost immediately, Detective James pulls away, tires squealing.

It's quiet for a minute in the temperature-controlled hush of the dark sedan. But then Agent Turner slings his arm over the seat back and levels a stony look at her. "Where have you been?"

Charlie's too numb to respond. She's breathing heavy, and

her head is pounding from tears and hunger. She can't even meet his gaze.

"Fine. You can tell us about your field trip later. But now we need to talk." Agent Turner sounds much colder than he did just a few hours ago. "We've found something."

INSTAGRAM POST #500

Not only does today mark our one-year
anniversary on the road, it also
commemorates our five hundredth post!
We still can't believe that this is our life,
and that you are our traveling buddies
and sweet community. Thank you,
thank you for following us this far—we
wouldn't be here without you. And where
exactly is here? Can you guess? Our
favorite Little Mermaid has always loved
orcas, and since our passports came
through and it's orca season in British
Columbia, we hightailed it north for
some super, natural BC vibes (yes, that's
their provincial slogan, and you'd better
believe we got it on a bumper sticker).
We hopped on a BC Ferry in Horseshoe
Bay (just north of Vancouver on the Sea
to Sky Highway—*highly* recommended)
and spent a few nights in stunning
Victoria (more on that soon). Then,
we took a smaller ferry to a secluded
little island. No hookups, so Sebastian
couldn't come, but do you see what we
saw? We are in awe. From the bottom of

our hearts: Thank you. #supernaturalbc
#hellobc #orcas #evaexplores

Always take the long way back,
Charlie & Eva

[IMAGE CONTENTS: A bright orange
kayak cuts through glacier-blue water.
A girl with long, dark hair curling over
her shoulders holds a yellow oar
across her lap. She's grinning from ear
to ear. On both sides of the kayak, the
sleek black-and-white bodies of orcas
arc out of the water.]

British Columbia was extraordinary. From the moment they crossed the border at the iconic Peace Arch between Blaine, Washington, and Surrey, BC, Charlie and Eva felt a unique connection to the province, the people, and most important, the place. Maybe it was because the geography reminded them of Minnesota: trees and rocky beaches and brooding skies. Or maybe they just liked the casual air, the way everyone seemed laid-back and outdoorsy—their favorite vibe. They considered staying through the end of September, or at least until it got rainy and miserable, as the locals were quick to assure them it would. But that was before everything went to hell.

Old grove forests, rugged coastline, and the charming buzz of seaplanes overhead punctuated their stay on Vancouver Island, and Charlie took notes on her phone as their neighbors in the campground encouraged them to check out Pipers Lagoon, Pacific Rim National Park Reserve, and Tofino on the far side of the island. They would have done it all if Charlie hadn't received a message on their third night from a kayaking outfitter promising an unforgettable orca tour in exchange for some positive press.

How do you know we're in Victoria?

Charlie messaged back. She didn't want to be standoffish, but the last thing they had posted was a picture in the sand dunes of Wisconsin taken over a week ago. No one should have been able to suss out where they'd gone next.

> Don't mean to be a creeper, but I'm friends with one of the groundskeepers at the campground where you're staying. She recognized your Airstream.
> —Jett

Charlie clicked through to the Instagram profile. Majestic Island Sea Kayaking was a legit company with what seemed like a good track record. They had a thousand followers and a handful of great pictures, including one of five grinning twentysomethings with tattoos and longish hair pulled back from their faces with leather bands. They seemed wholesome and fun-loving, and since seeing orcas was the point of their Canadian sojourn, Charlie accepted.

Charlie and Eva loaded their backpacks, dragged the tent out of storage, and left Scout with the camp manager for their twenty-four-hour excursion. They had to take a little walk-on ferry that was more private boat than public transit, and that wove between a scattering of smaller islands en route to their final destination: a spit of land with a sharp cliff jutting out of the sea on one side and a dense, evergreen forest on the other. A lacy mist hovered just above the water when they pulled up to the only dock, and as they stepped through the damp clouds and onto the mossy boards, Charlie felt like they had sailed straight into a thin place. It was timeless here, sacred somehow, and she wouldn't have been the least bit surprised to see a longboat appear out of the fog carrying a First Nations hunting party from another age.

"Welcome! Bienvenue! Willkommen!" One of the guys from the Instagram photo greeted them with warm handshakes and bad pronunciation, and escorted them to the coarse sand beach at the end of the dock. He had blond curls, sinewy muscles, and cheekbones that could cut glass, and Charlie sensed Eva melt a little beside her. Never mind that he was clearly closer to thirty than twenty. "I'm Jett," he said, giving them a dimpled smile, "and I already know that you're Charlie and Eva."

Jett, yeah right, Charlie thought, but she smiled back and let him give them the tour—though calling it a tour was a bit generous. There was a rack for a half dozen worse-for-wear kayaks, a pair of cedar pit toilets, and a hard-packed dirt path that led to a small clearing with a handful of walk-in, self-registration campsites.

"I've taken the liberty of registering you and setting you up in the primo site," Jett said, reaching for Eva's hiking pack and slinging it over one shoulder. "Rico and I will get you all settled if you'd like to take a little time to explore the island. The view from the north side is breathtaking. You can practically see all the way to Alaska."

"We'll set up our own site, thanks," Charlie told him, a blister of unease bubbling just below the surface. Something didn't feel right, and she couldn't decide if it was the fact that they seemed to be completely alone on an isolated sliver of land with two strangers, or if it was simply the mysterious island itself. She hadn't expected it to be quite so desolate.

"Suit yourself," Jett said, shrugging. "The boat comes back in twenty-four hours, and in the meantime, Majestic Island is our playground. We'll kayak in the morning, and tonight we'll feast on sockeye salmon and Okanagan peaches."

"It's just us?" Charlie asked, looking around the empty clearing and realizing that there were only two small pup tents set up: presumably one for Jett and one for Rico. "I figured we'd be a part of a group."

"We wanted to give you the royal treatment." Jett smirked as if this was something truly special and not at all alarming. "It gets cold here early, so you can get set up and we'll start a fire soon."

It was cold already, and Charlie zipped her fleece all the way to her chin to ward off the chill. Beside her, Eva's cheeks were pink, her eyes a little wide and glazed. Charlie watched her for a moment, worried about Jett and the yet-to-be-seen Rico. But then Eva swallowed hard, and Charlie *knew* in the way that only a mother can—Eva wasn't lovesick, she was just plain sick.

"You okay?" she asked when Jett took off to help Rico with some unexplained task. Their guides had already swept a spot for their tent, and Charlie unrolled it with a snap of her wrists.

"What do you mean?"

"I mean, are you feeling okay? You look a little off." Charlie straightened up and shoved back her sleeve so she could lay the soft plane of her inner arm against Eva's neck. The girl shivered. "You're warm. Why didn't you tell me you weren't feeling well?"

"I was fine this morning," Eva murmured. "It came on fast."

"I have ibuprofen in my pack. I'll get set up here and then

you can rest for a while. We can skip kayaking tomorrow and head straight back. Maybe they can call the boat or—"

"I'm fine," Eva cut in, forcing a smile. "It'll be fine. We came here to see orcas, and that's what we're going to do. I just need to sleep."

But a good night's sleep turned out to be tricker than they'd imagined. The temperature dropped much quicker than expected, and they huddled in their tent while Jett struggled to get the fire started. When the logs finally caught, they belched smoke that clung to the low-hanging tree limbs and wreathed their tents in a thick gloom that made them cough and sputter. And dinner turned out to be cold smoked salmon and bruised peaches from a brown paper bag that Rico had to excavate from the depths of his tent. It was almost comical, how inept their guides seemed to be, and how slapdash the entire experience was. Charlie figured they'd laugh about it someday, but when deep dark descended on their tiny camp and the fire smoldered to embers, everything changed.

It was the flash of something bright and glassy in Rico's hand, the way Jett gave Charlie a look over the orange coals and then motioned for her to come. Eva had crawled into the tent hours ago, achy and feverish, incapable of stomaching even a nibble of their cold meal. But Charlie felt too vulnerable to turn her back on the men and sat sentry in an old lawn chair between their guides and the door of their compact three-person tent.

"Come on," Jett whispered when she didn't budge from her post. "There's a pod that frequents the far side of the island. Sometimes they hunt at night."

Charlie didn't like the idea of hiking in the dark any more than the thought of leaving Eva alone—and sick—on an uninhabited island. "I need to stay with her," she said, hooking her thumb over her shoulder at their tent.

"Nah, she'll be fine. We won't be long."

Rico materialized from the shadows and tipped Charlie out of her lawn chair with a laugh. He was heavier than his counterpart, and though his face was round and happy, the sound of his giggle set her teeth on edge. But because the two men were their only hope of getting off the island, and because she didn't trust them enough to let them out of her sight, Charlie gave them a tight smile and fell into step behind Rico while Jett took up the rear.

The path to the other side of the island wove through dense trees and over smooth rock faces that were slick with lichen. When Charlie slipped, Jett was there to right her, his hands low on her hips in a touch that was far too casual, too familiar to make her think he was just being nice. Dread puddled in her stomach. In her thirty-some years, Charlie had been pushed up against brick walls and bathroom stalls, kissed and groped and held close against her will. She knew all too well how these things could twist into something ugly and out of control, how afterward she might wake in the morning with bruises on her wrists and scrapes in places that fingernails and belt buckles had raked across. Charlie never suffered the indignity of a 911 call or a rape kit on a cold gurney beneath glaring ER lights. But she was a woman, and all too aware of how Jett was taller, Rico bigger. They always were. They could take little bites of her and no one would ever have to know.

Deep down, Charlie had feared this. It was why Eva was back at the camp, tucked in her sleeping bag and oblivious to the way the night had tilted. Charlie had followed the men, intentionally letting them take her farther and farther away from her daughter and the temptation of her smooth limbs, raven hair, perfectly bowed lips.

Rico led the way, and there was something off about his

gait. It was exaggerated and clumsy, and Charlie doubted it was because the night was dark and the terrain unfamiliar. He was on something, she was sure of it. But just when she was about to feign exhaustion and insist they go back, the trees thinned and cleared altogether, and they emerged on a thin strip of pebbled beach.

The moon was full and fat in the sky, casting a golden glow on the expanse of dark water before them. Small waves criss-crossed the channel as currents swept around the tiny islands, and the moonlight dancing between the crests and troughs made the ocean seem alight with magic. Above them, a billion stars flickered in a liquid galaxy. Charlie must have gasped at the sight, because Jett snaked an arm around her and pulled her to him.

"Look for surface activity," he told her, his mouth almost touching her ear, his breath hot and suggestive. "Exhales, dorsal fins, blows. There are several resident pods here."

Charlie froze, the spell broken, and calculated whether it was better for her to stay put or pull away. Every nerve ending sparked with the understanding that she had to play this very carefully. As she hesitated, Jett's fingers curled under the hem of her fleece, tickling the place where the waist of her jeans met her warm stomach, and after a wrought moment of indecision, she slipped from his embrace and rushed to the edge of the water, pointing. "There!"

Of course, there was nothing to see. They indulged her for a while, pretending to study the bay like the tour guides they supposedly were, but when Rico tired of the charade, he went to lean against a boulder at the trailhead. Jett took Charlie by the hand and tugged her away from the coastline toward the trees.

"I should get back," she said, going with it, hoping that she had misjudged him and that was exactly where they were headed. Back to the little campsite and the tent where she could curl up next to Eva and calm her banging heart. Back to a place of tenuous safety. But after just a few steps, Jett stopped short and spun to face her. Before she could react, he cupped her head in his hands and kissed her, parting her lips with his tongue and pinching her jaw with his thumbs until her mouth opened to his.

Something sharp and bitter exploded on her tongue. Jett was taller than her, and pressed tight against him, Charlie could feel the hard curve of his every muscle. She couldn't overpower him, but she struggled and pushed anyway, choking on the chalky tab that he'd slipped into her mouth with his kiss. She coughed and turned her head, spitting out what was left of it onto the rocky beach.

Jett dropped her as if stung. "Goddammit! Did you just spit it out? That was good stuff!"

"What did you give me?" Charlie croaked.

"Nothing if you spit it out."

"Tell me what it was!" Even though she was shaking so hard her teeth chattered, Charlie's fear was galvanizing into a pure and steely fury.

"Chill out. We thought it's what you wanted. You came for this, remember?"

Charlie couldn't even respond. She came for this? She wracked her mind, trying to read a hidden meaning in their messages, in her acceptance of what she believed was a casual invitation. How had she ended up here? And what had Jett tried to slip her? Acid or ecstasy, maybe PCP? Beyond a little weed in high school, Charlie was virginal when it came to drugs.

Jett reached for her. "It's fine," he said smoothly, trying to gather her into his arms again. "You don't have to—"

"Don't touch me!" Charlie didn't mean to scream, but her words echoed off the craggy rocks, the expanse of dark water.

"Hey," Jett held up his hands in surrender, yet he didn't move away. "Whatever. Be a bitch."

There was no real venom in his voice, but in the moonlight, Charlie could see that his eyes were cold and glazed. She didn't trust him, not for a second, and she backed away slowly, her hiking boots sliding on the damp stones. "Don't touch me," she said again, softer. And then she took off, sprinting for the path. Rico was there, and he put out a hand as if to stop her, but he was high and miscalculated the distance. Charlie evaded him easily, and tore down the trail, impervious to the switch of branches as they lashed against the exposed skin of her hands, neck, and cheeks. She twisted her ankle and almost went down, but she sucked in a cry and kept going, putting as much distance between her and the men as she could.

But what good would it do? They were alone on the island with nowhere to go and no one to call for help. In a matter of minutes, Charlie had sprinted past the dock and the pit toilets into the clearing where their tents crouched beneath the sweeping evergreens, despair hot on her heels. There was a utility knife in her pack, but it was dull and rusty, hardly a weapon. And they had no phone signal out here, not even a single wavering bar. Charlie and Eva were well and truly on their own.

When her fingers began to tingle, Charlie wasn't sure if it was adrenaline or the dust that had dissolved on her tongue. Either way, she was terrified and murderous, a blunt edge that could hardly see past the next second and her staggering need to keep her daughter safe. Working quickly, she unzipped the tent to check on Eva (sleeping soundly) and rummage for the knife (right where she left it). Then she sat cross-legged in front of the closed tent flap, her knife and her rage the only things between Eva and a brutal world.

The rest of the night was a shadowed smudge of rustlings

and whispers and fears. Charlie wasn't sure if she was hallucinating or dreaming, if the flecks of drug that had dissolved on her tongue were powerful enough to pull her under even though she fought with everything she had to stay alert, awake, afloat. There were moments of clarity—an owl hooting in the trees, the snitch of a zipper, Eva talking in her sleep—and then long stretches of flickering lights, menacing sounds, uncertainty.

Until: "Mom? Mom, did you sleep out here?" Eva's hands on her shoulders, the fizz of laughter in her voice. "You're freezing!"

Charlie bolted up, and pain pooled at the base of her skull. She was parched and tender, her back sore from the uneven ground and her hands so stiff with cold she couldn't form fists.

"Oh my gosh. Did you guys *drink* last night?" Eva's smile quirked as she reached to pull a twig from Charlie's hair. "Wow. I mean, *wow*. I've never seen you quite so . . ." She flapped her hands in Charlie's direction as if her appearance needed no explanation.

"Are you okay?" Charlie's icy fingers cradled Eva's cheeks. The girl's eyes were clear and luminous in the morning light, her skin warm, but not hot.

"I'm fine! I told you all I needed was sleep." Eva stepped carefully out of the tent and wrapped Charlie in a hug. "I'm more worried about you. You have scratches all over your neck. What did you *do* last night?"

Charlie held her daughter at arm's length and studied her face, ignoring the questions she couldn't begin to answer. "You're sure you're all right?"

"Great! And I can't believe we're going to kayak with orcas today!" Eva squealed. Then she leaned close and whispered: "It's okay if you like Jett."

Charlie's eyes pricked with tears, but she blinked them away before Eva could see them. Over her daughter's shoulder she could see Jett unzip his own tent and crawl out, yawning and stretching with his fingers interlaced over his head. She watched him for a moment, and when he glanced over, she flinched. But Jett's gaze slid away, and he smiled as if nothing had happened.

"Who's ready to see orcas today?" he called, clapping his hands twice.

Eva jumped up, giggling. "Me!" she half shouted, her enthusiasm zinging through the small campsite. "Pick me! Pick me!"

Charlie couldn't watch. Taking a shuddering breath, she turned to the tent and began to zip up the flap. When her knee rolled onto something sharp, she looked down and realized it was the knife she had clutched for most of the night. It was stained and ineffectual, half-buried beneath dried evergreen needles and bits of loamy earth. Charlie stared at it for a minute, uncertain about everything. Was it all a bad dream? What *really* happened last night? She couldn't say for sure. And because the morning fire was already starting to crackle behind her, and she could hear Jett talking about instant coffee and maple brown sugar oatmeal, she palmed the knife, flicked it closed, and tucked it in a pocket on her thigh. She wiped both hands over her face and finger-combed her hair. Then she stood slowly, with only the slightest hint of a wobble.

Eva was okay, and that was all that mattered. It was the only thing that had ever mattered.

CHAPTER 8

SUNDAY

When Detective James turns into the parking lot of the marina, Charlie is pulled taut between elation and terror. Half of her is convinced that the authorities have given in and are going to let her take the *Summer Moon* out to search for her daughter. The other half fears that they've found something she will be required to identify. *Please, dear God*, she thinks. *Don't let it be some*one.

It's been a quiet drive, punctuated only by the intermittent click of the blinker and the drum of Agent Turner's fingers on the console until Detective James tells him to stop. Now Charlie feels wound tight as a spring and just as restrained, and before she can stop herself, she blurts: "Did you find Eva? You have to tell me."

Detective James says, "We don't, actually," at the exact moment that Agent Turner looks over the seat back at her and says, "No." His brown eyes are immense and unexpectedly reassuring, and Charlie suddenly wants to grab his arm in both of her hands just so she has something to hold on to. Instead, she laces her fingers together in her lap.

"Thank you," she says softly. "I thought . . . I mean, maybe you . . ."

"We have some leads," Agent Turner admits, and by the sharp huff from the detective in the driver's seat, Charlie surmises that

the FBI agent is going off-script. It's cold comfort—she suspects
Detective James doesn't like her very much, though they're
probably just playing Good Cop/Bad Cop with her—but she's
thankful for Agent Turner's honesty anyway. She needs all the
allies she can get, even if they're pretend.

"We've actually set up our mobile command center in the
boathouse," Agent Turner continues. "The building is not really
in use, and it made sense for us to be as close to the search effort
as possible."

It did make sense. Still, Charlie wonders how her fellow
mariners feel about the prolonged presence of law enforcement
at their little haven. Of the roped-off parking spaces near the
small building, the extra security, the *Summer Moon* lashed to
the floating dock and wrapped in a garland of drooping police
tape. Spring is the best, most hopeful time of year on the lake,
and Eva's disappearance—as shocking and horrible as it is—has
a ripple effect that radiates consequences for anyone even tan-
gentially involved. It's painfully obvious when Charlie steps out
of the refined sedan and onto the gravel of the parking lot. Instead of music drifting from the rows of docks and the low hum
of chatter as her friends get their boats ready for summer, it's a
ghost town. Only Weston and Thea are visible from their slip in
the very last row. They're watching the newcomers, and when
Charlie looks in their direction, Thea raises her hand in greeting
and then presses it over her heart. Charlie is too choked up to
even lift a finger in reply.

The inside of the boathouse has been transformed. The glass
cases have been pushed to the side and the desks hold industrial-
looking printers. There are folding tables filled with laptops and
bulky charging stations outfitted with durable handheld radios.
Cords snake across the floor, and a handful people sit on metal
chairs in front of oversized screens. They're typing dutifully or

riffling through stacks of papers that Charlie can't even begin to guess the purpose of.

All this for one missing girl. She's heartened, and then her stomach bottoms out. If all these people—plus the coast guard and others that she likely doesn't even know about—haven't found Eva yet, what are the chances anyone will?

But Charlie doesn't have time to dwell on this alarming thought because Agent Turner puts a hand between her shoulder blades and directs her past the beehive of activity to a room at the back of the building. It used to be a catchall, a narrow storage room that housed all the odds and ends the Landing Historical Society couldn't bring themselves to toss, but it's been cleared out. All that remains is another folding table and yet more dented metal chairs. Agent Turner motions toward one and Charlie sinks into it slowly, perching on the very edge.

"What did you find?" she asks, because no one else is talking.

Detective James ignores her question entirely. "We'd like to record this interview." He's typing something on a flat keyboard clicked into a tablet. On top of the portable setup is a small camera that blinks to life at the touch of a button. Charlie stares at the red light for a moment, realizing that someone at one of the computers she just passed is probably right now staring at her face on his screen. She blinks, wondering if she looks like a monster or just a grief-stricken mother.

"Do I need a lawyer?" Charlie's not even sure who she's asking. The person on the other side of the recording? Detective James?

It's Agent Turner who answers. "You haven't been charged with a crime."

Not yet, Charlie thinks, filling in the pregnant pause after his words.

"But you have every right to an attorney," the FBI agent continues. "Would you like to call one?"

"No. I don't want to waste any more time. What do you want from me? I'll tell you anything." Charlie has no idea if her cooperation is seen as disingenuous or sincere, and she doesn't really care.

"We'd like to talk about Eva Explores," Detective James says, stepping to the door and accepting a thick folder from a young officer. He closes the door with a thud and fans through the papers, arching his eyebrows at whatever he's seeing on the pages. He sits down next to Agent Turner, across from Charlie, and places the closed folder neatly in the middle of the table. "Whose idea was it to start the account?"

Charlie squeezes her eyes closed. She doesn't want to talk about this with them. Not because she has anything to hide, but because it isn't relevant. They're barking up the wrong tree. But she gathers her thoughts anyway and begins. "Eva wanted an Instagram account for her thirteenth birthday. I thought she was too young for social media, so we compromised. We started a joint account. It was called the Sutton Girls."

Agent Turner rolls his hand, encouraging her to continue.

"So I took this picture of Eva and it kind of went viral. We were at Gooseberry Falls, and the water and the light . . . Everything just blew up from there." Charlie lifts one shoulder, uncertain of how to explain what had happened to them. What they let happen.

"Is this the photo?" Detective James opens the folder and takes out the top sheet of paper. It's a printout of their first ever Sutton Girls post, the waterfall shot that started it all. At the bottom of the picture their short caption—the somewhat pretentious Anaïs Nin poem—is printed. And beneath that, the first of what she knows are hundreds of comments.

"That's it," Charlie whispers.

"So you took photos of your teenage girl and put them online for the world to see."

It feels as though Detective James has slapped her. "It wasn't like that."

"Lots of people post pictures of their children." Agent Turner comes to her rescue, but Charlie doesn't need help. She's savoring the ache. She needs someone to blame, and it might as well be herself.

"I took lots of pictures of Eva over the years," she says when she can trust herself to talk again. "I take full responsibility for that. But there were rules. I mean, I didn't write them down or anything, but we were careful. I usually posted pictures of her back, her feet, her hands. The photos were kind of abstract, you know? I didn't post her full face."

Detective James slides the folder toward himself and carefully extracts a sheaf of papers that have been clipped together. He peels them off one by one and places them on the table. There's the left side of Eva's face. The right. Her perfect, grinning mouth behind a three-scoop waffle cone dripping with hot fudge sauce. Just the glint of her mischievous blue eyes with a tartan blanket pulled up to the bridge of her nose and a fire roaring behind her. Someone has collected and printed every partial face shot that Eva and Charlie ever posted. The detective keeps laying them out, filling up the table with Eva's lovely features until he runs out of room and has to stack them on top of each other.

"Never her full face, huh?"

"We know you tried to keep her hidden, Charlotte, but I think you can see how easy it would be for anyone to know exactly who Eva is and what she looks like." Agent Turner catches her gaze and holds it. "You know you're both very recognizable."

Charlie just nods.

"Your daughter is a pretty young woman," Agent Turner continues. "And you have a lot of followers. It's not outside the realm of possibility that someone would become obsessed with her. Has she ever had a stalker? Anyone who gave her unwanted attention or made her feel uncomfortable?"

"We both have," Charlie admits, the pit in her stomach expanding to a gaping black hole. "Nothing too serious. We always blocked them immediately."

"Have you ever met one of them in person?"

There were so many accounts that they flagged and messages they deleted without reading past the very first line. But they had also come face-to-face with people who would do them harm. Charlie thought of Majestic Island. Of the shrill troll who thought it was her God-given job to track them down. And the guy who somehow figured out they were at the rodeo in Cody, Wyoming. Nothing serious had ever happened—praise the Lord—and they'd always felt safe enough. Truthfully, their life on the road didn't seem much riskier than a run-of-the-mill existence. The statistics are well known: most car crashes happen close to home; most violent crimes are committed by someone who intimately knows the victim. Still, Charlie and Eva put themselves out there in a way that opened the door to danger. She knew it.

"Yes," Charlie says carefully. "We met some weirdos. But we were never hurt. We never had to file a restraining order or anything."

"Lucky for you."

Charlie wants to glare at Detective James, but she knows her every movement is being recorded. She tips her head so the bill of her baseball cap obscures her eyes and fights to keep her expression neutral. He's trying to get under her skin and doing a damn good job.

After a beat of silence, Charlie says: "The Instagram account has been more or less defunct for six months. And even if we were posting every day—even if we thought that Eva had an active stalker—what are you suggesting? That someone kidnapped her off the boat while I was sleeping in the cabin? I mean, come on."

"How long were you sleeping?" Agent Turner tents his fingers on the table and leans forward. "I've listened to the nine-one-one call, and you say that you went belowdecks to nap. How long would you say you were down there?"

Longer than she would like to admit. Forty-five minutes? An hour? It could have been more. "I don't know," Charlie says, because she's ashamed. But then she offers: "Half an hour?"

"That's a long time. Long enough for a life raft to float completely out of sight?"

"I don't know." It's true, she has no idea. But all at once she can picture Eva taking the raft out of the seat compartment and pulling the red handle. It would inflate in seconds, snapping to life like a kernel of popcorn over a campfire. Did it hit her in the head? Knock her out and then toss her overboard? Most important: *Why?* Why in the world would Eva inflate the life raft on a beautiful spring day with her mother only steps away?

Charlie wrings her hands beneath the table where the recording device can't document it. "We need to focus on the raft. If it's gone, she had to have taken it. I put it in the seat compartment myself just a couple of weeks ago. I *know* it was there."

"We found the raft," Agent Turner says without warning.

It's the empty moment before an explosion, the second of nothingness before the world detonates into a million pieces. Charlie can't breathe—for a single heartbeat she can't even *see*—and then reality comes rushing at her like a tidal wave. "You found the raft?" she cries, her voice breaking. "What about

Eva? I mean, was there evidence that she was there? Where did you find it? What does this mean?"

"It washed up onshore several miles northeast of your last known location. The coast guard didn't expect to find it there, which is why we were so surprised when a hiker came across it this morning." Agent Turner leans back in his chair and crosses his arms over his chest, watching Charlie thoughtfully. He obviously thinks she knows more than she's letting on.

"I don't understand. How did it get there?" Charlie is hyperventilating but trying to sip tiny breaths through her mouth like Frank taught her so many years ago. She must be doing okay, because neither of the men move to help. Even Agent Turner is distant, cool and austere as unanswered questions trouble the air between them. If they found the raft and Eva wasn't in it, how would they ever find her? "Do you think . . . ?" She can't finish.

"Do you have a good relationship with your daughter?" Detective James's inquiry is abrupt and jarring. Charlie feels as if he has jerked her in an entirely new direction.

"I love Eva. She's everything to me."

"That's not what I asked. I want to know if you have a good relationship. Can you talk? Do you share things with each other? Does she trust you?"

He can't know how much these questions hurt in light of the last several hours. Before going to Piper Berkley's house and meeting with Peter Cole, Charlie would have answered without pause. Yes. Definitely. Charlotte and Evangeline Sutton, unstoppable mother and daughter duo, are the best of friends and confidantes. They know everything about each other and share their innermost thoughts and feelings. They traveled the country—and beyond—together, and shared some of the very best and worst experiences of their lives. But Charlie is so confused by everything that's happened and all that she's learned, that she stalls for a moment. Detective James swoops right in.

"Were you on bad terms with your daughter? It's our understanding that you were at odds about Eva Explores. Did you fight yesterday?"

"How do you know—"

"It doesn't matter," Agent Turner says. "Just answer the question."

Charlie slides back in her chair, as far from the men across the table as she can get in this small, suddenly suffocating room. "I wanted to be on the road for one more summer," she says as simply as she can. "Eva didn't. We worked it out. When we took out the *Summer Moon* yesterday, we were in a great place."

"We've been conducting interviews. Multiple sources confirm that Eva was not actually in a 'great place' lately." Detective James swipes through several screens on his phone, and then lifts the fingers of his left hand into air quotes to read: "'Eva was frustrated with her mom. She was counting down the days until college.'"

Charlie's mouth goes dry. "Who told you that?"

"And: 'Eva mostly keeps to herself, but everyone knows that her mom is kind of controlling.'" Detective James waggles the phone at her. "Would you like me to read more?"

The tear that slides down Charlie's cheek is hot and humiliating. She does not want to cry in front of these men, but her heart is ravaged. Not just because Eva said those things—*thought* those things—but because Charlie didn't know it. How could they have drifted so far apart? How could the young woman who had once lived inside her body, and then willingly spent two and a half years in a vintage Airstream trailer with her mother, hide a hurt so big from the person who loved her most?

"I didn't know," Charlie whispers. "I didn't know that she felt that way. That she resented me so much."

"Did you make a lot of money running Eva Explores?"

Once again, Charlie is whiplashed by Detective James's interrogation. "What?"

"It's a simple question."

"Not at first," she manages. She's so numb, the words tumble as quickly as her tears. She doesn't do anything to stop either of them. "The first year was really hard. But then we landed a couple of big accounts. Our trip to Maui changed everything."

"Ballpark it for me. Would you say you made six figures annually?"

Charlie considers, nods.

"That's a lot of money for a couple of women living in a camper."

"We saved most of it. Put it away for Eva's college tuition. She wants to be a writer."

"Like mother, like daughter." Agent Turner doesn't sound like he's mocking her, and when Charlie glances up, his mouth is a thin line, but there's something in his eyes that looks like compassion.

"So would you say," Detective James goes on, "that quitting Eva Explores was a huge financial hit? And that if you continued with the account, your income opportunities would have likely increased? I mean, you were on the road—pardon the pun—to true Instagram fame and fortune."

"We didn't do it for fame. Or the money."

The detective grins at her. "That was just the cherry on top, right?"

"What are you saying?" Charlie finally brushes the backs of her hands over her cheeks, wiping the evidence of her grief away.

"The raft was slashed, Charlotte." Agent Turner puts his palms on the table, on top of all those pictures of Eva, and levels Charlie with a look so intense she can't tear herself away. "Someone punctured it with a knife. If Eva was in that life raft, she didn't survive."

Charlie dies a little at his words. But even as despair spreads through her, she fights it.

"You think I did it," she says. She'd considered the similarities between Eva's disappearance and that old murder case, but it was so ludicrous. So far-fetched. "You think I slashed the life raft and put Eva in it." Charlie feels as if she has floated away from her body and can see the situation from the perspective of these officers. They've just established motive. She was the only person with means and opportunity, and now the motive is crystal clear. People kill for money and for love. But *murder*? Do they really think that she put her daughter in a ruined lifeboat and left her to die on Lake Superior? Because she was so enraged that Eva wanted to give up their burgeoning social media fame?

"Don't stop looking for her," Charlie says, suddenly frantic. "You can arrest me if you want to, but please don't stop looking for Eva. I don't know what happened, but she's out there somewhere, I'm sure of it."

"I'm sure you know exactly what happened to Eva," Detective James says, standing. "And in light of the fact that you're a flight risk . . ." He reaches for his duty belt and rests his fingers lightly on the pouch that holds a pair of handcuffs.

"Flight risk?" Charlie chokes.

"You snuck out of your house and borrowed a neighbor's truck so we wouldn't know you had left the property."

"I did that because I didn't want to drive past the camera crews. I wasn't *running*."

"And lying to law enforcement is obstruction of justice."

"Lying?" Charlie can hardly breathe. "But—"

"I'm not sure cuffs are necessary, Mitchum." Agent Turner's voice is clipped and professional. "She's not exactly a threat."

"Eva's out there," Charlie jumps in, trying to make them listen to reason. "I didn't hurt my daughter. I have no idea why the life raft was taken or how it wound up on the beach. I swear to you, I didn't do anything to it."

"Keep talking, Sutton."

Charlie knows it's a warning, but she keeps going anyway. "Eva has a boyfriend—someone I didn't know about until an hour ago. Maybe he has something to do with this. Find him. You have to talk to Lennon at Mugs. Here . . ." she slides her hand into the pocket of her jeans and takes out the tattered scrap of paper with Lennon's phone number scrawled on it. Thrusting it at Agent Turner, she tries again. "I don't know why she didn't tell me about him, but I think Eva was keeping a lot of secrets."

Agent Turner takes the paper and gives Charlie a tight smile, but he doesn't try to stop Detective James when he steps around the table.

A knock on the door pulls him up short and irritation melts across his features. She can tell he's taking pleasure in this—Detective James truly believes that Charlie is capable of hurting her daughter—and a part of her can't blame him. She, too, would hate anyone with the capacity to harm a child. She just doesn't know how to make him believe that she's not someone who could.

While Charlie stands in awkward, strained proximity to Detective James, Agent Turner opens the door and has a hushed conversation with whoever is on the other side. Charlie can't see the new arrival because he or she is hidden behind the door, but after a quick exchange, Agent Turner swings the door wide.

"Mitchum," he says, leveling a look at his provisional partner, "you should hear this."

Officer Mia Grady is standing on the threshold, looking like she hasn't slept a wink since Charlie last saw her. Her ponytail is crooked, there are dark hollows beneath her eyes, and her uniform is wrinkled—Charlie wonders if she even bothered to change it after spending the night in the Morrows' driveway. The young policewoman seems nervous to be interrupting her superiors, and her eyes widen when she clocks the tension in the room.

"I didn't—" she mumbles, but trails off when Agent Turner steps out of the way so that a second person can shuffle in.

Charlie immediately recognizes the Landing High School guidance counselor, a fresh-from-college, striking Latina woman in a khaki pencil skirt and a white blouse. She was welcoming and incredibly helpful when Eva rejoined the public school system, and Charlie can't help but give her a wan smile, even though she can't begin to guess at what Elena Alvarez is doing here.

There are a few beats of wrought silence, and then Agent Turner introduces the two women. "Ms. Alvarez has something she thinks we should see."

Charlie can tell that Detective James is itching to get out of this room and throw her in a cell where she belongs, but he crosses his arms over his chest and raises a single eyebrow. It's the closest they're going to get to a greeting.

"You sent us to the school after our night shift," Officer Grady begins, addressing Detective James. "We talked to the principal and to some of Eva's teachers, just like you told us. And we searched her locker. No computer."

"What about the Cloud?" Agent Turner asks.

"Eva changed the password to her school account. They can't access the files yet, but they will."

Agent Turner nods, encouraging Officer Grady to go on.

"So, when Ms. Alvarez heard that we were looking for Eva's laptop, she showed us something."

"Right," Ms. Alvarez says, picking up the thread and sliding the strap of a messenger bag off her shoulder. She goes to set it on the table but can't seem to bring herself to cover up all the printed pictures of Eva. Instead, she rests the leather satchel on a chair and unzips it. She lifts a black, one-inch binder from the depths of her messenger bag and clutches it to her chest for a moment, seemingly wrestling with herself. "These are all of Eva's college application essays," she explains. "She missed the early application cutoffs because of her time on the road and is focusing on schools with rolling admissions and late deadlines. Eva really wants to get into a school with a strong creative writing program, and she's using the essays as a sort of practice for her future portfolio. It's been a great exercise for her, but I also think it's been . . . cathartic."

"How many essays are in there?" The question slips from Charlie's lips. She knows she should remain silent, but the thought of Eva's words in that binder is haunting. Charlie doesn't consider herself a great writer, but she has a lot of experience—and a steady stream of requests for articles from popular magazines and websites to prove it. She's asked Eva dozens of times to let her help with the college essays, or at the very least, proofread them. Eva hasn't shared a single one.

"Fifty," Ms. Alvarez says.

"Fifty college application essays?" Detective James scoffs. He's clearly skeptical about what relevance Eva's musings may have to his open-and-shut case.

"She talks about a lot of things in here." Ms. Alvarez pats the binder. "I'm sorry, Charlotte, she told me that she wasn't sharing them with you. I tried to encourage her to show you a few of the more . . . *interesting* essays, but she said she wasn't ready yet."

"And you think her writing will shed some light on her disappearance?" Agent Turner reaches for the binder, and she hands it over with an air of reluctance.

"It's not just that. There's this." Ms. Alvarez peels a Post-it Note off one of the essays and hands it to Agent Turner. "This note was on the last essay she turned in on Friday afternoon—just a couple of days ago. I didn't see it until today because I hadn't had a chance to read the essay yet. When I found out Eva was missing . . ." Ms. Alvarez trails off and gives Charlie a small, sad smile.

But Charlie can't tear her gaze from Agent Turner. As he reads the note, something shifts in his face. It's subtle but obvious—a tightening of his jaw, a hard gleam in his eyes.

"What does it say?" Charlie breathes.

Agent Turner doesn't answer.

PART II

Eva

COLLEGE APPLICATION ESSAY #1

Discuss an accomplishment, event, or realization that sparked a period of personal growth or a new understanding of yourself or others.

Everyone loves a good rags-to-riches story. The miraculous transformation, the exciting shift from one thing to another. There's poetry in the metamorphosis, a sort of savage delight as we observe the journey through the chrysalis. What we often forget is that when a caterpillar magically transforms into a butterfly, it emerges from the cocoon exhausted, shivering, and wet. Beautiful, but fragile.

I am that trembling butterfly, the proverbial ugly duckling turned stately swan. Mine is a redemption story, and if you believe everything you read, a happily ever after. But before we get there, we have to start here.

When I was in eighth grade, a group of classmates cornered me in the girls' bathroom during lunch. There were eight of them, and one of little (big) old me, and when they circled up, I was sure that they'd taunt me from their overused playbook. You know, toss a few hateful names my way (Miss Piggy, Solid Sutton, Evangeline the Blubber Queen—my perennial favorite), and pinch handfuls of the rolls around my waist until I cried. It was a thing we did. Fun times.

Unfortunately, my tormentors were feeling creative that day, and instead of the same old, one of the girls grabbed the overflowing garbage can from the corner and set it in front of me. (Did I mention our janitorial services were seriously lacking?) I thought they might make me crawl inside the stinking heap of paper towels and trash, but they had a better idea: Since I was such a fatty fatso, I needed to eat my way through whatever I could find among the used tissues and balled up sanitary pads. Dear reader, I found seven wads of chewed gum, a stale granola bar, a bruised apple, a half-eaten and very soggy sandwich, an empty foil bag of potato chips (they made me lick it out), and a bottle of cloudy, half-drank Gatorade to wash it all down.

Of course, now I'm skinny (not really, I'll always have an "athletic" build), pretty(ish), and popular (nearly 250K ~~followers~~ friends on Instagram), so none of that matters, right? The way they laughed at me while I stuck my tongue in a potato chip bag to get the last few crumbs was erased forever the moment I read a comment from some total stranger saying: *Heeeyyy gorgeous!*

Yeah, right. The world doesn't work that way. Or at least, the human heart doesn't. There are two things they don't tell you about rags-to-riches, old-to-new, redemption stories that leave a cruel past far behind in the dust. Number one: the journey is painful. It hurts like hell, friends. And number two: no matter how beautiful the butterfly, deep inside she will always be that gross, squishy, untouchable caterpillar that the cool girls ran screaming from. The transformation is skin-deep, even when a quarter million fans will swear that what they see is the only thing that matters.

CHAPTER 9

SATURDAY

When she reaches over the side of the *Summer Moon* and takes his hand, Eva's life begins again. His grip is strong, his palm calloused because he's the kind of man who isn't afraid of work. And she isn't afraid of anything with him by her side. So even though it's completely insane, even though it will break her mother's heart into a thousand tiny pieces, Eva puts her foot on the edge and jumps.

Zach catches her, both hands going around her waist. And then she's slamming into his chest with more force than either of them anticipated.

"Whoa," Zach says, falling back a bit.

But he's grinning, and she's grinning, and she throws her arms around his neck and kisses him deeply. He tastes of spearmint gum and desire, and Eva knows that she could die in this moment and never regret a single thing. The boat is rocking softly, the rope that has lashed Zach's shitty old speedboat to the *Summer Moon* is creaking, but all of that disappears in his arms.

"I want you," Eva murmurs, her lips against Zach's mouth.

He pulls away so he can look into her eyes. "She's asleep?"

"Yup."

"And you gave her the pills like I told you?"

Eva disentangles herself from his embrace and straightens

her bunched-up shirt so she doesn't have to look him in the eye. "Yes, of course." No, absolutely not. She agreed to do this crazy thing—so she's certainly not without blame—but Eva could never drug her mother. That's a bridge too far. Besides, she didn't have to. Charlie *never* drinks, so two large glasses of chardonnay on top of a terrible sleep did her in as surely as a couple of crushed Ambien would. Alcohol has a devastating effect on Charlie—clearly because of her own mother's addiction—and Eva knows that the psychological effect of "overdoing" it will leave Charlie exhausted, remorseful, and confused. Eva regrets that, but it was better than drugging her mom. The pills Zach had given her went overboard.

"And you're sure she doesn't know about us." Zach puts a finger under Eva's chin and tips her face toward his. He searches her eyes, as if trying to read everything that's transpired since they last talked several hours ago.

She could get lost in all that stormy blue. His hair is the color of summer wheat and just a touch too long, and she reaches up to twine her fingers through it. He's not handsome in the traditional way, but his jaw is strong, his shoulders broad. There's something bewitching about the way he moves, smooth and powerful like a jungle cat. "She doesn't know about us *yet*. But she will soon enough."

Zach's smile is uneasy. "I'm going to board the *Summer Moon* and make sure everything is okay."

"Why?"

But he doesn't answer. Eva watches as he steps casually between the two boats, wobbling only a little when a wave swells beneath them and makes the watercraft sway. The buoys that are slung between the hulls squeak a bit as they rub against each other, and Eva can't help but wonder if the sound will rouse her mother. She checked on her only minutes before Zach arrived, crouching beside her on the floor in the cabin and secretly wishing that Charlie would wake up. Wouldn't it be better that way? If Zach showed up and they had no choice but to confront this thing between them?

This is my boyfriend, Eva would say. *It's true, he's twenty-four and I'm seventeen, but it doesn't matter, Mom. We're in love.*

She'd employ every cliché in her arsenal: age is just a number, the heart wants what it wants, love is blind—or, in this case, love is oblivious to a seven-year age gap and the fact that she's still technically a minor. For just a few more months.

"Your mom won't understand," Zach had insisted when they were still plotting. "She'll find a way to keep us apart. Do you know if I sleep with you, it's considered statutory rape?"

"We'd have to have sex first," Eva purred, straddling him as he sat on a blanket beneath a tree. They were in a hidden clearing only a few yards from one of Eva's favorite trails, but it was cold, and she wasn't afraid anyone would stumble across them. Zach was emphatic about keeping their relationship a secret from her mother, so they always met in solitary places.

It was the only obstacle between them, the fact that Eva was ready to tell the world and Zach argued they couldn't. But when Charlie began to press Eva about committing to one more summer doing Eva Explores—and she simply *refused* to let up—Zach hatched a plan that was guaranteed to get Charlie's attention.

"We'll disappear for a couple of days. She takes you for granted, Eva. She doesn't listen. It's time that she starts to take you seriously."

It took months to wear her down, but when graduation was only a week away and Charlie began to prepare Sebastian for their imminent departure, Eva knew she had to act. She wanted Zach to be at her graduation ceremony, and she did *not* want to hit the road only days later. Of course, Zach's plan seemed un-necessarily dramatic to her, the sort of subterfuge that belonged in a cheesy made-for-TV chick flick, but Zach swore it was ro-mantic. They'd disappear into thin air, and then before Charlie really started to worry, they'd be back with some ultimatums. No more Eva Explores. Charlie had to accept that Eva was in love with an older man. And she had to stop treating Eva like a baby. She was an (almost) high school graduate and a grown woman.

"What are you doing?" Eva calls when she realizes that Zach is taking a long time on the *Summer Moon*. She can't see what he's up to because the fishing boat is so much higher in the water than the 1980s relic of a speedboat where she waits im-patiently.

"Shhh!" he hisses over the side. "You forgot this." Zach throws down her backpack. It's followed quickly by the light jacket Charlie had insisted she take, and a bulky yellow duf-fel. When Eva catches the duffel, she almost tosses it back. But Zach is already lifting himself over the side, unraveling the mooring line from a cleat on the side of the *Summer Moon* as he comes.

"Why did you take the life raft?" Eva asks as he steps lightly into the speedboat and pushes off.

Zach shoots her a crooked grin. "Just look at this piece of shit," he says, smacking the side of the boat. "We need it a lot more than your mom does."

Eva can't argue with that, so she hauls in the buoys and stores them beneath the bench seat at the back of the boat. Then she tucks herself under Zach's arm and snuggles close as he speeds away. Her heart twists a bit at the thought of Charlie waking up alone on the *Summer Moon*, but she's comforted by the knowledge that she defied Zach in one small thing. Well, two. The pills and the note she wrote explaining things to her mother. She had left it tucked behind a loose dial on the helm. Charlie couldn't miss it.

Mom—

I'm safe. See you soon.

—E

Zach would have a conniption if he knew, but Eva understands her mother better than he does, and she's sure that Charlie will call out the National Guard if she believes her daughter is in any sort of danger. Better to put her mind at ease. It's one of the reasons Eva agreed to Zach's crazy plan in the first place. Slipping out from beneath her mother's watchful gaze for a couple of days sounded like heaven itself.

The sun dips lower in the sky, melting honeyed rays across the water as they make their way northeast toward the Canadian border. Of course, they won't go that far—Zach has a truck waiting for them in a small harbor on the farthest edge of the Superior National Forest—but a part of Eva wants to just keep going. Into Ontario, through Thunder Bay, and up to the Canadian Shield. Charlie always talked about taking Sebastian to Lake Nipigon so they could discover their very own private island. They'd live out the rest of their days writing poetry and coaxing good things from the soil, just like Annie Dillard. But that was Charlie's dream, not Eva's.

"Where are we going again?" Eva asks, burying her face for a moment in Zach's neck so she can ground herself in him. He's warm and smells of soap and sunshine. "Little Elk?"

"Little Moose," he tells her, dropping a kiss on the top of her head. "Population one hundred and twenty-two. At its peak. I doubt you could even find it on a map."

They're headed for Boundary Waters territory, and the tiny town where Zach spent his first few years. His family isn't there anymore, but they still own a house on the outskirts with a single bedroom and a pump out back that draws from a cold, clean well. Zach assures her it's not much, but it sounds perfect to Eva. Quiet and unfussy, a place where they can be alone. She pictures an embroidered tea towel draped over the handle of a vintage Chambers oven, a colorful quilt on a spindle bed. She imagines Zach as a towheaded little boy, and because she was just thinking about Annie Dillard, she remembers a quote: "Nothing moves a woman so deeply as the boyhood of the man she loves." It's so true, she squeezes Zach until he protests.

"Hey, ease up a bit. You trying to crush me to death?"

"I just can't wait," she tells him.

"Don't get your hopes up," he says, easing out of her embrace. "I told you the cabin's not much."

Eva can't tell if her enthusiasm has dampened the mood, or if something else is bothering him. Zach can be like this: sullen and a bit unpredictable. He can switch from hot to cold as easily as turning a faucet. Usually, she's pretty good at keeping him on an even keel, but when she looks back and realizes that the *Summer Moon* has disappeared on the horizon, Eva has to suppress her own misgivings.

She shuffles to the bench and grabs her backpack off the floor where Zach has stashed it behind the captain's seat. Before he arrived, Eva was sure she had tucked her phone in the main compartment. But when she unzips it and rustles around inside, it's not there. Eva tries all the zippers—every pocket and possible hiding place—before starting all over again. This time, she lifts her overnight things out of the bag and puts them on the bench beside her. Her toiletries bag, a few changes of clothes, and school-issued computer are all present and accounted for. But after riffling through her backpack twice, she has to admit: her phone's not there.

"I think I left my phone on the boat!" She has to raise her voice over the wind that is beginning to pick up. It was such a calm day, but as dusk approaches, Eva can tell that it's going to be a wild night. The lake beneath them is agitated and grumbling. She's glad that she doesn't get seasick.

"What?" Zach sounds distracted.

"My phone!" She shifts so that she can drape one arm over his shoulder and tuck her head next to his. "I was sure I put my phone in my backpack, but I must have left it on the boat. You didn't see it when you boarded the *Summer Moon*, did you?"

Zach shakes his head. "Sorry. No biggie though, right? I have a phone if we need it."

Eva's not satisfied, but there's not much she can do about it now. She slides back on the bench and reaches for her jacket. It's getting chilly as the sun slips down the horizon, and she's grateful to have extra clothes. Pulling off her jean shorts, she snags a pair of joggers from her backpack. She even remembered her Carhartt beanie, and she tugs it over her ears, tucking her unruly hair back so that it no longer whips her in the face as they race over the growing waves. She'd ask Zach to slow down a bit, but she knows he's trying to make the harbor before dark.

Eva is used to running away. She knows exactly how to pack everything small and tidy, thrust it in a corner, and hit the road. And she knows full well that the running *works*—it puts distance between her heart and whatever problem is making it splinter. The problem is, running doesn't fix a damn thing, and although Eva could escape everything that happened when she was a kid in Duluth, this particular run will require a return.

She's not sure how to do that. And as the distance between Zach's speedboat and the *Summer Moon* increases, Eva can feel the pull like a hook in her gut.

They've been racing up the coast for well over an hour when Eva can't take it anymore. She balls the cuffs of her jacket in her palms and crosses her arms to ward off the cold, then raises her voice so she can be heard over the wind and the waves. "I think we should turn around!"

Zach pulls back on the throttle abruptly, nearly pitching Eva off the seat. She manages to keep her feet beneath her as he slams the boat in neutral, but strikes her shoulder on the back of his captain's chair.

"What was that for?" she howls, rubbing her upper arm.

Now that they are no longer skimming across the surface of the water, they are suddenly rocked by the full force of the waves. The boat plunges port and starboard, listing dangerously before bobbing back up again. Eva has never been afraid of water, but her stomach roils with the surging lake beneath her. She had no idea the water had gotten so rough.

"We have to get to the closest marina!" Zach shouts back, ignoring her request. "We're not far—I need you to take the wheel."

Eva was just a little girl when Frank taught her how to skipper the *Summer Moon*, but it's been several years since she felt comfortable in the captain's chair. Still, when Zach slides an arm around her waist and trades places with her, she finds she knows exactly what to do. One knee on the seat, the other leg planted firmly beneath her, she slowly lowers the trim as far as it will go and tries to match her speed to the waves. It's getting truly dark, the sky and the water have whisked into a foam of smoky ink that makes it hard for Eva to see where she's going, but Zach lifts his arm beside her cheek and points the way.

"Head in that direction, but keep us at a forty-five degree angle to the wind," Zach tells her.

"What are you doing?" she yells when she can feel him move away. She doesn't dare to look over her shoulder for fear she'll lose sight of the spot his finger marked on the charcoal smudge of horizon.

"Getting life jackets and bailers! Securing our gear!"

The wind is howling too loudly for Eva to track what Zach is doing behind her, but she can feel him shifting, hauling seat covers off and digging through the bowels of the boat. She doesn't remember seeing any life jackets, and a needle point of fear pricks her chest. Once, she and Charlie were caught on the Apgar Trail in Glacier during a summer storm. It was scary enough to hike with the mountain on one side and a sheer cliff face on the other, but as towering thunderheads blotted out the sun and the wind stirred up dust devils on the trail before them, Eva knew a moment of pure, sinking terror. Just like that afternoon, every nerve ending in her body sparks neon bright, and then, suddenly, the world around her becomes clear and focused. She can't head straight for the coast as the seas are following—she'll bury the bow if she rides down a crest—so she turns the boat slightly and rides perpendicular to the place Zach marked for her. They'll get there, slowly.

"Did you find them?" Eva calls without turning her head. There's a sudden whoosh behind her and she panics at the sound. "Zach!"

"I'm here," he says after a moment. He pulls one of her hands off the wheel and slides it into the arm hole of a life jacket. She can smell the must even over the spray of ice-cold lake water, but she doesn't care. Zach pulls the life jacket to her shoulders and then she switches hands—one on the steering wheel, the other in the life jacket—until he can clip the buckles. The life jacket is loose, but it's on, and Eva is happy to have it.

They trade places, Zach manning the boat with his own life jacket secure, while Eva stands gripping the handrails so she can help watch the water for debris. She worries about Charlie on the *Summer Moon* by herself, but then calms when she remembers that her mother is accomplished on the water, a skilled captain who's been navigating Lake Superior for over twenty years. No doubt she woke long ago, found Eva's note, and headed back to the Landing marina. She'll be furious, and perhaps a little scared, but Eva can remedy that as soon as she and Zach dock. A quick call will alleviate Charlie's fears, and they can sort out the rest in the morning.

Eva reaches out to twist her fingers through one of the straps on Zach's life jacket, wanting to connect herself to him even though the lurch of the water makes it impossible to be close. She pushes on him as they rock and sway, and he pulls her right back, a tug-of-war that somehow feels more intimate than an embrace as they creep closer and closer to the dimly lit shore and the place where Zach has promised safety. A fresh start.

She doesn't know that if she could feel beneath his life jacket, she'd find a fixed-blade hunting knife tucked in the waistband of his jeans. It's sheathed in leather but dusted with filaments of yellow polyurethane.

She doesn't know that behind them the life raft is cartwheeling over the waves, leaking air so quickly it began deflating even before it had a chance to fill.

CHAPTER 10

Eva is damp and shivering when they pull into Little Moose. Zach was right, the town isn't really a town at all. It's a smattering of dilapidated houses clustered among tall stands of pine, fir, and spruce. A blink-and-you-miss-it sort of place that reminds Eva of similar forgotten hamlets all over the country. She's seen her fair share. She and Zach could be anywhere from the East Coast to an island in the San Juans. It's a disorienting feeling.

"What are you doing?" Eva asks when Zach switches off the headlights. He even puts the truck in neutral so they drift down the road in near silence. The dark is close and suffocating.

"A lot of these places are abandoned," he tells her, "but I know every single person who still calls Little Moose home. People will talk."

"Am I a secret?" Eva forces a laugh, but the truth is, it's been a grueling night, and she's homesick and uncertain. She's starting to understand that sometimes getting exactly what you want only makes you realize you didn't really want it in the first place.

When they finally made it to the tiny marina, Eva was disheartened to learn that Zach didn't have a permanent boat slip. They had to haul the boat out on a trailer. It was dismal and stormy, the lake choppy—even on the shore side of the breakwater—and Eva had to stay on the boat while Zach went to get his pickup. She swayed with the rhythm of the seething water, alone and a bit scared, and felt every unspoken worry churn in her stomach. What if she was making a terrible mistake? What if Charlie never forgave her? What if Zach didn't come back?

He did come back after what felt like forever, in a beat-up truck that Eva didn't recognize, and towing a rickety, aluminum trailer. It took Eva several tries to get the boat centered between the carpeted bunks, but she eventually got close enough, and Zach towed the boat—dripping and only slightly crooked—out of the lake.

The marina was abandoned and gave off an almost haunted vibe, and Eva wasn't comforted at all when Zach drove through a graveyard of old boats on blocks and unhitched his trailer at the very back of the desolate lot. They left the boat half-hidden in the trees and tucked beneath a moldy tarp.

Now, Little Moose is emanating the same spooky, deserted aura, as if the known world has dissolved around them and they are caught in some sudden apocalypse. Eva half expects zombies to shamble out of the trees. The hair on her arms stands up, even though the vents are pumping dry heat into the cab of the truck.

"Why don't you want anyone to know we're here?" Eva asks, trying to keep her voice nonchalant.

Zach glances over and seems to realize that Eva is struggling. In the dim glow of the dashboard lights she can see him smile gently and reach for her hand. He laces his fingers through hers and then lifts her knuckles to his lips. "Because I want to keep you all to myself. Because I don't want nosy neighbors bothering us. Not when we finally have a chance to be alone."

A warm tingle zings right through her, and Eva unbuckles her seat belt and slides across the truck bench to lay her head on Zach's shoulder. Everything is going to be okay. It has to be.

The house on the farthest edge of Little Moose is exactly

how Eva pictured it: neat and square on a patch of pretty land at the end of a long driveway. It's hemmed in by forest and totally secluded. Clouds are scudding quickly across the night sky, unveiling and then hiding the bright gleam of a full moon. But even by nothing but that sporadic light, she can tell the home has been well cared for, and she's grateful that it's set far apart from the shabby hovels they just passed. It could use a good power washing and a fresh coat of paint, but she can't complain. And she doesn't protest when Zach drives to a shed near the back of the property and lifts the wooden garage door to drive inside.

With the truck safely tucked away, Eva grabs her backpack and Zach his duffel, and they jog across the lawn to the front door. Standing just off the porch, Eva studies the house while Zach fumbles for the key in his pocket. It looks exactly like a child's drawing: a white house with a black door framed by two black-shuttered windows and a sagging front porch. The roof is a perfect triangle. For a moment she imagines staying right here. A pair of rocking chairs, a hanging basket or two spilling over with red geraniums. She'd find curtains for the windows, maybe in a homey buffalo plaid. But that makes her think of Sebastian, and she's speared with a longing so sharp she gasps.

"You okay?" Zach swings the door open wide, and then preempts the answer to his own question by saying: "Welcome home."

The squat bungalow is certainly not home, but Eva steps over the threshold with a sense of relief. She's cold and exhausted and, for some reason she can't quite pin down, deeply unhappy. She can feel tears forming in the back of her throat and in her hot, stinging eyes. But then Zach wraps his arms around her from behind, smoothes her hair off her shoulder, and peppers her neck with kisses.

"I can't believe we did it," he murmurs against her skin. "It's just me and you."

They've waited so long for this, dreamed about it so fervently, that Eva feels herself melting into his chest. When a tear slides down her cheek, she wipes it away before he can see it, and then spins in his embrace to wrap her arms around his neck.

"I need a shower," she whispers.

Zach laughs. "You're in luck. The electricity was shut off a long time ago, but the water heater is gas. I'll have to turn on the valve and then give the tank time to heat up, but you should be able to take a shower in an hour or so."

"An hour?" Eva groans. "I'm cold and tired and hungry and—"

"Shhhh . . ." Zach tilts away and presses a finger to her lips. "I can take care of all three of those things."

But it turns out that Eva is too exhausted and queasy to eat anything, so Zach leads her through the kitchen-and–living room combo and down a short hallway to the only bedroom in the simple house. It's just like she pictured it: a wrought-iron bed with a quilt in a faded rainbow of pastels. There are mismatched nightstands, one on either side, and a dresser painted robin's-egg blue with an oval mirror hanging above it. She catches a glimpse of herself in the warped glass—beanie still skimming her eyebrows, cheeks hollow and shadowed by the faint moonlight coming in through the window—before Zach leads her to the bed and begins to tug down the zipper on her jacket.

Eva's heart stops beating for a moment, and she can't tell if it's from panic or longing. She lets him slide off the coat, then puts up her arms obediently so he can lift her tank top over her head. Zach carefully undresses her down to the black bralette and matching panties she chose so intentionally nearly eighteen hours ago.

Eva stands before him, trembling and unsure of what comes next, but Zach just bends to kiss her on the cheek. Then he draws back the covers and makes her lie down, tucking her beneath the heavy blankets. She'd protest if she could. Pull him down next to her and kiss away the childlike feeling of being wholly in his keeping. But his hands are pinning her arms down, and she can feel exhaustion dragging her under even though closing her eyes is the last thing she wants to do.

"I have some things to take care of," Zach whispers, pressing his cheek to hers. "I'll join you in a bit. Just get some rest."

Eva tries to protest, but he covers her mouth with his own. And then he's gone. The bedroom door closes, a thud followed by a soft click, and then a second, metallic snick. Somewhere in the depths of her weary mind, Eva wonders where he's going and why. She thinks, briefly, that something about the door didn't sound quite right. But the pillow is soft, the bed layered with a well-worn sheet, several thick blankets, and a quilt on top of it all that sinks her deep into the sagging mattress. Her limbs feel weighted. For the first time in hours she is still, and though her body continues to rock with the memory of Lake Superior in spring, she is sound asleep in minutes.

．．．．

When Eva wakes in the morning, the sun is pouring in the bedroom window, filtered through the gauzy, floor-to-ceiling sheers. It's a milky, early light, the color of warm cream. But the air in the bedroom is sharp-edged and cold, and Eva draws the blankets up to her nose, fully aware of where she is and why. She dreamed all night of this boxy, practical house and the man in it, and she's breathless at the thought of Zach stirring beside her. She feels so grown-up.

Still, romance seems far-fetched when her bladder is screaming for attention and her mouth feels thick and fuzzy. Eva wants to sneak out to use the bathroom without waking Zach, but when she chances a glance at the far side of the bed, the quilt is flat and the pillow smooth and undisturbed. Not only is Zach not in bed with her like he promised, it seems he slept somewhere else entirely.

Irritated, Eva throws off the covers and hops out. The wide-planked, wooden floor is icy beneath her bare feet, but she's pleased to see that at some point in the night Zach must have brought in her backpack. It's propped beside a ladder-back chair in the corner of the room, and he has neatly unpacked the contents on the seat. There's not much to choose from, but Eva grabs a pair of jeans and a sweatshirt from the small pile, and clutches her toiletries bag to her chest. She forgot socks altogether, as she had been wearing sandals on the boat yesterday. Unfortunately, her footwear is nowhere to be seen, so she tiptoes across the room to the door. It's unlatched, open just a couple inches. Eva peers through the crack, but all she can see is the hallway and a sliver of the living room at the end. The whole place feels empty somehow. Hollow.

She pulls the door open slowly, thankful that it doesn't creak, and then annoyed with herself for being so skittish. Why is she sneaking around? Zach brought her here—*wanted* her here. Last night he had said, "Welcome *home*."

"Zach?" she calls, her voice dropping like a rock in the cavernous silence. "Zach?"

He doesn't answer, so she hurries to the bathroom—the only other door—at the far end of the hall. The porcelain toilet seat is freezing, and though she only turns on the hot tap, the water that dribbles out is lukewarm at best. There's a shard of old, blue soap veined with grit in a dish beside the sink, and because there's nothing else to use, Eva washes her hands and her face with the pungent, antiseptic bar.

Teeth clean, cheeks scrubbed raw, and more or less ready for the day, Eva carries her toiletries bag back to the bedroom. The door has drifted closed in her absence, and Eva puts her hand on the doorknob to push it open. But the knob feels strange in her palm, and it's not just because the tarnished metal is cold. It takes Eva a minute to realize that there's a silver keyhole in the middle of the knob facing the hallway. When she curls around to see the other side, it's smooth as a polished stone. The handle is installed backwards and intended for an exterior door. Instead of locking the bedroom door from the inside for privacy, the door can be locked from the outside.

It can lock someone *in*.

A simple architectural mistake, Eva tells herself, but the hallway warps for just a moment and she has to lean against the wall to clear her head. A part of her wonders if a key in the lock was the second click she heard as she was falling asleep last night. But that doesn't make any sense. Why would Zach lock her in only to leave the door open this morning? She shakes off her doubts and pushes the bedroom door wide to toss her toiletries bag on the bed.

It doesn't take Eva long to search the rest of the house. It's really only four rooms: a kitchen with a small table beneath a window, a living space arranged around a potbellied stove—a brown couch with a dusty afghan, an ancient armchair—and the bathroom and bedroom behind. A tidy, tiny square. Zach had told her it was primitive, but this is like something out of a different era. Eva can picture Ma Ingalls at the farmhouse sink, up to her elbows in tin dishes. They can't stay here, not for long, and a part of Eva is relieved.

She'd give *anything* for her phone. She's twitchy and anxious right now without the familiar heft of it in her pocket. It would be a window to the real world that feels a universe away. Although she probably wouldn't have coverage this far out in the boonies anyway. Eva peers out the broad kitchen window and is greeted by the sight of a small, emerald-green yard, speckled with dandelions and surrounded by dense, northern Minnesota forest.

Heavy footsteps on the porch followed by the front door creaking open yank Eva out of her reverie.

"Good morning, sunshine!" Zach says, stepping over the threshold with a small bowl in hand.

"Where were you?" Eva's too anxious about their bewildering situation to play nice. "I woke up and you were gone." She doesn't mention that he was never beside her to begin with. It's a confusing, complicated detail that she's not ready to unpack.

"Getting breakfast." He holds up a chipped cereal bowl filled with soft-hued eggs as evidence. They're pale pink and green, some with tiny tufts of feathers still attached to the shell.

"Where did you get those?"

"There are a couple of half-wild hens that claimed the old potting shed as their roost ages ago. I know where to look."

Eva can only stare at him. At his lopsided smile and the somewhat dazed look in his eyes. She can tell he's thrown off by her frosty reception and can't seem to figure out why she's upset. Zach looks more like a little boy than a grown man with his cheeks pinked by the chilly morning, and though she has a dozen questions she'd love to pelt him with, she moves to take the bowl from his hands instead.

"Do you like them scrambled?" she asks stiffly, uncertain how to act.

"*I* was going to cook breakfast for *you*." But Zach lets her take the bowl and begin rummaging around the kitchen.

On the counter beside the sink there's a pair of paper grocery bags that Zach starts to unpack while Eva searches for a frying pan. She didn't notice the bags last night, and doesn't think there's a grocery store nearby, so he had to have tucked them in the back of the truck before their disappearing act. Out of the corner of her eye, she sees him unload a loaf of bread, a bag of apples, and a square carton of butter. There are also potatoes, a block of cheese, a cylinder of mixed nuts, and carrots with the greens still attached. In no time, the counter is overflowing with food, much more than they could ever eat in just a day or two.

Eva places a cast-iron skillet over one of the burners and reaches for the butter to grease the bottom. "That's a lot of groceries," she says, slotting her first two fingers through one of Zach's belt loops and giving it a brief tug. She hopes she sounds sexy, teasing, because what she really wants to do is shake him. The entire front room is bathed in cheerful, morning sunshine, but Eva feels wreathed in twilight.

"I know you like to eat."

But that doesn't really answer her question.

They toast the bread on forks over the open flame of the gas burner and make sandwiches with the scrambled eggs. Eva is surprised by how hungry she is—ravenous, really—and she finishes Zach's breakfast when he assures her he doesn't want another bite. They clean up in silence, side by side in front of the large sink, while Eva tries to make sense of their strange predicament.

This isn't at all what she imagined it would be. Zach's job as graphic designer and web master for his father's company allows him ample time and space to travel, but Eva had pictured a much more modern retreat. After a long, lazy morning in bed, maybe Zach would've commandeered the armchair, balancing his computer on his lap as he got a little work done. And Eva could curl up on the couch with Netflix, flirting with him across the room until he gave up altogether and crossed the room to join her.

She feels like his sister in this flat, functional space, and Zach isn't doing much to disabuse her of that particular notion.

"I should text my mom," Eva says when the dishes are put away. "I'm sure she's worried sick."

"We don't get service out here," Zach's back is turned to her, but she can almost see the line that forms between his eyes when something rankles. She just doesn't know what she's said to put him on edge.

"Maybe we could go for a drive, then. There's got to be a coffeeshop or something nearby."

"A coffeeshop. You're kidding, right?"

Now she's annoyed. "It's not like we drove off the edge of the earth. We're still in Minnesota."

"In the middle of *nowhere*. In an old mining town that the rest of the country forgot. There's nothing out here, Eva."

"Then let's leave."

Zach spins on her so quickly, Eva backs up into the counter. But he immediately softens when he sees her cowering, and folds her against his chest so gently, she automatically squeezes him back. Even though he feels different in her arms.

"I don't want to leave," Zach says. "We just got here. I know you're a little nervous, but we're figuring it out, just me and you. I don't want you to call your mom and let her change your mind. We agreed to this, remember? Just a couple of days . . ."

Just a couple of days.

"I need to be back in time for the senior breakfast on Wednesday, for sure," Eva reminds him. "Then rehearsal's on Thursday and Friday is graduation. You're coming, right?"

"Mm-hmm," Zach murmurs, turning away.

But what can she do? Eva tamps down her fears and decides to go with the flow. She's here, with Zach, something she's wanted since almost the first moment she laid eyes on him nearly five months ago in Mugs. Peter had just given her the job, and Eva was still learning the ropes, but unlike other customers, Zach never once made her feel stupid. He sat by himself in the corner, laptop open on the table and nursing a cup of coffee that she kept refilling over the course of several hours. He ordered strawberry-rhubarb pie, and then much later a cheeseburger with French fries, which made her laugh because everything was backwards—but Zach just gave her his signature crooked grin and said that he hadn't planned on staying so long, but what choice did he have when the service was so extraordinary?

He didn't feed her one-liners or make her feel like her body was an all-day buffet, served up and available for his viewing pleasure. Instead, they talked about her travels, her writing, her close and complex relationship with her mom. Eva was really *all* they talked about, but when she sheepishly admitted who she was, Zach just gave her a blank look. He had no idea she was *that* Eva, the Evangeline Sutton of Eva Explores. He had never heard of it. Zach wasn't even on Instagram.

Maybe that's why she fell so hard. To be wanted—maybe even loved—for who she was, totally detached from social media fame, was something Eva hadn't experienced in a really long time.

Still, the house in the woods is small and boring, and their getaway feels off. Eva doesn't know what to do with herself in this oddly liminal space.

"We could hike," she suggests, but she only has her Birkenstock's along. They wouldn't make it far. "Play a game?" There's a faded checkerboard on a small table beside the chair.

"I have to chop some wood," Zach tells her, catching her chin for a quick kiss. "It's going to be cold again tonight, and we'll want to start a fire."

"I'll come with you."

"Nah. It's dull work. Stay here."

But when he disappears behind the detached garage, Eva slides on her sandals (which Zach placed neatly beside the front bench) and opens the door. She releases a shallow, pent-up breath when it swings wide, though she doesn't realize until it's open that she was afraid it might be locked.

The porch is creaky and Eva steps lightly, sticking to the edges where the boards are still nailed flat. She's not sure why she's trying to avoid detection, but her heart is fluttering in her chest and her senses ablaze. There's a cardinal trilling in the trees, and beneath his song the warble of several fat robins. The world is lush with springtime. But circled by the thick forest, the small yard is shadowed and almost gloomy.

Wishing she had socks and tennis shoes, Eva picks her way across the dewy grass to the gravel drive. It curves away from the house, cutting a path through the trees to where it connects with the highway. Even from a distance she can see it's an old road, streaked with cracks that have been filled and refilled with sticky tar, and crumbling to dust at the rim where it meets the forest floor.

Zach had said Little Moose was an old mining town. Iron ore? Copper? Eva doesn't know much about Minnesota's natural resources, beyond the origin of the infamous Black Beach where taconite—waste rock dumped for years by iron mining companies—washed ashore and turned the sand obsidian. She wishes she would have researched this mysterious town a bit more before agreeing to Zach's plan.

At the place where the hidden driveway meets the road, Eva steps onto the split concrete and spins a slow circle. In one direction, the hamlet of Little Moose clusters around the highway like grapes on the vine. The houses are compact, close together, and seem deserted. There are a few old cars parked on the grass, but it's hard to tell if they're in working order or not. In the other direction, a cement ribbon cleaves the forest in two before disappearing over a small rise.

This is the true north, rugged and unspoiled, fresh and exhilarating. It's also just a tiny bit terrifying. Because Eva is a mere speck out here, a bit of nothing on a planet so fierce and wild it's a wonder she's allowed to exist at all.

She loves it.

This is the high she and Charlie chased on the road, the feeling that they were insignificant and yet somehow belonged. There are at least a dozen places that feel like home to Eva's soul, and she decides that this is definitely one of them—even if it is kind of eerie.

Eva extends her arms high above her head, interlacing her fingers and stretching out the muscles in her arms and back. Which way should she go? Toward Little Moose or the trees? She won't be gone long, she just needs to walk the ache out of her legs, take a few minutes to clear her head. It's not like she could get lost out here—there's exactly one road and one way back.

But Eva takes just a couple steps in the direction of the houses when a sharp whistle shatters the quiet morning. Adrenaline punches her heart into her throat, but when she whips around there's nothing to see. No cars, no people. When it happens again, she spins toward the cabin she's sharing with Zach, and realizes that he's standing in the middle of the drive. His feet are planted firmly apart and he's clutching an axe in one hand. His face is a mask of fury even at this distance. Zach doesn't say anything, but he lifts his hand and motions for her to come. *Now.*

Eva's not the kind of girl who's used to getting bossed around (for all her flaws and foibles, Charlie is a rather open-minded mom), but her blood runs cold at the power radiating off the man she loves. A part of her wants to run, but what choice does she have? Where could she possibly go? Eva glances around one last time, looking maybe for a car, for someone to see her and know that she's here. She wants *someone* to know where she is. But the highway is silent. Eva steps off the road and makes her way slowly down the lane toward the place where Zach waits.

And in the house on the corner, a curtain falls closed. The man has what he wants: a photo of a girl with long, dark curls. She's lithe and lovely, a sprite maybe, or a changeling who has emerged fully formed from the trees.

COLLEGE APPLICATION
ESSAY #23

Some students have a background, identity, interest, or talent that is so meaningful they believe their application would be incomplete without it. If this sounds like you, then please share your story.

They used to call me the Little Mermaid, but honestly, I'm more of a cross between Daniel Boone, Cheryl Strayed, and Katniss Everdeen. No, I'm not a folk hero, American icon, or master archer—though I love to wax poetic about my views on trailblazing and colonialism, self-discovery, and societal inequality—I draw these comparisons for purely superficial reasons. What do Daniel, Cheryl, Katniss, and I have in common? We're survivors.

It's true. I can read a compass, tie a homemade tourniquet, and douse for water (but only with a forked hazelnut branch and only west of the Mississippi—you can take that one up with God). I've also mastered the impossible

knot (it's actually a very simple double fisherman's knot—

easy to tie, incredibly difficult to *un*tie), can identify

dozens of edible mushrooms and plants that grow across

the continental US, and make a roaring fire with nothing

but a bit of flint, a stone, and some dry moss. But while

these self-taught (and Google-enhanced) survival skills are

helpful to be sure, the kind of surviving I'm talking about

is a little less corporeal.

My mom doesn't know that I know her mother was a

raging alcoholic. She doesn't think that I wonder about my

father and what my life would be like if he was a part of it.

And she hasn't yet realized that the questions I have about

my life and who I am and where I fit cannot be answered

by another punishing hike that leaves us lathered in sweat

and triumphant. Sometimes we treat the world as a Band-

Aid and our experiences in it the salve that is meant to heal

our hurts. And it helps, it really does. There's a reason why

standing beneath the moon on a cold winter's night can

change everything. But as lovely and incomprehensible as our wild world is, it can't *fix* everything. Believe me, I've tried.

I'm a survivor because I take pieces of myself and share them with an open heart and open hands, even though there are times I want to hide. I'm a survivor because I've spent much of my life lonely, but I keep hoping for connection, for someone to see me as I truly am and not as just the person they believe me to be. I'm a survivor because I know the steps to take to ensure my own safety and well-being, and I'm capable and confident to carry them out—even when it might hurt the person I love the most. Even when those steps might lead me to a place I've never been.

My talents are varied, but they have always centered around a theme that, quite frankly, needs to be enhanced. Transformed. I know I can survive; it's time for me to *thrive*. I can't claim to know what that looks like yet, but you'd better believe I have the tenacity and capacity to find out. You're going to want a front row seat for this.

CHAPTER 11

Zach tries to contain his fury when Eva returns from her brief excursion, but she can feel anger coming off him in waves. It's disconcerting, and a little scary, and she marches right past him and toward the house before he can confront her. She feels like a child waiting for a reprimand, and that's not how a girlfriend—a peer—should feel. Eva hates it, and for a few panicked, confusing minutes she hates him, too.

"Why?" Zach demands. "Why did you leave? I told you to stay in the cabin."

Eva bites her tongue, but she can feel Zach hot on her heels. "Did anyone see you?"

"I was gone for five minutes," Eva says tightly, hurrying up the steps to the leaning porch. "I wanted some fresh air."

"Did you talk to anyone?"

"Stop it!" Eva whirls on him, losing control. She hates for Zach to see her like this—shrill and unhinged, not at all the chill girl she wants to be—but she can't help it. "Stop acting like you can tell me what to do. This was supposed to be fun—a chance for us to get away and spend some time together. But I feel like a prisoner here!"

Her tirade extinguishes the fire in Zach's eyes. He sighs heavily and rubs one hand over his face. The other is still clutching a rusty axe, and he stares at it for a moment as if he's forgotten he was holding it. Very deliberately, he sets it against a porch column. "You're not a prisoner, Eva. But I need you to listen to me: no one can know that we're here."

"Why?"

He reaches for her, then seems to change his mind. "You have to trust me on this one, okay?"

"I don't think so. My phone is gone, I'm a million miles away from . . . *everything*, and you're not talking to me! What is going on?"

Zach seems torn between rage and regret. He's trembling, and less than twenty-four hours ago Eva would have pressed herself against him and kissed his angst away. Now, she crosses her arms over her chest to stop her own hands from shaking. They're caught in a standoff on the narrow front porch, leaning away from each other as if this is the end of whatever it is they've started.

Finally, Zach says, "Go take a shower. Turn the water on and let it warm up for at least five minutes. I'll finish up outside, and when we're both done, we'll talk."

It's not quite what she hoped to hear, but it's better than nothing, so without another word, Eva spins on her heel and lets herself into the small house. She slams the door behind her just so Zach will know beyond a shadow of a doubt that she's seriously pissed off.

Eva wants to hold on to her indignation, but Zach is right—although it takes a while, the water eventually warms up. It's amazing what a hot shower can do, and she takes her time, letting the scalding spray wash away the last twenty-four hours along with the grit on her body. Unfortunately, no amount of scrubbing can erase the decisions she's made or the consequences she can feel crouching just out of sight. There will be a reckoning, Eva is sure of that. She feels small and so very stupid.

Pulling on leggings and an oversized flannel, Eva wraps her hair turban-style in a threadbare towel and shuffles into the living room. Zach is stacking wood next to the potbellied stove.

"Feel better?" he asks, standing up when she lingers just behind the couch. He brushes his palms self-consciously on his jeans and has a hard time meeting her gaze.

"I need socks." Eva won't give him the satisfaction of an affirmation, but she wiggles her bare toes at him, offering one small way to make amends.

"I've got you." Zach seems relieved to have something tangible to do, and he steps carefully past her to disappear in the bedroom. A moment later he emerges, a pair of tube socks in hand.

They're clean and white, and come halfway up her calves, but Eva doesn't care. She scrunches them down around her ankles and then goes to sit cross-legged on the couch.

Zach stands in the middle of the room for a few minutes, apparently deciding what to do, where to go. In the end, he sinks to the edge of the couch next to Eva, his knee just touching hers. She doesn't pull away, but she doesn't say anything either. She's not going to make it easy for him.

"Look," he says after a few tense seconds, "no one can know that we're here. My dad doesn't know we're here, and if he realizes . . ."

Eva has to restrain herself from rolling her eyes. "Then let's leave. You're twenty-four, Zach. Let's rent a room somewhere. Or better yet, let's go home. This was all a huge mistake."

"We're not leaving."

"Excuse me?" Eva is halfway to her feet before Zach's arm shoots out. He snags her by the wrist and yanks her back down. Her first (and only) boyfriend has never laid a hand on her in anger before, but the sharp tug leaves Eva's shoulder howling.

She blinks back tears, but they have nothing to do with the ache in her joint—she can't believe that he would hurt her, even unintentionally. Eva rubs her shoulder with one hand and backs into the farthest corner of the couch. Suddenly, she doesn't trust him.

"I'm sorry, Eva. I just need you to *listen* to me." Zach's eyes are wide and hurt as he inches closer to her, hands up to assure her he's safe. "Just listen. Okay?"

Eva's mind is whirling, but he's between her and the door, and even if she got away from him, where would she go? She has no idea where she is, or how to find the nearest town. Little Moose certainly doesn't count. And in a pair of sandals, she wouldn't make it very far. Eva has no choice but to collar her fear and rein it in, or this thing could go sideways fast. "Fine," she says, and is proud of herself for keeping her voice calm.

"I love you," Zach whispers, sliding even closer. He lifts his hands to her face, slowly, as if he's afraid she may bat them away. But Eva doesn't move, and he cups her cheeks in his palms, then kisses her mouth so tenderly, so sweetly, that for just a second she has to remind herself that he's acting crazy.

"You know that I love you"—Zach pulls back, searching her eyes—"right?"

Eva doesn't dare to look away. She can't even bring herself to breathe. Instead, she lets herself get lost in those eyes that she was sure she would love forever, and says, "I do." She can't tell if she's trying to convince him or herself, but it doesn't really matter.

Zach rubs his thumbs across her cheekbones and squeezes his eyes shut, exhaling a shuddering breath. "Okay. Good. Then we can make it through anything."

A dozen questions queue up on Eva's tongue, but she swallows them all. She can tell that there is only one way through this, and it's Zach's way. For now. So she keeps her lips pressed tight and waits for him to start talking.

"I was born in this house," Zach begins after a heartbeat or two. "Well, I was born in a hospital, but we lived here for the first two years of my life." He gives her a sheepish grin that she simply can't return. If he's trying to lighten the mood, it's not working.

"My dad worked in the mine before it was shut down." Zach picks up the story when Eva doesn't crack a smile. "Everyone in Little Moose did. Mining is boom or bust, you know?"

Eva doesn't know, but this is the first information Zach has offered up about his family. He's been frustratingly tight-lipped about his background, and although it seems like a strange time to break his silence, better late than never. She pulls her knees up to her chest and wraps her arms around them. "Go on," she says.

"I'll spare you the details, but mining in Minnesota has a tough history." He holds up one finger, counting. "There are always groups who are concerned about the environmental impact."

Like me, Eva wants to say, but she bites her lip instead.

Two fingers. "Then, the steel recession led to layoffs, idling . . . automation. Why pay a man when a machine can do it for free?" Zach's mouth tips into a half smile as he holds up three fingers. "Low foreign steel prices." He makes a fist, dropping his hand into his lap. "My dad's family has been mining the Mesabi Range since the late 1800s, but our mine closed permanently when I was two."

"So you left."

"Sort of. My dad is . . . a man of many talents. An entrepreneur of sorts. He bought up most of Little Moose because the houses suddenly weren't worth anything and he wanted the community to have a chance. Most people took the money and moved away."

"A modern-day Robin Hood," Eva murmurs. "So your family is the reason Little Moose is a ghost town."

"No. The government is. Besides, it's not a ghost town. A few remain." Zach lifts one shoulder. "Not many."

Eva chews on her lip for a moment. She wasn't sure what she was expecting, but it wasn't this history lesson. "I don't understand why it matters if your dad knows we're here or not."

"It's complicated. *He's* complicated."

"You sound like you're trying to convince yourself."

Zach runs a hand through his hair, mussing the blond waves. Then, in one quick exhale he says: "My dad is dangerous."

At this, Eva laughs. "You can't be serious."

"Come here." Zach puts out his arms, and after a moment of hesitation, Eva gives in. She folds herself against his chest where she can listen to the familiar rhythm of his heartbeat. "There are some things you need to know about my family. But for now I just need you to stay quiet and hidden and *here*."

Eva thinks about the small apartment Zach rents in Duluth, and how he never, not once, took her there. "I don't want my landlord to see us," he claimed. But that was a feeble argument because who would even know that Eva was only seventeen? It's not like she bore an "underage" tattoo. And even if they did know, who would *care*? She wasn't some twelve-year-old Lolita—she was days away from her high school graduation and mere weeks from her eighteenth birthday.

She thinks about how after their first meeting Zach never came back to eat at Mugs. The day after Eva served him, she finished her shift and found him leaning against a fence across the street from where she'd parked the truck. He was waiting for her. And she never stopped to wonder how he knew that she would be at work that night. Or when she would get off. Or what vehicle she drove. She was too breathless at how the streetlamp grazed his cheekbones, and the way he looked at her when she raised her hand to wave.

Eva thinks about their dates, always outside of Landing or in some secluded spot. Parking on snowy roads when it was cold or hiking obscure trails when the weather warmed up a bit. They avoided people and places where they would be recognized and remembered. Zach said it was because he didn't want them to be bothered by her fans, or by those who would snap pictures of them like homegrown paparazzi. Eva had admitted once that it happened, that people sometimes took furtive photos and uploaded them to fan sites. He looked downright horrified at the thought.

She pulls back now and stares at Zach—at the five-o'clock shadow on his strong jaw, the lips she loves to trace with her fingers, the scar that bisects his left eyebrow and makes him look rugged somehow—and remembers the day that he took her phone and disabled all tracking apps and devices. It seemed romantic at the time, a gallant gesture that protected their privacy and made it easier for Eva to claim that she was hanging out with a school friend or staying late at work. She didn't even question him. And because Charlie trusted her daughter implicitly, she never checked the apps. She never found out.

"I think I want to go home," Eva says quietly.

"Eva—"

"This isn't what I thought it would be."

"Evangeline, listen to me. I love you, and I want us to be together . . ."

But she's no longer listening. The more Zach proclaims his devotion, the more it grates. Her mind is catapulting from one missed red flag to another. Eva wanted this—an intimate weekend getaway without her mother's interference—and she let the lure and lust of first love blind her. She can see that now.

"We need to go back. I want to hear all about your family and your father, Zach, I really do. But not here. Not like this." Eva pushes up from the couch and squeezes his fingers when he catches her hand. She gives him a small smile. "Take me home."

"I can't." Zach swallows hard.

"What do you mean, you can't?"

"Three more days," he says, standing so that she has to look up at him. "We have to hide out here for three days, and then we can go anywhere we want and do anything we want."

She laughs, but it's uneasy. "What are you talking about? I graduate on Friday. I have a million things to do. You know that."

"Don't do this," Zach whispers, squeezing his eyes shut and tugging her against him.

"Do what?" Eva feels a tear spill down her cheek and wipes it against Zach's T-shirt. "I'm not doing anything. I just want to go home. Take me home. *Please*."

"I can't. Not right now. I have to make sure that . . ." He swallows hard. "I need to know that you're safe."

"What do you mean, *safe*?" Eva tries to wiggle out of his embrace, but his arms stiffen.

"Just—"

"Let go!" she gasps, when he holds her tighter.

"Stop, Eva." Zach's voice is broken, his words choked and reluctant. "We're stuck here for a while. If you'd just trust me . . ."

But she's past the point of listening. She feels trapped, frantic, and she bucks in Zach's arms, cracking his chin with the back of her head. He lets out a rough gasp of surprise.

It happens before Eva realizes what's going on. He sweeps her into his arms and begins to carry her toward the back of the house. "I can't reason with you right now, but when you calm down we'll talk, okay?"

"No!" she screams, wasting her voice, though she knows no one can hear her. No one is going to come and rescue her. "No! Don't do this, please! Zach, you can't do this!"

"Please, Eva. I'm *rescuing* you."

Zach almost trips when they make it to the hallway, and she uses every ounce of her energy to writhe and struggle in his arms. But it's no use. He's several inches taller, at least fifty pounds heavier. Every muscle on his body is neat and defined, carefully maintained with free weights and long runs that he takes every morning before dawn. Eva always thought that if she found herself in a precarious situation, she'd be able to battle her way through. She even felt sorry for the women who seemed to just give up instead of fighting back. She would never roll over and play dead. But after only a couple of minutes, Eva is spent and sweaty, her heart beating so hard and high in her chest that her vision begins to blur at the edges.

When they make it to the bedroom door, Zach nudges it open. Stepping inside, he puts his mouth against her temple. "This will all be over soon," he says.

Then he lowers her onto the bed and hurries out the door. Before she can get her feet beneath her, he's shut it. And as she lunges for the handle and her fingers brush the cold knob, she hears the same click that she heard last night. A faint, metallic pop that means she's locked inside.

From the other side Zach says, "I love you, Eva. Don't forget that."

CHAPTER 12

SUNDAY

Eva pounds on the bedroom door until her hands are red and throbbing, but Zach does not come back. She screams his name until her throat is scraped raw. Nothing. Blinded by fury and fear, she abuses him with every obscenity she can think of, every cruel and ugly thing that her imagination can conjure. But he ignores her.

So, she switches to pleading.

"Remember when we hiked to the frozen waterfall?" she says, her damp cheek flush against the cold door, her voice breaking. "It was the first time you told me you loved me. And I couldn't say it back. I could hardly even look at you. But you held me close and said that you'd wait for me. You'd wait until I could say it. You promised not to push . . ."

There's a sound in the kitchen, a soft thump followed by a shuffle. Eva presses her fingers against the wood and squeezes her eyes shut. Hoping. Praying.

"You kept your promise," she begins again. "And just a couple of days later, I said it back. Do you remember where we were? On the street in the dark after my shift at Mugs. I smelled like fryer grease and stale coffee, but you kissed me anyway. I said 'I love you' and I meant it. I meant it so much."

The slide of something against the hardwood floor. Movement that Eva can feel through Zach's thick socks, reverberating in the soles of her feet.

"I still do," she says, raising her voice. Can he hear her in the kitchen? "I still love you. I love you, Zach!"

The slam of the front door hits Eva like a bullet to the chest. For a moment, she can't catch her breath, and the room tilts wildly around her. When she finally does manage to gasp, it turns into a sob, a howl that surely Zach can hear even outside. Where is he going? How can he just leave her here? Sliding down the door, Eva lands in a broken heap on the floor and cries until she has no tears left. Until the sleeves of her flannel are soaked through, and her eyes are swollen and sore.

Zach was her first real friend, her first love. The person who made her believe that she didn't have to be Evangeline the Blubber Queen anymore, but she also didn't have to be the Little Mermaid. She could just be *Eva*, a girl who loved the outdoors, writing, and every book fit to print. She didn't have to wear makeup or make sure she sported the right label so that she was forever honoring her influencer contracts. Maybe best of all, she could be loved for all the things she truly was—and *wasn't*.

Was it all a lie? Did Zach feel anything for her, ever? And if it had all been some elaborate ruse, *why*?

When she's cried herself dry and is hollow and exhausted, Eva pushes herself up from the floor and shuffles over to her backpack. Her computer is tucked inside, and even if there's no Wi-Fi, maybe she can write a note or somehow document what's going on. If something happens and . . . but she can't think like that. She can't let her mind go to a world where someone would someday have to search for forensic evidence on her hard drive.

But before she even grabs the backpack, Eva can see that her computer is gone. She should have noticed the way her bag slouched against the chair this morning, limp and empty. Eva snags it by a strap and flings it across the room with a scream.

Why would he take it? What on earth would Zach want with her computer? Accepting that he took it makes Eva wonder about her phone. She *knows* that she put it in her backpack when she was still on the *Summer Moon*. Did he take her phone, too?

Eva spirals through their escape, and in light of her abduction (imprisonment?) everything changes. The pills Zach told her to give her mom. *"Just to help her fall asleep and stay asleep."* His insistence on checking the *Summer Moon* after she disembarked. *What was he doing?* Their long boat ride at dusk on a stormy, menacing night . . . Everything changes when she looks at it through the lens of what she now knows: Zachary Brennan is not the man she thought he was.

"I'm here," Eva whispers into the quiet of the room. It's a prayer perhaps, or a wish. "I'm still here."

Without her computer, Eva feels desperate to find *something* to help. The bed is unmade, and she rummages through it frantically, yanking off the blankets and sheets to check under the mattress and between the headboard and the wall. It's clean, and beneath the bed there is nothing but dust bunnies. Next, she tears through every drawer in the bureau. They're all empty, except for the bottom one, which contains an old, musty afghan and a handful of mothballs. The bedside stands are equally vacant. For a moment, the desk lamp looks promising, but when Eva picks it up, she realizes it's light as a feather and made of plastic. It would be an utterly useless weapon. *Weapon?* She can hardly believe that she's thinking like this.

Escape would be so much better. Rushing to the window, Eva pulls back the curtains only to find that the sash has been nailed to the frame. Someone has painted over the nail heads so that they look like part of the casing, but she can feel them when she runs her fingertips over the wood.

It's chilling. The understanding that someone installed an exterior door in this tiny, interior bedroom. That they methodically, intentionally nailed the only window shut and then painted over the evidence.

Eva's not standing in a bedroom. She's standing in a cell.

Panic claws at her, and for a few blinding moments she is sure she will die of pure terror. Her stomach revolts and she dry heaves, choking on bile. There's nothing she can do, nothing she can use to improve her situation by even a degree, and she's never felt more helpless or hopeless in her whole life. She's entirely at Zach's mercy.

It feels like defeat to crawl onto the bed, but once Eva's stomach has stopped spasming, it's all that she can manage. She wraps herself in the tangle of blankets, shivering so hard that even the heavy layers don't diminish her chattering teeth. Almost the moment her head hits the pillow, her body begins to shut down. Eva has tried fight, and now all systems are taking flight. She doesn't want to sleep—it doesn't feel safe or wise—but it's as if a boulder is pressing her deeper and deeper into the bed. Just opening her eyes feels like a distant impossibility.

In seconds, Eva is unconscious.

· · · ·

The light in the room has changed when Eva opens her eyes. It's gray and muted, no doubt from the sun sinking beneath the line of tall trees that surround the old house. She knows exactly where she is, and the dread and despair that flood her veins is no surprise. Eva doesn't feel teary anymore, but she also doesn't have a renewed sense of hope. Her dreams were of long halls and closed doors, of captivity.

For a few moments she lays perfectly still, wishing herself somewhere—anywhere—else. But in the silence, she realizes that she didn't simply wake up on her own; something broke through the tight web of her nightmares. It's noise and movement, something frenzied happening, and then all at once there's a key in the door.

Zach flings it open so hard the door slams against the wall behind it. "Eva!" he half shouts. "Come—you have to come right now."

He crosses the room in two long strides and tears the blankets off her. Eva is terrified to let him touch her, but it all happens so fast she can't even open her mouth to protest. Before she can blink, Zach has pulled her from the bed and deposited her on her feet. One hand around her waist and the other tightly gripping her upper arm, he ushers her toward the door.

This is what Eva wanted—*freedom*—but not this way. She tries to shake him off, but something fundamental has changed in Zach. Without even thinking, he presses her against the bedroom wall and holds her there, his face only inches from hers. His eyes are wild. Afraid. "*Stop it*. I need you to listen to me. There's no time to explain."

Eva's woozy from the sudden change in circumstance, but Zach doesn't give her the chance to talk back anyway.

"He's coming. My dad is coming. Someone must have seen you when you went out this morning. Or the cameras are still active . . . I don't know. But you have to get out of here. *Now*."

"What?" Eva tries to protest as he wrenches her away from the wall and pushes her into the hallway. His hands are around her waist, guiding, pushing her toward the cabin door.

"There isn't time, Eva. Just listen to me: the keys are in the ignition of the truck. Head back the way we came. Through Little Moose, and then turn south at the first stop sign—it's ten miles or so down the road. That'll take you to highway one."

"First you lock me up and now you're sending me away?"

Eva finally finds her voice *and* her strength. Twisting out of Zach's grip, she hits him in the chest, hard, with both palms. Then all at once her hands are fists and she's pounding him, over and over again, until he catches her wrists and wrestles her arms behind her back.

"Stop. *Please*. Just listen to me."

They're both spent and heaving, and when Zach lays his forehead against hers, Eva doesn't pull away. She can't. He's trembling beneath her, his skin clammy and warm. He's terrified, she can smell it on him, something harsh and acrid like a freshly snuffed match.

"I thought you loved me," she manages after a few shaky breaths.

"I do."

"I don't believe you."

"We don't have time for this." He pulls away from her and very carefully releases his hold on her wrists. He looks like he wants to gather her to him, but instead he cups her chin in one hand and levels her with a look of pure desperation. "You have to listen to me, Evangeline. You have to *run*."

Zach's voice is a blade, clean and sharp, and though so many things have passed between them, Eva knows in her bones that his words are true. If she was frightened before, it's nothing compared to what unfurls inside her now.

"You can do this." Zach kisses her once, on the cheek, then spins her around and together they run for the door. "I'll hold them off."

"Them?"

Zach ignores her. "Drive fast and head straight for the Ely Police Department. Turn east, then south. Get on 169—it'll take you there in forty minutes or so."

"What am I supposed to tell them?" Eva trips over the

threshold and nearly plunges headfirst onto the porch, but Zach catches her and keeps her upright.

"It doesn't matter. Just get somewhere safe."

"What about you?"

Zach scowls. "Don't worry about me. Just get out of here."

"But—"

"Eva, *go*!"

She stumbles on the cold grass, her stockinged feet slipping on the lawn and becoming instantly wet. Strips of fog wreath the trees, and a light breeze lifts Eva's curls off her neck, sending a full-body shiver down her spine. Her hair is still damp, she never even had a chance to brush it, and she knows she must be a sight: tangled mane, bloodshot eyes, no shoes. No coat, either, and nothing at all to identify herself and lend credence to the preposterous story she's about to tell. She'll pull into Ely—a town she's only crossed through once or twice—looking homeless and unstable. Eva doesn't even know what to say. How can she explain the last twenty-four hours of her life?

But as she nears the shed, Eva realizes she might never get the chance to tell her story. She can hear the roar of an engine in the distance. Someone is revving the motor, driving fast on that long lick of road that splits the forest in two. The sound makes her stumble, and at the very moment that Zach shouts her name, the air fills with the squeal of brakes and the crunch of gravel. Frozen to the spot, Eva watches the flash of black between the underbrush, until adrenaline bucks hard in her chest and she comes to her senses. She sprints the last few yards to the cover of the shed, her heart galloping.

The garage door has already been lifted and Eva slips inside, pressing herself between the truck and the wall and dropping into a crouch. Past the bumper of the truck she watches as a black SUV tears down the drive, slamming on the brakes and pulling to a stop only feet away from where Zach stands. A cloud of dust billows over him, and before it has a chance to dissipate, the doors of the SUV are wrenched open and three men jump to the ground.

Two of the men are in combat fatigues, tactical cargo pants and camouflage shirts with pockets beneath a khaki vest that can only be body armor. Their hair is close-cropped, and the driver is wearing reflective sunglasses, even though clouds have completely obscured the setting sun. There's no military base around here—at least, not to Eva's knowledge—but even if there was, these men don't give off an official vibe. There is nothing safe about them. But they pale in comparison to the man that jumped from the passenger seat.

He's dressed in dark pants and a white button-down shirt with the sleeves rolled to his elbows. His shoulders are broad, but his hair is streaked white and his belly soft. There's nothing immediately intimidating about him, but the casual way he walks toward Zach emanates such power, such authority, Eva flattens herself against the truck. The man—the way he holds himself and moves through the world and so clearly calls all the shots—is menacing.

Words are exchanged, but Eva is too far away to hear. When the white-haired newcomer turns away from Zach, she feels a moment of relief, but then he brings his arm around with the full force of his body and backhands Zach across the face. He crumples to the grass and doesn't move.

Eva's hand is slick with tears, her finger throbbing between her teeth. She doesn't even realize she's biting it until the pain registers, and then she only clamps down harder because she's afraid if she starts screaming she won't stop. Even though she was furious with Zach only minutes before, she can't stand to see him lying on his side, one arm thrown over his head and the other curled against his stomach.

Is this Zach's *father?* The man who so indifferently turns from the heap of humanity at his feet and shakes out his fist? The thought makes Eva's head spin.

But she doesn't have time for sympathy. The white-haired superior barks an order, and at once the two men in fatigues leap into action. One jogs toward the house while the other heads directly for the shed. For her.

Eva has mere seconds, and she casts around looking for an escape. There's a door in the back wall of the shed beside a leaning workbench, but piles of junk are stacked in front of it. She could never move it all in time, and even if she did it would make an unholy ruckus. Eva could jump in the truck and try to drive away, but she instinctively knows that in order to get out of the shed, she'd have to run over the man striding closer and closer. In this moment, she wants to be the sort of person who could do that, but she isn't. Eva can hardly bring herself to squash a spider when one scuttles across her bedroom floor; she knows she won't be able to floor the gas when she's staring down a living, breathing man in the rearview. And what if they chase her? What if that SUV forces her off the road? Her only other option is to do what Zach told her to do: run.

Eva's barefoot and breathless, but she's also fast, and she prays for strength as she launches herself off the dirt floor of the shed and sprints for the open garage door. She has surprise on her side, and by the time the man in camo realizes what's happening, she's several paces ahead of him and racing for the trees. He shouts and starts after her, but Eva's already in the shadow of the forest.

When she breaks the cover of the canopy, it's instantly cooler and darker, and Eva wishes she had her well-worn hiking shoes, a windbreaker, a compass. Although she barely feels the rocks and sticks that tear at Zach's socks, she knows that the cloth will be shredded and useless in no time. But she'll take her chances.

Looking over her shoulder is a risk, but Eva has to know where her follower is. She's surprised to see that the trees slowed him down more than she would have anticipated; she's pulled ahead of him as he fumbles through the thick ferns and shrubs. Eva is smaller, lighter, and she would bet far more experienced off-trail than her pursuer, and she uses it to her advantage. Because she is wearing nothing but leggings and a flannel, and the man is clothed in a full, bulky uniform, she sets her path toward the thickest underbrush. He'll get snagged on every branch while she breezes through. What she really needs is a hill, something sloped that she can climb like the rim of a bowl. Most people don't know to spiral upward, to point their downhill foot outward to avoid rolling an ankle. Eva has seen many a novice hiker slide on scree and twist vulnerable joints because of improper footing. She can almost picture her stalker tumbling down a ravine while she scurries away.

It's this wisp of a daydream that takes Eva down. She's scanning her surroundings, looking for a rise or fall in the landscape instead of watching where she's going. But the boulder is half hidden by brush anyway, and in the growing darkness Eva might never have seen it at all. When her shin cracks the sharp edge as she runs, the pain is dazzling. It explodes through her leg and drops her as surely as a bullet would. She knows she should be afraid, but the agony radiating through her bones overrides even her longing for escape. Eva gasps in the growing twilight as hot blood soaks through her leggings and turns the forest floor beneath her black.

"Got you."

The man crouching over her brings reality into stark focus.

Eva tries to scream, but the air is pinched out of her chest by shooting pain and unbridled fear.

"You didn't have to run," he says, tsking at her. "Doesn't matter how fast you think you are, how tricky. I would've caught you in the end. But it looks like you learned your lesson."

Eva whimpers when he lifts her leg and squints at the wound through her torn leggings.

"You'll need some stitches, for sure. Is it broken?"

When she doesn't respond, he pinches the soft flesh of her calf to get her attention. "Hey, can you move your foot?"

Wheezing, Eva lifts herself to her elbows and carefully flexes her foot back and forth and side to side. She doesn't want to give this stranger the satisfaction of obeying, but she also doesn't dare to defy him—not when she's prone on the ground, injured. Not when she can see the dull glint of a gun tucked into the belt at his waist, a hunting knife strapped to the other side. He's about her mom's age, square-jawed and freshly shaved. Up close, he's generic-looking and doesn't seem so frightening. In fact, he's holding her leg gently, studying her with what seems like concern.

"Let's get you out of here," he says with a sigh. "Though you certainly didn't make it easy for me." Then he slides his arms beneath her and picks her up as if she is a small child, like she weighs nothing at all.

The man marches back to the clearing, Eva's trembling body in his arms and her blood staining the sleeve of his dusty uniform.

COLLEGE APPLICATION ESSAY #28

Henry Drummond is quoted as saying: "The people who influence you are the people who believe in you." Share about someone who has influenced your life. How have they helped to shape the person you are becoming?

It should come as no surprise that the person who has shaped me the most is my mother, Charlotte Greer Sutton. I could write much more than a mere five hundred words on all the various ways she has molded me into the woman I am. But I fear the vast majority of these essays will focus on the inspiration of the applicants' beloved parental units, so I'd like to turn my gaze in another direction.

Because I was bullied as a preteen and spent the bulk of my formative years on the road in a vintage Airstream trailer with my single mother, I wasn't afforded many opportunities to make friends. Sure, I can have a stimulating conversation with a total stranger, and often enjoy thought-provoking exchanges with "friends" that I meet online, but an in-real-life bosom buddy? Not so much. Six months ago I would have told you that I don't even know how to make an honest-to-goodness friend. I wouldn't have dared to try.

But then Zach came into my life. Our relationship evolved in the most natural, unassuming way. I didn't even realize he was becoming my best friend until we were wholly invested in each other's lives and completely inextricable. I'll be the first to admit that I'm no relationship expert, but it seems to me that the best friendships are often the ones that take you by surprise—and sometimes between two people who seem ill-fitted at best. I suppose they do say opposites attract.

I knew Zach was someone special when, a few weeks after we met, he took a damp paper towel (we were having an impromptu picnic in the front seat of his car) and began to gently, almost tenderly, wipe it across my cheeks, my forehead, my closed eyes. "What are you doing?" I asked him, too stunned to move. And he said, "I want to see *you*."

My skin is freckled. I've spent years in the sun and wind, hiking trails and swimming and even dirt-biking when given the chance, and the elements have left their mark on every inch of me. I'm tough and muscled instead of thin and willowy. And goodness knows I'll never be a porcelain-skinned supermodel. But when Zach looked at me, makeup-free and stripped down to my essence, I realized that I would never *want* to be.

When someone sees the real you—and not just accepts you, but *loves* you for who you really, soul-deep, are— it changes everything. Suddenly you don't have to act anymore, to be something and someone that you're not. It frees you up to live authentically and wholeheartedly. And though I'm still learning to live in this new (old!) skin, I'll be forever grateful for the man whose influence is allowing me to be, well, *me*.

CHAPTER 13

They speed down the highway, through a warren of gravel roads and two-track lanes that cut precariously close to the trees. Eva is stretched across the middle seat of the dark SUV, her leg wrapped in an old towel that the soldier commandeered from the house back in Little Moose. Of course, she doesn't know if he's actually a soldier, but because she also doesn't know his name, she's come to think of him as such. He's wearing the uniform after all.

When the soldier looks over the passenger seat from time to time to check in on her, she makes sure to avoid his gaze. She's not sure what he's looking for. Is he afraid she'll whip a weapon out of her ruined leggings? He's already patted her down and confirmed that she's not hiding so much as a tissue. Or maybe he's worried about her jumping from the moving vehicle. Unfortunately, not only are the child locks engaged in the back doors (Eva quietly tested them), she's completely in-capacitated. Her shin is so swollen it bulges from between the folds of torn fabric when she dares to remove the blood-soaked towel to peek. She doubts she could put any pressure on her left leg at all right now, and the thought fills her with dread.

At least she's alone with the two soldiers. The white-haired man and Zach are following the SUV at a short distance. The older man is behind the wheel of Zach's truck, and her (former?)

196

boyfriend slumps in the passenger seat. She can't see them well, but the light of the dash creates a halo out of the old man's snowy hair behind the steering wheel.

Eva has dozens of questions, but pain and fear prevent her from asking a single one. Instead, she tries to focus on mapping their route, clocking turns and looking for landmarks so that somehow she can find her way back to civilization when this is all over. They're driving farther and farther into the wild, until Eva is sure that they have left the known world behind entirely. She worries that even if she manages to escape, she'll never make it home.

When they finally stop in front of an old field gate, Eva feels dread splash through her like ice water. The soldier who carried her out of the woods hops out to swing the gate wide so they can drive through, but instead of getting back into the vehicle, he walks slowly in front as they crawl down a small ravine, over a shallow creek, and around a sharp bend. Almost immediately, Eva can see that there's a second fence and another gate. This one is chain link, towers over the soldier's head, and is topped with razor wire. A guard in matching camo fatigues stands holding an AR-15, which he swings behind him so he can shake the soldier's hand.

"Welcome home," the driver tells her, twisting around so he can grin at Eva. He hasn't said a word to her, hasn't even acknowledged her presence, and his declaration now sounds ominous. This is *not* her home. Eva is not staying here.

In seconds, the guard has entered a code into the keypad near the gate, and they're driving through the perimeter. The guard waves almost cheerfully and tries to catch a peek of the inside of the SUV, but the windows are tinted and the evening smudged charcoal around the edges. Eva is relieved to be hidden.

They drive through more forest, but it thins as the vehicles climb a small rise. And there, at the top, Eva can finally see their destination spread out before them. The bones of an old homestead stretch across the gravel lane. To the right there's a sprawling white farmhouse with a wraparound porch and golden light glowing in every curtained window. It's warm and welcoming, with black rocking chairs, an oversized porch swing, and a chocolate lab standing sentinel in front of the apple-green door. To the left, there's a red barn with peeling paint and a smaller, sun-bleached shed. There are freshly tilled gardens cut in neat squares, and wild lupine rimming the outbuildings. The whole scene is completely incongruous with the guns and camo, the razor wire and security. Eva can't make the pieces fit.

But behind the foremost, idyllic scene, a new tableau unfolds. In the glow of several yard lights, Eva can see a trio of what look like new Morton buildings. They're set like wooden blocks in a row, with small windows, doors on either end, and worn paths leading deeper into the property. There are no utility doors and no sign of machinery at all, but figures move back and forth across the darkness, walking and talking and carrying out tasks that she can't begin to guess at. Beyond the buildings, everything becomes a bit of a blur, but if Eva squints, she can make out rows of trucks, wooden structures, and acres of dark forest.

"What is this place?" Eva doesn't realize she's spoken out loud until the driver of the SUV laughs.

"We'd tell you, but then we'd have to kill you."

"Don't tease her," the soldier who chased her scolds. "I'm already afraid she's going to die of a heart attack before Tamar can take a look at her leg." Turning to Eva he says, "Welcome to our little slice of the American dream: the Gates of Zion. But that's kind of a mouthful—we just call it 'The Gates.'"

Eva isn't sure what she suspected, but it certainly isn't this. This is a bustling community in the middle of nowhere, well cared for and almost normal-looking. If she is going to be trafficked or held for ransom or recruited for some crazy cult, she would have predicted a much darker, more menacing setting. Not a farmhouse with rockers and pretty, patterned curtains in the windows.

"This is as far as you come," her soldier says when they pull around the farmhouse and come to a stop beside a small building. It's hidden behind the big house, but there's a brick path that leads from the pocket-sized structure to the back door. It looks like an oversized garden shed that has been repurposed, and the tiny windows beside a narrow door are glowing. "They're expecting you."

Eva has no idea who *they* are, but her heart seizes. "Please," she says, finally finding her voice. "I just want to go home. Please let me call my mom."

"That's not up to me." The man hops out of the passenger side and opens the door so he can reach Eva. Without hesitation, he grabs her off the bench seat and hoists her into his arms. The movement is so sudden and jarring, a wave of nausea rushes over her. Eva pinches handfuls of his uniform in her sweaty palms and tries not to throw up as he strides across the lawn. She wants to resist, to kick and fight back, but she's underestimated both his easy strength and her own overwhelming fatigue. Instead of freeing herself, she swoons, so that when he steps over the threshold of the shed, Eva's world is tilting and out of focus.

There are voices and hands, the caress of warm air that smells of laundry detergent and floor polish. Eva doesn't even know she's cold until her skin prickles at the change in atmosphere, and she wishes for a blanket, a roaring fire, a mug of something hot and steaming. Almost immediately, one of her wishes is granted when she's lowered to a stiff mattress and a blanket is pulled across her upper body.

"I'll let you take it from here," the soldier says to someone that Eva can't see. Then his hand is heavy on her shoulder for a moment. "You'll be good as new in no time," he tells her, but she's not reassured. "I'll see you around."

By the time the room stops spinning and Eva can take in her surroundings, a woman is already at work on her leg. The stranger is wearing a long, denim skirt, a red, cable-knit sweater that looks handmade, and a severe bun that drags her hair away from her sun-spotted face.

The woman is straddling a stool beside a wooden chair that contains an amateur-looking surgical kit. A few gleaming silver instruments, rolls of gauze, and a dark bottle of iodine are all laid out on a bleached white towel.

"No," Eva says, taking it all in. She pushes herself up on her elbows and is rewarded with another head rush that makes the room tip.

The woman picks up a pair of slender scissors. "You'd rather I leave this gaping open?" She motions to the gory mess that is Eva's shin. Blood still seeps from the flapped open, V-shaped wound, and her leggings are soaked through. The towel is un-salvageable. "You'll have an infection by tomorrow."

"Then I should go to the hospital," Eva shoots back, trying to keep her head lifted.

A second pair of hands press her back into the pillow, and Eva finds herself looking at a girl about her age. She is also dressed in a long skirt and thick sweater, but her waist-length, dirty-blond hair has been woven into a single braid that curls over her shoulder. Her eyes are a pale, icy blue, and they glare at Eva.

"Be still," the girl hisses. "You're lucky she's looking at you at all. If I had my way—"

"Rachel!" the woman interrupts. "*Enough.*"

The girl—Rachel—bites her bottom lip, but when the woman turns her attention back to Eva's leg, the girl rolls her eyes. It's a look Eva can read perfectly, even in her diminished state: *you don't belong here* and *I hate you.*

The snick of the scissors fills the charged air between them, and Eva winces as the woman cuts at the fabric of her leggings. The lycra is stuck to her skin in places, glued by dried blood and matted with dirt and leaves, and the tugging makes her eyes water. Still, she curls her body so that she can see what's going on—she doesn't trust Rachel or the woman.

"Can you move your foot? Your knee?" The woman helps Eva point and flex her toes, then bend and rotate her knee. After a few minutes and some more poking and prodding that makes Eva gasp in agony, she says, "I don't think it's broken. But you do need stitches to close the wound."

Eva's stomach clenches into a fist, but before she can squeak out a single word, the woman goes on.

"I'm going to be honest with you: I don't have any local anesthetic. So you have a choice. Either Rachel can hold you down, or I can give you a light sedative. I don't have many pills left, so I'm not going to waste one trying to force you to take it, but it's yours if you want it. It'll make you drowsy and forgetful. You likely won't remember anything about the procedure at all."

Eva is panicked at the thought of taking anything from this woman, but the alternative is laid out beside her in all its sharp and shiny glory. She feels trapped in a horror movie, though the perpetrators of her worst nightmares are a dowdy middle-aged woman in desperate need of a decent cut and color and a teenager with an attitude problem. It's obvious to Eva that Rachel would love nothing more than to hear her scream while the other woman diligently stitches up her leg with what might be fishing wire and a sewing needle.

Apparently sensing her hesitation, the woman gives Eva a thin-lipped smile. She seems tired, and there's something resigned in her gaze.

"I'm Tamar," she says, as if an introduction might help. "I worked for twelve years as an ER nurse before coming here. I was good at my job. Believe me, I know what I'm doing—even if I don't have a sterile procedure room and scrubs to back me up."

Eva considers her, and because she's terrified and lonely and soothed by that one small smile she says, "I'm Eva."

Tamar nods. "I know."

A ripple of concern lifts the hairs on Eva's arms. *Tamar knows her?* But she doesn't have time to ask.

Reaching behind her, Tamar grabs an amber pill bottle and unscrews the cap. Eva can tell that the bottle is nearly empty, but the woman tips one pill out and extends her hand. "I promise this isn't poison or whatever other horrible thing you might think it is. It'll just help you sleep."

Eva studies Tamar's face, but if there is anything sinister hiding in the stranger's eyes, Eva doesn't have the capacity to unravel it out. She's scared and hurting, cold and exhausted. So she reaches for the tiny blue pill, and when Rachel hands her a glass of water, she swallows it down.

The last thing she remembers before everything goes blurry and gray is Rachel leaning over her, smirking.

. . . .

Eva wakes with a thirst so profound it is all-consuming. The need for water, for *something* to soothe her parched mouth and throat is so intense she is wild with it. She flails, and falls half-way out of the narrow bed before she remembers. The shooting pain in her leg does much to bring back the awful night, but then Rachel heaves a dramatic sigh from across the room and throws reality into sharp focus.

"It lives," Rachel says dryly. She pushes herself up from a narrow, wooden bench, and takes a few steps toward the place where Eva cowers, suffering. "You slept for nearly twelve hours."

"Water," she croaks, ignoring her leg, Rachel's sneer, and the details of her prison now bathed in morning light.

Rachel blinks and purses her lips, as if trying to decide whether or not to oblige. Finally, she says, "Beside you." She flicks her wrist in the direction of a small table next to the bed.

Eva lunges for the glass waiting there and gulps half of it gone. Lukewarm water spills down her chin and onto her dirty flannel, but she doesn't care. The tall glass is empty in moments, and she falls back onto the pillow, gasping a bit for breath.

With her most urgent need met, Eva begins to absorb new information. Her leg is hot and she can feel her pulse beat throughout her calf, but she can tell it's bandaged tightly. There's nothing she can do about it now. So she turns her attention to her surroundings.

The shed is bigger than she first realized and has been turned into a living room of sorts. There's a battered couch against the back wall, and an assortment of mismatched armchairs. Rachel was sitting across from Eva, on what looks like an old church pew. It's been painted white and softened with a few lumpy pillows in an assortment of clashing patterns. The cushions look like practice projects from a beginner sewing class. And Eva herself is shoved into the farthest corner of the building on a pop-up cot—it seems everything has been shifted to make room for her temporary bed. Tamar and her terrifying array of surgical instruments are gone; Eva is alone with the blond teenager and her almost tangible disapproval.

Her head is thick and throbbing, but even so, it's clear that they—whoever *they* are—have intentionally isolated her from the rest of the inhabitants of . . . the Gates? Did the soldier call this place the *Gates of Zion?*

"I'm supposed to take you to the bathroom and get you cleaned up," Rachel says, crossing her arms over her chest and glaring at Eva with obvious disgust. "And I have chores to do."

Her meaning is clear. *Move it.* But Eva's not sure she can. "Why didn't you wake me?" she asks, stalling for time as she eases herself up. Her head swims and her vision is shot through with pinpricks, but now that Rachel has said the word *bathroom*, it's all Eva can think about. When was the last time she ate? Drank? She has no idea what time it is, but her stomach is hollow and her bladder full. She feels like she's been hit by a truck and left for dead.

"I tried," Rachel huffs. "I would have jabbed you with the scissors if Tamar hadn't taken them."

Eva stifles a shiver at the thought, and carefully swings her feet over the side of the bed.

"You're not supposed to put any weight on it," Rachel says, watching her. "The tissue over your shin is very thin and can easily tear. But Tamar didn't have Steri-Strips, so she had to stitch."

There are no crutches that Eva can see, and it's evident that Rachel isn't going to help. "So what am I supposed to do?"

Rachel shrugs. "I'm just telling you what Tamar said. You can do whatever the hell you want."

Eva is on her own. She wobbles a little when she stands, but the dizziness passes quickly, so she takes a step. Flames of pain lick up her lower leg, but Eva steels her expression and even manages to give Rachel a tight smile.

"Great. It can walk." Rachel spins on her heel and crosses the room in two big strides. It's so easy, so painless, there's no way she's not rubbing it in—her mobility is a taunt. Swinging the door open, she steps outside and holds it for Eva. "Come on. I don't have all day."

"Aren't you afraid I'll run?"

Rachel laughs. "*No*," she says pointedly. "And if I was . . ." she reaches beside her and produces a long-handled garden hoe. It must have been resting against the outside wall of the shed. The blade is V-shaped and vicious-looking, and Rachel wields it like a weapon.

"What? No guns for girls?" Eva says through gritted teeth.

Something in Rachel's gaze hardens, and in one whirlwind movement she swings the hoe like a bo staff and whips it at Eva's leg. She stops a single inch short. "I'm supposed to be planting today." Rachel leans in and closes the gap, rapping Eva's bandages with the wooden handle.

The thump sends a jolt of electricity through every bone in Eva's body. She sucks a few shallow breaths between gritted teeth and wills her eyes not to water with the pain.

"But I'm not about to let a little gardening get in the way of my responsibility to keep an eye on you. If I have to maim you further, I will."

Rachel's eyes are as cold and glittering as a sheet of Lake Superior ice in February, and Eva doesn't doubt her for a second. This strange young woman would love nothing more than to hurt her, Eva is sure of that.

It's going to make escaping so much harder than it needs to be.

CHAPTER 14

MONDAY

Eva spoons the last bite of cold oatmeal into her mouth and resists the urge to lick the bowl. She hasn't eaten anything since scrambled egg sandwiches with Zach over twenty-four hours ago, and considering the terror, trauma, and uncertainty of the hours since, she feels completely hollowed out. She's still hungry, of course, but it's more than that. There's a hole in her heart where Zach is supposed to be, and she prods the depth of it carefully. Eva misses him (where is he?), but it's a bit of a blank space, smooth-edged and neat. When she dares to think about her mother—about Scout and the house by the lake, Sebastian and Frank and her little yellow room that sparkles like a ray of sunshine even on cloudy days—the gap is a ragged, savage thing. Huge and gaping, it's enough to gobble her whole if she lets it.

But Eva can't think like that. She can't let herself be dragged under by grief. So she carefully places her spoon in her bowl and folds her hands in her lap to stop herself from throwing them both across the farmhouse kitchen. She imagines how the ceramic would shatter against the wooden floor, how the spoon would clatter. Then she fantasizes about the heft of Rachel's blond braid in her hands—and how easy it would be to use it to throw her to the ground.

Eva is clean and fed, dressed in a frumpy dress that puts her in mind of the *Handmaid's Tale*. It's ankle-length and shapeless, a pale, bleached blue that matches Rachel's eyes almost perfectly. Eva blushes, thinking about Rachel and the blasted dress, about the way that her enemy stood there while Eva stepped out of her clothes and sponged off her body with a faded washcloth and a half-used bar of what could only be homemade soap. It smelled, predictably, of lavender.

"You can't shower," Rachel had told her. "You're not allowed to get the sutures wet for forty-eight hours. But God knows you need to wash up. You reek."

Of course, Rachel wouldn't leave the bathroom. Instead, she locked the door and stood against it as she watched Eva undress. "*Everything,*" she warned when Eva paused for a moment in her underwear.

"I'll wash them out," Eva said, turning her back to Rachel—even though she was loathe to do so—and reluctantly peeling off her bralette. She was almost desperate to hang on to something that was recognizably *hers*, but Rachel grabbed it. When Eva looked over her shoulder, she could see Rachel toss the bra in a bag.

"Your things are headed for the burn pile," she said, her mouth a thin, prim line.

"You can't burn my things!"

"Stop me."

So Eva had no choice but to put on the shapeless, secondhand panties (they were too big), the Fruit of the Loom shelf bra (it pinched under the arms), and the ugly, shapeless dress that had been laid out for her on the bathroom counter. Someone had thought it all through. Someone had chosen to put Eva in the most humiliating, ill-fitting getup imaginable. Eva had her money on Rachel. She was a vindictive, coldhearted snake.

"I get to babysit you *all day,*" Rachel says now, resting her chin in one hand on the kitchen counter. She's staring at Eva, drumming the fingers of her other hand on the butcher block countertop.

"Am I a prisoner?" Eva dares to ask.

The corner of Rachel's mouth tips into a faint smile. "Sure. You were supposed to be a recruit, but we've gone off-script now, haven't we? I'll tell you this much: you're either in or out. And you're sure acting like you're out."

"I don't even know what *in* means. What is this place?"

Rachel looks thoughtful for a moment, as if she's deciding whether to share more with Eva. In the end she shrugs.

"You'll find out soon enough."

"Where's Zach? I want to see him."

"That's not going to happen."

"Why not? I—"

"Wash your bowl," Rachel interrupts, turning her back on Eva. "We have to get going."

Eva slides off a wooden stool and heads to the sink. The house is huge, rambling, and filled with enough furniture for a horde. Eva counts fourteen chairs at the dining room table. The living room—which she can just see beyond a wall with a towering china hutch—has a brown leather sectional that looks well used. And the mudroom that they walked through to get into the house was lined with a long bench and open lockers with enough hooks, boot boxes, and baskets for an elementary school classroom. Eva hasn't seen the second floor, but the wide staircase and massive footprint of the first floor indicates a warren of bedrooms and more bathrooms. A study? A library? A den of horrors?

She wants to ask Rachel more questions, to find out anything she can about this place and the people who live here, but she's still seething about the way Rachel stared her down when she was naked and hurting. Eva's afraid she won't be able to be subtle, to carefully draw out the answers she wants with flattery or simple kindness. And there's no doubt in her mind that animosity will only make Rachel intentionally misdirect her. Or clam up entirely. Eva knows that Rachel would revel in any chance to frustrate or shame her.

Still, questions line up and jostle for attention. What is this place? Where is everyone? Is Zach okay? Why can't she just go home? What has she gotten herself into?

Eva turns on the tap and grabs a scrub brush to wash out her oatmeal bowl, but she goes slowly, using the chore as an excuse to take in as much as she can about the farmhouse.

It's clean, almost oddly so, but there is no decor at all. No pictures on the walls or knickknacks to give it any character. They passed one photo in the hallway on their way in: a picture of the man with white hair at the center of a gaggle of people—adults, children, and babies in arms—but Rachel ushered her past so quickly Eva didn't have time to really look. She couldn't even tell if Zach was in the photograph. Back at the cabin he'd said, *"My dad is coming."* Is the man with the white hair his father? Is Rachel his sister? The thought makes Eva shudder.

"Are you really that incompetent?" Rachel is suddenly beside her, tearing the bowl from her hands and giving it a quick once-over with a rag. "It's one bowl. One spoon."

Eva feels a sharp retort like salt on her tongue, but she bites it back. Instead, she steps meekly away from the sink and lowers her eyes. She can bide her time. Let Rachel think she's a nervous little mouse. Let the bitchy blonde underestimate her.

"It's practically noon," Rachel mutters as she quickly towels off and puts the bowl away. Someone had left it sitting out for Eva hours ago, and Rachel made her eat the cold, congealed oatmeal. Eva was in no position to complain. Now that she's no longer starving, she can see that the farmhouse is laden with food. Fruit piled in a basket, fresh loaves of bread wrapped in tea towels on the counter, an entire chocolate cake with thick frosting beneath a glass dome. The refrigerator is double wide and industrial, and when Rachel opens it briefly to grab an apple, it's packed with everything from gallons of milk and blocks of cheese to dark Coke bottles lined up in neat rows. Eva's mouth waters at the thought of a Coke (in a bottle!), but Rachel slams the door shut without offering her a drink or an apple.

"We have to work fast. The radishes, peas, and lettuces are all in, but we need to plant beans, broccoli, and carrots today," Rachel says, taking a loud bite of the apple in her hand. "Lunch is at one, so we have just under two hours."

Gardening. Eva has been locked in not one, but *two* rooms, kidnapped, stitched up without anesthetic by a retired nurse, and stripped of her clothes and belongings, and this snarky stranger expects her to plant some *vegetables*? Eva glances around the kitchen, looking for a phone, a computer, *anything* that she could use to contact the outside world, but Rachel already has her by the elbow.

Pinching tight, she says, "You'd better work fast. The Gathering is after lunch on Mondays, and then I hear Dad wants to talk to you."

"Dad?"

It's not really a question, but Rachel takes the bait. "Didn't you meet him?" Her eyes glitter. "Oh, you must not have. People don't quickly forget Abner Brennan."

There's something about the way she says his name that makes Eva wither inside. But she repeats it to herself over and over—*Abner Brennan, Abner Brennan, Abner Brennan*—stamping it on her brain so that she will never forget. So that someday when this is all over, she can tell the world who he is and what he's done. She just doesn't know what that is yet.

Eva realizes that escape is out of her reach right now—she needs to learn more about where she is (the geography, the layout of the compound, and the people), but she is also not nearly as mobile as she would like to be. Each step, each time she puts weight on her bad leg, it feels like her shin is being ripped open. The way the pain zings white-hot across her calf makes her wonder if Tamar was wrong. Something feels very broken in her leg.

But whether or not Eva is ready to run, it feels perverse that Rachel expects her to slot into life at the Gates without batting an eye. She wants to claim exhaustion, to show Rachel that it's simply impossible for her to do chores, but before she can speak a single word, the girl drags her toward the back hallway and the mudroom.

Eva stumbles a step or two, landing hard on the heel of her bad leg and sending a current of agony straight up her spine. When she cries out and nearly falls, Rachel puts a hand to her mouth in mock distress.

"Oh, I'm sorry! Did I move too quickly? I forgot all about your leg. It's so hidden under that dress . . ."

Curling her hands into fists, Eva sets her jaw and refuses to give Rachel the satisfaction of seeing her fingers tremble. There's nothing she can do about the tears shimmering in her eyes, but she blinks them away and stares Rachel down. "You can go slow or you can carry me," Eva says, her voice quiet but steady.

"You can crawl," Rachel snaps back. But after a few tense seconds she turns and walks to the back door, pausing to wait for Eva on the threshold.

It's another beautiful spring day: cool in the shade but warm in the sun. The air is filled with birdsong and rich with the scent of earth and forest: plush and musky and everything Eva loves about Minnesota in May. It's Charlie's favorite sort of day. But just the thought of her mother makes Eva's heart seize. What is Charlie doing right now? Where is she? Does she know what happened? Regret is a boulder that threatens to crush her, and Eva has to push all thoughts of her mother—and home—away.

The walk from the back of the house to the gardens (across the dirt road and to the far side of the big, red barn) seems interminable. Rachel hurries ahead, seemingly confident that Eva can't go far or fast, and begins to carry supplies from a small lean-to greenhouse attached to the side of the barn. It would be the perfect time for Eva to bolt, but she's nauseous and barely hobbling. So she shuffles after Rachel, and when she reaches the farthest edge of the large patchwork of plots, she sinks gratefully to the ground.

Rachel has set out a crate with gloves, trowels, and packets of seeds, as well as several black trays filled with delicate seedlings. The wicked-looking hoe is once again in her hands, and as Eva watches, she stabs it into the ground and begins scoring a thin line in the earth. Eva can't imagine how Rachel expects her to help, but before she has a chance to ask, the morning is torn in two.

A sharp crack echoes off the trees.

It's quickly followed by a second, and then a third. One more. When an entire volley of retorts accompanies the sudden flight of several dozen birds from the canopy of the surrounding forest, Eva's brain finally catches up with her ears. *Gunshots*.

Her reaction is raw instinct, a primal urge that compels her to make herself as small as humanly possible. Eva is out in the open, a prominent target in any position, but she flings herself down anyway and covers her head with her hands as gunshots ring out across the shallow valley.

They're not hunting—they can't be. Eva knows that any quarry the shooters might be tracking is long gone by now. The incessant rat-a-tat of bullets—automatic weapons?—ensure that any deer, elk, or black bear are either racing through the underbrush or riddled with holes by now. She should *run*. She should . . .

But Rachel's laughing. At first, Eva is convinced that Rachel is *crying* and they are united in their fear, but a quick glance dispels that fantasy. The gunshots persist—lesser now, but still puncturing the perfect morning—and Eva's captor is nearly bent double with glee.

"Good God in heaven, you're pathetic," she says. "Look at you!" Rachel screws up her face and cowers, covering her head with her arms in a mockery of Eva's protective pose.

Eva can hardly hear her over the rush of blood in her ears, but Rachel is clearly unaffected by the gunshots, so Eva slowly pushes herself up. Squinting toward the back of the property, she realizes that beyond the row of Morton buildings and the makeshift parking lot, there's a tall, wooden fence of sorts. The shots seem to be coming from behind it.

"What's going on?" Eva asks, her voice breaking. She doesn't want to need Rachel for anything, but she has to *know*.

"Training," Rachel responds with a smirk. It's not much.

"Training for what?"

"War."

War? Eva thinks of the soldier who chased her and brought her here. The camo and combat gear, the tall fence with the razor wire. Underneath and in between the barrage of constant discharge, she can now make out the sounds of shouting. Men are yelling quick, terse words that she can't quite discern.

As Eva studies the compound she can see a sort of camp take form. Behind the house and the barn, the buildings look like barracks. And beyond the makeshift wall there's camouflage netting slung from high branches and what looks like a climbing wall.

Eva is shaky and sick to her stomach, but she struggles to her feet anyway. It feels dangerous not to be upright, ready to flee, with such uncertainty around her.

"Rachel!"

Eva's head snaps in the direction of the sound. It's the man with the white hair, and he's emerging from a side door in the barn. He strides across the grass toward the gardens with a grim look on his face.

Even at a distance Eva can feel power crackle around him like electricity. He's unusually tall, well over six feet with broad shoulders and thick arms. His dress shirt is cuffed and rolled to his elbows, and his forearms are covered in pale hair that makes him appear to glow in the morning sun. But it's his face that makes Eva's breath catch in her throat. His features are chiseled and severe, his skin permanently bronzed from a long life lived outdoors. He'd be almost handsome if it wasn't for his eyes— they are black holes, pits of gravity that draw her to him even as they make her feel panicked and exposed. The gunshots were better than his gaze on her.

"Dad," Rachel says, and the word on her lips sounds both sacred and a little terrifying.

Eva flicks her eyes to the girl and realizes that she is standing straight and still, her back a rigid line that betrays a barely concealed fear at the sudden presence of her father. She's clutching the handle of the hoe in both hands, her fingers white-knuckled.

"I'm sorry," Rachel continues. "We didn't get as far as we were supposed to. She slept late and I couldn't wake her. I tried, I—"

"Rachel . . ." He's close enough to touch her now, and as Eva watches, Rachel flinches just a bit. It's a single full-body tremor that whispers from head to toe and then dissipates when the man reaches out and brushes her cheek. "I'm not upset about the garden. But I do question why you've dragged our guest out here so soon after her accident."

"I thought . . . Tamar said . . ."

"Is Tamar in charge?" he asks, pinching Rachel's chin almost tenderly. Eva recognizes that move—it's classic Zach, and the thought makes the earth shift under her feet.

"No." Rachel lowers her eyes.

"No, she's not. Remember that, Daughter. And consider how you would like to be treated if you were a stranger in a strange land. Miss Sutton is our guest, not our prisoner." At this, he turns toward Eva, and she shrivels beneath the force of his full attention. "Hello, Eva. It's nice to finally meet you, my dear."

When he extends his hand, Eva reaches out not because she wants to, but because she can't imagine doing anything else. Her fingers are dwarfed by his massive hand, and in the warm grip of his welcome she feels embraced and important and *seen*.

His eyes crinkle at the edges when he says, "I'm Abner Brennan; you can call me Abner. It's my pleasure to welcome you to the Gates of Zion. We are so blessed to have you here."

For the first time since Zach yelled at her back at the cottage, Eva *does* feel welcome. Abner is smiling at her with his impenetrable eyes, and she could nearly forget that he is someone to cringe away from. But when she glances at the snug knot of their hands, she can see that his knuckles are purple and split.

This man hit Zach. Viciously.

Rachel is trying to bully Eva into submission, and Abner has apparently decided to use a softer, but no less manipulative approach. He's trying to make her feel welcome so that she'll let her guard down. She's just not sure what he—or Rachel—wants from her.

Eva shivers a little and Abner's expression changes. The congenial half smile melts off his face and his eyes become hooded. "Are you okay?" he asks.

"I'm dizzy," Eva admits, pulling back her hand so she can

wrap her arms around herself. It's not a lie. Neither is: "My leg hurts."

He softens. "Of course it does. I hear you hurt yourself quite badly. Come. I'll take you inside and get you something to drink. Have you been given anything for the pain?"

Eva shakes her head, panicked at the thought of going anywhere with this man and confused by his behavior. But he's already slipping an arm around her waist, and when he lifts so that she doesn't have to bear her full weight on her wounded leg anymore, she feels a rush of relief. It's clear he likes her like this: needy and docile.

"That's better," he murmurs. And then he's leading her away from the gardens, away from Rachel and her bladed tools, her cruel smirk.

"What am I supposed to do?" Rachel calls, her voice almost plaintive.

"Finish planting." Abner doesn't even turn around. Instead, he gathers Eva closer and walks her toward the farmhouse. "I've got you," he says, only for her ears. "You're going to be just fine."

Eva thinks about Zach slamming the door of the bedroom at the house in Little Moose. Of the way the key clicked in the door when he locked her inside. She thinks about hiding in the garage and then running through the forest, her heartbeat a drum in her chest. Her mind flashes through every horrifying moment since the second she reached for Zach's hand on the *Summer Moon*. And though she has endured more horrible things in the last few days than the entirety of her life before, nothing compares to Abner Brennan's arm around her, his breath in her hair.

COLLEGE APPLICATION ESSAY #41

Pick a quote that describes a lot about you and explain why you connect with it. Choose a quotation that admissions officers won't see over and over and stay away from individuals who are constantly quoted.

"You've got to jump off cliffs all the time and build your wings on the way down."

Annie Dillard

I have jumped off cliffs. Literally and more than once.

In the Pacific Northwest, I dove off a thirty-foot ledge into a glacier-fed river and nearly drowned. The water was so cold, so incredibly shocking in its intensity, that when I broke the surface, I gasped. It was a natural reaction, my body believed it was the most logical thing to do, but clearly, a deep breath while fully immersed in a body of water is ill-advised. I swallowed a mouthful of ice-cold water, and half of it ended up in my lungs.

It's amazing to me how something can be so cold it burns. It's amazing to me that from the top of the ridge, the boulders beneath the bottle-green water looked like tiny pebbles. And it's amazing to me that even though it would have been easier to sink, everything inside me wanted to *rise*.

I have jumped off cliffs. Figuratively, more times than I can remember.

I am not risk-averse, and though my more natural tendencies might lean toward inertia, my mom made sure that I would never find myself flightless and floundering. My mom is an adventurer and risk-taker, and everything I know about wing-building (and all the rest) has come from her.

In some ways, we could not possibly be more alike. We love the new and novel, we live for the next opportunity to step far outside our comfort zones. And over the years of living and adapting and becoming the women that we were always meant to be, we have become something new entirely. Yes, I am her daughter, but I am also her sister, her best friend, and, at times, her competition. I am her biggest fan and her toughest critic, her eager devotee, and a vicious detractor. She raised me the very best way she knew how.

And yet. People can change a lot in two and a half years. I was barely fifteen when my mother and I hit the road full-time in a vintage Airstream trailer, and seventeen and a half when we made Landing, Minnesota, our home. I am no longer the naive, bullied little girl who spent many nights curled up beside her mommy. And I am no longer the delicate fledgling she still seems to think that I am. How do you tell the one who taught you everything that you can take it from here?

My mother gave me these wings, but I think she's afraid to let me fly. And so I take to the sky in secret when she's not looking. When I can dream and plan and explore the woman I am becoming in my own right. It's far from perfect, but there's joy in that, too. In the way that I fall and mess up, ding a wing and rise again. It's glorious and heartbreaking. It's a cliff I never dreamed I would have to throw myself from.

I wouldn't change a thing.

I would change everything.

*507 words. Close enough, Mrs. A? If not, can you help me find some words to cut? I feel this one in my bones and each time I hit delete I die a little . . .

CHAPTER 15

Abner takes Eva into the farmhouse. In the kitchen he pauses, grabbing a Coke from the fridge and a couple of ibuprofen from the cupboard beside it.

"I'm sorry I don't have anything stronger," he says, offering her the two blue pills. "I'm sure Tamar has a prescription or two, but she's pretty possessive of her medicine cabinet."

"It's okay," Eva demurs, accepting the medicine as if it means nothing at all. In reality, she's practically buzzing at the prospect of a little pain relief. And a Coke! What she would give for some onion rings from Mugs to go with it. But she yanks her thoughts back from the edge before she loses it completely and focuses on the ibuprofen. Her leg is keeping time with her heart, a sickening twinge of agony for every single beat.

Abner screws off the top of the Coke bottle with a satisfying pop. "Here," he says, offering it to her.

"Thank you." Eva is ashamed of the gratitude she feels. Pain relievers? Coke? She wants it so bad she's trembling. *Why is he being so nice to her?*

Two pills in her palms and then on her tongue. A long swig of sugary caffeine that hits at the base of her skull like a drug. "Thanks," Eva says again, meaning it. "I feel better already."

"I'm glad to hear it. You're our guest, Eva. I'm sorry if Rachel

221

made you feel differently. If *last night* made you feel differently."
He cringes. "It wasn't supposed to be that way."

Eva isn't sure what he means. The horrifying approach of
the SUV? The way he backhanded Zach so casually? Or maybe
he's talking about the frightening race through the trees and
how his soldier hunted her down like an animal.

"It's okay," Eva says, not meaning it.

"No, it's not. We're better than that. You must be scared to
death."

The fact that he's named it, that he's willing to admit how
this all must feel to Eva, is enough to undo her. Tears glint on her
eyelashes and she resists the urge to sob. "I don't understand."

"Of course you don't, but I think I can remedy that," Abner
says kindly. "And I also think I can help you with that leg. A vicious bout of sciatica forced me to use crutches several years
ago. Why don't you wait here while I see if I can track them
down?"

Eva nods, quietly elated at the thought of crutches. Anything to take the pressure off her leg.

Abner disappears around the corner in the living room, and
Eva hears a door open, followed by the sound of heavy foot-
falls on stairs. Of course there's a basement. She wonders what's
down there and wishes she would have feigned unease at the
thought of being alone. Maybe he would have taken her along.

But then it hits Eva that she's alone in the vast house. Glanc-
ing around to make sure that no one is hiding in a doorway or
down a hall, Eva hobbles back toward the mudroom and the
photo on the long wall.

It's a canvas as big as a coffee table and filled with dozens
of people. There's Abner at the very center of the shot, holding a giggling toddler on his hip. Eva can't tell if the child is a
boy or a girl, as he or she is sporting a pair of corduroy overalls

and has genderless, short curls the color of a copper penny. But every other woman or girl in the picture is easily identifiable by her dress. The garments are ankle-length and universally unflattering, a sort of uniform that renders them all similar and shapeless.

The gaggle of people around Abner and the toddler are all young, and there are so many small children that Eva wonders briefly if he runs some sort of home. But there are pairs of twenty and early thirtysomethings, and as Eva studies the picture, she thinks that she can group them into families. She would bet that there are five grown children with their spouses and kids gathered around. Rachel is there surrounded by a gaggle of preteens. And then—Zach.

He's on the edge of the group, separated from what Eva assumes to be a sister by a sliver of blank space that makes it look as if he has been photoshopped in. The way he leans away from the cluster of his family speaks volumes. His smile looks fake, and doesn't reach his eyes, and Eva's heart contracts in spite of herself.

"I see you've found the most recent Brennan family portrait."

Eva starts, and the sudden jerk of movement sends her leg into spasms.

"I didn't mean to startle you," Abner says, putting a steadying hand on the small of her back.

Her skin boils where he's touching her, but Eva doesn't dare to move.

"Here," he says, passing over a pair of aluminum crutches with his free hand. "I tried to adjust them for your height, but we may have to tweak them a bit."

Eva accepts the crutches and uses them as an excuse to pull away from Abner. She's never needed crutches before, but she's seen it done enough, and when she slides them under her arms and shifts her weight to the hand grips, the stress on her leg is almost immediately alleviated. Eva can feel the muscles in her jaw soften in relief.

"Good?" Abner asks, smiling. His mouth pulls slightly to the right side, just like Zach's, and Eva can't stop herself from recoiling a little.

"You have a big family," she says, so he won't ask her about the sudden chill in the air.

"Eleven children." There's an entire symphony of pride in his voice. "Five in-laws, and a baker's dozen of grandchildren. We have three sets of twins." He points them out to Eva, but she's barely paying attention. "Sadly, my long-suffering wife passed away a few years ago."

"Where does Zach fit?" Eva sneaks the question in while he's still admiring his descendants.

Abner slides just his eyes to give her an assessing look, and for a moment Eva is convinced that he won't answer her. But then he admits, "Zechariah is fifth in line."

Zechariah. Not Zach. It's a dusty, old-fashioned biblical name—a small side step from the much more common *Zachary* and yet somehow vastly different, infused with significance. If he had introduced himself as Zechariah instead of Zach at Mugs the afternoon they met, would Eva have paused? Would she have asked him questions about the origin of his unusual name and discovered more about who he was and where he'd come from? Would she be here right now, a veritable prisoner—no matter what Abner says—on a compound in the woods of Northern Minnesota?

"Where is Zach?" Eva dares to whisper, rebelling with that one small syllable. It feels like a dangerous question, but Abner just ignores her.

"Come," he says, holding out his arm in the direction of the kitchen. "Let's sit down. I have a bit of time before lunch and the Gathering."

Eva has so many questions but she isn't sure that Abner will want to answer them. Or that he'll be truthful if he does.

His office is beyond the living room, in a wing that looks over the far lawn. They are on the opposite side of the property as the barn and the gardens, and looking out the tall windows, Eva can see a lush, rolling yard that descends gently to a wall of trees. It's postcard perfect, downright pastoral, and paired with the floor-to-ceiling bookshelves that surround Abner's desk, Eva is momentarily convinced that nothing sinister could be at play in such a lovely setting. But then she reads the spines of a few of Abner's books. There are theological treatises shoulder to shoulder with books that warn of dark agendas and hidden enemies, as well as socialism, Marxism, and tyranny. It's a paranoid, threatening collection.

"Do you like to read?" Abner moves behind the expansive desk and motions for Eva to take one of the armchairs across from him.

"Yes," she says, sinking onto a nubby cushion and leaning her crutches against the other chair. She's distracted, and clearly Abner can tell. He seems mildly annoyed.

Eva's off-balance, incapable of decoding Abner's unexpected warmth. It feels insincere, manipulative. What does he want from her? Questions bubble to the tip of her tongue, and before she can stop herself, she blurts out: "Why am I here?"

At this, Abner laughs. It's throaty and rich, an intoxicating sound and completely unexpected coming from so powerful and serious a man. "You're bold," he tells her. "I like that. But as a seventeen-year-old Instagram influencer and not-yet high school graduate, you're really in no position to question me."

"You know who I am?"

Instead of answering, Abner pulls a phone from his pocket and uses face ID to unlock it. He taps and scrolls until he finds what he's looking for. Then he turns the screen so Eva can see it.

She's looking at a picture of herself and Charlie. They're crouching on an outcropping of stone over what looks like a bottomless canyon. The sun is setting behind them, so they are bathed in shadows, but it's a gorgeous, impressionistic shot layered with the colors of a southwestern twilight. Eva remembers setting up the camera. She remembers that just behind them, where it looked like the earth fell precipitously away, there was a ledge. The danger was just an illusion.

"This is one of my favorites," Abner says, smiling indulgently as if Eva and Charlie are his children, or at least people he can take personal pride in. "I can actually see your faces. Kind of."

Eva is still trying to catch up. "You follow Eva Explores?"

"Just because we choose to live a simple life doesn't mean we are completely detached from the rest of the world. Yes, we are fully independent and off the grid, but we do like to know what's happening on the outside. In fact, we take it all very seriously. Would you believe several of my sons are computer geniuses?"

Eva doesn't know what to say, so she says nothing at all.

Abner continues. "We have Facebook pages with hundreds of thousands of followers—more than you, my dear. We also have popular podcasts, weekly live streams that attract viewers from all over the world, and fans on every continent. We may look like backwoods hicks, Miss Sutton, but if you—or anyone—believe that's all we are, you're profoundly underestimating us."

"Who's us?" Eva asks, finding her voice.

"The Family of Zion, of course." Abner grins, and the expression makes Eva think of shark-infested waters.

"So you're a cult." Eva is shocked when the words tumble

from her lips, but instead of becoming angry, Abner laughs
again.

"Is that what you think?" Before she can even draw a breath,
he answers his own question. "I suppose it must look like that
to you. But no, we are not a cult. We are a lifestyle, a movement, a flock of true believers who have had a glimpse behind
the curtain. We know what we have to do. And we are going to
change the world."

The fervor in his eyes scares Eva even more than his hand on
her body or the sound of gunshots. "What do you mean?"

Abner waves his hand as if swatting at a fly. "Never mind."

"But what am *I* doing here? There's been some sort of mistake. I don't belong here. I—"

"You are the proverbial fly in the ointment. Wrong place,
wrong time. You can thank Zechariah for that."

At the mention of his name, Eva goes still. What happened
to him? Why won't they let her see him? But she doesn't get to
ask any questions because Abner is still talking.

"You're right. You aren't supposed to be here. At least, not
like this. We had hoped you might . . ." He shakes his head.
"Zechariah shouldn't have taken you to the cottage. It was a
mistake. And now I'm left to clean up his messes once again."

Abner slaps both hands on the desk with an air of finality.
Their conversation is done. Eva can tell that even before he says,
"I think that's enough for now."

"What about Zach?" Eva asks quickly. At the very least she
wants to know where he is. How he's doing.

"Don't worry about him."

Eva is dismayed when Abner stands and begins to move toward the study door. "When can I go home? Can I please just
call my mom? She must be worried sick . . ."

Heaving a sigh, Abner reaches for Eva's crutches and holds

them just out of reach. He's clearly annoyed with her and ignores her questions altogether.

Eva is scared to ask, but they've come this far. Her voice only trembles a little when she says: "What are you going to do with me?"

"For now, you're going back to the shed. It's the safest place for you while we figure out what to do. Don't worry, I'll have Rachel bring you some lunch." He hands her the crutches and swings the office door wide. "Then I think you should join us for the Gathering."

A bolt of defiance zaps through Eva and she lifts her chin to refuse him. They'll have to carry her, kicking and screaming, to this *Gathering*. But just as she opens her mouth, she thinks: Zach. Maybe he'll be there. Maybe he's regretting what he's done, how he's entangled her in this sheer madness. Maybe he'll help.

"Did you want to say something, Miss Sutton?"

Eva shakes her head, lowers her eyes. "It's just a lot to take in."

It's evident that Abner prefers his women this way: nervous and shy, more than a little scared. Whatever it is he enjoys in the Instagram photo of her and Charlie, it isn't their bold pose, the way they look as if at any moment they may topple off the edge—and that they couldn't possibly care less. Those gutsy women don't belong in a place like this, where long skirts make sprinting impossible, and girls are clearly meant to be seen and not heard. Eva thinks of the way that Abner so casually dismissed Rachel, his own daughter, and decides that if she wants to get anywhere, she must learn how to blend into the background.

She can do it. And while she plays the part of a cringing wallflower, she'll continue to collect information that will help her get away. Eva already knows that the Gates isn't as isolated as she first thought it was. The dizzying, half-delirious ride through the forest and to what felt like the very edge of the map had made her feel utterly alone, but thanks to Abner, she knows there's technology and Wi-Fi, a way to connect with civilization beyond the razor wire fence. All she needs to do is find a way to use it.

COLLEGE APPLICATION
ESSAY #50

The lessons we take from obstacles we encounter can be fundamental to later success. Recount a time when you faced a challenge, setback, or failure. How did it affect you, and what did you learn from the experience?

It has taken me a very long time to realize that I have spent the majority of my life as the object of every verb. My father (a man I never met and who made it crystal clear to my mother that he wanted nothing to do with his spawn) left me. The kids at my middle school (who needed someone to pick on and somehow decided I was the most appealing target) bullied me. My mom (who truly is the best but can be so overbearing it's practically criminal) coddled me. But maybe the most significant example of my objectification is how Instagram made me.

Who knows why the algorithm sprinkled pixie dust on us

that day, but from the moment my mom and I uploaded a photo of thirteen-year-old me in Gooseberry Falls, my life has never been the same. Perhaps in a college application essay I shouldn't share that I am an Instagram star of sorts. But I know you'll look me up. Go ahead, I'll wait. I'm the intrepid girl who grew up zigzagging around a map, tracing paths and eventual destinations in the bougie charm of a renovated vintage Airstream we named Sebastian. It's true, I've hiked nearly every mountain range in America, hit forty-four of fifty states, and know at least half a dozen national parks with the familiarity of a park ranger. But what people don't realize is that behind the scenes I was jerked back and forth by the whims of an ever-growing audience, and a mom who always—*always*—knew what was best.

Pictures were taken *of me*. Decisions were made *for me*. And because I loved our life on the road—and it saved me from the things that scared me—I happily went along with everything. But what about when I want to be the subject of the verb?

I have to be honest and say that the lessons I'm learning are in real time. This isn't a past tense journey for me, but one that I'm walking every moment. Even realizing the importance of my own autonomy and independence was hard won, and something I have to remind myself to fight for daily.

I'll be forever thankful for our memory-making, life-making, *me*-making years on the road. And I'll always love the girl with the frizzy braids and freckled skin who grew up in such extraordinary circumstances. But it's time for me to decide.

Evangeline Sutton is no longer the Little Mermaid who wore fins for her fans but longed for legs to carry her away from a life that was her past, not her future. Eva will study and learn and write. About the adventures she lived, and the ones yet to happen. Eva will continue to explore, in her own time and in her own way. And this particular journey will be a quiet one.

This time, you won't find me on Instagram.

Hey, Ms. Alvarez! I'm done. I think fifty is my max—I've said everything I needed to say, and then some. It's been good practice. Thank you for reading my ramblings and offering your feedback. It's been really helpful, and you're cheaper than a shrink. ;-) Sorry to subject you to all this drama, and I know I'm all over the place when it comes to my mom. Am I crazy or do all girls have a love/hate relationship with their mother?!? Wait. Don't answer that. lol —E

PS-Gone for a few days,
but I'll be back early next week.
See you soon!

CHAPTER 16

Eva fights panic when Abner leads her back to the little shed behind the farmhouse and locks her inside. She can't stand the thought of being confined again—of being at the mercy of whoever holds the key—and even when he's gone, it takes her a while to regain control. Her sobs are bitter and leave her feeling wrung-out and hopeless. She has a plan! (Sort of.) She knows what to do! (Not really.) But none of that hard-earned and only slightly affected confidence erases the fact that she's in an unimaginable position.

It's the week of her high school graduation. Eva's supposed to be sleeping in, going to rehearsal and the class brunch afterward, and daydreaming about her future. It's true, she doesn't have a tight group of close friends at Landing High, but she isn't *dis*liked. Everyone is nice enough, and though her class is a mismatched assortment of kids, they have fun together. Prom was a blast (she wore a pink confection of a dress with black Chucks), and she screamed herself hoarse at the hockey playoffs (they lost in overtime). Eva wasn't bullied. Not once.

Crying on the cot in the shed, Eva is stabbed with regret. The whole point of settling in Landing was so that she could have a taste of the high school experience. And she threw it away when she fell head over heels for an older guy. A guy who dragged her halfway across the state and rendered the graduation gown hanging over her closet door useless.

A guy who is now incognito. Eva still shivers at the thought of Abner backhanding his son, but she's also angry at her so-called boyfriend for abandoning her in this deranged place. Rachel loathes her, Abner acts like he's buttering her up, and everyone else avoids her like she's a prisoner. Which, she supposes, she is.

When Eva has calmed down enough to think clearly, she realizes that she doesn't have much time before Rachel is supposed to come and bring her lunch. And then she's expected at the Gathering, whatever that is. This may be her only opportunity to inspect the shed. Eva wants to make use of every remaining minute.

Abandoning the crutches beside the door, she wipes away her tears and limps around the small space looking for chinks in the walls of her makeshift cell. After a quick but thorough investigation, Eva guesses that the space is used as a meeting place of sorts (there are stacks of notebooks and cups filled with an assortment of pens on a low shelf) and there is absolutely no way out. The only door is locked from the outside with a thick padlock. And the two windows are not only tiny, but not built to open at all. Even if she had something to smash the glass, she'd need to find a way to dismantle or destroy the wooden frame between the small panes. Then Eva would have to crawl through the shards of broken glass, drop to the ground on her wounded leg, and hike without a compass or any idea of where she's going, only to face a razor wire fence. Never mind the uniformed guards, the arsenal of weaponry, and the fact that she may be miles from anyone who could possibly help her. But there *has* to be a way. She just needs to keep her wits about her until she finds it.

At one o'clock, the sound of a bell ringing echoes across

the compound. At least, Eva assumes it's one—there's no clock in the shed. But she hurries to one of the windows and watches through the dirty glass as a door in the front of the barn is flung open and children pour out. There are twenty or so of them, ranging in age from preschool to junior high. Two women are the last to emerge—one of them looks like Tamar—and they each have smaller kids either by the hand or in their arms.

The barn must be a converted space, a school of sorts by the look of it. Eva would love little more than to follow them down the sloping hill toward the barracks, but in less than a minute they are out of sight, heading for the back of the property. They don't spare Eva or the shed a single glance.

As Eva watches, Rachel comes into view. She stalks after her siblings, her nieces and nephews, and heaven knows who else. Eva wishes she could get her attention, but the shed is too far away for Rachel to notice her trying, and she soon disappears.

Since there's nothing left to see, Eva flops down on the bed and lifts her bad leg to the pile of pillows she's arranged there. It feels good to elevate it, and with a couple of ibuprofen on board, it's starting to bother her less. In a couple of days she's sure she'll be good as new, and learning as much as she can about the patterns of the people within the Gates is an important part of formulating her escape plan. Eva slides one of the notebooks she found from between the stiff mattress and the metal frame of the cot and pokes a pen out from the spirals. She jots down a few notes about the number of kids and teachers, the timing of the meal, and where everyone goes to have it, adding to the details she has already scribbled down.

As she's writing, it strikes Eva that Rachel is not in school. Has she graduated already? Are teenage girls not allowed to go to school in the Family of Zion? Eva can't help but be fascinated by her cultish counterpart. Rachel is close to her age, young and pretty and full of spirit—even though that very grit is often directed in cruel ways at Eva.

Rachel's jealous. The realization hits Eva like a slap, but the moment she thinks it she knows it's true. What has it been like for Rachel to grow up on this compound, isolated from the rest of the world and all the grubby beauty that it holds? Has she ever tasted salt water on her tongue, or walked a city street to the soundtrack of traffic and shouted conversations in a dozen different languages? Has she sat in a dark movie theater with her hands greasy from popcorn while the opening credits roll? What about a high school crush, that last-day-of-school feeling, a frozen pizza at midnight just because?

Eva feels a pang of pity for Abner's overlooked daughter, but it doesn't last long. The sound of a key in the padlock sends her scrambling to hide the notebook.

"Potato soup today," Rachel announces, coming into the shed, "but I spilled some of it on the way."

Eva sinks back to the cot in the nick of time, the only evidence of her subterfuge a slight squeaking of the rusty springs. Rachel doesn't seem to notice.

"There were ham buns, too, but I couldn't carry everything, so I guess you'll just have to make do."

Eva sits up, trying not to roll her eyes as Rachel passes her a half-empty bowl of soup. Rachel's other hand is free, and she produces a spoon from her dress pocket. She could have easily carried a bun, and Eva tries not to be spiteful. But then Rachel produces a chocolate chip cookie from her other pocket and tosses it onto the cot between them.

Is this a peace offering? She considers not acknowledging it. But then she realizes that there's no way that Rachel herself had time to eat. It's only been a matter of minutes since Eva watched her follow the school children deeper into the compound. She grabs the cookie, stuffing it into her own dress pocket.

"What about you?" Eva asks, pausing with her spoon suspended above the bowl, even though the aroma of the soup is making her mouth water. "Have you eaten?"

Rachel looks taken aback. She seems so thrown she answers honestly, "No," she admits, and then quickly adds, "I'm not hungry."

Eva doesn't know her well enough to press her, so she lets it go and lifts a bite to her mouth. Unlike the oatmeal she ate several hours ago, the soup is hot and studded with chunks of soft potatoes and carrots. She's starving. She just wishes Rachel wouldn't have "spilled" half of it on the way over.

Sinking to the edge of one of the chairs, Rachel watches Eva eat. It seems something has shifted slightly in the air between them, and after a few minutes she asks, all in a rush, "What did you and my dad talk about?"

Eva takes her time chewing, realizing that if she's careful, she may be able to tease more information out of Rachel. "He told me about your family," she says truthfully. "About how Zach—I mean, Zechariah—is the fifth of eleven kids. Where do you fit?"

Rachel pulls her bottom lip between her teeth, thinking. Eventually she sighs and says, "I'm number seven."

"How old are you?"

It's an innocuous question, and Rachel answers easily. "Nineteen. You?"

"Seventeen. Almost eighteen."

"Old enough," Rachel murmurs.

"For what?"

Rachel laughs. "Old enough to marry. But I doubt that's what Zechariah had in mind. Did you sleep with him?"

Eva nearly chokes on her soup. This is not a conversation that she wants to be having with Zach's sister, and besides, she was supposed to be the one asking questions—not the other way around. "That is *none* of your business."

But Rachel won't be deterred. Leaning forward, she props her elbows on her knees and knots her hands together. She gives Eva an earnest, concerned look. "Hey, I'm trying to help you here. If you slept with him, you're already married in the eyes of the Family. Doesn't matter if you want to be or not—it's a done deal. If you haven't . . . Well, you have more options."

"Are you kidding me?" Eva's stomach has turned, and the scent of the soup suddenly makes her nauseous.

"I wouldn't lie to you about this. But you and Zechariah better have your stories straight. If you say he *didn't* have sex with you, but he says you *did*, Tamar will have to do an exam and—"

"Oh, my God." Eva slams her back into the wall behind her, trying to get as far away from Rachel as she can. "You're kidding me. That can't possibly be true."

Rachel sits up straight, a smug little smile on her thin lips. "I'm *not* kidding. But I'm sure you'll find out for yourself soon enough."

Eva is furious, her blood carbonated in her veins. The thought of being forced to share intimate details with Abner Brennan—or Rachel or Tamar or *anyone*—obliterates the self-control she's been fighting so hard for. She wants to smack the superior look off Rachel's face, but before she can land a verbal punch, Rachel stands.

"Had enough?" she asks, and without waiting for an answer, she takes the bowl from Eva and sets it on the small table beside the cot. "Good. We should get going. I have to set up for the Gathering and I guess you might as well come along."

The walk from the shed to the row of barracks at the back

of the property is long and arduous, but Eva is still frothing at the thought of Abner knowing about her sex life, and manages to nearly match Rachel's swift pace. She's gotten the hang of the crutches, and as she jabs them repeatedly into the ground, she wonders if the aluminum aids could be used as a weapon. If she swung them hard enough, would they do any damage? Of course, they'd be useless against the stronghold that is the shed, but could she protect herself with them? Could she hit someone? Beyond the unintentional playground scuffle, Eva has never hurt another human being in her life. She's not sure that she could do it. If she had to whip her crutch at Rachel's head, could she follow through?

Rachel pulls a few paces ahead, and Eva can see that her yellow braid is starting to fray at the edges. Soft wisps of downy hair frame her face and tickle her neck. They make her look much younger than her nineteen years, and even though she's fuming, Eva feels a quiver of compassion for the young woman. Rachel is so unhappy. So trapped—even if she doesn't know it and would never describe it that way. In another time and place, could they be friends? For just a moment, Eva pictures backpacking with Rachel, the steady climb and near euphoria at the summit. The feeling of a shared experience that levels every playing field. But that's just wishful thinking.

As they near the first Morton building, Eva realizes that she misjudged it a bit. People are milling around outside, stretching in the early afternoon sun and talking in small groups gathered on the grass. The double-wide doors of the structure are thrown open, and beyond the glass Eva can see that it's a cafeteria of sorts—not a bunkhouse—filled with folding tables and a surprising mixture of people. The teachers and children are there, plus more women in dresses. They must be the cooks and cleaners of this unusual place, the cogs that whirl behind the scenes to keep everything running. And, at tables separate from the women and children, are more men. Some of them are dressed in combat fatigues, but others wear jeans and T-shirts, regular, informal clothes that somehow make them look incredibly out of place at the bewildering Gates of Zion.

Where does everyone live? Just ballparking the number of people in the cafeteria and on the lawn, Eva would guess there are easily a hundred people here. Maybe more. They can't all crowd into the farmhouse, and unless families are packed like sardines in the remaining Morton buildings, Eva can't imagine where they fit.

But here, below the rise, Eva can see more of the property—and it's even bigger than she thought. Before the wall of what can only be the training grounds, there are trails peeling off into the trees. Do they lead to smaller homes? More buildings? Eva wishes she could pepper Rachel with questions.

"We're outside today," Rachel says suddenly, pointing to a trail that cuts between the first two buildings and carves through the forest. "In the amphitheater. Dad will be live streaming the Gathering so that everyone is on the same page when . . ."

"When what?" Eva asks, but it's clear that Rachel isn't going to say anything more. The pinched look on her face reveals that she's already said too much.

"I have to carry equipment down, and it's going to take you a while to navigate the stairs, so I'm going to let you find your own way. Sit in the very back row on the left side so that I can see you when I walk in."

Eva can't believe her luck. She's sure that Abner would be furious if he knew that Rachel was just going to leave her, but before she can mentally celebrate this small victory, Rachel's hand shoots out and snag's Eva's wrist.

"There are a hundred and sixty-two people here who know

who you are. You stick out like a sore thumb. Never mind the fact that there are cameras all over the compound. Someone is always watching, Eva. Don't even think about trying to run."

Eva swings her crutch, dislodging Rachel's grip on her arm. "I thought it was pretty obvious that I *can't* run."

Rachel just glares. Then she turns on her heel and leaves Eva alone in the shadow of the low-slung building.

People are finishing up their lunches and trickling down the trail on their way to the Gathering. Eva watches them, trying to make eye contact, trying to connect with anyone who might give her even a scrap of information, but they all determinedly avoid her gaze. The women shuffle past hurriedly, a docile breed of maidens with their eyes downcast and their prairie dresses obscuring all obvious suggestions of their femininity. And while the men go slow, taking their time and laughing with one another, they ignore Eva as if she doesn't exist at all. When a small child reaches for her and giggles, a young teenage girl sweeps the toddler into her arms and rushes away.

Still, she feels their attention on her—a hundred-and-sixty-two pairs of eyes plus the cameras that she can now see mounted on the corners of the buildings and in the trees. Eva has no choice but to follow the crowd toward the wide path and the Gathering.

Because she's slow, most people hurry past, pouring around her as if she is nothing more than a stone in a stream. So Eva takes her time, pausing every once in a while and making a show of being sore and exhausted. No one stops to help her, and soon she's alone on the path.

The trail through the trees is wide and well-trodden, but it cuts sharply so that Eva can't see where she's going. However, she can hear when the Gathering begins. Rachel must have taken a different way down because she hasn't passed Eva, but a loudspeaker of sorts is clearly working, and Abner's voice peals across the compound.

"No mission too difficult, no sacrifice too great!" he shouts, and when the microphone screeches, several birds take flight.

A chorus of voices answer him as one: "We are liberty at work!"

Eva stops in her tracks, chilled by the litany and the force of their intent.

"We build, we fight, we strike for freedom!" Abner continues.

"Our rights we will defend!"

"The war is won, but the combat rages on!"

"Onward soldiers!" The final rallying cry echoes across the forest. And then, the invocation devolves into a chant that sounds like a battle cry in the throats of everyone gathered: "On-ward! On-ward! On-ward! On-ward!"

Eva had intended to bide her time and do what Rachel told her to, but the war cry from the trees is otherworldly. She's gripped by a horror so pure she can only think one thing: *Run.*

Wheeling away from the Gathering and the people assembled there, Eva begins to retrace her steps. She scampers up the track, swinging her crutches as quickly as she can, wondering if she should just abandon them altogether. But before she can make it out of the trees and into the sunshine of the open compound, someone grabs her from behind. Eva cries out, but her shout is smothered by the chanting that continues from the amphitheater.

"Eva!" Her name, whispered in her ear. "It's me."

She knows his voice, the feel of his breath on her skin. "Zach?" She twists in his arms, and when she sees his face, she gasps.

The skin over Zach's cheekbone is split like a ripe peach

and crusted with blood. One eye is black and blue, and so swollen it's little more than a slit. His lip is purple and puffy, his neck speckled with pinprick bruises . . . Eva watched Abner strike his own son, but this seems like far more damage than a wicked backhand could do. It looks like Zach's punishment did not end when they arrived at the Gates.

In spite of herself, in spite of the terrible situation he's put her in, Eva feels a wave of affection wash over her. Only days ago she thought she was in love with him. Turns out, love can't switch to hate as quickly as she imagined.

"What happened?" She reaches out to brush his cheek, but before her fingers can graze his skin, he seizes her hand.

Watching the trees, Zach pulls her off the trail and into the underbrush. When she wrestles with the crutches, he wrenches them away and half carries her deeper into the covering of the forest.

"What—"

He sets her down and presses his fingers to her lips to silence her. "We don't have much time," he says, his voice low and his face so close to hers that Eva could tip toward him a single inch and touch his forehead with her own. "We're in a blind spot. None of the cameras can see us here, but you're supposed to be at the Gathering. If you don't show up soon, people will notice."

"Where have you been? Why are you—"

"I'm being punished," Zach interrupts. "I'm being held in a room in the basement of the farmhouse, but my father doesn't know that I learned to pick the lock years ago. I have to get back before the Gathering ends."

Abner went into the basement to get the crutches. Zach was *right there*.

"Let's go," she says. "Right now. You and me. Let's run." She's tried so hard to stay calm and clearheaded, to think rationally.

But everything inside her is rebelling. The chanting at the Gathering has stopped, and Abner is talking quickly and forcefully. She can't make out the words, but in some ways that's scarier than the rallying cry of his followers. What is he saying? She didn't think Rachel meant it when she said they were training for *war*. Now she's not so sure.

"We'd never make it," Zach says sadly. "I'm so sorry, Eva. I'm so very, very sorry. You have to believe me that I never intended for this to happen."

"What is this place?"

Zach frowns, a deep line appearing between his eyes. "My home. It wasn't always this way. But my dad stopped trusting the government and started talking about how our values were under attack. I was in fourth grade when he pulled us out of public school and started homeschooling us. It's been a steady march to this—" He sweeps his arms, indicating the compound, the cameras, the speech they can still hear from the Gathering— "ever since."

"He's—"

"A domestic terrorist. A homegrown radical. A self-proclaimed prophet, but really nothing more than a cult leader and psychopath. Take your pick."

"But he's been . . ." Eva casts around, trying to figure out how to describe her encounters with Abner.

"Nice to you?" Zach supplies. "It's an act, Eva. It's all designed to make you feel safe and accepted. Like a part of the family. Look, there's a whole process. First you were identified as a potential recruit." His good eye softens. "Then it was my job to persuade you. Successful leaders inherently know how to manipulate through extreme displays of affection so recruits will be receptive to their core beliefs."

"You identified me? You *love bombed* me?" Eva's reeling,

but the term floats to the surface all the same. She listened to enough true crime podcasts on the road to know the steps an abuser would take to gaslight his target. "You're sick. This is *sick*."

"I know," Zach whispers. "I know and I'm sorry."

"Too little too late," she says, regret coiling in her stomach. "Why? Why did you take me to the house in Little Moose? If you were afraid Abner would come, why would you take me there?"

"I was trying to protect you. It would have been perfectly safe if you'd stayed out of sight."

"Don't make this my fault. I'm here because of *you*."

"I know. It's all my fault." Zach says all in a rush: "I don't know how much you've pieced together, but my father has a massive following. The Family of Zion is much more than whatever you think it is—it's a way of living, an ideology that appeals to people all over the world."

"I don't understand." Eva pulls away, and this time Zach lets her go. She studies his face, searching his eyes for answers.

"It's a revolution, Eva. They want civil war. And not just here. They don't like the way the world is going, and they've been building toward revolution for decades. They're tech savvy and have learned how to use the internet to finance, network, coordinate, and recruit. They're also heavily invested in social media platforms and online forums. And in order to make their message mainstream—to reach more people and turn them toward the cause—they need—"

"People like me." All at once, Eva can see how appealing she must have seemed to Abner and his acolytes: a popular, pretty, girl next door with followers from all over the planet. She—and Eva Explores—attracted outdoorsy types who love their country and the freedom of wide-open spaces. The sort of people who live off the grid and who prize liberty and autonomy, free will and independence. There were definite crossover points that could be exploited. "But I'm—"

"Not like that. I know. As I got to know you, I understood pretty quickly that it wouldn't work. I should have just backed away." Zach brings his hands up to touch her cheeks, briefly, before balling them into fists at his side. "But then I fell in love."

At this, Eva laughs. She takes another step back, putting her bad leg down so she can stand unsupported. On her own. "I don't want to hear it," she says through gritted teeth.

"I know. But I was under so much pressure to deliver . . ."

"Am I supposed to feel sorry for you?"

"Getting away was *your* idea," Zach snaps back. "You were feeling suffocated by your mom, and when you brought up going away for a day or two, everything just fell into place."

Did she? Did Eva bring up the idea of sneaking away? She can't remember.

"I planned to lay low in Little Moose until everything settled down. I just wanted to keep you safe, Eva. The cabin seemed like the best bet. I figured we could work it out after we were free and clear."

"You *kidnapped* me. I would have never gone with you if I knew the truth."

Zach runs a hand over his face and flinches as he disturbs various wounds. "It wasn't supposed to be like this. We were going to run away together. We could have *both* escaped . . ."

"You *lied* to me." Eva is shaking with outrage and grief. "If you would have just told me, if you would have trusted me enough to—"

"I know, Eva. You're right. You're right about everything."

When he tugs her into his arms, Eva doesn't push him away.

She wants to—she doesn't trust him or love him or even *like* him—but he's all that she's got right now. For just a moment she clings to him, pressing her head into his chest and wishing that they could rewind the clock.

"Look, there's so much more I could tell you, but we're out of time. I need you to just lay low for a couple of days. The Uprising is tomorrow. Do whatever Rachel tells you to do. Stay out of the way and—"

"The Uprising?" Eva murmurs into his shirt, her mind snagging the word. "What's the Uprising?"

"The beginning of the end."

"You can't be serious." Eva tilts her head back to study his face, but his features are carefully blank.

"I don't want to scare you, Eva, but everything is going to change. Here—at the Gates—they're just the tip of the spear. When they begin the Uprising, there are regiments all over the country that are poised to follow suit. It's a country-wide coup, a chance to sow chaos and shift the balance of power. People will die, Eva."

Eva can feel herself shutting down. It's more than she can handle or even begin to understand. Rachel was right; they're planning for war.

"Every book burning and protest, every alt-right rally and rumble of unrest has been leading to this. It's unstoppable. But it's also the perfect opportunity for us to escape. The cabin in Little Moose—"

"Was a place to hide out," Eva cuts in, putting the pieces together. "But your father found us instead."

"Please, just hang tight for a few more days. When everything explodes, I'll come for you and—"

"What do you mean, 'when everything explodes'? You're just going to let that happen? And you expect me to 'hang tight,' knowing that . . . that your father is planning an *uprising*?"

Zach pushes her hair out of her eyes and tucks a strand behind her ear. "There's nothing we can do, Eva."

She searches his eyes for the man she thought she fell in love with. He's in there somewhere, quiet and kind, thoughtful and serious. But there's nothing left for her here if Zach has already given up. Eva's heart is torn for the agony of his broken face, the thrashing he must have endured for taking her to Little Moose. She understands that her very presence—as anything less than an enthusiastic ally—was an extraordinary threat to Abner and the plans of the Family of Zion. Zach risked *everything* to be with her, even if what they shared was nothing more than a pitiful facsimile of love. A part of Eva wishes that she could comfort him.

But she's not about to give up.

"Okay," she tells Zach, pretending to soften. She doesn't know exactly what the Uprising is yet, but it fills her with a quiet dread—and a steely resolve to *do* something. Anything. "I'll be quiet. I'll wait for you." What she wants to do is scream: *What about my mother? What about the people of Landing? And Duluth and Manhattan and Leavenworth and Portland and every other beautiful place that I love?* But she doesn't. She forces a taut smile, and Zach presses his lips to hers, briefly.

"Go," he says. "Head to the amphitheater and the Gathering. Tell Rachel that you fell. I'll come for you."

Eva turns, picks her crutches up from the forest floor, and begins to make her way back to the trail. She doesn't look over her shoulder.

She doesn't say, *Don't bother. I'll already be gone.*

PART III

The Sutton Girls

INSTAGRAM POST #1001

Not going to lie, friends, it has been a
RIDE. Thank you for joining us as Eva
Explored (see what we did there?) so
much of this beautiful country we call
home. Cue the "Star Spangled Banner,"
"America the Beautiful," and let's throw
in some "Born in the U.S.A.," because
who doesn't love a little Springsteen?
To say that we have loved these years
on the road would be an obscene
understatement, but it's time for us
to put Sebastian out to pasture (on
blocks) and reenter the so-called real
world (do we have to?). Thank you
for following our journey, for keeping
Sebastian's tank—and our bellies—
full, and for taking our suggestions
to get outside and connect with this
beautiful world seriously. We have
loved your stunning pictures, generous
tags, and heartfelt stories about your
own experiences on the road and in
the wild. The adventure is far from
over. It's your turn now.

#findingroots #yourturnnow
#evaexplores #evaexplored

Always, ALWAYS, take the long way
back,
xoxo—Charlie & Eva

[IMAGE CONTENTS: Charlie and Eva
sit on the fold-out stairs of Sebastian,
their silver Airstream trailer. Charlie
is on the top step and Eva is two steps
below, nestled between her mother's
blue jean–clad legs. Eva's head rests on
her mother's knee, her long curls
half-obscuring her face. Both women
are dressed in colorful Nordic sweaters
and heavy boots, and snow blankets the
ground in front of the trailer. Charlie is
leaning down to kiss the crown of her
daughter's head.]

Comments
Newest First

shellyblake Is it true? Is Evangeline Sutton missing?

ellawatts Praying for you Eva!!!
    shellyblake @ellawatts So it's true then.
    ellawatts @shellyblake I don't know. But prayer
never hurts!

shellyblake @ellawatts Cuz thoughts and prayers are the best we can do.

ellawatts @shellyblake Not picking a fight here! Praying for you, too!!!

betty.lost.cause I read the entire thing is a publicity stunt. It's STAGED, everyone. Wake up! Stop believing everything you read! Charlie and Eva are attention whores.

> **ellawatts** @betty.lost.cause Please don't spread rumors . . .
>
> **betty.lost.cause** @ellawatts Praying for me too?
>
> **shannagirl** @betty.lost.cause For real? Oh, man, that's low . . .

sandradee32 We love you Charlie and Eva! We miss you! #thelongwayback #comeback #evaexplores

zoefit07 Why are they reporting her name? Isn't Eva a minor? I thought there was a law about that or something . . .

> **betty.lost.cause** @zoefit See? Publicity stunt.
>
> **marinscott** @zoefit07 They have to report the names and publish pictures of missing minors. Duh. How else would people know who to look for?
>
> **zoefit07** @marinscott Eva's young and pretty and white. 'Nuf said.
>
> **marinscott** @zoefit07 Is she? I think she looks Latina. Maybe Middle Eastern? At least partly . . .
>
> **betty.lost.cause** @marinscott She's clearly Jewish.

tristan.speaks I love them so much. Their account was

like my whole life for a while. #livingvicariously If Eva is
really missing, that's so so so sad.

marinscott Is there something we can do? I mean,
to raise awareness or something?

>   **marinscott** Never mind. Just saw it on the news—
>   and I'm on the East Coast. The whole world is about
>   to know.

CHAPTER 17

CHARLIE

MONDAY

Charlie wakes at dawn in the cavernous quiet of an empty house and stares at the ceiling of her lakeside bedroom. It's not lost on her that the water-stained walls of the Landing jail could have been the first thing she saw this morning, and she feels a twinge of gratitude that she's in her own bed. She's also thankful for seven hours of drug-induced sleep, and the fact that Agent Turner promised he'd meet her at eight. His reluctant, almost grudging agreement to let her help is the only reason she took the prescription and allowed herself to rest in the first place.

"I know my daughter," Charlie had said the night before—after Ms. Alvarez left the temporary command center. Eva's note had upended everything. *Gone for a few days, but I'll be back early next week.* That tiny, one-line PS changed the entire investigation, and coupled with Eva's essays and her effervescent gushing about her new boyfriend, it was enough to shift Charlie from the prime suspect in a suspicious missing person case to a victim herself. The pieces were starting to fit, but none of it squared with Charlie. "Something's not right here."

"Face it," Detective James sighed, putting his fists on his hips, "Eva's a runaway. She took off with her lover. It's a common occurrence, Ms. Sutton."

"She wouldn't do this. I'm sure of it." Charlie sounded insistent, but she wasn't so convinced anymore. "Okay, maybe she *would*. Maybe she *did*. But something is still wrong."

"Maybe you need to rethink this *disappearance*." Detective James began sweeping the papers strewn across the folding table into a neat pile. Thwacking the stack against the tabletop, he straightened the edges and then tucked them all back into the file folder. "The note says: 'Back soon.' Maybe she just doesn't want to talk to you right now."

His words had stung. Many of the essays had stung. Charlie wanted nothing more than to have a heart-to-heart with Eva so she could determine where to draw the line between Eva's true feelings and typical teenage angst. But those conversations were for another day. First they had to find her. "Fine," Charlie said, swallowing all her quick retorts. "Why would she turn off location services on her phone?"

"You're very persistent."

Charlie stifled the urge to scream. "Yes, you're right. She hid things from me. But something is still wrong. I *know* Eva—I know she's in trouble. What about the life raft? You said someone slashed it with a knife. Why?"

"Seems like you don't know your daughter very well, Ms. Sutton," he said, ignoring her questions.

Charlie felt something in her chest ignite. "Are you a father, Detective James? Have you ever parented a teenager through the chaos of hormones or helped them navigate the gap between childhood and being a full-fledged grown-up? There's no road map, no instruction manual. We are *all* capable of doing something so completely unexpected and out of character that the people closest to us would never believe it. So if you're expecting my seventeen-year-old to act rationally in a situation that we clearly can't begin to fully understand, I think *you're* being completely irrational."

"Charlie, let me assure you, this case is far from closed." Agent Turner had jumped into the fray, ignoring a sideways glance from Detective James. "Eva is a minor and we don't know who she's with. Boyfriend or not, there are suspicious details surrounding her disappearance."

"Even if she's a runaway?" Charlie was still sizzling from her tirade, but Agent Turner's kind nod helped.

"Thank you," she said at the exact moment Detective James headed for the door and called over his shoulder, "I'm going to let you take the lead on this one, Turner."

When the detective had stalked out of the room, Charlie turned to the FBI agent. "Can he do that? Can he just abandon this case because he doesn't like how it's turning out?"

"He's not abandoning the case. He's just frustrated," Agent Turner said. "Cases like this are hard on everyone. No one wants Eva to be hurt, or worse. But this," he held up the binder, "definitely changes things. Some of the urgency is gone."

"Not for me."

"Which is just one of the reasons we're not done here." Agent Turner grabbed the file folder and set it on top of the binder already in his arms. "I'll canvas tomorrow. Talk to this Lennon girl—the server at Mugs. And I'll chat up some of her teachers and friends. Someone knows something about this secret boyfriend."

"I'm going with you."

"That's not how this works."

"But I know my daughter." Charlie didn't want to beg, but she would if she had to. "Maybe I'll be able to see things that you can't. Spot inconsistencies or something out of the ordinary."

Agent Turner crossed his arms and narrowed his eyes slightly.

"Maybe people will open up to me more willingly than they would to you. I mean . . ." Charlie indicated herself, her worn baseball cap and faded sweater, and then arched an eyebrow at his smart navy blazer and paisley tie. They were a contradiction in terms. "We're talking about Landing, Minnesota, here. Know your audience and all that."

Agent Turner considered her for a long moment. "You can ride along," he said eventually. "Time is of the essence, and if you can open doors that I can't, so be it. But if I catch so much as a whiff of trouble, I'll drop you on the sidewalk so fast your head will spin. This is a fact-finding mission. Period."

Now, Charlie all but jumps out of bed, eager to see Agent Turner and get started. For the first time since Eva went missing, she feels like she has a purpose, and she showers quickly, dresses casually, and brews a pot of coffee as if her life depends on it. Scout scampers from room to room, catching her energy, and barking occasionally when Charlie drops her hairbrush or trips over her own two feet.

"We're going to find her," Charlie tells him as she scoops kibble into his bowl. "Our girl is going to come home."

By the time there's a knock on the door, Charlie is well-caffeinated and practically bubbling with ideas.

"I did some checking," she says, opening the door with one of Sophie's leftover blueberry biscuits in her hand. "Lennon graduated from Landing High a couple of years ago and works at Mugs while studying accounting online."

"Hello to you too." Agent Turner steps into the house and follows Eva to the kitchen, pausing to give Scout a scratch behind the ears.

"So if we head to the high school now," Charlie continues, checking her watch, "we can talk to some kids before the tardy bell at eight thirty. That feels less intimidating. Nonthreatening is the way to go—don't you think?"

"Maybe, but—"

"And after that, around midmorning or so, we could head to Mugs and interview Lennon. She'll probably have a break around then—"

"Charlotte." Agent Turner puts up a hand to stop her, but his tone has already done the trick. "Slow down. How do you know these things about Lennon? Were you up all night?"

"First of all, no." Remembering her manners, Charlie grabs the plate of biscuits from the counter and holds it out to Agent Turner. He takes one. "I slept nearly seven hours last night. As for how I know those things, haven't you ever Facebook-stalked someone, Agent Turner? And don't forget that Eva works at Mugs, too. I know the general schedule."

"Please, Charlotte. Call me Jude."

"Then I'm Charlie."

Jude takes a bite out of his biscuit and studies her. After a moment, he says: "Facebook? I thought you were more of an Instagram girl."

"Facebook has more personal information. Where you live, who your relatives are, all the places you've gone to school . . . Lennon's profile was wide open."

Jude tilts his head toward her in a gesture of respect. "Have you ever considered a job as a research analyst?"

Charlie takes a bite of her biscuit and asks, around a full mouth, "Are you flirting with me?"

"No." Jude's laugh is quick and resonant. "Absolutely not. I'm just thankful that the tenor of this investigation has changed. I'd be lying if I didn't say that today feels very different than yesterday. And I think if she's out there, we're going to find her."

• • • •

After their impromptu breakfast, Charlie walks the path through the trees to Sophie's house and Jude picks her up there. While a cop is no longer stationed on her driveway, the flock of reporters at the end of the lane remains, and Jude takes the long way into town, bypassing the news vans.

Charlie holds last year's Landing High yearbook (a part of the welcome package when Eva enrolled in December) on her lap with the names and pictures of certain kids circled in permanent marker. She was indiscriminate in casting her net, marking anyone who she could even vaguely remember Eva mentioning. A boy named Luke in her science class. A girl called James. She flagged Piper, and then found a picture of her surrounded by other girls, so she looked them up and circled all of them, too.

But in the end, Jude disregards all of Charlie's half-baked suggestions and careful "research." Instead, he drives straight to Mugs.

"We know Lennon has information," he explains. "So that's where we begin. Always go with the sure thing, Charlie."

At quarter after eight on a Monday morning, Mugs is nearly empty. The before-work-and-school crowd has dissipated, and the Bible studies, mom groups, and casual coffee dates won't start to cluster around tables until closer to ten. In the entryway, Jude leans in to tell Charlie to let him take the lead, but his gentle warning is unnecessary. The memory of the bustling cafe and the newscaster trying to thrust a microphone in her face less than twenty-four hours ago is more than enough to silence Charlie. She follows him into the dining room, just happy to observe.

"Lennon Ahoka?" Jude walks right up to a strikingly pretty native girl with a waterfall of dark hair. She's clearing a table but glances up as he approaches.

The corner of Charlie's mouth lifts as she realizes that Agent Turner did his homework, too. Of course he did.

"Yes?" The girl's face is friendly and open, but her smile wavers a little when she sees who called her name. Jude is wearing dark jeans and a cream-colored sweater today, but he still exudes a casual authority. There's absolutely no mistaking that he's law enforcement, or the fact that there's a gun holster low on his hips. "How can I help you?"

"Agent Jude Turner of the FBI," he says, offering his hand with a disarming, close-lipped smile that somehow conveys both friendliness and gravitas. "I'm sure you've heard about Evangeline Sutton's disappearance."

Lennon's eyes cloud over, but it's nothing more complicated than grief. "Is she okay?"

"We sure hope so," Jude says with a nod. "This is Eva's mom, Charlotte."

"Charlie," she says, stepping forward and shaking Lennon's hand. It's trembling just a little. "Thanks for being a friend to Eva. I hear you're rather close."

"Work friends." Lennon lifts one shoulder. "We're kind of a weird breed. Besties when we're on the clock, but I didn't ever see her outside of work. I mean, we meant to, it just never happened."

Charlie can't help but love this kind, sincere girl. She's warmed by Lennon's obvious affection for her daughter, and wishes that Eva would have pursued friendship with her instead of a romantic entanglement with a stranger.

"It's come to our attention that Eva has a boyfriend," Agent Turner jumps right in. "Someone that Charlie didn't know about."

"Peter told me you'd probably reach out. But there's not much I can tell you." Lennon shoots Charlie an apologetic look.

"I only saw him once. And Eva didn't really talk about him. I mean, not directly. Just casual things like, 'I'm seeing him tonight.' You know how it is."

Charlie doesn't really know how it is, but she gives Lennon a reassuring half smile all the same. "Do you know his name?"

"Just his first: Zach."

"What does he look like?"

"Well," Lennon plays with her apron strings, twisting one around her index finger and then letting it unfurl. "It was a long time ago. But he was cute enough. Blond, kinda tall. Bit of a Prince Charming type—generic-looking. He seemed older to me."

"How much older?" Jude scribbles notes on a pad that he's pulled from his pocket.

"Twenties?"

Charlie's heart stops and then thuds painfully back to life. Her seventeen-year-old was seeing a twentysomething? Eva—sweet, inexperienced Evangeline Rose—was dating an older man? "Early twenties or late?" Charlie almost chokes on the question.

But Lennon just shrugs. "I don't know. But he's definitely out of high school. He has a job. Something to do with computers or the internet or something."

"This is good, Lennon. You're doing great." Jude exudes a professional warmth that clearly puts Lennon at ease. "Did you catch the name of the company he works for? Even the description of a logo would help."

"He was just here that once. He sat in a corner booth and typed on a computer. If there was a logo on his bag or something, I didn't see it. I wasn't really paying attention."

"Does Zach live in Landing?" Jude asks as he continues to write.

"No, he drove up from Duluth, I think."

"That's a long way to come for a cup of coffee." Charlie knows she sounds shrill, but she can't help it. Why on earth would a twentysomething drive all the way up the coast from Duluth for lunch at Mugs? It's a nondescript, small-town diner. There's nothing in Landing to draw Zach here. Except Eva, apparently.

Jude ignores Charlie's little outburst. "Did Eva and Zach see each other often?"

"Oh, almost every day," Lennon says. "He was here all the time. Well, he never came into Mugs, but he picked her up after shifts a lot."

"Do you know where they would go? I'm guessing not back to Duluth . . ."

Lennon's eyes fill suddenly with tears that threaten to spill down her lovely cheeks. "I don't know. I'm really sorry. I wish I could tell you more."

"You've told us a lot," Jude assures her. "Thank you. And I'm sorry to upset you, but I have just a few more questions if you're up for it."

Lennon takes a shuddering breath, pulls out a nearby chair, and sinks into it. "Okay if I sit down? I've been up since five."

"Of course." Jude slides into a chair across from her and rests his forearms against the edge of the table. "We're almost done here. Just trying to get a better understanding of Eva's relationship with Zach."

"Do you think he may have something to do with her disappearance?" Lennon seems almost afraid of the answer.

"We're simply gathering information at this point."

He asks her several more questions, but Charlie has kind of stopped listening. It's obvious to her that Lennon doesn't know anything truly valuable about Zach, and also crystal clear that Zach worked hard to keep his identity a secret. Why would he never step foot in Mugs again after his first meeting with Eva? Why would he drive over an hour—each way!—to see her on an almost daily basis? What was a twentysomething doing with a seventeen-year-old high school senior? It makes her blood boil.

"Thank you for your time." Jude pushes back his chair to stand, and Charlie tips back into reality.

"Yes, thank you, Lennon." Charlie reaches for another hand-shake, but in the end she can't help herself—she wraps Lennon in a hug. The girl is close in size to Eva and smells of griddle breakfasts and strawberry shampoo. Charlie breathes her in for just a moment before pulling away.

On the sidewalk in front of Mugs, Charlie paces back and forth while Jude taps something into his cell phone. Their visit with Lennon didn't unearth the sort of groundbreaking intel Charlie hoped it would, and she's already whirring with the desire to move on. Maybe the school will provide more insight. Maybe Jude can shake down those high school kids until some-one remembers something relevant.

"Landing High next?" Charlie asks, hoping to hurry him along.

"Nope."

"But I thought—"

"We have a lead, so we'll follow it."

"We do?" Charlie can't think of a single pertinent scrap of in-formation they obtained from Lennon—at least, not something that brings them any closer to finding Eva.

Jude nods. "Mugs doesn't have security cameras, but Len-non said that employees have to park in the alley or around the corner. Did Eva usually drive your truck to work?"

"Yes."

"And is it a dark gray extended cab?"

"I don't get what my truck has to do with anything."

Jude walks to the corner and motions for her to follow. Mugs is at the very end of Landing's pint-sized main street, and across from the wide, bay windows of the side of the cafe, stand a row of neat houses. They're boxy and quaint—Charlie once heard that the city gives the owners an annual stipend to plant tulips and generally keep their yards tidy. But before Charlie can ask what the homes have to do with anything, Jude steps off the curb and begins to cross the street.

"Where are we going?"

"Canvassing. Lennon said that because Eva came to work after school, there was rarely room for her to park in the alley. That leaves the street. If Eva parked here, it's possible that one or more of these houses have motion-activated security devices."

Charlie realizes that she missed a lot of pertinent information when she zoned out. She jogs to catch up. "You think someone's personal camera may have caught Eva and Zach?"

"Maybe. Maybe not. If we're really lucky, we'll get some footage of his car. Make, model, even a partial license plate— that would be a coup. The cameras don't have great range, but these houses are practically on the sidewalk."

He's right, the front lawns are postcard-sized, and Charlie feels a surge of hope. It's sadly short-lived. No one is home behind the first door they knock on. But as far as Jude and Charlie can tell, the homeowners don't have a security camera anyway. The second house definitely doesn't have a camera, and neither does the third. By the time they reach the fourth house, Charlie is convinced that any data they might collect wouldn't be helpful anyway. The house is too far down the block, too far away from Mugs. Surely Eva didn't park this far away.

When an elderly woman answers the door, Charlie's hope is extinguished entirely.

"I do have cameras!" the lady exclaims when Jude explains

their presence on her front porch. "Two of them. My son set them up for me."

Jude fills her in on Eva's disappearance and their desire for any footage that might feature her.

"I've seen that poor girl on the news. Good thing my plan saves video for sixty days," the woman tells them proudly. "I'd be happy to help in any way I can."

Charlie wanders away while Jude gives her a business card with his email address and careful instructions on how to share the data. It feels like a long shot to Charlie, especially as she doubts that the elderly woman—sweet as she is—will be technologically savvy enough to be of any help. Jude had told Charlie that a search warrant could be submitted to the security company if the homeowners were uncooperative, but that could take days. Weeks? They don't have that kind of time.

Charlie falls into step beside Jude as they make their way back to his truck, but she struggles to match his long stride. He's clearly energized, satisfied with the progress they've made. Charlie doesn't feel the same way.

"You okay?" he asks, pausing to let her catch up.

"I thought we'd learn something," Charlie admits.

"We learned a lot. It's been a good morning."

Charlie stops entirely and crosses her arms over her chest. "Has it? Because it feels like we're no closer to Eva than we were last night. I just can't believe this is it."

Jude gives her a strange look. "This isn't *it*, Charlie. The evidence response team has gone over your boat with a fine-toothed comb and are now examining everything they collected. While you and I are out here, my computer forensic experts are trying to crack Eva's cloud password so we can gain access to her school computer. And just because we don't have her phone doesn't mean that we can't obtain her records. We've already submitted an affidavit to the US attorney's office for a search warrant. There's an entire team working to—"

"I'm sorry," Charlie interrupts, rubbing her face with her hands. "I know. I know you're doing your job. I don't doubt that you're very good at it. It's just . . ."

"Hard." Jude sighs. "It's really hard. Look, I think you should talk with our victim specialist. She's an amazing woman who I think could be very helpful as we navigate this situation. She should be here this afternoon; I'll send her straight over."

Charlie wants to protest, but she's exhausted. Instead, she starts to nod, but when Jude doesn't say anything more, she looks up and realizes he's not paying attention to her anyway. His eyes are glued to his phone.

"She sent it," he says, a thread of disbelief in his voice. "Mrs. Henderson from down the street. She sent the security camera footage."

There's a beat of silence as Charlie takes in the news. She wants to be even-keeled, realistic, but hope inflates in her chest anyway. "Bravo, Mrs. Henderson!" She can't stop the grin that spreads across her face. "Let's see what's on it."

SIT TIGHT PODCAST
TRANSCRIPT EPISODE 302

What happened to Evangeline Sutton?

Jane: Good morning and welcome to *Sit Tight*, the podcast where we circle up to chat about all the latest gossip and the shifts that are shaping the cultural zeitgeist. I'm your host Jane Castle—

Chelle: And I'm Chelle Valdez. Together we explore the ins and outs of everything from Bitcoin to the latest TikTok trend so you can decide when to dive in—

Jane: And when to sit tight. This morning we're stepping out on a bit of a limb to talk about a developing story. You'll remember that last month we dug deep into the world of social media and, specifically, the impact it has on kids.

Chelle: Not gonna lie, I was stunned by some of the research we unearthed. In case you need a refresher, we focused on a study released by the American Academy of Pediatrics.

Jane: Basically, it said that tweens and teens who use social media are at risk for everything from cyberbullying and grooming to internet addiction and sleep deprivation. As if we didn't already know that.

Chelle: Those episodes rocked my world and had a huge impact on the way that my husband and I plan to introduce social media to our own tweens.

Jane: Me too, Chelle. That's probably why the news of Evangeline Sutton's disappearance hit me so hard.

Chelle: If you don't know who Evangeline Sutton is, you must be a new listener to the show. Welcome. We're so glad you're here! But if you've been with us for any amount of time, you know that we're huge fans of an Instagram account called Eva Explores. We've been following them since pretty much day one and have long considered Charlie and Eva's brand of social media fame the gold standard of authenticity, connection, and inspiration. Because isn't that what social media at its best is designed to be?

Jane: I certainly think so. I'm an optimist, so stick with me here, but beneath the corporate greed and behind-the-scenes string-pulling that happens on all social media platforms, I have to believe that the initial driving force was a desire to share ideas, create beauty, and build bridges between people. We long for togetherness, and social media has the power to bring us together.

Chelle: In a perfect world. And, honestly? Charlie and Eva Sutton were my perfect world!

Jane: Seriously, I'm so shook about this. I thought they were the ones to look up to, the success story that got every aspect of this Instagram-fame thing right. But in case you haven't heard the news, it's being reported that Evangeline Sutton is missing. Here's what we know. After two and a half years on the road and active online, Charlie and Eva stopped posting on Eva Explores. The details of their departure from Instagram are spotty, to say the least, but many of their fans—us included—have waited with bated breath for what we hoped would be their triumphant return.

Chelle: Instead, it appears Eva went missing on Saturday afternoon from a boat in the middle of Lake Superior. Our hearts are broken for her family and friends—and even for her fans. There's not much else to report at this time, but her sudden disappearance and the months of silence on Eva Explores has us asking: What went wrong?

Jane: I can't help but believe that this news is connected to her online fame. How could it not be?

Chelle: Let's consider the possibilities. There are four as far as I can tell. One, Eva harmed herself. Jane, I can see the look on your face and I agree wholeheartedly: it's too awful to think about. But we don't know what happened behind closed doors. We don't know what she endured or how she may have suffered to present a picture-perfect life to all her fans.

Jane: Oh, it just guts me. Okay, two?

Chelle: Two, Charlie harmed Eva. To me, this is probably the worst. A mother is supposed to love and protect, to give her very *life* for her children. It's hard for me to imagine the Charlie we believed we knew, doing something to Eva, but again—

Jane: We don't know what happens behind closed doors. Ugh. I can't stand it. Okay, I'm going to hazard a guess about the third possibility. *Someone else* harmed Eva. Someone we don't know, but who obviously knows her. Maybe an unhinged fan? A stalker? Or someone who hated the Sutton girls for reasons we may never learn.

Chelle: This theory seems the most implausible to me. A stranger? Really? In the middle of the lake? We know that the coast guard was sent to an undetermined location and returned with Charlie. Alone. If someone wanted to get their hands on Eva, it would have been a much simpler endeavor on land.

Jane: I agree. And you know what that means: life wasn't as perfect as it seemed for the Sutton girls.

Chelle: I think you're right, Jane. Of course, option four is that this could all be a terrible accident, but that doesn't seem very likely either. Eva was an accomplished young woman, a world-class hiker, biker, swimmer, and adventurer. It seems far-fetched to imagine a sunny excursion could have ended in such unexpected tragedy. And yes, we know that it was warm and beautiful off the coast of Landing, Minnesota, on Saturday.

Jane: I'm simply wrecked by this. I feel like a little girl who has just learned that her favorite fairy tale is nothing but lies and broken promises. I believed that we could be involved and engaged in social media in a healthy way—and I used Charlie and Eva Sutton as shining examples of how it could be done.

Chelle: I suppose nothing is quite as it seems. And no matter what happened—no matter what we learn in the coming days and weeks—I have no doubt that Charlie Sutton will never forgive herself for exposing her daughter to the world in such a questionable way. I can't decide if we should feel sorry for her or be furious with her. What do you think? Weigh in by checking out our Instagram stories—we'll be sharing some of your responses. Thanks for joining us on *Sit Tight*. And stay tuned for more after this word from our sponsors.

CHAPTER 18

EVA

MONDAY

Eva makes it to the amphitheater just as everyone is beginning to disperse. The Gathering wasn't long, but it was clearly invigorating. As she turns the final corner on the path, she can see the entirety of the Family of Zion rapt in celebration. That's really the only word for the way they hug one another, sway in ecstasy, and laugh as if the world is a truly beautiful, miraculous place. If she didn't know any better, Eva would believe that she had stumbled upon a wedding reception or milestone birthday party—not the final rally before a potentially catastrophic uprising. If she didn't know any better, she'd be tempted to hurry down the slope and join them in their revelry.

"Where were you?" Rachel's sudden appearance at Eva's elbow makes her jump.

"You scared me," she accuses, but Rachel's having none of it.

"You were supposed to sit in the last row so I could keep an eye on you."

Eva marks the low, wooden benches that surround the natural amphitheater. The ground slopes away rapidly, making it possible to see every corner from the platform at the bottom of the pitch. There's no way she can claim to have been there all along, hidden among the crowd.

"I fell," she says instead, using Zach's homemade excuse. It's paper-thin, but it's the best she's got.

"And it took you half an hour to get back up?" Rachel's gaze darts to Eva's injured leg, but it's hidden beneath her long dress. Her brows knit together. "Do I need to get Tamar?"

Is Rachel *concerned* about her? "I'm okay," Eva says, but before she can offer anything more, Rachel cuts in.

"I'm supposed to be looking out for you. If you've done something, it's on *my* head."

Eva feels a burst of pity for the young woman before her. Rachel is in a truly impossible situation. She didn't choose this any more than Zach did. "It's fine," Eva says, resisting the urge to lay a calming hand on Rachel's arm. "I fell, and when the shouting started, I wasn't in much of a hurry to get back up."

Rachel stares at her for a long moment, obviously trying to discern if Eva is telling the truth. But then someone bumps into her from behind, and Rachel spins around to see a young man in fatigues give her a sheepish smile.

"Sorry, Rach," he says, a shallow dimple making his mischievous grin irresistible. "You okay?"

Eva watches her blond warden melt before her eyes. Rachel softens so quickly, so immediately, it's almost embarrassing. But the boy either doesn't notice the change in her or doesn't care. It seems he likes it.

"I'm fine," Rachel says, giving him her own warm smile. "It's crowded, and people are excited."

It's true. As the Family of Zion begins to leave the way they came, there's a bottleneck at the mouth of the trail where the three of them make an unlikely cohort. The leader's daughter, the young conscript, and the outsider. People give them searching looks as they pass, and Eva can tell from their loaded glances that they know exactly who she is. She wonders what Abner told them. Is she a guest like he asserts? Or a prisoner? Eva doesn't believe for a second that anyone here would actually *kill* her, but by the volume of weaponry and ammunition displayed at what amounted to a riotous family meeting is alarming. She backs away from the trailhead and the press of people, and Rachel and the soldier follow.

"Are you going . . . ?" Rachel leaves the question open-ended.

Eva realizes it's because she's there. She's not supposed to know about the Uprising, the final checkmate in a game the rest of the world doesn't even know it's playing. So she pulls away from Rachel and the man a little more, pretending to be absorbed in watching the Gathering disband.

"I am," he admits, and Eva can feel his eyes on her like a brand. She doesn't so much as blink, and he goes on. "But don't worry about me. I've trained for this. I know what I'm doing."

"I know you do." It's practically a whisper, but Eva can still hear it. She can also hear when Rachel takes a shuddering breath. Are they together? Is this boy Rachel's *betrothed*? It's strange to even think such a word, but somehow it's the right one here. Rachel goes on, "I just wish you didn't have to. Let me talk to my dad. He'll listen to—"

"No. We get one shot at this, Rach. I want to be there. And I don't want to waste any time with your father, asking him about reassignment. I want to ask him for—"

You. Eva can practically taste the sweetness of the word in the air, but the soldier doesn't say it. She feels like she's gone through the veil and emerged in another time—an era when a woman's father had to be consulted before she could, what? date?—but the cell phone that suddenly trills in the hushed forest glade is decidedly modern. Eva almost salivates at the sound, and when the boy pulls an iPhone from his pocket, it's all she can do not to lunge across the space between them and rip it from his hands. She's *this close* to civilization, to a single call that could make all of this madness stop.

"John here," he says, accepting the call and stepping away from Rachel.

Eva watches him hungrily, wondering if she could slip the device from his pocket when he's not looking. Speculating about whether or not it has a passcode and if she could find a way to crack it. Then Eva realizes that John has coverage out in the middle of nowhere. How?

She must have voiced the question because Rachel snorts a short laugh. "We're not complete yokels," she says. "We may be completely off the grid, but our solar field keeps us up and running twenty-four seven, three sixty-five. We even have our own mobile cell tower. Don't look so surprised."

"You're not giving away all our secrets, are you, Rachel?"

Abner must have walked up from the other side of the amphitheater. He appears behind them and lays his large hand at the base of Rachel's neck. It looks like a fatherly gesture, but Eva can see how Rachel tenses beneath his touch.

Licking her lips, Rachel turns to give Abner a bright smile as she tries to subtly slip out from beneath the weight of his palm. He just slides his fingers down to grip her shoulder. "Of course not," she says. "I can't stand her. I wouldn't give her the time of day if she asked."

"Is that so?" Abner stares at his daughter for a long moment. Then he shoots a glance to John, who is still talking furtively on his (lovely, magnificent, amazing) cell phone. Finally, Abner turns his attention to Eva. "She's our guest," he reminds Rachel as he studies Eva. "It's your duty to be kind to her."

"She has been," Eva assures him. She isn't particularly fond of Rachel, but the memory of Zach's ruined face is still fresh in her mind. She refuses to be the reason Rachel may be punished.

"If you say so." Abner seems unconvinced, but after a few seconds he lets his hand drop from Rachel's shoulder. "And how are you doing, Miss Sutton?"

"Not so great," she says, improvising as she goes. The truth is, her leg is feeling better. It's still stiff and throbbing, but the fire has gone out of it. She just doesn't want Abner to know that. Eva leans weakly on her crutches and gives him a brave half smile.

"Rachel, I want you to take Eva to the house and get her some ice and another dose of ibuprofen. We don't want her thinking we're completely heartless. And perhaps you could cut yourselves a slice of Anna's chocolate cake."

"I thought that was for tonight," Rachel says pointedly.

But Abner just laughs. "I've raised such a rule follower! Tell me, Daughter: Who is in charge here?"

"You." The word on Rachel's tongue sounds almost holy.

"And who just told you to cut the cake?"

"You."

"So I expect to be obeyed. We only live once, girl. Might as well have our cake and eat it, too." He pats her back, but it isn't a gentle tap. Rachel pitches forward and Abner laughs again. "Guess I'm feeling the power! It's flowing through my veins."

The thought of power—supernatural, sacred power like he implies—flowing through the veins of someone like Abner Brennan makes Eva feel delirious. He's handsome and charismatic and engaging, but he's the most dangerous person she's ever met. He's the beguiling glint of sunstone in the split second before the poisonous bite. He's immutable. Inevitable. She can't look away.

"Hello, Father."

Eva is startled by how John addresses Abner, but even more so when he strikes his fist against his chest and inclines his head in a sort of bow. Abner accepts the fealty with a nod and repeats the motion, a movement that looks as if he is stabbing himself in the heart. Perhaps this was the thump that sounded after Abner had cried, "No sacrifice too great!" She can't help but wonder if they mean those words very literally.

"Is John . . ." Eva starts to ask the question but trails off when she realizes that she probably won't get a straight answer anyway.

But Abner surprises her. "John is not my biological son, but I am the spiritual father of all who are adopted into the Family." He gives her a sly, sideways look. "You may call me Father if you'd like."

Eva's breath catches in her throat. By the way he's looking at her, she would swear that he *knows*. He knows that she never met her own father, that she grew up with no one but Charlie to call home. But of course, her life was online for the world to see. Her Eva Explores followers knew that she and Charlie were alone in the world, and Abner already admitted that he followed their journeys.

She doesn't know what to say, so she doesn't say anything at all. If she neither accepts nor rejects his offer, he can't take offense.

Abner gives her an almost imperceptible wink, apparently acknowledging her shrewd play. But Eva stares at her feet, pretending to be too shy to meet his gaze.

. . . .

The chocolate cake is thick, fudgy, and clearly not from a box mix. Eva tries not to moan at the first decadent bite and cuts her eyes to Rachel to see if she's being watched. She is. It's unnerving to have her every move observed and dissected, so she swallows carefully, sits back, and pretends to fuss with the bag of ice on her shin.

Eva's sitting in one of the ladder-back chairs at the enormous dining room table, leg propped on the bench beside her and an old plastic bag filled with ice melting all over her bandages. The wound has bled through a bit, and she worries that her stitches have torn. But she doesn't want Tamar to come back and mess with anything, so she hides the stain from Rachel—who's sitting with her own slice of cake at the far end of the table—and pulls down the hem of her long dress.

"It's really good," Eva says, giving in and taking another generous bite. "Did you make it?"

At first it doesn't seem like Rachel will answer, but then she sighs and says: "My older sister Anna did. She could open a bakery in New York City and there would be a line around the block just to get in."

"Why doesn't she?" Eva drags the tines of her fork through the whipped chocolate frosting and pretends not to care about the answer.

"She has an eighteen-month-old. And she's pregnant with her second. Anna's place is here."

Eva wants to ask how old Anna is—but Rachel keeps going.

"We *all* belong here. The work of the Family of Zion is more important than a bakery. It's more important than anything. Besides, when Anna bakes for us, she's answering a higher calling."

If she had all the time in the world, Eva would follow this rabbit trail for as long as Rachel indulged her, but getting lost in the weeds of Anna's bewildering life is not productive. Rachel's talking; maybe Eva can get her to talk about things that matter.

"Do you believe that?" she asks casually, catching Rachel's gaze and holding it. "Do you believe that being here is a higher calling?"

"Of course." Rachel doesn't even pause to think about it,

but her expression doesn't match her words. There's something wistful in her eyes.

"And that higher calling is to . . . what?"

Rachel pushes her cake back and forth across a chipped plate, then uses the back of her fork to pick up the crumbs. She licks it, and Eva realizes that the girl hasn't had a single real bite. Rachel has played with the cake—tasted a bit of frosting and collected the crumbs—but that's it. Is she punishing herself? Inflicting a sort of personal penance?

"We're called to restore this broken world," Rachel finally says, "by returning society to the common equity of moral law. We've strayed so far . . ."

It's obviously a talking point of sorts, something that has been drummed into Rachel's head for years. Common equity? Moral law? *Who's* strayed so far? Eva is fuzzy on the details. "I don't know what that means."

Rachel heaves a sigh, but she seems to be invested in the conversation now. In making Eva understand, or maybe exonerating herself through explanation. "It means our country—this land that was created to be a city on a hill—has become so corrupt, the only thing that could possibly fix it is a revolution."

"And that's the Uprising."

"What do you know about it?" Rachel's anger flashes bright, but Eva has planned for this.

"I overheard people talking about it after the Gathering." It's a perfectly plausible explanation and leaves Zach out of it entirely. She glances at the dining room floor and taps her good foot softly against the boards. Is he beneath her right now? Is there a vent in the room? Can he hear their conversation? If Rachel ever discovers that Zach found her, that they talked, Eva wonders what would become of him.

"So you meant it literally when you said the Family was getting ready for war," Eva continues.

"It's been a long time coming. And when it's over, we're going to remake the country into something beautiful and fair and just."

The words are out of Eva's mouth before she can consider the consequences. "This country—this world—is *already* beautiful and fair and just. It's also really messy and messed up, but I think that's part of life. You can't have light without the dark, the high without the low, the beauty without the brokenness."

"You sound like a false teacher," Rachel says, pushing her cake aside. "Tell me, Eva: Do you believe in God?"

"I do," Eva says, meaning it. "And I think he's the definition of love."

"Sounds like something a social justice warrior would say. What about the Old Testament? What about blood in the streets and the commands to wipe out entire wicked nations?"

Eva's spine tingles. "So we're a wicked nation."

"How can we expect God to bless something that has become so evil?" Rachel sounds sad. "Before the resurrection: judgment."

It hangs in the air between them, the specter of righteous judgment played out as a terrifying holy war at the command of a man like Abner Brennan. Clearly, it fills Rachel with something akin to pious resignation. To Eva, it sounds like hell itself.

"I don't think you get to make that call," she says quietly. She feels small and fragile in the face of such anger. Such hatred. Eva thinks about the thousands of miles she and Charlie crossed, taking in as much of the country as they possibly could. Over those years together, they talked about the fraught history of this nation they loved (the genocide that cleared the land for new settlers, the slavery that built it from the dirt up, the injustices and intentional silencing of marginalized voices) and wrestled with the magnificence of a place and a people that—at their best—kept learning and growing and trying. Mistakes were made. Over and over. Again and again. And yet, "It's not that simple."

"It is. People keep complicating things that are black and white. Well"—Rachel slides her chair back—"no more. *Everything* is about to change."

"I don't want to be here," Eva whispers.

"Yeah, tough luck with that. You're not going anywhere." Rachel grabs her plate and then comes around the table to take Eva's, too. It doesn't matter; Eva's lost her appetite anyway. "Everyone is focused on the Uprising, so you're kind of an afterthought right now. But there will come a point where you'll have to make a choice. If you're not for us, you're against us."

I'm against you, Eva wants to scream. *I'll always be against you, and nothing will ever convince me that this is the way to change* anything. But she holds her tongue, and when Rachel clatters the dishes in the sink and motions for Eva to follow, she does so obediently.

As they walk to the shed, Eva chances one last question: "What about Zach?"

"You love him, don't you?"

Eva doesn't know how to answer.

"Thing is, you don't even know him."

Eva's pretty sure that Rachel doesn't know her own brother very well either, but she arranges her face to look crestfallen. It isn't hard. Her logical next questions are: "Where is he? Is he okay?"

"He's a traitor," Rachel says simply, unlocking the padlock on the shed door. "He has to atone for betraying the Family. He was supposed to recruit you, not try to run away with you."

"But—"

"But nothing. Family first. Always."

When Rachel locks her in, Eva throws her crutches across the small room and stifles a scream. The shed feels more like a cage than ever, especially when school lets out for the afternoon and the children of the Family come tumbling out of the barn door. Eva can see them from the window, and she wishes she could be out there with them. She wishes she could scoop them up and take them away from this terrifying place and these hate-filled people, but when they come racing toward the big farmhouse, she can see that they're smiling. Grinning and laughing, actually happy as can be in this isolated little world that's been created for them. Is it a safe haven or a pressure cooker? Maybe both.

If school is out, dinner has to be fast approaching. Eva looks to her soup bowl and finds it sitting on the small, bedside table, the leftovers inside congealed. As she looks at the still life of the bowl, glass, and tarnished spoon, her mind catches on something. She wanders over and reaches for the spoon, not knowing what she wants to do with it until it's in her hand like a tool. A *tool*.

Hurrying to the door, Eva realizes that the hinges are on the inside. She can't unlock the padlock from within the room, and the windows are an implausible escape route, but if she can get the pins out of the door hinges, she'll be able to take the entire door off.

Eva's shaking with adrenaline, but she turns the utensil around and uses the handle end like a flathead screwdriver, wedging it between the pin and the hinge. The end is tapered, thin and worn smooth from years (decades?) of use. Still, Eva's afraid it won't fit, but tapping the spoon a few times with the heel of her hand forces it into the crack.

The pin is old and rusty—it obviously hasn't been removed or changed in ages—but after several minutes of knocking the spoon gently and easing the pin up and up, Eva has managed to expose an entire inch. It will take time, coaxing it out millimeter by millimeter, but it will work.

Eva doesn't even realize she's crying until the tears splash on her shaking hands. She's going to do it. Tonight, when everyone else is asleep, she's going to take the door off the shed and escape. Beyond the pristine farmhouse lawn is a seemingly infinite forest, a road that goes only God knows where, and a country that doesn't know what's about to hit it. But Eva doesn't care how far she has to go. She'll crawl back to Landing if she has to.

Everything depends on it.

EVA EXPLORES (#1 FAN PAGE)

We're your one-stop shop for all things Eva and Charlie. Merch (unauthorized but super cool), dishy details, and copycat adventures. #evasexplorers

Hey, #evasexplorers, Dara here. I know everyone is super upset about the news, and trust me, I get it. I can't eat or sleep. But now is not the time to turn against each other. There is no US or THEM. And isn't that what Eva Explores taught us all along? That there's room for everyone? Stop dividing into Team Charlie or Team Eva. We're all Team Sutton Girls. Besides, assumptions are mere speculation and nothing more. The truth will come out sooner or later, and we're going to need each other when it does.

I'm turning off comments on this post and encouraging you all to put up a green square in honor of these women we've grown to love. I can't imagine what they're going through right now. So let's show them we're here—that we are holding them in our hearts—by turning everyone's feeds green for our favorite adventurers. It can be a photo of the great outdoors or just a green wall in your house. Be creative and use the hashtags: #evasexplorers (as per usual) and #greenoutforEva

Thanks, Explorers. Fingers crossed that wherever Eva is, she's just decided to take the long way back. —Dara

PS—I know green ribbons are for mental health awareness, but it seems very fitting, no? I know Eva Explores was brilliant for my personal mental health, and the Sutton girls often talked about the healing properties of spending time in nature. Perhaps there will be even more to discuss when all is said and done.

[IMAGE CONTENTS: A green square. When you look closer, you can see that it's a close-up of thick, emerald-colored grass.]

CHAPTER 19

CHARLIE

MONDAY

When Jude turns onto Lakeside Road, he gives Charlie a sidelong glance and says, "Do you want me to drop you at the neighbor's house again?"

"No." Charlie's staring out the windshield, gaze loose and unfocused, but she can already see the herd of reporters at the end of her driveway. "Let them take a picture."

"Are you sure?"

"Doesn't really matter much, does it? They'll print what they want to print. Say what they want to say."

Jude opens his mouth as if to encourage her, but instead of arguing, he just lifts one shoulder. "Okay."

The morning has been a roller coaster of emotions, and Charlie is definitely on the descent. Sure they have some porch camera footage from a sweet old lady, but what good is that going to do? Charlie needs cold, hard facts. A promising lead. She's never been apart from Eva for so long, and she's starting to feel her daughter's absence like a missing limb.

Are they too close? Is that even possible? Charlie isn't the sort of mother who ever wanted to be her daughter's best friend, but is it her fault if it happened anyway? She loves her girl like a storm, an avalanche, a force of nature that cannot be held back. Her love is inevitable. And destructive? Did she push her daughter away with her constant need to pull her close?

As they near Charlie's driveway, she realizes that the reporters are focused on something off the road—no one even flinches when Jude flicks on his blinker and nudges carefully through the crowd. By the time a few cameras swing toward the cab of the truck, Charlie can see that Frank and Sophie are standing on the driveway near the bottom of the short hill. They've dragged two garbage cans to opposite sides of the lane and strung an old fishing rope between them. Frank is tying orange ribbons all along the length.

Charlie rolls down her window. "What's going on here?" she asks.

Frank gives her a grim smile and walks over. He's clutching a roll of bright ribbon in one hand and a pair of scissors in the other. "Good morning, honey," he says, leaning up to kiss her forehead. She ducks a bit so he can reach. "Did you sleep okay?"

"Fine. I'm more interested in what you and Sophie are doing."

"Keeping the hoodlums off the property." He glares toward the vans. "I'd flip 'em the bird if it wouldn't end up on the news. Can't have an old guy like me being a bad example for the kids."

"Certainly not." Charlie smiles in spite of herself.

"Mr. Morrow, if you would like an officer stationed on the property, I'm sure we could swing it for you," Jude offers. "At least at night."

"Nah, this'll do the trick." Frank hooks a thumb over his shoulder at their makeshift barrier. Then he hollers: "Soph! Let the rope down so they can pass."

Sophie unhooks one end of the long rope and lets it drop to the ground so that Jude can roll over it.

As he eases down the driveway he says, "They're good people."

"The best," Charlie agrees.

"I'm glad you have a support system."

"You make it sound like I'm going to need it." Charlie keeps her eyes carefully trained on the lake spread out before her, the sun glinting off the surface of the water like a scattering of golden coins. She loves days like this, when Superior looks like a lost treasure.

Jude puts the truck in park and turns it off. Facing Charlie, he waits a few heartbeats until she gives him her attention. "You *are* going to need them," he says, watching her carefully. "No matter what happens, no matter how this turns out, you'll need good people around you. You and Eva both."

Charlie's thankful that he includes Eva, that he talks about her in the future tense instead of implying that she's never coming back. Still, she doesn't like the seriousness of his tone. "Let's find this Zach guy," she says, slapping her hands on her thighs as if to dispel the solemn mood in the air. She reaches for the truck door, but Jude puts a hand on her arm to stop her.

"This is where we part ways, Charlie. I'm glad you could help today, but my team will take it from here. We'll analyze the recordings and contact you if there's anything you can do to help."

"Please don't shut me out of this." Charlie doesn't want to beg, but she will if she has to. "Please. Let me help."

"You already have. And I promise: I won't leave you in the dark." There's a note of finality in his voice, and Jude turns to swing open the driver's-side door. He jumps down to the gravel before Charlie can open her mouth to protest.

Hurrying to unbuckle her seat belt and follow him, Charlie jogs around the truck only to find that he's already talking to Frank and Sophie.

"Keep an eye out for Lauren, she's our victim specialist. She should be here in the next hour or so," Jude says. "Charlie, if you could send me Eva's work schedule for the past sixty days, that would really speed up the process. We have a lot of footage to go through, and anything to help us narrow it down would be much appreciated."

She reluctantly accepts the business card that he hands her.

"Take care of her," he tells Frank. And then he's back in the truck and pulling out.

Charlie watches him drive away, feeling powerless and empty. She can't decide if it was better to peek behind the curtain and be allowed to ride along with him this morning, or if it only made matters worse. Of course, she's no FBI agent. Charlie's not even very good at solving the mysteries in the paperbacks she loves to read. But it feels wrong to be shut out of the investigation into her own daughter's disappearance. She's not law enforcement or coast guard or a trained diver. But she's Eva's mom. That should count for something. Maybe everything.

When Jude's truck has disappeared beyond the bend, Charlie sucks in a shuddering breath and heads toward the porch. Her feet are heavy, her head stuffed with cotton, and she feels herself sway just a bit. In an instant, Frank and Sophie flank her, arms linked behind her back as if they are ready to prop her up. To catch her if she falls.

"Thank you," Charlie says, resting her cheek against the top of Frank's head.

"For what?" He gives her a little squeeze. "Just doing my job."

. . . .

Lauren looks to be mid-fifties, trim and fit, with platinum blond hair that falls to her shoulders and a no-nonsense manner. Charlie would bet money that she's a former agent, but Lauren does not match the picture she'd painted in her mind. Someone soft and maternal would not have offered Charlie much comfort at all. She's in the market for competent powerhouses with an uncanny ability to get results, and Lauren fits the bill. Still, Charlie has zero desire to talk to her.

"I'm here to assist in any way I can," Lauren says after a stilted conversation over coffee. "My job is to offer support, make referrals, and ensure that you know your rights."

"Agent Turner wants you to babysit me." Charlie doesn't mean to be so blunt, but she's really past the point of caring.

Lauren laughs, and the sound in the small kitchen is unexpected. "You don't need a babysitter, Charlotte. I'm just here to help."

"Thank you for the offer, but I'm doing fine."

"Okay then." Lauren takes another sip of her coffee. "Is it all right with you if I spend a little time with Frank? You're not the only one impacted by what's happened here."

Charlie feels chastened, even though Lauren is being nothing but patient and kind. "Of course," she says, pushing back her chair and bringing her own coffee cup to the sink. She pours the dark liquid down the drain. "I'm sure Frank would love the chance to talk a bit. I haven't exactly been around." Charlie is struck by the sudden understanding that she's been a shitty mom *and* honorary daughter. Poor Frank. He must be in ruins and holding it together for her sake.

"What will you do?" Lauren asks. It's a simple question, but Charlie can tell there's much behind it. Lauren is clocking her self-care, trying to gauge how she's *really* doing. "Could you snag a nap? Go for a walk? Find something to eat?"

"A walk," Charlie says, deciding the moment the words leave her mouth. Outside, away from here. She'll put on her hiking shoes—the lightweight, quick-drying ones—and walk the shoreline down to Black Bear Park. "Will you be here when I get back?"

Lauren shrugs. "Would you like me to be?"

Charlie doesn't answer. In the living room she squeezes

Frank's shoulder, then grabs her hiking shoes off the rack near the door. "I'll be back soon," she says. "Why don't you keep Lauren company in the kitchen for a while?"

Frank gives her a bit of a funny look, but when she smiles, he relaxes a little. "You okay?" he asks.

"No." It's honest, and she can tell that Frank feels the same way. "But we're going to get through this. Right now the FBI is looking at that house cam footage—hopefully they'll turn up something concrete."

"One step at a time," Frank says, repeating a mantra that he often said when Charlie was young and first came to live with him and Hattie. When she tried to race ahead, to skip the hard parts, he reminded her that the only way to get anywhere was to put one foot in front of the other, one step at a time.

It makes her throat tighten now, because she doesn't want to go through any of this. But he's right, and she knows it. "That's why I'm going for a little walk," she says, crouching down to pull on her shoes. "I'll be back soon. Spend some time with Lauren, okay?"

"Be careful," Frank calls as she slips out the door.

The day is both cool and warm, in the way that only spring days can be, and Charlie can feel the promise of summer in the way the sun kisses the skin on the back of her neck. If Eva were here, she'd grab some sunscreen from the cupboard above the washing machine and chase after Charlie to rub it in.

"Never go out without protection," she'd joke.

Charlie prays that chutzpah is alive and well in Eva at this very moment—wherever she might be.

The siren call of the lake is tempting, but Charlie's feet carry her somewhere else entirely. Sebastian is locked—a habit they formed on the road and hadn't been able to break, even in safe, provincial Landing—but there's a magnetic key holder tucked in an alcove between the propane tank and the hitch. Charlie locates it easily and palms the key, suddenly desperate to be inside the trailer.

The interior of the Airstream is familiar, if stuffy and a bit close. It reminds Charlie of days that started out cold and then got hot while they were out adventuring—they often returned to a closed-up Sebastian and this exact stale air. It smells faintly of laundry detergent and yeast, even though they never once baked bread in the tiny trailer oven.

A few weeks ago, Charlie opened everything up, throwing the windows wide so the cool, spring air could scourge everything clean. She washed the bedding, mopped the floor, and began to stock the cabinets with necessities for the road. But Eva had balked, and the ensuing standoff was so bitter that Charlie had locked everything back up again and stayed away just so Eva would stop cold-shouldering her.

Now, there's a crate on the table filled with things that Charlie never had time to unpack. Cleaning supplies are mixed in with a bag of wild rice (the Sutton girls love their Minnesota wild rice, even if they poke fun of how on the nose their devotion is), a twenty-four pack of their favorite lime sparkling water, and a few canned goods, among other odds and ends Charlie picked up during their months off the road.

Charlie had no agenda when she decided to open up Sebastian, but there's a clear and obvious task before her. Taking a can in each hand, Charlie opens the latched pantry and stacks them neatly inside. The glass cleaner and anti-bacterial wipes go under the sink. The water bottles can be lined neatly in the fridge, whether it's on or not.

The crate is nearly empty, and Charlie has grown used to the thick air when there's a staccato of raps on the trailer door.

"Come in," she calls, forgetting for a split second where she is and what's going on. She could be anywhere: the Tetons,

Yosemite, the Great Smokey Mountains. Eva could be just outside the door, playing with Scout.

But she's not.

"Charlie?" Lauren pops her head into the trailer, and the expression on her face is enough to bring Charlie crashing back to reality—to the precarity of the situation they're in.

"What's wrong?" she asks, nearly dropping the stack of new dishcloths she's holding.

Lauren schools her expression into a mask of calm neutrality. "They found something. Agent Turner wants you to come as soon as you can."

• • • •

"Thank you so much for sharing Eva's work schedule," Jude says as he grabs an extra folding chair for Charlie and sets it down in front of one of the computer consoles. They're in the main room of the boathouse, and though it's still a hive of activity, Charlie would swear that there are fewer people here today than she saw yesterday. She wonders if they're already reassigning resources.

"Oh," she says belatedly. "I'm glad it helped."

"Immensely. We're working on isolating all the clips that were recorded before, during, or after Eva's shifts, and pulled out some stills that might help us identify Zach."

"You guys are fast."

He nods, turning back to the computer. "Okay, let's start with some specifics. Looks like our Zach is tall—assuming Eva is five foot seven like you've already said—he's well over six feet."

A screenshot appears on the console. It's a bit pixelated from being enlarged, but there's absolutely no mistaking that Eva is standing on the sidewalk in front of an old, black sedan. She's wearing jeans and her puffy winter coat, her curls hidden beneath a thick beanie. Behind her is a man. His face is turned

away from the camera, toward the street, but he towers over
Eva. His hair is blond, or maybe light brown, and his shoulders
square.

"Do you recognize him?" Jude asks, zooming in even farther.

"No," Charlie says. But maybe she does? "He could be any-
body. Tall, blond, built like an athlete. That's half the men in
this state."

Jude flicks through a few more stills. The man—Zach, she
assumes—reaches out to grab the string of Eva's apron. Charlie
hadn't realized she was still wearing it, but the next few frames
show him tugging, Eva turning, and the apron coming off in his
hands. The movement has pulled the couple closer, and the last
screenshot shows him tilt his head toward Eva.

"They kiss, don't they? Is that why you're showing me stills
instead of the video?"

"I want you to focus on *him*, not the two of them as a couple," Jude says. "I know it must be really confusing to see your
daughter with a boyfriend you didn't even know existed, but
we need to identify this guy."

"Then let me see the actual footage. Let me see how he moves,
if he has any tics or characteristics that seem familiar to me."

Jude doesn't respond, but he types a few commands into the
keyboard and a video pops up. It's the same scene as the pictures Charlie just saw, but this time she can watch Eva and Zach
move. There's her daughter's familiar, bouncy walk. She lands
on the balls of her feet as if she's poised to run at any moment.
And behind her, a young man, moving much more intentionally. Slow and almost fluid. When he reaches out for her apron
strings it seems like an afterthought, a tiger pawing lazily at a
toy. The unraveling that happens—the way Eva spins with the
slight tug and ends up in his arms—is all her.

They do kiss, long and deep, and it's hard for Charlie to

watch. Not because of the intimacy of the moment, but because Eva so clearly and deeply trusts this man.

"I don't recognize him." Charlie squeezes her eyes shut and rubs her forehead with her fingers. "Do you have any footage of his face? Does he ever look directly at the camera?"

"We're still isolating scenes and enhancing everything we can," Jude says. "I just wanted to get your initial reaction in case he was someone you could immediately identify. A friend of the family or something."

"No, I don't think I've ever seen him." Charlie can practically taste Jude's disappointment. It's sharp and bitter on her tongue.

But he doesn't give anything away. "I'll print some of these out so you can take them back to Frank. Let him have a look. And Sophie, too. Maybe someone will recognize him."

"Agent Turner?"

The sound of his name and the urgent tone make Jude's head snap up.

"I think you should see this." A man with a neat goatee and tortoiseshell glasses motions Jude over to a console at the very end of a long table.

"Stay here," Jude tells Charlie. But the second he's out of his chair, Charlie's up and following. If they've found something, she wants to know.

"What've you got, Dan?" Jude leans over the table to get a better look at the screen. If he's noticed Charlie standing a few feet away, watching and listening, he doesn't let on.

"I've been looking at footage outside of the range you gave us," Dan says. "And I got a few hits. It seems he came to Landing more often. Not sure what he was doing, but he liked the road beside Mugs. Sometimes he'd just sit in his car."

"License plate?"

"No. The angle is all wrong. We can only see the side of the car. But look at this." Dan clicks on a file and opens it. The screen fills with a picture of the blond man, leaning against his dark sedan. There's a cell phone pressed to his ear, and he's talking animatedly. His eyes are wide, his mouth open; Dan freezes the frame mid-sentence. He taps the screen and says, "This is the first full frontal view we've found. Look familiar?"

Jude squints at the picture, moving in closer and then backing away. Charlie still doesn't recognize the man, but it's helpful to see his full face. At this distance he's generic-looking, with hair that's just a touch too long—it grazes the line of his heavy brow on one side. She's ready to ask Dan to print this photo off for her, too, but then Jude sucks in a breath through his teeth.

"Is that—"

"That's what I was wondering," Dan cuts in before Jude can finish. "All those boys look alike, but we don't see this one very often. It's been a couple of years at least."

"Get the Brennan file for me," Jude says, snapping to attention.

Something has changed in the atmosphere. Energy crackles through the air like electricity, and all the hair on the back of Charlie's neck stands up. "Who's Brennan?" she asks.

Jude whips toward her, the look on his face assuring her that he'd forgotten she was there at all. "Thanks for coming, Charlie," he says, taking her lightly by the elbow and steering her toward the door. "You've been very helpful."

"I haven't been," she protests. "I haven't done a thing. And what about those printouts?"

"Go home."

"You know him." Dread pools in Charlie's stomach, oily and slick. Because if an FBI agent recognizes Zach, it can't be good. "You have to tell me who Brennan is. Is that Zach's last name? Did he call himself something else? Was he pretending to *be* somebody else?"

"Charlie, stop. Let us do our jobs. I know you're trying to help, but *go home*."

When she opens her mouth to fight back, Agent Turner takes her by the wrist. His grip is firm, enough to pull her out of the spiral she was in. "I'll call you soon," he promises, and then he opens the door and ushers her out into the afternoon. Without any of the pictures he promised.

Charlie stands on the grass for a moment, breathing heavy and wondering if she should pound on the door until they let her back in. But then she realizes that she has a name. *Brennan.* It doesn't ring any bells, but Charlie's resourceful and pretty accomplished online. She can do her own search. And when she finds Brennan—whoever he is—she won't stop at anything to get her daughter back.

CLASH CONTINUES OVER MINING PERMITS

Duluth, Minnesota—The US Bureau of Land Management and conservation groups have reached a stalemate regarding two prospective permits that would allow copper-nickel mines in the Mesabi Range of Minnesota to open.

The conservation groups challenged the permits, citing potential catastrophic environmental harm as well as significant impact on local endangered species, including the gray wolf and northern long-eared bat. "It's irresponsible to pretend that the opening of these mines won't have a horrific effect on biodiversity in the area. In light of growing concerns over climate change, allowing these permits to pass would be a significant setback when we need to be making gains," said Leigh Watson, the director of Minnesotans for Environmental Conservation. Her group has been working tirelessly to oppose the companies requesting the permits.

Doug Penning, spokesman for Brennan Mining disagrees. "Our land is rich in natural resources that the people of this country should be able to use. It's devastating to our economy and our independence to depend on imports of raw materials that we have in abundance. Let's put the good people of Minnesota back to work."

The iron ranges of Northern Minnesota have a long and storied history. But in the 1980s the steel industry faced global challenges that greatly impacted the mining of taconite (a lower-grade iron ore that requires more processing and is found throughout the Minnesota mining ranges). The ensuing layoffs, automation, and idling changed the face of mining in Minnesota forever. Local communities were greatly impacted, and generations of miners suddenly found themselves out of work.

Now, Mr. Penning said his clients are turning their attention to copper-nickel, another natural resource that is found in Minnesota. In fact, it's believed that Minnesota has the largest known undeveloped deposit of copper-nickel in the world. "This is the next wave of mining. It's modern, safe, and will revitalize communities all over the state."

Many disagree. "The water pollution that will undoubtedly be caused by these open pit mines is a price that's simply too high for our beautiful state—and our world—to pay," said Ms. Watson. "Heavy metal water pollution is devastating to the environment, and will forever alter the region's forests, lakes, and waterways. These permits cannot go through."

As the debate rages on, tensions are ratcheting up between those who support the mines and their opponents. Neither seems willing to give a single inch as communities all over the country watch and wait as these decisions set precedent for the future of mining far beyond the borders of Minnesota.

CHAPTER 20

EVA

MONDAY

When the sun begins to slant across the grass outside the shed, a bell tolls over the compound. It sounds like an old dinner bell, the kind a prairie woman might clang to call her children for dinner. And that's exactly what it is. From inside the house and around the grounds, the kids come running. The little girls hitch up their skirts to sprint—their scuffed tennis shoes seeming out of place beneath their long dresses—and the boys hurry to catch them. Even from the stuffy cage of the shed, Eva can feel the excitement sizzling through the air. It's clearly dinnertime, but it's more than that, too. Something is going on.

Eva expects to remain locked up while the Family gathers in the sprawling cafeteria building, but as the adults trickle more slowly from the house, Rachel hangs back on the steps. When everyone else is gone, she comes to the door of the shed and unlocks it.

"You like watching us?" she asks Eva, her eyes glittering and unreadable.

Eva takes a step back from the window, realizing that of course they could all see her silhouetted in the frame. The dusty pane of glass is dirty, but it's not opaque.

"Just curious, I guess," she says. The truth is, she was count-

ing people, clocking sizes and ages and taking stock of what—
who—she's up against. She plans on using the spoon to take
the door off tonight, and rather than sneaking past the Morton
buildings and the training grounds at the back of the property,
she'll skirt the farmhouse lawn, keeping to the trees. Eva wants
to know who might spot her and if she could take them down.

"Well, don't gawk at supper." Rachel swings the door wide
and holds it for Eva with mock gallantry.

"I'm coming?" Eva doesn't want to go. She doesn't want to
spend time with these people or hear more about who they are
and what they're doing. The more she knows, the more they'll
see her as a liability. The more she knows, the more she feels
crippled by fear.

"You're one of us now."

"What if I don't want to be?"

"You don't have a choice."

Because she doesn't want to draw more attention to herself
or make Abner feel like he has to come and teach her a lesson,
Eva grabs her crutches and follows Rachel. She spent most of
the afternoon walking back and forth in the shed, stretching
her leg, and putting it up between exercises to help with the
swelling. She can walk without the crutches now—not quickly
or without pain—and the bleeding has stopped, but she doesn't
want Rachel to know that.

By the time they make it to the cafeteria, it's teeming with
people. Men, women, and children line the tables, keeping to
a loose set of unspoken rules that seem to govern their meal-
times. Some families appear to be seated together, but for the
most part the men and women are separate, with the children
gathered at the tables closest to the doors. Drawing the stares
of dozens of people, Rachel lifts her head and leads Eva to one
of the only open spots at a table in the middle. Eva sits on the

very end of a low bench with Rachel beside her and her back to a table full of soldiers. She can smell the tang of their sweat and beneath that the loamy scent of earth. There were, blessedly, no gunshots in the afternoon, but these men had clearly been doing *something*.

Eva wants to turn around and look for Zach, but she doesn't dare. Is he still locked in the basement? How much longer will he have to *atone*? A shiver travels down her spine at the arcane word. It's hollow, resonant. It even *sounds* scary, like the echo of a struck bell. All she can do is say a prayer that he's safe.

Abner steps to the head of the room and a hush instantly falls over the crowd. It's sobering how readily they obey him; all he has to do is stand up to command their full attention. Instead of looking at Abner, Eva furtively studies the people around her. They are all rapt, their focus wholly and devotedly on their leader. They don't just listen to him, they love him, and it's written all over their faces.

"Tonight marks an end," he says, his voice rich and hypnotic. "But also a beginning. This is the last meal we'll share before the world undergoes a miraculous change. A sacred, long-awaited change. There will be birth pains, to be sure, and for some of us, this may be the final meal we enjoy together on this earth. But our treasure is not hidden here, and this is not our home."

Murmurs of assent rise like bubbles in champagne. In spite of Abner's heavy words, the people around Eva are fizzing with what looks like joyful anticipation. The woman across from Eva closes her eyes in ecstasy as a single tear trails down her cheek.

"And so we feast tonight," Abner continues, "and rejoice in the Family and in what we've been called to do. What a joy, what a privilege we have been given. This evening we say with conviction: No mission too difficult, no sacrifice too great!"

"No mission too difficult, no sacrifice too great!" The people in the cafeteria don't shout this time, but their voices mingled as one are a boom in Eva's chest all the same. She trembles.

"Onward," Abner says quietly, his hand raised in a fist. And then he whispers: "Onward." The fist goes to his chest, covering his heart, and everyone mimics the movement. The thump falls heavy in the room, marking Abner's words with a solemnity that Eva can feel in her bones.

He prays, but she's no longer paying attention. Her hands are shaking so badly she has to clasp them in her lap, and even then, Rachel elbows her in the ribs. The meaning is obvious: *Get it together.* But Eva can't. She feels like she might pass out. It's the press of bodies, the magnetism of Abner, the fact that these normal-looking people have planned an act of violence that they hope will change everything. Eva is still trying to figure out what they hate so much that they would be willing to sacrifice for. To harm—to *kill?*—for. It's beyond her comprehension. She wants to scream, to grab Rachel by the shoulders and shake her out of whatever spell Abner has cast. But the girl is utterly bewitched. They all are.

The prayer is interminable, but as soon as Abner says "amen," platters of food are carried from the kitchen. There's roast and mashed potatoes, glazed carrots and rolls that are so fresh from the oven they're almost too hot to touch. Eva's stomach growls in spite of her predicament, and as the food is passed, she fills her plate, realizing that she'll need her strength for what's to come.

Rachel angles her back so that Eva is shut off from the rest of the table, but Eva can't decide if it's intended as a slight or a form of protection. Is Rachel shielding her from the bald curiosity and furtive glances of the rest of the family? Or is she boxing her out? Whatever the reason, Eva refocuses on her food—and the Family around her.

The animated conversations in the room jumble together, a cacophony of words and laughter that makes it nearly impossible for Eva to learn anything. But after she's had a few bites and taken the edge off her hunger, she realizes that if she leans back just a bit she can hear the men behind her. The tables are so close that if she tips too far she'll brush against the uniformed back of a soldier. She can feel the warmth of his body through her dress. And the deep staccato of his voice is easy to pick out over the whispers of the women at her table.

"It all comes down to land. *Our* land. The Fifth Amendment states that 'private property shall not be taken for public use without just compensation.' But how is telling us what we can and can't do with *our* land just?"

Eva's not sure his argument holds, and someone from farther down his table must agree because there's a lull as the soldier listens to a comment or question that Eva can't make out.

"You're missing the point. Land is just the beginning. It's the tip of the iceberg. When a government begins to exercise eminent domain over our God-given property, there's no incentive to stop. Pretty soon they're telling us how to raise our kids, what to put into our bodies, and what to believe. Enough. It has to end somewhere."

"It ends here." Another voice, and then several murmurs of assent.

"The time for talking is over," the man behind Eva continues. "And I for one am more than ready to get my hands dirty."

A few fists pound the table as his companions laugh their agreement.

"Not hungry?" Rachel glances over her shoulder and juts her chin at Eva's plate. "Not processed enough for you?"

Eva realizes her fork is frozen in midair, a swirl of mashed potatoes poised and ready for her mouth. She takes the bite. "It's delicious," she says, but the truth is she can't taste it at all. She might as well be eating sawdust.

Rachel's lip curls in a half smile, and there's something that borders on pleasure in her eyes.

She cares, Eva realizes. *She cares what I think. She wants me to understand.*

Eva doesn't, not at all, but she smiles anyway and tears off a corner of her roll. There are things about Rachel that Eva can't help but admire, even though her best qualities—her loyalty, spunk, and iron will—are a source of constant frustration for Eva here.

"You would love California," Eva murmurs. She's been consoling herself by daydreaming about some of her favorite places. A little island called Guemes in the San Juans, the peak of Haleakala at sunrise, a grubby ice cream stand south of LA with the best Rocky Road she's ever tasted. She'd give anything to be there right now. Sand between her toes and the scent of salt water and sunscreen. Rachel would fit in perfectly. Well, minus the ankle-length dress and bad attitude. Eva can almost picture it: Rachel's blond hair whipped by the wind as they straddle surfboards just off the tawny curve of Laguna Beach. Rachel looks like she was made for the sand and the sun, for wild water and taco trucks and long nights around a lazy, flickering fire.

But Rachel's nose crinkles. "California is a hellhole," she says, but there's no real heat in it. "I would hate it."

"Maybe," Eva agrees, sad that their moment of connection is popped as easily as a soap bubble. As Rachel turns away again, Eva says, "You don't even know what you're missing."

She's talking to Rachel. To all of them. But nobody hears her.

. . . .

Although Eva is trusted enough to attend supper in the cafeteria, the Family's goodwill ends there. Nobody talks to her.

Nobody even tries to make eye contact. And as Eva is escorted back to the shed, she feels a rush of pure panic.

"I can't do it," she says, breath high and quick in her throat. "I can't go in there again."

"You have to." Rachel sounds dispassionate, but there's something uneasy in her gaze. She seems to hold the padlock key loosely, reluctantly. Maybe she's thinking about California.

"Please." Eva catches her free hand and holds it, weaving their fingers together and willing Rachel to have a little compassion. "I'm going crazy. It's hot and awful in there. Can I just see Zach? I don't even have to talk to him, it's just that he's the only person I know. Please, let me see him. Let me see that he's okay."

Rachel looks down at their hands, at the tangle of their fingers locked together. Eva's are dark from long hours in the sun and the genetic contribution of a father she never knew. Charlie once told her he had skin the color of warm cedar, and she couldn't help but—briefly—love him for the way he reminded her of the forest in summer. Rachel's hands are pale in comparison, smooth and unblemished as newly fallen snow.

Eva knows that Rachel has barely left this compound. She can see it in the surety of the girl, in the way she thinks she knows things she can't. Those years on the road, and all the people they met, taught Eva that nothing is ever as simple as a theory—and people are even more complicated still. If Rachel would just *listen* for a while, she might realize that good and evil are not as effortlessly defined as Abner would have her believe. She might grow to learn that people's stories are knotty and complex and unimaginably beautiful, even when they don't look like everyone else's. Maybe especially then.

"No," Rachel says, finally pulling her hand away. Their fingers stick together in the warm evening air, and Eva doesn't make the unraveling easy. "You can't see him."

"Why not? Is he okay?"

Rachel sighs. Then she says quietly, "Tamar is with him. She's taking good care of him, I promise."

Eva thinks about the injuries she saw only hours ago. Zach was beat up, but she didn't think he needed the care of a nurse. Did Abner discover that his son snuck out of whatever make-shift basement cell they're keeping him in? That he found Eva?

"I'm supposed to tell you that Tamar will be by in the morning to check on your stitches." Rachel unlocks the padlock and opens the door to Eva's own prison.

"The *morning*? You're locking me up all night? Alone?" Eva sounds frantic—and she is—but she's also leaning into it. She doesn't rein in her alarm because she wants to know what to expect. Who might stop by and when and why.

"I'll come back to take you to the bathroom later," Rachel says, crossing her arms over her chest. For the first time, she seems conflicted about her role as Eva's caretaker and warden. Eva doesn't even know why Rachel has been given this particular job—because they're close in age?—but it's obviously taking a toll on her. "Look, I know this is hard. But it'll get easier. You'll get used to it."

"I don't want to get used to it. I want to go *home*." Tears gather on Eva's lashes. She tried so hard to be calm and atten-tive, a wise observer so that when the opportunity presented itself to escape, she'd be ready. But right now she feels just like a little girl who wants her mother. Who wants this madness to end.

Rachel touches Eva's arm for just a moment. "Trust me, after tomorrow, you'll be glad that you're here. The Gates is the safest place in the world for you."

After Rachel leaves, Eva scrubs angrily at her eyes and hur-ries to the cot. Reaching between the frame and thin mattress, her fingers connect with the soup spoon. She hid it there, beside her notebook, in case Rachel realized her lunch dishes were still sitting on the small table and decided to take them back to the kitchen. Thankfully, Rachel hadn't noticed the dirty bowl, and Eva didn't have to explain the missing utensil. She clutches it now, running her thumb along the blunt edge and wishing the hours until dark to pass quickly.

"Help me," she prays, pacing the shed and believing that the God she speaks to and the one the Family invokes are not one and the same. The God she believes in said to love your neighbor as yourself and pray for those who persecute you. So she does exactly that, asking that Abner's efforts are frustrated at every turn, that the Uprising will fizzle out like a snuffed flame. And then, when she has run out of words, she says, "Help me find my way home. *Please.*"

When night begins to fall and long shadows cloak the compound in a thousand shades of gray, vehicles begin a slow procession from the back of the property to the gates. Eva can only see a small portion of their progress, but she presses her face to one of the tiny windows anyway, unconcerned about whether or not she can be seen. She's riveted by the strange parade, the back of her neck slicked with fear as cars and trucks and every manner of transport files one by one down the lane. They honk once when they're just out of Eva's line of sight, and she imagines that Abner and his children—except Zach—are on the porch of the farmhouse keeping watch. Perhaps even blessing each vehicle and its inhabitants as they leave the Gates of Zion for destinations unknown.

Eva wishes she had learned more. Where they're going and why. What they intend to do. Wreak havoc, she knows, but how? In the murky twilight she can't make out license plates (they're probably obscured anyway), but she grabs her notebook and scribbles down as much detail as she can in the dying light. Make and model when she can recognize them, and colors and descriptions when she can't. It isn't much, but it's something.

Dark blue Dodge Ram

Old red minivan w/rust over driver's-side wheels

White Camry w/dented rear panel

Rachel comes back much later to escort her to the bathroom. Eva's buzzing with adrenaline and doesn't have to pretend to be flustered and upset. Rachel seems preoccupied, quiet and jumpy, clearly unnerved by the seemingly endless column of fighters that were just deployed. She gnaws on her thumbnail, a bad habit that Eva hasn't seen her indulge in until now.

"Where are they going?" Eva chances as Rachel leads her back to the shed in silence. They haven't said a single word to each other, and it grates on Eva more than it should.

But Rachel doesn't respond. She just locks Eva up again, refusing to make eye contact, and shuffles slowly back toward the house.

Eva knows that she should wait until everyone is asleep, until all the lights in the farmhouse are extinguished and the compound is still. But she's itching from pent-up energy, her stomach sour with misery. She has to go—*now*—and almost as soon as Rachel has closed the back door of the farmhouse behind her, Eva is making her preparations.

She rips the notes she's taken out of the notebook and folds them into the pocket of her dress. A full water bottle that Rachel gave her after an earlier bathroom break goes in the other. There are no more supplies to be had, nothing that she can carry and use to either help her or protect her. It's an isolating feeling, and Eva has to beat back the loneliness that threatens to immobilize her. She wishes for a compass—just that one, small thing would be such a boon—but she's grateful that it's a clear night and the stars out here are spilled across the sky like cut diamonds. Easily recognizable and ready to light her way.

South and east. Eva believes that if she just keeps moving south and east she'll hit a road eventually. It's the only plan she's got.

There is no electricity in the shed and therefore no light, so Eva has to fumble around in the dark for the door hinges. Her heart is jackhammering in her chest, but she finds that if she holds the pin between the thumb and forefinger of her left hand, she can guide the end of the spoon with her right hand to the gap between the metal. It's slow, painstaking work, and by the time she has the first pin out, she's sweating through her dress. She wishes for her own clothes. For her hiking shoes. Even a ponytail holder for her wild mane of curls that keep getting stuck to the side of her damp neck and cheeks.

With the middle hinge free, Eva moves to the bottom. She saves the top for last, thankful for Frank and the bits of construction know-how he shared with her throughout the years. Because the door doesn't quite reach the threshold, she slides a few of the notebooks beneath to catch it when it falls.

When the final pin taps up and out into her waiting palm, Eva has to suppress a sob. The full weight of the door pushes into her chest, threatening to crush her, but the padlock still holds one side in place, and she shifts the whole slab of wood to balance it against the waiting notebooks. A curl of cool night air slips in through the gap, and Eva laps it up, her heart full and hopeful for the first time in days. She can ignore the hot throb in her leg, the way she feels dizzy and frightened and so very alone. She's finally *free*.

Eva only has to crack the door ten inches or so to slide out, and as soon as she's clear, she heaves it carefully back into place.

Something is obviously wrong with the door—it's crooked and barely balanced in the frame, but if anyone glances out a window to look at the shed, the illusion will hold up in the dark. By morning, it won't matter. She'll be long gone.

Savoring this tiny act of insurrection, Eva turns her face to the night sky and gulps in fresh mouthfuls of forest air. The path before her is crisp and new as a blank sheet of paper, mysterious and unknowable, but for just a moment, Eva ignores the impossibility of her journey and relishes the challenge. She can do this. She *has* to do this.

And then, from somewhere beside her, a single word. "Eva?"

She whips around, every nerve ending alight, and comes face-to-face with Rachel.

"I came to talk," she says, her blond hair loose around her shoulders and glowing softly in the moonlight. She looks like an angel, and for a second, Eva hopes—prays—that she is. "I snuck out because you looked so afraid earlier. I thought you could use . . ."

A friend. Rachel doesn't say it, but the word is dense as fog in the space between them.

"Rachel," Eva says, her voice breaking as she wills the girl across from her to understand. "I can't stay here. You know that, right? You know that holding me here is wrong, that what's happening here is *wrong*."

For a few heartbeats, the two girls stand in the darkness and stare at each other. Eva's blood pumps fast and furious in her veins, matching Rachel's as she raises a hand and presses it over her heart as if to hold it in place. Eva swears she sees a wisp of tenderness in the movement, the crack of an open door.

But then Rachel takes a step back from her and draws a mighty breath. "Abner!" she screams at the top of her lungs. "Dad! Come quick! Eva's trying to escape!"

VOICE MAIL
784-555-4042

"Ms. Sutton? This is Zechariah Brennan. You don't know me, but Eva does. Look, I'm so sorry for what I've put her—and you—through, but I don't really have time for apologies. Eva's in trouble. I—"

CHAPTER 21

CHARLIE

TUESDAY

The phone call comes in around three a.m., after Charlie has fallen fitfully asleep. The shrill ring in the stillness of the dark living room jolts her awake, but when she fumbles for her cell phone on the coffee table, it crashes to the floor and cartwheels under the couch.

"Dammit!"

Charlie had succumbed to exhaustion less than an hour before the phone rang, and in those few, restless moments of sleep she feared exactly this: missing something important. Missing Eva. Her brief nightmares were all about Eva being just out of reach—on a cliff, in the water, being spirited away by a nameless, faceless evil—and Charlie was always, agonizingly, a second behind. A hair's breadth too late to save her.

"Dammit!" she cries again, rolling awkwardly off the couch to scrabble across the floor for her phone. It's stopped ringing, but that only makes her search harder. "Please," she whispers, fumbling. "Please, please, please."

When she finally reaches her phone, the pad of her thumb slides across the screen and sparks with pain. The screen protector is spiderwebbed with cracks and her thumb is bleeding.

The missed call is from an unfamiliar number, and hope

plays tug-of-war with dread in Charlie's chest. Agent Turner? Detective James? Some other unknown entity that's trying to find her daughter and is calling with news? She doesn't have long to wonder. As she's studying the phone, an alert for a new voice mail pops up. Trembling, Charlie clicks on it.

It's only thirteen seconds long—and it ends abruptly—but Charlie listens to it over and over, memorizing the handful of words and the urgent cadence of the stranger's voice. At some point, Scout appears beside her and lays his warm head in Charlie's lap as if he knows that she needs the comfort. She buries one hand in his scruff as she mouths the scant sentences over and over again.

Zechariah Brennan.

Zechariah.

Not Zach. For a minute Charlie is completely frozen, incapable of discerning what to do next. She has a *name*, but then she realizes that Jude already knows that much. He had said, "Get the Brennan file for me." Charlie had first assumed Brennan was a first name, and though she tried several internet searches, she hadn't turned up a single pertinent scrap of information. Later, when she tried "Zach Brennan," there were over three million hits. Most of them for Zachary Brennans scattered all over the world. An accountant in Portland, a minor league baseball player in Japan, a real estate agent in Minneapolis. Nothing pertinent. At least as far as she could tell.

Now what? Should Jude be her first call? Zechariah? In the end, Charlie does the simplest thing and hits the phone icon on the bottom of the voice mail message. She holds her breath, longing to hear him on the other end of the line, but it rings out. Once more she hits the call button, but before it can even connect, she hangs up. Zach's voice on the message was raspy and strained. He sounded furtive, hidden. Like Eva wasn't the only one in trouble. Maybe calling him back made the situation *worse*.

Digging Jude's business card out of her back pocket, Charlie taps out his number. "Pick up, pick up," she mutters. He promised he'd keep his phone on him. He promised he'd answer her call.

But Jude's number goes to voice mail after only four rings. Charlie tries three more times, finally leaving a terse message after the last attempt. "It's Charlie. Call me."

Out of options, Charlie jumps to her feet, her heart pounding a syncopated rhythm in her throat. It isn't until she's standing that the full weight of what Zach said washes over her like a tidal wave. *Eva's in trouble.* She should be horrified, but the silky feeling that pours into her chest is something different entirely. It's *joy*.

If Eva is in trouble, it means Eva is *alive*.

A sob escapes her lips, but Charlie doesn't even try to stop it. She cries in the stillness of the lakeside house, Scout pressed tight against her legs. "Eva's alive," Charlie tells him when she can talk again. "Our girl is alive."

Scout whines and rubs his head against her knee as if he can understand what she's saying.

"Now all we have to do is find her."

. . . .

Sunrise is little more than a smudge of velvety light over the water when Charlie decides she's waited long enough. Surely someone is at the makeshift headquarters, brewing coffee or preparing reports or doing God knows what to get ready for another day of searching. As she hops in her truck, she realizes that she doesn't even know where Jude sleeps. At the little motor inn on the outskirts of town? In his truck? Or maybe he drives back to

Duluth. Maybe that's why she couldn't get ahold of him during the night—he was sound asleep in his bed at home. The thought makes her skin prickle with something that feels a lot like fury.

This early in the morning, the end of the driveway is blessedly vacant of news vans, and after Charlie lets down Frank and Sophie's makeshift barrier, she doesn't bother to put it back up. She doesn't plan to come back anyway; not until she's tracked down Zechariah Brennan, and Eva is safe and sound and *home*.

The streets of Landing are sleepy and still, and Charlie ignores the posted speed limits and barely taps her brakes for stop signs. She realizes it's probably pointless to race—the boathouse will likely be dark and empty—but when she pulls into the marina parking lot, it's a hive of activity. Cars line the lot and light streams from the windows of the boathouse. Jude's truck is among the vehicles, and so is an armored tactical van and a long, black truck with a gold seal on the door. Bile bites at the back of Charlie's throat. They've called in the cavalry. *Why?*

"Where is Agent Turner?" Charlie asks, bursting through the door moments later. There are people everywhere—it's a hub of determined activity, the atmosphere crisp and purposeful—and before she can take a single step, someone has lightly taken her by the arm.

"Excuse me, ma'am, but you're going to have to leave."

"It's fine," Jude says, noticing the commotion. He straightens up from where he was bent over a computer and crosses the space between them. "She's with me."

Concern carves a line in his smooth forehead, and he tugs her off to the side, away from the door. "What are you doing here? It's barely seven."

"You didn't check your voice mail," Charlie blurts. "Zach called. He called me several hours ago and I tried to call you, but you wouldn't answer. He said that Eva's in trouble."

"I need to hear the message." Jude takes off across the room and motions for her to follow. Over his shoulder he asks, "Was the number blocked? Did you try to call it back?"

"I did, once, but he doesn't sound . . ." Charlie casts around for the right word and lands on, ". . . *safe*. I didn't know if calling back was the right thing to do."

"It's okay, you did great." Jude clears a space for her at one of the tables next to a computer and the same guy with tortoiseshell glasses from yesterday—Dan, she remembers. Charlie wonders if they've all been here all night. Jude says, "I want you to play the message for us."

So she does, laying her phone on the table and letting the message run multiple times. Dan records it and taps the number into his computer. Then his fingers are flying over the keys, searching and referencing and working the sort of technological magic that Charlie can only begin to guess at.

"Who is this guy?" she asks, sliding her phone back into her jacket pocket and watching Dan out of the corner of her eye. "This *Zechariah Brennan*?"

At first she's afraid Jude won't answer her. He sits back in his chair and runs one hand over his face. She can hear the faint scritch of his five-o'clock shadow and see the dark half-moons under his eyes. Until this very moment, Agent Jude Turner has been nothing but the picture of professional calm under pressure, composed and imperturbable, expertly aloof. Now, his humanity is showing. It both scares Charlie and comforts her.

"Zechariah Brennan is peripheral," Jude says eventually, meeting her gaze. "A secondary character that we would take no notice of if it wasn't for his father."

"Okay . . ." Charlie draws out the word, willing him not to stop there. She can tell that he's calculating, trying to decide what to share and what to hold back. So she presses, "What do they have to do with Eva?"

"We can't know that yet. But in light of everything we've learned in the last few days, we feel confident that when Eva left the *Summer Moon* on Saturday, it was with Zechariah Brennan."

"Who's *peripheral*." Charlie uses Jude's own word. "You're going to have to give me more than that."

"I know." He puts his hand, palm up, in front of Dan. Without even taking his eyes off the computer screen, the tech grabs a file folder from the far side of the computer and slaps it in the agent's hand. Jude clears a space in front of them and places the folder flat on the table. "Maybe something in here will ring a bell for you."

"Desperate times and all that," Dan pipes in.

Jude ignores him. "Let's start at the beginning. This is Abner Brennan." He flips open the file and taps his fingertips on an eight-by-ten glossy at the top of a sheaf of papers. "Look familiar?"

Charlie pulls the picture closer. It's an older man in what appears to be a studio portrait. She'd peg him at late sixties, with a headful of white hair and startlingly blue eyes. He has the look of someone who was handsome in his youth and who was still convinced he possessed a certain irresistible charm. He didn't. Something about him made a shudder trip down Charlie's spine.

"No," she says. "I don't recognize him."

"What about now?" Jude flips the photograph over and begins to lay out a collection of printed newspaper articles. Scanning the headlines, Charlie can see there's one about a book burning and another highlighting a counterprotest. Something about a contentious mine shutdown and a lawsuit against the Bureau of Land Management of Minnesota. Over a dozen articles, and the name Abner Brennan is in every one.

"I saw some of these last night," Charlie admits. "I googled 'Brennan' because you said the name."

"Abner Brennan has been on the FBI's radar for at least a decade. He became a person of interest when he started inserting himself in community government elections touting a 'return to values' platform with a very aggressive agenda."

"Values are good," Charlie says, trying to follow.

"Guess it depends on what your values are." Jude flips to another page and scans it as he speaks. "Abner Brennan's values are anti-immigrant, anti-LGBTQ, and anti-Semitic."

"Just to name a few," Dan hops in. "Abner Brennan is a domestic radical. But it's much more complex than that. He's a fundamentalist and reconstructionist with a heavy dose of white nationalism and anti-government rhetoric thrown in. Some people say he's a cult leader."

"I don't understand."

Jude gives her a wry smile. "Most don't. But he's a homegrown would-be terrorist who thinks our country is evil and that it's his God-given job to return America to a state of obedience and purity."

"Where does Eva fit in?" Charlie can hardly get the words out.

"We're not sure yet, but obviously Zechariah is his son." Jude locates another picture and passes it to Eva. Pointing to a young man at the edge of the photograph, he says, "Fifth of eleven children. The four older brothers are all married and seem to have taken on roles in their father's empire. Social media, podcasting, public speaking and the like. Zechariah kind of slipped below the radar. We didn't really know what became of him."

"And, frankly, didn't much care," Dan says. "Keeping tabs on the rest of the Brennans keeps us busy enough."

"Does any of this mean anything to you?" Jude studies Charlie carefully. "Have you ever met the Brennans or had any interactions with them online? We're looking for *anything*—any connection, no matter how small, matters."

Charlie's head is spinning, and though she hasn't eaten anything for hours, her stomach churns as if she might throw up. "I don't think so," she says slowly.

Even on the road, she and Eva weren't isolated from the headlines. They knew about the mass shootings, the protests and counterprotests, the racially motivated violence, and political posturing. On a literal mountaintop it was easy to believe that this country they loved was as sublime as the view before them. But coming back down always meant a return to the real world. Crime and overdoses and screaming pundits, yes, but also quiet inequalities and generational wounds and living paycheck to paycheck. There was so much hurt. But the Brennan family doesn't sound familiar to her at all.

"The Brennans flirt with violence," Jude continues, his voice softer now, as if he realizes how hard this is to hear. "They're big supporters of extreme gun rights and use a lot of charged language in their propaganda, encouraging their followers to commit acts of violence, but then asserting that they didn't actually mean what they said or wrote."

"They mean it. Every time." Dan's jaw is a rigid, angry line. "They don't even bother with the subtlety of dog whistles."

"Eva wouldn't willingly be a part of anything like this. Did he kidnap her?"

Jude sighs, closing the file with a snap. "We don't know. But we recognized Zechariah in the door cam footage from yesterday, and the message you received this morning confirms it. It certainly looks like Zechariah—Zach—is Eva's boyfriend. And that changes everything."

"Why?" Charlie slides to the edge of her chair, imploring Jude and Dan to see things the way she suddenly does. "If you know who he is, you know where he lives. Let's go get her. She must be with him. We can just go to his house and—"

"It's not that simple." Jude looks pained. "The Brennans have several properties and shell companies that hide the money they take in from contributions."

"Contributions? From whom? To what?"

"To their cause. People are more than happy to support them. We can only guess at both their net worth and where they've set up home base."

"They're training for civil war," Dan says, and Jude shoots him a look that could kill.

"*War?*"

"Something is going on," Jude admits. "There's been chatter for weeks, and our intel points to . . . something."

He's sparing her, trying not to scare her too much with what he knows, but somehow that's even worse. Charlie pictures every worst-case scenario. "Like what? A bomb? A mass shooting?" she asks.

"A major domestic terrorist event," Dan confirms. "Thing is, we're not just facing one threat. Our surveillance suggests—"

"We need to find Eva," Jude interrupts, cutting a sharp look Dan's way.

Horror rakes across Charlie's heart, leaving deep wounds in its wake. "Eva would *never*," she whispers, trying to make them understand.

But Jude is already shaking his head. "We don't think Eva is an accomplice, Charlie. We think she's a victim. But if she's associated with Zechariah Brennan in any way, she's in trouble."

"We have to find her."

"That's exactly what we're trying to do." Jude scoops up the file and taps the edge against the table authoritatively. "We're thankful for your help and for sharing the message. Dan will be able to glean a lot of useful information from it, I'm sure."

At this, Dan snorts a short laugh and salutes.

"I'd like to put a temporary tap on your phone so we can listen in if Zechariah calls back." Jude stands, and Charlie gets the impression that he's getting ready to dismiss her. A quick phone tap and she'll be gone.

"I don't want to get in the way," Charlie says, quickly rising so she can look him in the eye. "But you can't just send me home. Not after this. Not when I know what I know. Is something happening *now*? Is that why you—"

The trill of her phone—which is set to ring just like an old rotary—stops Charlie cold. It's buzzing in her pocket, against her hip, and her trembling hands can't dig it out fast enough.

"Quiet!" Jude shouts, raising his hands and waving frantically at Charlie's phone. The sound in the room stops as cleanly as if a cord has been cut, and in the ensuing hush the ringtone is shrill and insistent. To Charlie, Jude says, "Answer it and put it on speakerphone. Lay it faceup on the table in front of Dan."

She nods, sinking shakily into the chair that he pulls out for her. Then Jude presses a finger to his lips for the rest of the room before giving Charlie a look that says *now*.

It's the same number. She knows the second she looks at the caller ID. Hope coils around her, fragile as a plume of smoke, as Charlie taps accept and says, "Hello?"

"Is this Eva's mom?"

It's not the voice they were expecting. It's not a man.

"Yes," Charlie manages, disappointed. "Who's this?"

"It doesn't matter. I shouldn't be calling you, but Eva's in danger. I can't just let her die. I mean, she didn't do anything. Not really."

The girl is sniffling softly—crying, Charlie thinks—but that doesn't matter at all. Charlie is hung up on one word: *die*.

It's like a siren is building in her body, a scream that will erupt and echo across the lake, but Jude grabs her by the shoulders and gives her a shake. She meets his gaze, the warm, brown intensity of his eyes, and reads what's written there. She clings to him like an anchor in a gale. *Be calm*, he seems to communicate. And *it's okay* and *you can do this*. *You* have *to do this*. So Charlie swallows the unholy shriek and wrestles her terror into submission.

"Where is she?" Charlie croaks. Perhaps she should say "thank you" or try to get the girl to stay on the line and keep talking, but everything boils down to this one essential question: *Where is Eva?* Charlie can't think of anything beyond simply this.

A long silence stretches thin across the phone line. The girl is still there, she hasn't disconnected the call, but Charlie is petrified that she will. After several taut moments, she opens her mouth to beg the disembodied voice, to argue and bellow and fight, but there's a sudden, feverish gasp of air on the other end.

And then, in one rushed breath: "Bayfront Festival Park. In Duluth. But you'd better hurry."

WELCOME TO THE
DIVERSITY EMPLOYMENT FAIR!

Duluth is excited to host the region's first-ever diversity employment fair designed to provide employers and recruiters with qualified professionals from a variety of experiences and backgrounds. Our mission is to connect businesses with skilled workers who will reflect the communities they serve and provide immeasurable benefits to the organizations they represent. This is a prime opportunity for prospective employees and potential interns to meet with nearly fifty area businesses in a variety of industries including science, consulting, financial services, technology, nonprofit, manufacturing, healthcare, transportation, and more. Recent high school and college graduates welcome, as well as seniors, women, minorities, persons with disabilities, and members of our LGBTQ and immigrant communities. Join us for this premier opportunity as we seek to enrich our job sector and our region.

*A variety of food truck and local vendors will ring the park, with businesses and organizations set up in the center.

CHAPTER 22

EVA

TUESDAY

Eva is sandwiched between Abner and a paunchy, middle-aged man he calls Buzz in the cab of a nondescript white van. Abner is in the driver's seat, Buzz up against the passenger door, and Eva is pressed hip to hip with two men who give her full body chills. The air is close and sickly sweet with the scent of sweat and fear, and the radio is tuned to a fuzzy AM station that alternates between classic country music and a predawn talk show. The host likes the sound of his own voice and laughs uproariously at his own jokes. Not that Eva can make out a single word he's saying over the rumble of her heart. It's drumming so hard and so fast the beats seem to overlap one another.

When Rachel screamed for Abner outside the shed several hours ago, he materialized almost instantly. It was as if he had been waiting in the shadows for just such an event. Was Eva that obvious? Were her intentions so easy to read?

At first, Eva had been sure that she'd get away with a slap on the wrist. The spoon would be confiscated, and Rachel would be instructed to be more careful with her charge. Maybe a guard would be stationed outside the shed door. But Abner's slow smile, the way his teeth glowed suddenly bright in the soft moonlight, wasn't kind. It was mercenary.

"I was willing to give you the benefit of the doubt, Evangeline, but I'm afraid I don't have the time or the patience to reform you. You are now a liability." Abner dipped his chin in a show of paternal disappointment, the universal gesture of "this is going to hurt me more than it hurts you."

Eva doubted that sincerely.

"What are you going to do with her?" Rachel asked, her voice hoarse and rimmed with urgency.

"Never mind, Rachel." Abner dismissed his daughter without so much as a glance in her direction. "Eva, come with me."

His hand fell heavily on her shoulder, his meaty thumb digging into the soft dip below her collarbone. It would leave a bruise, but Eva didn't so much as squeak. She didn't dare to. Something had changed in Abner. There was purpose to his every movement, a serious zeal that poisoned the air around him.

As they rounded the corner of the shed it became apparent why Abner had been so quick to appear. The column of vehicles was long gone, but there were three more parked where the driveway curved down to the barracks at the back of the compound: the black SUV that Abner had used to collect her and Zach from the cottage in Little Moose, a silver truck, and a white utility van. The van was old and faded and looked like the kind of vehicle used for deliveries. Besides the cab, there were no other windows, and the double-wide cargo doors at the very back were chained and padlocked shut. A small, seemingly select group of men surrounded the trio of vehicles.

"You're taking her with you?" Rachel jogged to keep up with Abner's swift pace. "B-but I thought she was supposed to stay here. Why—"

When Abner spun on Rachel, he dragged Eva painfully with him. She was left tilted and aching as he clenched her shoulder even tighter, his fingers curled like claws. "How dare you question me," he said, his tone low and dangerous. "My own daughter."

Rachel looked as if she'd been slapped, and Eva flinched, waiting for Abner to raise his hand and follow through. She'd seen him do it before. But from somewhere behind him one of the men cleared his throat.

"Abner, we're late," he said, his voice spectral in the darkness. It was impossible to know who spoke or how Abner would respond to the light rebuke.

Eva steeled herself for his rage, but instead Abner's grip loosened a little. "Go to bed, Rachel," he said, those four simple words infused with an absolute power that brooked no argument.

Rachel caught Eva's gaze, her eyes desperate and her cheeks glistening in the moonlight. Was she *crying*?

If Eva had felt fear before, it was nothing compared to what overwhelmed her when Rachel spun on her heel and ran back to the house. Her legs gave out entirely. But Abner must have felt her falling, because he swept an arm around her waist and then picked her up as if she weighed nothing at all.

"She's coming with us?" a man questioned from somewhere behind them. But Abner didn't even bother to answer. He just wrenched open the driver's-side door of the van and thrust Eva inside.

They drove for hours. There had been frequent pit stops along the route, winding roads that led to small clearings or old homesteads that looked abandoned. At every one, Abner and Buzz left Eva in the cab of the van, her hands lashed to the steering wheel with zip ties. One sojourn was nearly two hours, and Eva fell into an exhausted, fidgety sleep with her head lolling against the back of the seat. She woke when she lost all feeling in her hands and her neck was so stiff it burned.

Now, the sun is a lump of glowing coal that hovers just above the horizon line, and Eva can recognize the familiar backroads of the area surrounding Landing. Her proximity to home draws a soft moan from her lips, and Abner shoots her a warning look. He and Buzz have more or less ignored her throughout the entire trip, and Eva suspects it's because they don't want to be reminded of the fact that she's a seventeen-year-old who doesn't deserve whatever it is they have planned for her. Because it can't be anything good, can it? Abner called her a liability. And what do you do with liabilities? You eliminate them.

"Where are you taking me?" Eva finally asks, her voice scratchy.

It seems Abner's heard her, though, because he responds, "It doesn't much matter, does it? Knowing won't change anything."

"Abner," Buzz says slowly, looking over Eva's bowed head, "maybe we could let the kid go."

"I thought I made myself clear."

Although the cab is stuffy, the atmosphere suddenly crackles with ice. It's obvious to Eva that this is the continuation of a conversation that's been going on for some time. It appears as if Buzz has been advocating for her. Why? She sneaks a glance at his face in profile and wonders. Is he a father? A grandfather? Maybe he's having second thoughts about harming an innocent teenager. Eva hopes so, but it's clear Abner will hear none of it. The realization extinguishes whatever scrap of hope Eva's been clinging to. Abner is cold and rigid beside her. He will not change his mind.

"I just want to know," Eva presses. If they've already decided that they're going to hurt her—to *kill* her?—things can't get any worse, so Eva isn't afraid of pushing. She feels hollow, scraped raw, but she says, "We're headed south. Toward Duluth? Are we meeting someone there?"

He glances at her out of the corner of his eye, seemingly impressed by her moxie, by the fact that she dares to even speak to him. It isn't lost on Eva that just hours ago Abner shut down his own daughter with a few forbidding words. But Rachel cares about his opinion of her. Eva has nothing to lose.

"I guess you could say we're meeting a lot of people in Duluth," Abner offers, humoring her. "And confronting some idolatrous systems that prop up wickedness in our world."

"Abner," Buzz warns, but the name on his lips is gentle, almost affectionate. "She won't understand."

"Maybe she doesn't need to. Maybe it's enough to know that she is a part of bringing about a new world order." Abner puts his hand just above Eva's knee and gives her thigh a little squeeze through her dirty dress. "You, my dear, won't even be a footnote in the history books, but *I* will know that you were there when retributive justice rained down. There's something poetic about that."

Eva can't help it, she jerks away from him so hard that the van lurches. But there's nowhere for her to go. Buzz is a brick wall on her right side, and Abner is now fuming on her other. His fist snaps out and grabs a handful of her tangled hair, dragging her head close to his.

"Don't fight me, little girl." Abner's breath is hot and putrid on her cheek. "I can make this very, very hard on you." His fist tightens, ripping hair from her scalp until her eyes water, and then he thrusts her away. Buzz is quiet and still on Eva's other side, but he doesn't give her even a glimmer of compassion. He looks pointedly out the window while she wipes silent tears.

A half hour from Duluth, Abner makes one last stop. This time he leaves the van running, and when the silver truck and black SUV pull up beside him, he doesn't even bother to close the van door while he talks with the other men. All the engines are running, and Eva can't make out what they're saying, but the occasional word lifts on the breeze and floats into the cab.

digital

delayed

ignition

The men look at their watches while someone stares at the screen of a cell phone and counts down from five. Then they all press a button at the same time, nod, and walk to the back of the van. There's a long, metallic scrape, and the whole vehicle sways. They've unlocked the padlock and opened the cargo doors for the first time on their entire journey, and as someone riffles around in the hold, Eva realizes that she knows what's back there.

Deep down, she's known all along.

. . . .

The clock on the dashboard says nine-twenty-nine when they pull off I-35 and turn onto West Railroad Street. Eva knows this area like the back of her hand: the bustle of South Lake Avenue and the inexorable draw of the Aerial Lift bridge, the beach on the far side of the canal where Charlie and Scout like to wade out far from shore on those rare, scorching summer days. She knows where to get the best ice cream, and she and Charlie once did an Eva Explores event at the outdoors store where over two hundred people showed up and crowded every aisle of the quaint space. This is home to Eva, and she feels a sinking, swamp-like dread when Abner drives past the convention center and the road to the aquarium.

The traffic is unexpectedly thick, and if Eva cranes her neck she can see that something is happening at the Bayfront Festival Park. There are hundreds (thousands?) of people out enjoying the beautiful morning, and the entire area is giving off a joyful, almost celebratory vibe. It's a Tuesday in late May, far too early for a concert or festival, but as Abner continues to roll closer to the venue, a sign comes into view:

DULUTH DIVERSITY EMPLOYMENT FAIR

There are tables and booths arranged around the park, and large banners that announce area businesses and prospective employers. Along the perimeter, Eva can see food trucks with long queues, a trailer emblazoned with the bold claim that Beans & Nosh makes the best iced coffee on the North Shore, and a small red tent that is serving up Belgian waffles and maple deer sausage. It looks like the job fair is just getting started, gearing up for a morning of meet and greets with hopeful employees. There are young people—recent college and high school graduates—everywhere.

Eva doesn't realize what's happening at first when Abner rolls down his window and says, "Booth seventy-four," to a man wearing a yellow safety vest. The event attendant is holding a clipboard and scanning a list, but Eva can't see his eyes behind the reflective aviators he's wearing.

"You're late," the man says, crossing something off. "Better get going. You're halfway around the perimeter to your right."

Eva's heart stutters to life and she draws a breath to say something—to call out, to scream, to do *anything*—but Buzz takes her by the jaw and wrenches her face toward his. If the look in his eyes isn't enough to silence her, the gun he holds in his lap is. Then the van is easing forward, the man with the clipboard already focusing on his next task. The moment is gone before Eva can harness a single coherent thought.

"You got the hat?" Abner asks. "The glasses?"

Reaching into the glove compartment, Buzz produces a baseball cap and a pair of oversized sunglasses, as well as a roll of transparent duct tape. They must have improvised back at the compound when Eva became part of the plan. She vaguely remembers things being taken out and put back in, of commotion and activity, but her senses had been muted by raw terror and disbelief.

"Yup," Buzz answers Abner unnecessarily. He's already pulling the worn baseball cap down over Eva's forehead. The sunglasses go on crooked, and then he's ripping off a length of the tape.

"Please, no—" Eva manages in the second before he slaps it over her mouth, using his thumbs to seal the edges against her cheeks.

"The windows are tinted, Eva, but if anyone decides to press their nose to the glass, they'll just see a girl in sunglasses and a baseball cap taking a moment to herself in the company van."

Eva can feel herself begin to hyperventilate beneath the duct tape and the low-slung hat. She can't believe that this is happening, that they're actually going to do this unimaginable thing. When she starts to shake uncontrollably, Buzz draws away from her, cramming himself against the passenger door as if he can't stand to touch someone so close to death.

Abner pulls into an empty space, parking behind a large delivery truck and in front of a van that looks similar to the one they're in. Eva doesn't think they're in spot seventy-four, but they are well concealed, and no one pays any attention at all to one more cargo van among dozens. They're on the outskirts of the park, past the main entrance and all the activity, but close enough that Eva can read the signs on some of the tables and make out the faces of several people. No one is looking in their direction. And if they did, what would they see? Nothing out of the ordinary.

"This is where we leave you, my dear." Abner turns off the ignition and grabs Eva's wrists. She struggles, trying to wrestle herself away from him, but Buzz pinches behind her elbows, thrusting her arms forward as if they're nothing but kindling. Two quick movements are all it takes to zip-tie her hands to the bottom of the steering wheel, and then Abner and Buzz duck down and secure her ankles to a metal bar beneath the seat. Eva can't move. She can't scream or motion for help or even try to make eye contact with a close passerby. She's imprisoned in the cab of the van, and she knows that it will soon be her coffin.

There's a bomb in the cargo hold.

Abner glances at his watch, and then gives Eva a grim smile. "You have just under twenty minutes, Evangeline. I suggest you spend it in prayer."

With that, Abner and Buzz wrench open their doors and hop out, but not before Abner hits the door lock and traps Eva inside.

Her face is slick with sweat and tears, and her hair clings to her damp neck. It's impossible to comprehend just how she got here, and every time Eva tries to grasp the gravity of her situation, it slips right through her fingers. She can't make sense of the fact that she only has nineteen minutes left to live (eighteen? seventeen?), but her heart swells in her chest as she thinks of her mother.

It's true, Eva realizes, that your life flashes before your eyes when the end is near. Her mind is a spinning slideshow of memories—literal mountaintops and quiet moments with their toes buried in the sand, and late nights whispering in the warm, safe belly of Sebastian—and if Eva closes her eyes she can almost feel Scout pressed tight against her hip and the gentle drag of Charlie's fingers toying with the curls that drape over her shoulder. She smells the smoky char of a lit grill, a smear of aloe lotion soaking into sun-warmed skin, Lake Superior on a fall morning when the wind carries a fine blade of winter sweeping down from the north like a prophecy. The tang of gasoline from a roadside pump in the desert. The moment when the edge of her spoon cracks the caramelized sugar on a perfect crème brûlée. The sound of Frank's low, husky laugh. Her first kiss. Like fireworks and falling all at once.

Eva doesn't want to die.

So she prays. No words, just her heart cracked open like a door, thrown off its hinges and turned inside out. *Thank you* and *more* and *please*. Love and longing, every mistake offered with open hands, fingers full and aching. Then a sudden, blinding, fleeting understanding of grace. She didn't deserve any of it, and she was allowed to live and love anyway.

When a soft clicking invades her desperate reverie, Eva ignores it at first. There's a jangly, grating scrape, followed by a soft pop, and then her eyes snap open at the exact moment that the driver's-side door is softly unlatched.

It's impossible to make sense of what she's seeing. Zach is slipping into the cab beside her, his face a ruined mess of black and blue, and a bent wire clutched in one hand. He presses a finger to his split lips, and then carefully eases the door shut behind him.

"Hey," Zach says quietly, although they are alone in the cab of the van. There's no one to hear them, and the tape over Eva's mouth renders her mute. Zach seems to notice it when Eva groans, and he reaches for a corner of her gag to begin to carefully peel it off. Her eyes must register the agony she feels, because he puts one hand on her shoulder to steady her. "Okay, I'm going to do it fast," he warns. And then he rips, immediately covering her mouth with his free hand to stop her from screaming.

"We have to be quick," he says.

"What are you doing here?" Eva is too shocked to fully register how much danger they're in. "How did you find me? How did you *know*?"

"Rachel," he says simply. "When she realized that they were taking you, she came to get me."

"*Rachel?*" Eva can hardly believe it. "But she ratted me out!"

"My sister is a complicated person. But she didn't want you to die." Zach rubs his hands up and down her arms as if to smooth away the awful word. "I slipped in the back of the silver truck when they were getting supplies and hid underneath some tarps."

"You've been here all along?" Eva thinks about the journey from the compound to the park, all those stops in the dark and all the frightening uncertainty. Somehow knowing that Zach had been near her every step of the way reframes the entire experience. She wasn't ever alone. "I can't believe you came for me."

Zach pauses for just a moment, wiping the tears that stream down her cheeks with his palms. He kisses her once, sweetly, on the mouth. "I love you, Eva. Always have."

From the waistband of his jeans he produces a kitchen knife. It's wrapped in a plastic sheath and Eva realizes it's the same knife that Rachel used to cut the chocolate cake the day before. Has it only been a day? Eva feels as if she's lived multiple lifetimes since she stepped off the *Summer Moon*.

Zach slides the knife between Eva's left wrist and the zip tie, and with one quick jerk it snaps. He frees her right hand and then bends to release her ankles. "Listen," he says when she's free. "It's going to get bad here really fast. I hid under those tarps with an entire arsenal of weapons. After the bomb goes off, members of the Family are stationed at the freeway entrances and all over the downtown area to pick off survivors. You have to find a place to hide. If you—"

"Wait." Eva puts a hand flat on his chest, stopping him. "What do you mean *you*? *We* have to find a place to hide. *We* have to—"

"Eva . . ." Zach starts, but Eva already knows what he's going to say. All at once she can see it as clearly as a snapshot. The bomb is in the van. The van can't stay here.

"Zach, no—"

"I don't have time to argue with you. This is how it's happening. You need to go now. You need to *run*."

"I won't leave you," Eva sobs, but Zach wrenches open the door.

"Yes, you will. We don't have time to clear the park. I need to get this van as far away from the crowd as I can."

"But there's only a few minutes—"

"I know. That's why I'm leaving now." Zach slides out of the van, pulling Eva with him. Almost the moment her feet touch the ground, he's climbing back into the van and slamming the door in her face. The engine roars to life, and in the midst of her anguish, Eva feels a second of gratitude that Abner forgot the keys in the ignition.

"Wait!" she screams, pounding on the window with her fists. Zach rolls it down quickly, his face wild with the knowledge of what he's about to do. There is an entire world contained in his eyes, but his hands don't tremble on the wheel. Zach is resolute. Eva steps on the running board and throws her arms around his neck, squeezing with every last ounce of her strength for a single, frantic heartbeat before Zach drags her arms away and pushes her back to the ground.

"I love you too," she says. She's not sure exactly what she means by it, or how the vicious unspooling of her heart can ever be mended, but it's exactly what he needs to hear. Zach's eyes fill with tears even as he smiles at her. And then he's pulling away.

VOICE MAIL
SA JUDE TURNER

"James, it's Turner. We have a situation developing in Duluth. Possible threat to life from a credible source related to the Evangeline Sutton missing person's case. We're en route from Landing but requesting Duluth PD presence at Bayfront Festival Park immediately."

CHAPTER 23

CHARLIE & EVA

By the time Charlie pulls off the interstate and turns toward Canal Park, she's lost sight of Agent Turner and the convoy of law enforcement vehicles. The waterfront district is purring with excitement on the cusp of a new season, and already vacationers and sun-loving locals are wandering the streets hand in hand, appreciative of this early taste of summer. It's another abnormally warm day, approaching seventy before ten a.m., but Charlie hardly registers the light pouring through her windshield or the cheerful, brightly dressed crowds. Instead, she's taking stock of her surroundings: the police cruiser that sits askance on the corner with two cops leaning against the doors, the unexpectedly sluggish traffic on a Tuesday morning, and the conspicuous absence of the FBI tactical van. She'd trailed the black truck at a distance for eighty-some miles before losing sight of it on the outskirts of Duluth.

After the second call from the unknown number, Agent Turner had told Charlie in no uncertain terms to go home and wait. There were phone calls to make and things to do, leads to be followed and places to go, because the woman on the other end of the line appeared to be a credible source with information on a clear and present threat to life.

339

Eva's life.

Of course, there was no way in hell that Charlie was going to just go back to the lakeside house and stare at her phone while her daughter was in danger. She swore to herself that she wouldn't get in the way—she would let Jude and his team do what they needed to do—but when the dust settled, she would be there for Eva. Being that girl's mama was what she had been put on this earth to do.

"I can't prevent you from coming," Jude told her as the room swirled around them. Agents were grabbing gear and car keys, checking guns and securing magazines of extra ammunition in their holsters. "And I know you'll probably do the opposite of what I tell you to anyway. But please, Charlotte, for the love of God, stay far away."

He must have seen the truth written in her eyes, because he pushed a heavy sigh through his teeth and added, "Be careful. Call me if you see or hear *anything.*"

Charlie sat in her car while they rolled out, the entire cavalry heading south toward Duluth and whatever was supposed to happen at Bayfront Festival Park. Then, when the last vehicle had rounded the corner and faded from view, she pulled out of the boathouse parking lot and followed them. Charlie still couldn't get a clear perspective of the whole picture, but the drive to the city was an hour and a half of time to think it out, to turn the situation over again and again like a kaleidoscope catching a ray of sunshine. Just as everything slid into tentative focus, it blurred again, leaving her wrung out and confused.

It came down to this: Eva had a secret boyfriend who wasn't the man he claimed to be. And that lie built on a lie landed her in a terrible situation with a very dangerous group of people. So Charlie would be there when everything exploded. She had to be.

Now, traffic crawls toward the Duluth Entertainment Convention Center and the Amsoil Arena, and then grinds to a stubborn halt. There's not so much as a hint of movement. A few people have opened their windows or even stepped out of their cars, but Charlie can see that the long line of vehicles is going nowhere. Leaving her truck running, she slides out of the cab and walks toward a man who's standing next to his minivan.

"What's going on?" she asks.

"I'm trying to get my kid to the job fair." He gestures toward a young man about Eva's age in the passenger seat. The boy shrugs, salutes, and turns his attention back to his phone. The man continues, "They've shut down the road. They're trying to turn people around."

"Why?"

"Beats me."

But Charlie is already walking away. Walking, and then jogging, and suddenly sprinting alongside the idling cars and toward the barrier that's been put up to stop the flow of traffic. There's a police cruiser jackknifed across the road, so Charlie cuts across a grassy ditch and through the arena parking lot. It's full of vehicles and people, but she ignores them all and races across Harbor Drive toward Playfront Park where Eva used to climb the monkey bars, and once knocked out a baby tooth when she fell. She hadn't even cried.

The pedestrian thoroughfare into the festival grounds is lined with balloons and crowded with people, and there's happy pop music thumping from a stand of portable speakers. No one seems to know that anything is wrong, that just outside of the park the police have set up a roadblock to prevent more people from coming in. Charlie swivels as she runs, scanning faces and searching for anything that will give her the tiniest clue about where Eva might be, but nothing seems menacing or even slightly out of the ordinary. It's a gorgeous late-spring day, and this multicultural job fair is an obvious, smashing success. All around her employers are passing out flyers filled with information about their companies, and prospective employees are perusing their fare as if each job opportunity is ripe with potential for a new future, a new life. The press of people is so overwhelming, Charlie wishes she had a bullhorn and a stage—if Eva is here, she likely won't know what to do with a cop or a plainclothes FBI agent, but Charlie is family and safety and *home*.

The sudden sound of an engine revving stands out among all the noise only because it is accompanied by honking. A few quick bleats at first, then whoever is laying on the horn presses it down hard and doesn't let up. It's muffled, a distant annoyance that makes a few people look up and shake their heads. But the honking is not coming from some disgruntled driver stopped at the traffic jam on West Railroad Street. It's coming from inside the park.

Charlie knows with a sudden, sickening certainty that she has to find the source of this commotion. The honking echoes around the warren of tables and booths and seems to originate near the frontage road that skirts the festival grounds. Charlie hurries in that direction even as the crowd around her begins to turn. A woman screams, a short peal of terror that cuts off almost immediately, but then more people begin to shout.

All at once the crowd is moving, a frenzy of fear and uncertainty that rolls like a ground swell across the wide green. It's like watching a storm slowly spin to devastating life.

"Run!" someone shouts. "Get out of here!"

And then a single, chilling word rips through the commotion: *bomb*.

"There's a bomb!"

"Bomb! Run!"

"It's a *bomb*!"

Men and women are running past her, flying toward the entrance to the park and away from the harbor and the little canal in front of the boat club and resort. Because the festival grounds are shaped like a baseball diamond and surrounded on two sides by the water of the Duluth Harbor Basin, there's only one way for people to run—toward the road and the traffic jam that they don't know has trapped them here. Charlie's heart stutters to a stop as she realizes that there's nowhere to go, nowhere to run to get away from a . . . *bomb*?

"How do you know?" Charlie grabs a middle-aged businessman by the lapels of his suit jacket as he tries to rush past. "How do you know there's a bomb?"

He shakes off her hands, panicked, but shouts over his shoulder: "There's a girl . . ." He waves one hand in the general direction of the frontage road next to the canal, but Charlie isn't paying attention anymore. *There's a girl.*

A girl. A girl and a white delivery van honking and zipping between trucks and tents and clusters of screaming people. Charlie sprints toward it. In no time her lungs are burning and her side feels torn open, but Charlie pushes herself harder. She has to make it to that van before whoever is driving it collides with the stage. Because that's where the van is heading, right? To the place where the most people will be gathered.

But as Charlie follows the erratic path, she realizes that the driver is not hitting people, they're *avoiding* them. And the area around the stage is virtually empty. This isn't a concert, and no headliner is setting up to play. In fact, the closer the van draws to the steely-blue sheet of the cold harbor, and the fewer objects and people stand in the way, the faster it goes.

Charlie grasps what's happening when it's too late for her to do anything at all. The van speeds down the final stretch of frontage road—there's nowhere to go and no turning back—until it hits the low rim of boulders that form the breakwater around the park. The force of impact doesn't stop the van or even slow it, but sends it careening through the air, a hunk of metal screaming across the spring morning and then slamming into the plane of dark water.

Charlie hits the ground before the van has sunk beneath the waves, the truth taking her out at the knees. She blinks at the spot where the lake is quickly devouring the van that she is sure holds her daughter, her body so numb she feels she may be dying too.

In seconds, there's nothing to mark the spot where the van went under except for a frothing of air bubbles. A sob tears free from Charlie's throat, but the keening cry of her shattered heart is swallowed by a moment of pure, negative sound, an inhale that warps time for a nanosecond before the harbor magnificently erupts. The plume of white water that blooms from the bay is a savage flower of foam and silt and debris. It's pale and murderous, a cloud of virulence that sprays ice-cold water and dust over Charlie's trembling shoulders. She cowers, tucking her head in her arms as the ensuing boom rips at her eardrums.

The air throbs in the aftermath, or maybe it's just Charlie's mutilated heart, trying to keep time in a world where Eva is nothing but mist. Charlie lifts her hands, palms up, and tries to catch her, but even as her fingers close, she knows it's useless. Her daughter—the better half of the legendary Sutton girls, Charlie's beloved Little Mermaid, her Evangeline Rose—is gone.

. . . .

They believed her. No sooner had Zach pulled away than Eva began to scream. "Bomb! There's a bomb!" She was sobbing, and the manic look in her eyes convinced the people around her so quickly it was as if she had lit a match and was holding the fuse in her hand. *"Run!"*

So they did. And then Zach began to honk the horn, and chaos ensued. Eva's understanding of homemade bombs was limited, to say the least, and she had no idea if Zach's plan— whatever it was—would work or how far the blast radius would reach if and when the device detonated. But getting as many people as far away as possible seemed like the best, most logical thing to do. Never mind that she felt like she was bleeding out herself, barely able to put one foot in front of the other or gather the breath she needed to shout.

While most people followed Eva's horrifying directive, as the crowd thinned before her she could see that some people were coming *toward* her. Law enforcement, guns drawn, ran at Eva as quickly as everyone else ran away. It was instinctual for her to put up her hands, a reflex born of too many cop shows and a love for spy movies and police procedurals. So she was unbalanced, arms high overhead, when the cargo van hit the breakwater.

Eva stopped as if she had been shot. The sound of metal hitting rock, and then just as quickly water, tore through her. The titanic splash that followed was shocking, but it was over in mere seconds, a wisp of time that left Eva frozen in place on the trampled grass of the festival grounds.

"Get down!" A Black man in plainclothes with his gun drawn grabbed Eva and pushed her to the ground. He covered her with his body. "If there's a—"

His words were obliterated by the blast, and Eva covered her face, her heart ruined by the knowledge of who was driving that van. "He's in there," she said, but it was whispered and use-less. It wouldn't change a thing.

Now she cowers under the unfamiliar man, cocooned beneath his arms and the warm tent of his body. He smells of sandalwood and sanctuary, and although she doesn't know him, she's suddenly, overwhelmingly grateful to be anywhere but on the compound of the Gates of Zion. This man is a stranger, but he is familiar in a way that makes her want to lay her head on his shoulder. Mingling with the understanding that Zach is gone is the fragile, budding belief that she is *safe*.

"Are you Evangeline Sutton?" he asks, rocking back on his haunches when the shock wave has settled. He keeps one steadying hand on her arm, and Eva pushes herself up, leaning against him because she doesn't think she can support her own weight. The water where the van had gone down is a foaming whirlpool of waves and debris; Eva knows with an anguished certainty that nothing could survive what just happened.

Then it hits her. "They have guns!" Eva says, bolting to her feet and spinning around. "There are so many of them and they're all over Duluth. But they have an entire arsenal and they're going to start shooting after the bomb goes off!"

"Slow down." He steadies her and ducks his head so that they are eye to eye. "Who has guns? Who's going to start shooting?"

"The Family," Eva spits, but she can tell that the name doesn't mean anything to him. So she tries, "The people of the Gates of Zion. Abner Brennan."

Recognition finally clicks and turns his gaze to stone. He waves someone over and passes Eva into the arms of a policewoman in uniform. "She needs a hospital," he tells her. To Eva he says, "They'll take good care of you. I'll see you soon. And I'll call your mom. She's so worried."

"My mom?" Eva's voice cracks at the mention of Charlie. She wants to see her so badly it's an all-body ache. But there's no time to dwell because the policewoman is ushering her away from the water and toward the entrance of the park.

As Eva is led away, she can see fear and confusion writ on the faces of everyone she passes. A patchwork group of officers in uniform and plainclothes try to herd the crowd toward the parking lot and away from the scene of the crime. They're a gloriously ragtag collection of humanity, men in three-piece suits and punk teens and worried parents. A small cluster of twentysomethings in camo T-shirts makes Eva's heart stutter, but they're not carrying guns—they're helping an elderly Asian woman. One has her large purse slung over his shoulder, and the other two are flanking her, arms locked around her waist as they help her hurry toward the park entrance.

"Let's get you out of here," the policewoman says, leading Eva to a cruiser. It's parked behind an armored vehicle with SWAT painted on the side in white block letters. Eva doesn't know what it's doing at the park or who alerted the authorities, but for the first time in days she feels like everything might be okay. Not good, maybe never again *good*, but okay.

Before she lets the policewoman put her in the back of the cruiser, Eva turns to take it all in. People are crying, hugging loved ones, and shaking their heads at the incomprehensible turn their day has taken. They don't even know yet what they've been spared, or how much danger they are still in. And yet, as Eva watches them, she can't help but love them. The girl with box braids and bracelets halfway up her arm who's comforting a towheaded little boy who seems to have lost his mother. The man who looks like a bank CEO, who's rolled up his sleeves and is handing out bottles of water to anyone within arm's reach. The cop with his arm around the shoulders of a woman in a soft pink hijab. It's a song, a symphony, and Eva closes her eyes for just a moment to listen. There's a genesis contained in every note.

VOICE MAIL
SA JUDE TURNER

"Charlie, it's Jude. Listen, we found her. She's okay. They're taking her to St. Luke's. More soon, but go. She's waiting for you."

CHAPTER 24

CHARLIE & EVA

TUESDAY AND BEYOND

Charlie can't quite believe it. She listens to Jude's message again and again, furious with herself for missing his call in the first place. She hadn't even heard her phone—her ears were still ringing from the blast—but as she stumbled to her feet, it buzzed against her hip. She tries to call him back, but he doesn't answer. So she retraces her steps, weaving through the throngs of people to where her truck is still stuck in gridlock. If anything, it's gotten worse as people try to flee the festival grounds. Charlie knows she's not going anywhere for a very long time, so she sets off on foot. St. Luke's is just under two miles away, and she'll run it if she has to.

She doesn't make it far. Near the freeway entrance, traffic is flowing better, and a guy with silver hair and Ray-Bans in a red convertible slows down to keep pace with her.

"Are you hurt?" he asks. "I heard there was a bomb."

"There was," Charlie confirms, though it's surreal to admit. "But I'm fine."

"Where are you going? Do you need help?"

He's a tourist from a small town in Iowa, and he insists on driving her to the hospital. He chats all the way, but Charlie absorbs exactly none of it. It doesn't matter; he's not making small talk, he's trying to distract her.

"Take care," he says at the brightly lit ER entrance. Then he adds soberly, "Be safe."

Charlie hurries into the building, skirting the reception desk and homing in on the cop she sees stationed in front of a swinging door. "I'm Charlotte Sutton," she tells him, her voice breathless and insubstantial. She may as well have run the entire way. "My daughter, Eva, was brought here. Evangeline Sutton?"

Recognition glints in his eyes, but he puts up a finger and turns his back to talk into the radio at his shoulder. After a moment, he asks to see Charlie's ID, and then he's pushing open the door and escorting her down the hallway. They stop in front of a glass-fronted room, but Charlie can't see inside because curtains have been drawn across the windows.

"May I . . ." Charlie can't finish, but the cop nods anyway.

The door is cracked open and Charlie steps through. She's half-hidden behind the pale curtain, but from here she can see the whole room. Eva sits in the center of a narrow hospital bed. It's her Evangeline Rose, hair tousled and tangled, skin uncharacteristically pale so that her freckles stand out even at a distance. She's wearing a dirty blue dress, prairie-style, with puffed sleeves and a Peter Pan collar. The skirt is hiked up to her thighs, and a nurse is examining a wound on her left shin. An IV snakes into one of Eva's slender hands, and an oxygen tube loops around her ears and into her nostrils. She's the same, but changed. It feels like a lifetime since Charlie last saw her on the deck of the *Summer Moon*.

Charlie must make a noise because Eva looks up, and when she catches sight of her mom, her whole face crumples.

"Mom?" It's a plaintive, childlike cry, and Charlie's heart breaks because behind that raw longing is an unmistakable vein of doubt. Eva's not sure how her mother will react. She's afraid.

Charlie is across the room in two strides, then sinking to the side of the bed and gathering her girl into her arms. If the nurse is annoyed by the interruption, she doesn't make a fuss, but lets Charlie cradle Eva as if she is a small child.

"I'm sorry!" Eva cries. "I'm so, so sorry. This is all my fault. I should have never—"

"Shhh . . ." Charlie soothes her. "Don't. You're okay. That's all that matters."

It is and it's not. They both know that the fallout from all of this will be far-reaching and profound. But for now, it's enough that Eva is safe and whole and wrapped in Charlie's embrace.

"But I—"

"Not now," Charlie says, her voice fracturing. "Are you hurt? What happened?"

"She has a pretibial laceration that has become infected," the nurse tells Charlie. "It will need to be cleaned out and resutured, but it should heal nicely. We're giving her a dose of IV antibiotics and some fluid—she's a little dehydrated."

Eva adds, "I'm fine. I'll be fine."

Charlie sits back and takes Eva's face in her hands, studying each detail. Her lips are dry, her skin raw. There are scratches on her cheeks and neck, and a bruise that's the exact shape and size of a thumb beneath her collarbone. But it's Eva's eyes that ruin Charlie. Her daughter looks tortured, like she's been to hell and back and thoroughly singed in the process. Getting her back is just the beginning, Charlie realizes.

A short rap on the door makes them all look up, and Detective James steps into the room. He gives them all a tight, serious smile, then crosses the room to shake Eva's hand. "Welcome home, Evangeline. We're thrilled you're back."

Charlie can tell he means it, and it floods her with a sense of gratitude.

"I hate to do this to you right now, I'm sure you just want to catch up with your mom, but I have some questions I need to ask."

"Anything." Eva sits up straighter, wincing at how the movement strains at her leg. "I want to tell you everything I know. I—" She stops abruptly, her eyes going wide.

"What is it?" Charlie reaches for one of Eva's hands, but the girl yanks it away and begins rummaging through the pockets of her dress.

"I took notes. I wrote down everything I could." She produces a sheaf of folded notebook paper and thrusts it at Detective James. "They—the Family—are planning an uprising. The bomb at Bayfront Festival Park was just the beginning. There's going to be mass shootings all over the city. They were supposed to start after the bomb exploded. What's happening out there?"

"You don't have to worry about that right now," Detective James says, taking the paper from her. His eyes widen as he studies the list. "There are makes and models here. Are you telling me that these are the vehicles?"

"Yes!" Eva tries to climb out of the bed, but Charlie and the nurse push her back down. "Yes, the number beside the description is the number of people in the vehicle. I could be wrong, I couldn't always see directly inside, but I also wrote down what the men looked like when I could. And some partial plates. I—"

"Thank you, Eva," Detective James interrupts. "We have lots more to talk about, but for now I have to go. You take care of yourself, okay? Get better. We'll talk soon."

The officer rushes from the room, and they can hear him shouting into his phone as he runs down the hall. The cop stationed outside pokes his head in to give Eva a thumbs-up, then closes the door behind him as if to say, *No one is getting through me.*

"Sounds like you're quite the hero, Eva." The nurse lays a hand on Eva's ankle and gives it a gentle squeeze. "We're going to have to clean up that leg, but I'll give you a few minutes with your mom first."

She slips out quietly, and Charlie and Eva are suddenly alone in the room. The only sound is the beep of the heart monitor and Eva's ragged breath, and then a thin wail escapes from her lips. "I'm not a hero!" she chokes out. "I lied and I hid things from you, and I ran away. I've never been so scared in my life. I'm so sorry, I—"

"Evangeline . . ." Charlie curls on the bed beside her and pulls her daughter's head onto her chest. "Baby, I forgive you. And I'm sorry if I made you feel like there were things you couldn't tell me. I'm sorry if I've been suffocating you. But listen, you're alive and that's all that matters right now. When that bomb went off, I thought I'd lost you forever."

Eva's fingers clutch at Charlie as she sobs.

"It's not okay," she cries, her tears wetting Charlie's shirt. "It will never be okay."

Charlie doesn't shush her or dissuade her. She holds Eva close and lets her say everything she needs to say. It's a love story and a tragedy, a thriller that Charlie can hardly believe is now a part of their personal history. It's unbelievable and all too possible, a world tipped sideways that needed just the slightest nudge to fall.

When it's all over, Eva is wrung out and limp, her body heavy against Charlie's. It reminds Charlie of when Eva was a toddler and she'd fall asleep in her mother's arms. Her weight somehow doubled in the moment before drifting off—the second before she let everything go and allowed herself to be simply, steadfastly held. So Charlie does the only thing she knows to do. She hangs on.

. . . .

Home feels different when Eva steps over the threshold a few days later. Scout is the first one to greet her, but Frank isn't far behind, and Sophie lingers in the doorway between the living room and the kitchen until hugs have been given all around and Eva motions her over. It's a happy reunion; there are balloons and flowers and a tiered chocolate cake that makes Eva's stomach flip. She realizes that she may never be able to eat chocolate cake again without thinking about everything that happened. For now, she can't stomach a single bite.

"I need just a few minutes alone with Charlie and Eva," Agent Turner tells Frank and Sophie when small plates of cake and glasses of cold lemonade have been passed around.

"Of course," Frank says, moving to leave, but Eva stops him with a hand on his arm.

"Stay," she says, then adds, "Please?"

"Anything you want." Frank puts his hand over hers and leans in to give her a kiss on the cheek.

"Let's go out back. I'd like to talk outside if that's okay." Eva begins to move toward the side door without waiting for an answer. It's new, this confidence, her ability to say what she wants and then follow through as if she's allowed to have an opinion.

"There are chairs on the lawn," Charlie offers. "The media can't see us there."

There were news vans at the end of the driveway when they arrived at the Morrows' lake house. CNN and Fox and MSNBC along with local reporters and people who just wanted to catch a glimpse of Eva. Whether she liked the distinction or not, she was being lauded as a hero because her careful notes allowed law enforcement to capture many of the members of the Family who were poised to take part in the Uprising. Most were apprehended before they could get off a single shot because the unexpected failure of the car bomb threw their plans into total chaos. The would-be soldiers didn't know what to do, so they watched and waited and were eventually identified when Detective James shared Eva's list with the Duluth PD, the FBI, and

Minnesota state law enforcement. They brought out the cavalry. And now everyone wants an exclusive with Eva.

There are thick clusters of cottony clouds in the sky and a cool breeze coming off the water. But the sun is warm on their backs, and as Eva sinks into one of the Adirondack chairs around their fire pit, she closes her eyes and takes a deep, steadying breath. She wasn't sure she would ever sit in these chairs again. Or see this view. Or smell the white musk and vanilla of her mother as she sank into the chair beside her.

"We're in your debt," Agent James says, repeating a familiar refrain. "I want you to know that because of everything you told us, we were able to derail most of the Family's plans for what they called 'the Uprising.'" He puts air quotes around the words, and the action feels dismissive to Eva. He continues, "The FBI has been following their activity for years—and we knew *something* was going to happen—but they mostly coordinated offline. They went old-school on us."

Eva doesn't respond to his little shrug and self-deprecating laugh. Instead, she says quietly, "But we didn't derail *everything*."

She doesn't feel brave. There were a handful of shootings across the country, including a standoff in Duluth when one of the squads in the convoy resisted arrest. An officer was injured. And there was a mass shooting at a grocery store in Idaho; another at a mall in Tennessee. A backpack bomb was detonated at a bus stop in California, and there was a hostage situation in Detroit. Each incident was tied to Abner Brennan and his Family, and though Eva knows the math doesn't add up—that she can't blame herself for something that she didn't even know about a week ago—she feels responsible.

Survivor's guilt, the FBI victim specialist says. But Eva doesn't need a fancy term to wonder if she could have, *should have* done more. Not just in the days since her abduction, but all the days and weeks and months before. Did she *ever* do enough to stop hate in its tracks?

Agent James leans forward to catch her eye. "That's not your fault. The casualties our country sustained were nothing compared to what they would have been if you hadn't done what you did. You were incredibly brave, Eva. I hope you know that. For what it's worth, you've helped put Abner Brennan—and a significant number of his associates—behind bars for the rest of his life. We have him on charges of domestic terrorism, hate crimes, and conspiracy to commit murder, along with kidnapping, unlawful detainment, and tax evasion. And that's just the tip of the iceberg."

Eva knows all that already. It's exciting, to be sure, but it's not a happy ending. Not by a long shot. "Zechariah Brennan is the real hero," she says. She knows her mom is still—and might forever be—nursing a grudge against her ex-boyfriend and abductor. Charlie doesn't yet fully understand what happened between them or how complicated the entire situation was. But in the end, Zach gave his life for her. For every single person at Bayfront Festival Park that day. And Eva is still coming to grips with it all.

"He is," Agent Turner agrees. "What he did was incredibly selfless. He was a courageous young man, even if it took him a while to see the light."

Charlie manages a single nod, and Eva's grateful for that small concession. It's a step.

"Our bomb techs have completed their investigation of the blast site, and I'm sorry to report it was frustratingly inconclusive." Agent Turner temples his fingers as he explains. "Most IEDs have some sort of a homemade countdown device—a kitchen timer or alarm clock or something—but they depend on a moment of connection to ignite. The water should have prevented that trigger from firing."

Eva's chest seizes with a moment of what-might-have-been. From the window of the cargo van, she can picture Zach swimming, the IED—*improvised explosive device*, she knows from more than her fair share of interviews with the FBI—sinking to the bottom of the harbor, stripped of all its awful power. What would her life look like now if Zach was still in it?

They are considering Eva's disappearance a kidnapping because she was not old enough to consent to what happened to her—even if she chose to go with Zach in the beginning. And then, when she wanted to leave, he wouldn't let her go. Of course she told them everything. About the drugs that Zach urged her to give Charlie, the note she left (and that he took), and being locked in the house at Little Moose. When Eva heard about the missing life raft from the *Summer Moon*, she realized that Zach must have inflated it and tossed it overboard during their nighttime trek across the lake. To frame Charlie? To make it look like Eva was the victim of an unfortunate accident? None of it looked good for Zach, but didn't his final act erase everything that came before? Couldn't there be forgiveness if he knew what he had done, and then quite literally did everything in his power to right it?

"I'm tired, Mr. James," Eva says, rubbing her aching eyes with her knuckles. "Do you need something else from me or can I go lie down now?"

"Sorry," the agent says, catching Charlie's gaze over Eva's head and giving her an unreadable look. "I don't mean to keep you. You've been so helpful in all our conversations, and I just wanted to keep you updated on what we're learning."

Eva doesn't tell him that they keep sharing the wrong news. She knows she probably shouldn't be curious, but a part of her is still back at that compound in the woods. They won't tell her what's happening there, what they've done to the Gates of

Zion and the people who live behind the fence. The women and children, those who didn't have a choice about what happened to them, even if it felt right. Like home. Eva thinks about them often. For better or for worse.

"I want you to know that Zach wasn't your only friend at the Gates." Agent James leans forward with his elbows on his knees. "In our interviews, we've learned that not only did Rachel free Zach the night before the Uprising, she was the one who called your mom and tipped us off about what was going to happen."

A hint of a smile crosses Eva's lips. Spunky, sassy Rachel Brennan stood up to her force-of-nature father. And won.

"I know she was your captor, Eva, but somehow you got through to her. She cared about you." Agent James pauses, tries again. "She *cares* about you."

Charlie catches Eva's hand and squeezes it tight. "Of course she does."

Eva can tell that there are more things her mom would like to say, but she blessedly keeps her mouth shut and pretends to be interested in the little waves that lick the shore.

Following her gaze, Eva is suddenly gripped with the need to be in the water. It doesn't matter that the air is cool and the water freezing. She wants to feel it between her toes and lapping up her ankles. Her wound is clean, properly stitched, and carefully bandaged—she can't get it wet, but she can stand on the shore.

Neither Agent James nor her mother stop her when she stands and walks to the low wall at the edge of the property. Her leg is stiff, and it stings a bit when she lifts it over, but by the time she's sitting on the stacked rocks to take off her shoes, she's forgotten entirely about her wound.

The first bite of Lake Superior water is icy and clarifying, a shot of pure, crisp solace that feels like a new beginning. Zach is in the mist of each wave as it bubbles up the shoreline and tumbles over the rocks, but so is she. Eva as a toddler with her toes in the foamy surf. As a preteen draped over a blow-up mattress with her mom on the other side. As a grown woman slicing through the water with a wicked freestyle stroke.

But the water that gives life can take it. The love that feels forever can fade. People are messy and broken and achingly beautiful, and life is never quite what it seems. And in this moment Eva has room for it all, for the new scars that she bears and the way that they will inevitably, inexorably heal. For the soft understanding that hope is a haven for every bruised and battered soul.

For now, it's all she needs.

EPILOGUE

Charlie and Eva wake to the trill of a redwing blackbird. It's a happy sound, quick and bright like water dancing over stones. The window by Charlie's head is cracked open, and the cool night air is quickly being replaced by a sticky, late summer heat. The moment the sun rises, the earth begins to bake. She had forgotten that, the way the cornfields trap the humidity and the dark soil seems to exhale in the light of a new morning. They'll have to shut the windows and turn on the air-conditioning or Sebastian will be a sauna by midmorning.

"Rise and shine, honey." Charlie props herself up on one elbow and reaches to tousle Eva's hair. She's cut it, and it barely grazes her shoulders, a glossy, riotous halo the color of a raven's wing. Charlie curls a strand around her finger and gives a gentle tug. "Wakey-wakey."

"Not yet," Eva murmurs, rolling over and burrowing deeper into her pillow. "Five more minutes . . ." But then she must remember, because she sits up, puddling the soft, floral sheet around her waist. "What day is it?"

"I think you already know." Charlie smiles, spinning out of bed and stretching as her feet touch the trailer floor. A short shuffle and she's in the galley kitchen, flipping on the coffee-pot that she prepped the night before. In seconds, Sebastian fills with the aroma of hot coffee. They grabbed muffins from a local grocery store last night, but Charlie feels like making pancakes, so she gathers the milk, flour, and eggs, and begins to whisk.

"I've got breakfast covered," Charlie calls over her shoulder. "Take your time. I'll throw batter in the pan when you're ready for it."

"Thanks, Mom." Eva sticks her head out of the small bathroom and asks, "What about a little walk this morning? Wye Cave isn't far, and I wouldn't mind exploring a few of those tight squeezes a bit further."

But Charlie is already shaking her head. "It's over an hour to Iowa City and we need to get you moved in by three. Then we're supposed to have dinner with Trinity's parents and—"

"Okay." Eva lifts one shoulder, a smile tugging at the side of her mouth. "I'll shower."

Charlie leaves the pancake batter on the counter and grabs a cup of coffee. She steps out into the misty Iowa morning in nothing but a pair of boxers and a University of Iowa sweatshirt and sits in one of their faded lawn chairs with her knees pulled up to her chest. It's hard to believe that she's bringing her daughter to college today, and then driving away to leave her in the hands of total strangers. But her hesitation is much more than typical, new-college-parent nerves.

It's been a hard summer. Lots of counseling and healing and backsliding. From the day she came home, Eva slept with Charlie in the queen-sized bed on the main floor of the lake house and didn't move back into her own bedroom until mid-July. She moaned sometimes in her sleep, and cried, and there was nothing Charlie could do about it. "Don't wake her," her counselor told Charlie. "Let her subconscious do its job."

So she did. And when Eva woke, they talked and fought and worked themselves to the bone undoing the knots that had been lashed tight around their hearts. They both felt misunderstood. They both found ways to walk a mile in the other's shoes.

Eva's acceptance letter from the University of Iowa came the day she was supposed to graduate. Her applications had been delayed because of her late arrival in the public school system, but even though she had been waiting on tenterhooks for news, Eva left the letter unopened on the kitchen table for a week. Charlie wondered which application essay she had used, or if those fifty reflections were just her own personal therapy sessions. An ongoing exercise in self-discovery. There was clearly more work to be done, as Eva was a hollow shell of herself in those early days, twitchy and quiet and scared. But one morning Charlie found the letter opened and spread out on the table with a single honeycrisp apple holding down a corner. It was the first step up from rock bottom.

"Pancakes?" Eva asks, poking her head out of Sebastian. "Do we have chocolate chips?"

They do, and Charlie makes a steaming stack and carries them out to the picnic table. Eva has set out the maple syrup and orange juice, two plates beside each other, and two slender glasses. They eat in silence for a few moments, quieted by melting chocolate and butter-crisp edges and the zest of cold juice, and then Eva asks, "Is Jude coming in the morning?"

Charlie nods. "He'll get in late tonight, then we'll pop over before breakfast to say goodbye." Warmth spreads through her limbs like water pouring across a flood plain. Jude is the best, most unexpected surprise from the worst thing that has ever happened to her. He was nothing but poised and professional while the FBI wrapped up all the loose ends, but around the same time that Eva moved out of her bed, Charlie's cell phone began to ding with incoming texts from Jude.

They were innocuous at first, bland and forgettable. Then

they started really talking, and before Charlie knew it, they were FaceTiming nearly every night.

"And then . . ." Eva prompts. "Remind me where you're heading."

"Colorado." It's a simple answer, because for the first time in years, Charlie doesn't want a crammed itinerary. There's a valley of red stone and rugged canyons tucked away between Colorado Springs and Breckenridge, and she wants nothing more than to stay there for as long as they possibly can. She feels herself blush at the thought of waking up with Jude in the bed at the back of the trailer. She wonders what it says about her that it's not something she's ever imagined before.

Charlie and Eva clean up quickly after breakfast, a sense of unanticipated urgency hurrying them along. They've waited eighteen years for this day, and though they could have never predicted the path it had taken them to get here, there's joy in each movement as they tear down camp and get Sebastian ready for the road.

The sun is streaming through the trees of Maquoketa Caves State Park, and the dappled light makes the Airstream glow like a postcard photo. Normally, Charlie would grab her camera and snap a few pictures, maybe have Eva push back a curtain from inside the trailer so that her graceful hand would be seen at the edge of the frame. But Eva Explores is no more.

Surprisingly, letting it go was a bit like unclenching her fists and taking a deep, purifying breath that rolled through every muscle of her aching body. Charlie's lungs expanded, her shoulders relaxed, her pulse slowed. Maybe they would tell their story someday, and maybe Instagram would be the medium they chose. Maybe not. Charlie still had her camera, and Eva still had her words, and maybe there were better ways to share and connect, to remind people to open their eyes and their hearts. To explore the world around them and smile at the people they met. To always take the long way back.

"Ready?" Eva says, and for the first time in months she's grinning, ear to ear, nose scrunched like she's a little girl again.

Charlie pulls her close, breathes in the scent of her still-damp hair, and tries to memorize the moment. Then she drops a kiss on her daughter's sweet forehead and takes her by the hand. "Let's go."

AUTHOR'S NOTE

I'VE NEVER WRITTEN AN author's note before because I've never had a reason to. But it feels wrong to send *The Long Way Back* out into the world without at least a fumbling attempt to share where this all came from and why.

When my children were young, we had a pop-up tent trailer that we dragged all across the country. Twice it went from our home in the Midwest all the way to British Columbia, where half of our family lives. Many more times than that it stayed closer to home, allowing us to enjoy the Midwest from campgrounds where we made lifelong memories. There is something truly unique about experiencing a place in this neighborly, outdoorsy way. Our kids made friends with strangers, and we spent long, lazy days exploring the exquisite world around us.

For most of my life I've believed two things: one, that we are (and always will be) better together; and two, that we are all (whether we realize it or not) worthy of love. I still believe those things, but my heart has broken over and over again as I've witnessed (and, sadly, participated in) the ways that we have been quick to divide into "Us" vs. "Them." To condemn those we disagree with and justify bald hatred of our neighbors (near and far) for no reason other than that they believe something different from us.

Much of these ugly confrontations happen on social media, and as I was conceptualizing this book, the intersection of our changing world and these opposing ideologies seemed to go hand in hand with our digital interconnectedness. While the Family is brooding and plotting, Charlie and Eva are exploring and adventuring—and loving it. Of course, their experiences are far from perfect, but they meet kind, generous people along the way and encounter the best the world has to offer. While the Family is rallying people to their cause online and stirring up dissension and dissatisfaction, Charlie and Eva are making connections and inviting people to embrace life and the beautiful country they call home. Eva Explores and the Family represent two sides of the same coin, living in a place that is beautiful *and* broken—they just choose to see different sides of it.

It was my goal in this book to show the humanity of all my characters, to be real and honest in my representation of them and why they believe the things they do. The *why* of it matters much to me, and I hope that as you read you may have felt a stirring of empathy for characters you may have wholeheartedly disagreed with. Everything comes from something, and though our past hurts will *never* justify or excuse hateful actions, knowing may help us understand, at least a little.

I wish that everyone could experience a cross-country trek in a trailer and the simple camaraderie of strangers sharing stories around a campfire. Maybe in listening to each other we would—at the very least—be nudged toward kindness. But maybe sharing stories could accomplish something even greater: the understanding that we belong to each other. I hope you are encouraged to take the time to listen to someone who sees the world differently from you, and look for areas of commonality instead of rushing to vilify. Our world needs good listeners. It needs our open hands and open hearts. It needs *you*.

Grace and peace,
Nicole

ACKNOWLEDGMENTS

EVERY TIME I SIT down to write the acknowledgments, I am stunned by the number of people who had a hand in "my" book. The truth is, it's never just *my* book, but a collaborative effort by so many talented and generous people that I find myself at a loss. My gratitude is deep and sincere.

The Long Way Back became a full and exciting possibility when I brainstormed the concept with my former editor, Daniella Wexler; my agent, Danielle Egan-Miller, and her assistant, Ellie Roth. We had so much fun tossing ideas around and pushing the envelope with where the story could go. So much of what landed on the page is because of the thoughtful (and, frankly, brilliant) suggestions of these three women. I wish I could plot every book with this dream team.

After some serious self-doubt and late-night uncertainty, friends Tosca Lee and Kimberly Stuart offered much needed feedback and encouragement. Sometimes "you're on the right track" is all you need to hear.

When I reached out to a childhood friend and FBI agent, he didn't hesitate to offer his help and expertise, and even went so far as to allow me to visit his office and meet his coworkers. The hours I spent peppering them all with every question and scenario that I could think of were instrumental to the writing of this book—and also just plain fun. I learned so much and grew in admiration and respect for the job they do. I'm forever grateful for their help and their service, even if I can't name them. You know who you are. And, obviously, any and all errors relating to law enforcement, a missing person investigation, or FBI procedures and protocol are mine and mine alone.

A trip to Duluth, Two Harbors, and the North Shore of Lake Superior was filled with new friends and plenty of people willing to share their stories and answer my questions. From the hotel concierge to the police officers who didn't flinch when I approached their cruisers, the good people of Minnesota were unfailingly friendly and kind. I adore the entire state (Skol, Vikings!) and think that Lake Superior and the surrounding area is one of the prettiest places on the planet. Thanks for welcoming this Iowa girl with open arms. And please forgive any mistakes, oversights, or inaccuracies in my descriptions of your beautiful state.

My Tall Poppy sisters are a source of companionship and camaraderie, and I'd be lost without their help, insight, and wisdom. This linking arms thing is awesome.

The team at Atria that polished this book and made it shine are the best of the best. Editor Kaitlin Olson, and Stacey Sakal and Kayley Hoffman caught my mistakes and inconsistencies and helped me keep Charlie and Eva true to character. James Iacobelli created a gorgeous, evocative cover that made me gasp when I first saw it. Yvonne Taylor worked with all my different narrative structures and ephemera (I'm sorry!) and designed a stunning interior that flows seamlessly. Publicist Megan Rudloff and marketing director Maudee Genao are fun and tireless and so very gifted at what they do. Anything good that happens for this book is because of their involvement. To all the behind-the-scenes helping hands (assistants and beta readers and everyone else), your work is vital, and I'm so thankful for you, even if I never knew the details of how you helped. A very special thank-you to Ifeoma Anyoku for answering all my questions and keeping me in line. It takes a village.

To all my readers, and especially everyone who welcomed *Everything We Didn't Say* with such warmth and enthusiasm: thank you. You make my job so much fun, and your encouragement keeps me dreaming up new stories to share. I hope I'm still doing this when I'm eighty, and if I am, it's all because of your generosity and kindness. A special shout-out to the Book of the Month and FabFitFun communities. Thanks for enfolding me with such warmth and welcome.

Finally, all my love and gratitude for my family. Every place that Charlie and Eva explored in this book is a place that we have personally enjoyed. I'm thrilled to have a family that loves adventures and the open road, and forever grateful for the memories we've made (and will hopefully continue to make). Aaron, you're my rock. Isaac, Judah, Eve, and Matthias, you are my inspiration. I've been doing this for over fifteen years now, and in that time my kids have gone from babies in my arms to (almost) grown-ups with their own lives, hopes, and aspirations. It's hard to believe. You are all my dreams.

ABOUT THE AUTHOR

NICOLE BAART is the author of eleven novels, including *Everything We Didn't Say* and *The Long Way Back*. The co-founder of a nonprofit and mother of five, she lives in Iowa with her family. Learn more at NicoleBaart.com.

READING GROUP GUIDE

1. Although Charlie and Eva are Instagram influencers, Charlie struggles with the whole concept of social media and wonders about its effect on her daughter. What do you think about social media? Do you think there should be age restrictions on certain apps? Why or why not?

2. In many ways, the Eva Explores account is an extravagant love story about a country that Charlie and Eva see as beautiful and filled with hope. When Eva meets the Family, she realizes that not everyone feels the same way. How do you see it?

3. It would be easy to vilify all the members of the Family, (and perhaps they all deserve it to one degree or another) but many of them act in ways that seem to contradict their beliefs. Why do you think this is?

4. Eva hides her relationship with Zach from her mother and makes a terrible choice to run away with him. Talk about a time you did something that you later regretted. How did the experience affect you?

5. In spite of the fact that she spent two and a half years on the road, when Eva meets Zach, she is still rather sheltered and naive. Do you think her unusual early teen years made her susceptible to his influence? Why or why not?

6. Does Charlie and Eva's life in their Airstream trailer appeal to you? Explain why or why not.

7. Why do you think Charlie went to such great lengths to make Eva's dream of traveling come true? Have you ever worked to make someone else's dream a reality? Share about it.

8. Throughout much of the book, Charlie worries that she has failed her daughter. Do you think she's a good mom? Why or why not?

9. They say love is blind, and many of Eva's poor decisions can be chalked up to the infatuation of first love. Do you remember your first love? How did it change you?

10. Even though she is scared and angry about her imprisonment at the Gates, Eva tries to understand her captors and even has compassion for them. In her song "Human Family," Maya Angelou writes: "We are more alike, my friends, / Than we are unalike." Do you agree or disagree? Why?

11. Obviously, what the Family has planned is horrific and categorically wrong. What do you consider to be acceptable methods of protest? How should we attempt to affect change when we disagree with systems or ideologies?

12. Cults often pursue people who are socially isolated, don't have strong family ties, and are curious and open to new ideas. In many ways, Eva fit the bill, and yet Zach knew right away that she would resist recruitment. Why? Do you think the Family is a cult? Why or why not?

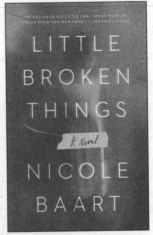
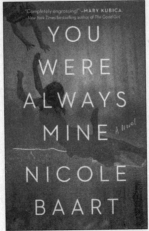